# A Silver LINING in EVERY Cloud

Cover photo credit: Arlyn Atadero Photography

Layout & Design by Tinyah M. Hawkins/Goofidity Designs

ISBN: 978-0-578-25394-7

Printed in the U.S.A.

# A *Silver* LINING in EVERY *Cloud*

BY
**CHARLES LYNN RUSSELL**

Dedicated to my beautiful wife Patricia,
who took me for better or worse fifty-four years ago

# ACKNOWLEDGMENTS

I could not have completed any of the eight novels without the support and assistance of my wife, Patricia. Her positive attitude has gotten me through the difficult times that, I assume, all writers confront.

I want to thank Doyle Russell, Mary Danna Russell, and Glenda Watts for proofreading *A Silver Lining in Every Cloud*. Also, Ruth Collins has not only proofread my last three novels but has taken the time to teach Patricia and me as well.

I could never thank Glenn Droomgoole enough for copyediting the book. I feel like someone learning to swim and being taught by a gold medalist swimmer. He has taken the time and patience to attempt to make my writing presentable.

# AUTHOR'S NOTE

First, let me thank you for your support of my novels. The eight books that I have written are all motivated by an actual event. This novel, *A Silver Lining in Every Cloud,* was born out of an incident in which a well-known racehorse trainer had a horse qualify for a rich futurity but died between the trials and the finals. Everything from that point on is fiction.

An earlier book, *When the Cactus Blooms,* the first of a two-book series, was inspired by a neighbor's dog who was old and arthritic, barely able to get around. Remembering his younger days, he carried a ball around with him. It was sad, reminding us that sometimes the memories are all that we have.

My most common response from readers is "Your books are so easy to read." I think many authors would take offense to that evaluation, considering it too simple or unsophisticated; however, those descriptions fit me perfectly. I'm not concerned that reading my work does not require a dictionary.

The setting for this novel is the top of the Texas Panhandle. Living eight years in this part of Texas gave me an appreciation for that area. The sky is bigger, the north wind is colder, the storms are more severe, and the people are honest and friendly. The focal point of the story is the High Plains Cattle Auction. In most cases I write about people and events that I know something about. My dad worked for thirty years at various cattle auctions, and from the time I was a small boy I accompanied him on many occasions.

I have spent considerable time around a racetrack, and when I write about the inside of the track at Ruidoso being slow for quarter horses in the 1960s and '70s, it is correct. I used a jockey in this book who rode during this time. You could find him at the brush tracks or New Mexico tracks, depending upon the time of year. He was one of the best, even though he never gained the fame that others did. I was a frequent presence at the brush tracks in the 1960s and '70s. You might drive off into a pasture or field and find horses tied to mesquite trees, but the location didn't take away from the fact that there were some good horses brought to these places.

I have attempted in all my novels to make the characters seem real while experiencing sorrow, joy, and challenges that we all face at one time or another. I have enjoyed writing each of the eight books, and I hope you are able, as you read this one, to be able to put aside any problems for a couple of hours and become an active participant in the story.

"Only in the darkness,
can you see the stars"

**MARTIN LUTHER KING, JR.**

# 1

## August 27,1968
# RUIDOSO, NEW MEXICO

 GRACE

I woke in a fog, thinking it was a bad dream. I reached to touch him and he wasn't there. It was no nightmare. I'd slept for the first time in five days, and my mind had blanked out the previous week's horror. He was gone and would never be there again. Just like that—twenty-five years and all that remained were the memories. We were on the verge of having success, which had avoided us for years and now this.

Wide awake, I thought of the past. I'd begged him for years to seek another profession but finally gave up, accepting the fact that he wanted nothing but to train racehorses. We'd done without, living in a travel trailer and going from one track to another. I'd worked part-time jobs in concessions and at pari-mutuel windows, depending on the track, to provide a little extra revenue.

I'd always heard that everyone should have one great horse in their lifetime. Ours came to us through a longtime friend last February. He brought us a filly that he'd purchased from a horse ranch in Oklahoma. He'd overlooked our dismal record of training mostly cheap claiming horses and, because of the friendship, we suddenly had a well-bred prospect. A beautiful thing, she lived up to her looks, winning two races leading up to the New Mexico Futurity.

Last Thursday, a dream came true as she posted the third fastest qualifying time of the 128 entries that were looking to secure a spot in the New Mexico Futurity and a purse worth $225,000. We'd celebrated by eating out at a nice restaurant and discussed the possibility of adding a substantial amount to our meager bank account. Excitement and anticipation of what the money would mean to us dominated, with neither of us interested in eating the expensive meal.

He woke me up sometime before dawn saying he had a terrible headache. We went to the emergency room. As we entered he collapsed, and everything after that was a blur. I sat and waited for hours, it seemed, until a doctor came in telling me he was sorry, but my husband didn't make it due to a brain aneurysm. Until some friends arrived to take me to their house, I sat in shock.

Now, with what seemed like an eternity of grieving, I had to make decisions. Lying in bed would not solve or change anything. I struggled from the bed and dressed.

Sitting at the kitchen table drinking coffee, I thought of the most pressing problem. Oliver Knox, the owner of the filly, was pressuring me to turn her over to another trainer. I'd begged him to let me finish the dream that Henry and I had harbored. He was coming by today to let me know. Somehow it was the most important thing in the world for me to lead Lady in the post parade and to have Henry's name on the program. Sadness covered me like a dingy gray overcoat. How many people paid attention to a forty-five-year-old widow?

I'd eaten little the last five days and was not hungry this morning. I left and drove the half mile to Barn C where our horses were stalled. My dad met me when I arrived, and at seventy-five his age was showing.

He hugged me. "Morning, Grace. You hangin' in there? I've got everything fed. Have you had breakfast?"

"No, I couldn't eat. Maybe later. How's Lady this morning?"

A package of Camels appeared, and he tapped one out—lighting it before he spoke. "Good. That's the sweetest little mare to be so fast. Good horses are supposed to be a problem. You know, crazy and everything. Not her. She doesn't have a mean bone. Have you heard from Oliver?"

"Afraid so. He's coming by this morning to give me the news. I'm hoping he lets us keep her. Of course, she belongs to him."

"It'd be a dirty shame if he takes her away from us. We've had her from the beginning of her career." He turned and limped back to the barn.

He'd gone down after my mother passed two years ago. He'd refused to move in with us, staying in the tack room at the tracks on our schedule. We'd fixed it up the best we could, and he never complained. He insisted on earning his keep by feeding, cleaning stalls, and doing whatever task that came up. I was fortunate to have him, especially now.

I put Lady on the walker and moved a chair out into the sunshine, but it was cold this morning. The filly would break into a trot occasionally but didn't kick-up or strain against the halter. She was a classy little thing. Lady seemed too simple a name for her. A white streak on her forehead and a white sock on her front right leg and on the back left leg was in contrast to her dark brown almost black color. She had a beautiful head with little ears and everything just fit on her. Even though she was small, her back end was wide with a long hip and a huge gaskin muscle.

My dad brought out a chair and sat down beside me. "She's something, isn't she? Just seven more days to wait."

"Do you think she'll do good?" I asked.

"We draw for the post position tomorrow. If we draw from the five out, we have a good chance. That stud horse of the doctor's is probably going to be the horse to beat. He dropped his cigarette on the ground and squashed it with his foot. "Did you hear from Luke?"

"He called again, but the reception was bad. He kept apologizing for missing the funeral. He's coming home for good."

"I'm proud of my grandson. We need him now, more than ever. It's a terrible war. Can you imagine them calling it a conflict? It makes me sick to read about the demonstrations when our boys are dying over there. I'm still mad that he was drafted right out of high school." He took out his pack of Camels, looked at it and put it back in his shirt pocket. "I'm smoking too much. I'm determined to cut back to a pack a day."

"Angie called last night. We talked for over an hour. She keeps insisting I come stay with them. We ended the call when she started crying. She always adored her daddy. I keep reminding myself how fortunate I am to have two loving children. It's all that keeps me going."

He took out his cigarettes again—not putting them back until he had one lit. "Has she gone back to work?"

"Yesterday. She said it was driving her crazy staying home and thinking. It helped seeing her customers. Most of them hadn't heard about her dad, and that was positive. She's still not able to talk about it. She enjoys her work in the salon and is good at her job. Many of the older ladies won't let anyone else touch their hair."

"What about the 'Leaner?'"

My dad was referring to Angie's husband, Evert, who was always leaning up against something because he was lazy. "He's still not working. I guess she'll have to support him from now on."

"She could've done better."

"I agree, Dad, but it's too late now. Maybe if she'd gone to college there'd have been a better selection."

"I've been putting this off, Daughter, but it's bothering me. What're you going to do now?"

"I'm just trying to make one day at a time. I haven't given it much thought. Everything was so sudden. I'm still having a hard time believing he's gone."

Before we could continue, Oliver drove up in his pickup. He had his wife with him, and they came over to where we were seated. "How're you doing, Grace? I know it must be tough on you."

"I'm still somewhat numb. Have you made a decision yet on Lady?"

He cleared his throat. "Yeah. I'm going to let you keep her. However, I have another trainer that's going to advise you. I want you to do what he says. You'll still receive ten percent of the purse. I owe that to Henry."

Confused—I hesitated trying to gather my thoughts. "Why?"

He looked at his wife. "Lynda and I will feel better doing it this way."

Lynda's head was bobbing up and down like one of those toy ducks you wind up. I couldn't think of anything to say.

Dad spoke up. "What's he going to do differently? Grace knows how Henry has been training the filly. It looks like it would make sense to continue and not make changes."

Lynda's tone was sharp and impatient as if she was talking to a child. "We made a decision, and if you don't like it we can take Miss Jet to another barn."

"No, that'll be fine," I said. She never referred to her as Lady since that was the nickname we'd given her.

They left and we sat in silence for several minutes. "I guess that's that," I said. My dad didn't curse, but I was tempted. It could've been worse. They might've taken the filly and eliminated any chance of me receiving the trainer's part of the purse. I needed that money desperately. How change happens so quickly, I thought. A short time ago we were friends—celebrating Lady qualifying for the big race. Now that friendship seemed to have disappeared, and they didn't trust me.

"You need to eat something. I'm going to the track café and bring you back some breakfast." He didn't wait for an answer.

I leaned back and closed my eyes. My dad's question returned—what was I going to do now? We had nine horses in our barn plus our pony horse. Six, including Lady, belonged to other people—three belonged to us. All were claimers except, of course, Lady. Of the three that we owned, all were cheap claimers not worth more than $2,000 and probably less. Our other outside horses were better but not by much, competing in $2,500-$3,500 claiming races.

Could I do it? I'd been involved in our operation, working alongside Henry. I was knowledgeable enough—but a woman trainer? We generally went to the fair in Albuquerque from here. It was a seventeen-day race meet and from there we would go home for a few weeks before heading to Sunland Park. Maybe if Lady was able to win or even place, I could take some time off with the additional purse money. Now was not the time to make decisions about the future.

We lived from month to month on our income and seldom had little remaining in our bank account. Most owners were good to pay, but sometimes one was late and we would be overdrawn. We still banked in Childress, our hometown, and thus far they'd been understanding.

I'd grieved the last five days to the point of weakness. Alone in my trailer at night was the worst time. The first few nights I'd wrapped a pillow in one of Henry's shirts and held it close, thinking that might help. I'd cried until I'd run out of tears. I'd loved Henry but just as important, he was my best friend, and we did everything together. We were a team.

Dad interrupted my despair. "Breakfast is ready."

He presented me with a paper plate with scrambled eggs, ham, and a biscuit. I was going to do my best to eat. "Thank you, Dad."

"We're going to make it, Daughter. I know it's tough, but think about Angie and Luke."

"Why did this happen, Dad? Couldn't we have a little time to enjoy our success? I mean it doesn't make sense."

"I read the Bible every day, Daughter. I don't know. We just have to have faith."

"Right now, Dad, my faith is weak. I don't understand. My whole world is upside down, and I'm angry."

"It's not a good time to understand. Let's give it more space." He lit another Camel.

# 2

## August 29, 1968
# TAN SON NHUT AIR BASE

 LUKE

I leaned back in my seat and took a deep breath as we lifted off, thankful to be alive after twenty-one months in Vietnam. The cargo of the plane was filled with body bags of soldiers less fortunate. Our destination was Los Angeles and then home.

I thought back to a few days ago when six of us struggled back into Long Binh Post, which was located about twenty miles northeast of Saigon. We'd been out seven days on a reconnaissance patrol looking for a battalion of Viet Cong. There were six of us that were dropped off in the jungle by a Huey, and we all made it back—which was a miracle. We reported to our commanding officer with information we'd gathered about the location of the enemy. After finishing, the Captain asked me to stay.

"Sergeant Ranker, I have news for you from home. I'm sorry to say it's bad. Your dad died. We received word the day after you left on your patrol. I'm terribly sorry."

I couldn't believe what he was saying. It couldn't be that Dad had died. I'd tried to talk but couldn't.

"I'm sorry. We tried to reach you but weren't successful."

I was exhausted and moved to a metal trunk to support my weary body. I'd just gone through seven days of nerve-shattering fear, and no emotion surfaced.

"You only have a short time left, so we can give you leave to go home. There would be no use for you to return to serve only a few weeks. Your service here has been exemplary, and the leadership you provided your men deserves recognition.

Several of your actions have been submitted by your men for medals to honor your leadership. I wish we had more men like you over here."

I'd been a platoon leader and had lost five soldiers out of the twenty-four. Those five would haunt me the rest of my life.

I'd called my mother and, of course, she wanted me home. Within twenty-four hours, the paperwork completed, I was on my way back to the States. My thoughts turned to Dad. Beginning when I was a small child, everyone accused him of being partial to me over my sister. They said I looked like him. We stayed together as a family even when he was at the track. My sister and I would enroll at whatever school was available, but this changed when my sister was a sophomore in high school and received her driver's license. She was two years older than me, and we started staying at home while my mom and dad were at the track, but of course, my grandparents only lived a short distance from us. Some people thought it terrible for us to be left on our own. We got along fine, however, and liked going to school in our hometown; a small town in the southeastern part of the Texas Panhandle. We lived on a farm which consisted of 110 acres of cultivated land and 300 acres of pasture that actually belonged to my grandparents. When my grandmother passed, Granddad started going to the track with our parents.

I leaned my head back against the seat and closed my eyes. Angry, depressed, and confused, I needed sleep desperately. I'd left my path to relaxation under my bed for the next solider, reminding myself I could do without the drugs. Trying to sleep, my mind turned to the last two years. I'd been drafted into the Marines in September of 1966, and since I wasn't enrolled in college, they didn't waste any time calling my number. By December, I was in Vietnam. It was nothing like I'd expected. I'd thought the people of South Vietnam would be thankful for our help and welcome us with open arms. Instead, they were suspicious of us and treated us more like intruders.

The veterans virtually ignored newcomers, giving us no respect.

This would continue until we'd gone through several months and fought alongside them and survived. The Viet Cong were experienced and knew the terrain. Many had been fighting since they were old enough to hold a gun. Most of our recruits served only one year and went home, being replaced by poorly trained boys, many just out of high school. Contrary to what the generals kept saying; we weren't winning the war.

I was involved in small skirmishes the first several months. My introduction to the horrors of war occurred on July 2, 1967, when I was involved in a sweep in the area north of the post of Con Thien, which was only two miles from the Demilitarized Zone. We were ambushed by an undetected North Vietnamese force ten times our size. Out of several platoons, made up of 292 Marines, only twenty-seven didn't require assistance to leave the battle. Almost a third of our men were killed. I happened to be in a shaded area when we were attacked which saved me. I carried this valuable lesson with me when I led my own platoon. I was one of the fortunate and retreated from the massacre on my own.

✳✳✳

Nineteen hours and several stops later we landed at the Los Angeles Airport. Several of my colleagues had family waiting for them, and the reunions were emotional with laughing and crying. I noticed several young people carrying signs that objected to the war. I'd been warned about this before leaving Vietnam and was not surprised. I tried to ignore them as I made my way into the terminal.

I scheduled a flight to El Paso and called my mother telling her I should be there by five p.m. She assured me they would be waiting when I arrived. By they, I knew she meant Granddad. I had wonderful memories of spending time with him when I was growing up. He'd had me driving a tractor by the time I was ten. We'd gone fishing frequently at several stock tanks in the area. My grandmother passed while I was still at home, and I'll never forget how he grieved over her loss.

From the time I can remember he read the Bible daily, which was strange since he seldom went to church with us. He never cursed or drank liquor. I assumed he had no vices unless you counted his Camels. His name was William but friends called him Willie.

I found a secluded place to wait for the call to board my flight. The question came out of nowhere. "What're you going to do now?" I'd thought of little else but surviving the last two years. Now—what about my future? College had never been a consideration when I finished high school, even though I'd received a scholarship offer to play football from a junior college. I was more mature now and with a GI Bill it would be free. Maybe I should go that route since it would give me time to decide what I wanted to do for the next forty years.

I had no girl waiting for me even though many of the men I'd served with did. There'd been someone in high school, but I'd received word that she'd married recently. I wasn't disappointed as I never expected it to last. The call to board my flight was announced, bringing me back to the present.

✲✲✲

We touched down in El Paso three hours later. Exiting the plane and entering the terminal, I saw no protestors. I spotted my mother before she saw me. When I started toward her, she called, "Luke," and came running. She hugged me—crying. "Thank God, you're home and safe." She stepped back, looking me up and down. "You've lost weight."

While she gave me the once-over, I returned the visual interrogation of her post-Dad image. Her short brown hair was swept behind her ears. Her dark complexion mirrored my own. The dark circles under her sad brown eyes gave away the grief. Rushing in for another hug, I wrapped her petite frame in my long arms.

Granddad strode forward, hugging me, Stetson in hand. A lanky cowboy with thinning gray hair stood eye-to-eye with me. Blue eyes faded to almost gray still shone with the love he felt. "Welcome home. It's good to have you back."

The walk to Mom's pickup was emotional with her stopping every few minutes to talk of Dad's passing. "I don't know what I'm going to do, Luke. I miss him so much already. I haven't been alone for twenty-five years."

"Mom, let's just get to the pickup, and we'll have plenty of time to talk of that later."

On the drive to Ruidoso, she told me about Oliver's instructions. I was aware of Lady's success and what it meant to my parents. Now that Dad was gone, evidently the relationship with Oliver had gone south. "Has the trainer who was supposed to help showed up to give you any suggestions?" It was hard to believe Oliver would want anything done differently since the filly had had great success.

"He's been by a couple of times but had no instructions. He's not one of the leading trainers, which makes it strange. The whole thing is confusing."

It was dark by the time we reached the track. The horses hadn't been fed since Mom and Granddad left early to come to El Paso. The barn was well lit, and I had my first look at Lady. Being around the track and horses growing up, I had a pretty good idea what to look for in a good horse, and she was everything and more I'd expect a stake's horse to possess. A sloping shoulder, a short back, a long hip, and a good front end. Of course, the powerful back end was her most impressive attribute. Being so well proportioned, she looked small but, approaching her, she was probably fifteen hands and would weigh a thousand pounds.

We went to Mom's trailer and talked until two in the morning— mostly about Dad. It was good to relive some of the memories, and I believe it helped Mom to deal with her grief. I kept the conversation away from Vietnam, which was not difficult. They seemed to understand it was something I preferred not to talk about.

With me and Granddad agreeing, Mom decided to continue training at least for the time being. Now was not the time to make changes. I declined the offer to stay with her, since she would've insisted I use her bed while she slept on the couch. I dropped Granddad off at the barn and went to a motel. It took several minutes of ringing the bell to wake the proprietor, who wasn't the least bit happy with his late customer.

"Hold your horses, I'm coming. You know what time it is?"

I looked at my watch. "Ten after two. I'm sorry for waking you. I just got back from Vietnam and was visiting with my mother."

"That's a waste of time over there. Did you kill a lot of civilians? I heard about the My Lai Massacre. What's the matter with you guys anyway?"

I just stood and glared at him until he looked away. "Sorry to bother you." I turned and left. I drove to the parking lot of a grocery store which was closed, getting as comfortable as possible in the seat of Mom's pickup. I tried to get my mind off my grief and the decisions I was facing. But, I couldn't sleep. After lying there for an hour, I realized what was wrong— my body was used to the drugs after stress. I'd taken the pills every night I was in the barracks for the last year. I didn't know what they were, except we called them downers.

I'd stayed away from the drugs for the first year. When I was given my own platoon and lost my first man, that changed. He was only eighteen years old. I'd done everything to protect him, not allowing him to be the point man on any of the patrols. After begging to be treated like everyone else, I gave in. He stepped on a mine and was blown to pieces. From smoking pot, I moved to harder drugs. All I knew was that they were sedatives and readily available. I never took them on patrol, to keep my mind clear. I made a mistake not bringing some of them home.

# 3

## September 2, 1968
# THE BIG DAY

 GRACE

I went to the kitchen and put the coffee on. Today was it. I was hoping for a nice, dry day but evidently that was not going to happen. It had stormed, raining off and on most of the night, and when I looked outside the porch light revealed the steps to the trailer were surrounded by pools of water. Lady had never run in the mud, and I had no idea how she'd handle it. The trainer who was to advise me came by each day and did nothing, and I continued to be confused as to his role in Lady's training.

The last five days spent with Luke had revealed a different boy from the one who went to war. He left with a mischievous grin and a positive attitude, and since his return, I hadn't seen him smile. He'd lost weight, at least twenty pounds, and was so nervous he couldn't sit still. I assumed it would take time to become whatever normal might be for him, which I hoped wasn't his present condition.

After two cups of coffee, I took my shower and dressed. The last ten days had taken their toll. My clothes didn't fit after losing weight. I stepped on the scales when I exited the shower, and they showed 112, which was thirteen pounds lighter than usual. The image staring back at me in the mirror revealed sadness and hopelessness. The moment we had dreamed about, and he wasn't going to be here. My eyes grew misty, and

I looked away—life went on. I owed it to him to try and move on.

I heard the knock and the door open, knowing it would be my dad. I finished putting on makeup and went to the kitchen, finding him with his coffee in one hand and a Camel in the other.

"Morning, Grace. Did you sleep any?"

"Not much. You?"

"No. I don't think it was the storm. Just anticipating today and what it means." He sipped his coffee. "I thought Luke might already be here. He's changed, Grace. We should've expected it. I can't imagine what he's been through. We have to do everything we can to help him."

"I know, Dad. I knew he'd be different but not to this extent. Of course, losing his dad is part of it, I'm sure."

I sat down at the table with my coffee. "What do you think about the race today? Do we have a chance? I'm worried about a sloppy track."

"The six gate's not bad. It just depends on how she handles the mud. Grace, what in the world is going on with this guy that's supposed to be advising you? He's done nothing."

"I know. It doesn't make sense. We may not even see him before the race. You do remember that we have another horse in today?" I was probably the only trainer who had a $3000 claimer in today as well as an entry in the New Mexico Futurity.

"Yeah. Big Time Boy's running in the first race. The six furlongs fit him, and I wouldn't be surprised if he won. Is Blaine coming today?" he asked.

"He called yesterday and said he'd be here. He's such a nice man. I wish all our owners were like him. He was the only one, besides Oliver, who attended Henry's service.

"Would you like some breakfast, Dad? I thought Luke would be here by now."

"Let's give him a little more time. I'll go feed and come back. He should be here by then, and we can eat together."

✳✳✳

Dad returned forty-five minutes later, and Luke still wasn't here. We had breakfast and went to the barn. By then it was good daylight, and I was getting worried. We took each of our horses out of the barn and walked them around for a few minutes. It wasn't raining now, but we'd had several inches during the night.

At a few minutes past nine Luke showed up. He apologized and said he'd finally been able to sleep a little. "I guess it caught up with me. How's Lady this morning?"

"Same as always. Laid back and acting like it's just another day. I hope she can handle a sloppy track," I said.

"I bought a program and form last night and noticed we had another horse in today." He pulled the program from his back pocket.

"Right. He's that big sorrel gelding on the walker. He's in for $3000 claim and going six furlongs. We think he has a good chance. His owner will be here. I want you to meet him. He'll probably come by the barn before the race. He owns a cattle auction at Dalhart."

My dad had been cleaning out a stall and came over. "Luke, have you had breakfast?"

"No, I wasn't hungry."

"I could use another cup of coffee. Let's go to the track café, and I'll buy your breakfast. We might have to relive some of those fishing trips when you were growing up."

They weren't gone but a few minutes when Oliver showed up with a serious look. "Is she ready, Grace?"

"I think so. She just doesn't get excited. To her it's just another day. We were fortunate to have drawn an outside gate."

"I need to tell you that we've made a rider change. Pate suggested it, and I agree with him."

Pate was the trainer who was supposed to be advising me. "Why would you do that? Kenneth has ridden her in all three of her races. It doesn't make sense to change now."

He looked off in another direction. "Grace, this filly belongs to me. I'm doing what I think will help her run a good race. If you don't like it, I'm sorry. That's the way it's going to be."

"Who's the new rider?" I asked.

"Wooten."

"The midget?" Of course, I already knew that. He was known to be crooked and was notorious for doing anything to win and even throwing races if enough money was involved.

"He's called that sometimes," he said, still refusing to look at me.

"What are you trying to do, Oliver? Lady has won three races with the same jockey and here you are changing riders in a stakes race worth over $225,000."

"I told you, Grace! She's my filly and that's the way it is."

I stared at him—dumbfounded. He turned and left, not giving me a chance to question him more about his decision.

✳✳✳

The morning dragged by with minutes seeming like hours. I told Dad and Luke about Oliver's visit, and they were as angry as I was. Finally, the call for the first race was announced. I was disappointed that Big Boy's owner hadn't shown but maybe he hadn't been able to come.

Luke had already saddled Gem, my pony horse. Handing me Big Boy's halter, we started to the paddock. We'd shortened his name which fit him since he was over sixteen hands. Big Boy was nervous in the saddling paddock, and I was glad to see Kenneth coming with his gear. He walked up without saying a word and threw the saddle on Big Boy. It was evident he was upset, and for good reason.

"I'm sorry, Kenneth. It was none of my doing. Oliver just informed me a couple of hours ago about changing riders. The whole situation's a mystery."

"It's not your fault—I know that. Of all the riders to take my place it would be that little crook. Something's going on, Grace. I don't know what it is, but it stinks."

I changed the subject. "Big Boy feels good. I think he'll give you a good trip. There's not much speed in the race so don't worry about rating him. If he wants to move to the front—let him."

"I love to ride this horse. He's honest and will give you all he has."

I gave him a leg up, and after making the circle the bugler sounded the call to the post, and they were on the track. Big Boy didn't need a pony horse, so I went down to the finish line. I was going to be optimistic and get close to the Winner's Circle. The horses came by in the post parade, and Big Boy was acting like a colt even though he was seven. Occasionally he would lunge forward, and when Kenneth pulled back on him he'd kick up.

Somebody touched me on the shoulder. It was Blaine, the owner of Big Boy. "What do you think, Grace? We going to the Win Circle today?"

"Maybe. I'd given up on you coming."

"We had a load of cattle come in last night, and I didn't get much sleep. It delayed my start this morning. How're you doing?"

"Just one day at a time, Blaine. I find myself hoping it's a dream. Maybe I haven't accepted it yet."

"Did you place a bet on Big Boy?" I asked.

"Sure. I got you a $10-win ticket also." He took it out of his shirt pocket and gave it to me.

"Thank you. How are the plans for the wedding going? I imagine Jimmie is excited."

"Yeah, my daughter talks of little else. I'll just be glad when it's over."

We stayed silent as the horses approached the starting gates. I assumed my dad and Luke were close, but I hadn't seen them. Big Boy had the two gate, and his odds were 4-1. They began loading, and I held my breath hoping that this nice man's horse would run well. The thoroughbred track was only six furlongs, so the starting gates were right in front of us.

The gates opened with a clang, and Big Boy broke well and took the lead. At the first call he was still in front, and by midway he had opened up by two lengths. The stretch run was wonderful as he kept extending his lead, running his heart out, as if knowing how important it was that he do well today. He crossed the finish line five lengths in front. For the first time in ten days, I was able to smile.

Blaine reached and hugged me. "Let's go, Grace. We need to get our picture taken."

Luke and my dad joined us as Kenneth and Big Boy returned to the Win Circle. Kenneth was all smiles. "He was at his best today, Grace. I think he ran this race for you."

He lowered his head, and I rubbed his nose. "Thank you, Big Boy."

We all had our picture taken, and Big Boy went to the test barn. Blaine cashed our win tickets, and we all returned to the barn to wait for the eleventh race.

The afternoon went slowly, and by the time the results of the ninth race were being announced, Luke, Dad, and Blaine had left. There was a huge crowd, and they wanted to find a spot to watch the race. I had just enough time for a bathroom break at the trailer. I should've gone before they left, leaving me alone.

I was only gone ten minutes, but when I returned, Oliver's pickup was there. I could see that he and the trainer were at Lady's stall. It was too early to get her out—the first call for her race hadn't been announced. Approaching them, I gasped when I saw Pate, the trainer, filling a syringe from a bottle.

"What are you doing?" I cried. "You can't give her anything!"

Oliver evidently hadn't heard me drive up and jumped. "Just calm down, Grace. We're just going to give her a little help today."

"You're breaking the law, Oliver! We'll all lose our licenses. Stop it, now!"

Pate squeezed the skin at the bottom of Lady's neck, locating the vein, and— before I could get inside the stall—injected whatever it was into her. I just stood there in shock, realizing what the trainer and rider change was all about.

# 4

# HIGH PLAINS
# CATTLE AUCTION

 JIMMIE LYN

I'd just gotten off the phone with my dad, and he was ecstatic. Big Boy had won his race at Ruidoso. I was pleased for him and especially for Mrs. Ranker, who'd lost her husband a few days ago. He'd begged me to go with him, but I had too much to do here.

I kept books at the Auction and was behind. That was just the least of it. In just twenty-five days Jimmie Lyn Waddell was going to become Jimmie Lyn Davis. I was involved in the planning of my big event and that occupied much of my time. It was happening—finally. At twenty-three, my family had about given up on me. I'd gone through college and several relationships before anything serious came along. Then it happened. I'd gone to the law office of Beckett and Becket in Amarillo on May twentieth to file on a company that owed us a large sum, which we'd been unable to collect.

At least for me, I think it was love at first sight. He was tall—my first observation. Of course, that was important since I was five-eleven if I slumped. If I stood erect, the dreaded six-foot label was there. He was the lawyer to whom I was directed. We hit it off immediately even though I discovered later that he was thirty, which didn't bother me in the least. He was six-foot-five and towered over me. I had to look up for a kiss.

It was a whirlwind courtship, which was fine. After all we were adults and knew what we wanted. We'd not had a cross word, and it was amazing how much we had in common. We'd been together almost every day since we met, with the 86 miles or hour and a half drive providing no obstacle for us. Most of the days I made the drive to Amarillo.

My dad and mom were divorced and had been for ten years but got along remarkably well. In fact, my mom couldn't resist being a part of the planning for my wedding. The invitations were going out this week and—living here my entire life—it was a long list. My future husband, Drake, had only been in Amarillo for six months and his list was short, mostly a few friends from work.

My mom, who thought she had to know every move I made, insisted on knowing all about Drake. I was able to satisfy her since he'd been very open with me in describing his past. He'd previously worked for a law firm in New York, which sent him abroad where he'd spent the last five years—two in Spain and three in London. He grew tired of living outside the United States and gave his company an ultimatum—move me back or I find a position with another firm. They refused and he quit, finding a job in Amarillo where he confessed to being very happy. Of course, he hadn't gone through a winter here yet. I smiled—that shouldn't be a problem. We'd be married by then.

It was five o'clock and time for me to get off. I made every effort not to expect any special consideration, working for my dad. My eight-hour day was eight hours. I didn't take more than my hour for lunch, and I didn't take off work unless necessary and then my check reflected it. Unlike some offspring, I liked working for my dad. My degree was in business, and I'd worked here off and on since junior high. You could say I knew my way around High Plains Cattle Auction.

My first stop in town before going to my apartment was at Mrs. Proctor's, who was making my wedding dress. She was a long-time family friend and a wonderful seamstress.

She met me at the door. "Jimmie Lyn, come in."

"I'm sorry, Mrs. Proctor, for not calling before coming by. I was anxious to see how far along you are."

"It's getting there. Let me show you what I have so far."

I followed her into another room where material was scattered everywhere. She picked up the white dress, holding it proudly in front of her. "What do you think?"

"Oh, it's beautiful. I wish I could do it justice," I mumbled.

"What do you mean, girl? Of course, you'll be beautiful. Just give me another week, and you can try it on. I can't wait to meet the groom. Tell me about him."

I hesitated, wanting to give her a good description. "He's tall and has dark hair and brown eyes. He's not skinny but thin is a better description. He smiles a lot and has a wonderful sense of humor. We like the same things. It's unbelievable but he doesn't like country music. Finally, I've found someone with good taste. He's a Methodist, like me. It seems we've spent all these years just waiting for one another."

"He sounds perfect!"

"I feel like we've known each other for years even though it's only been a little over three months. I'd about given up. Being so tall, I'd been picky and eliminated any prospect that wasn't taller than me. I couldn't see myself marrying someone I had to look down on."

"Well, I'm happy for you. You're a beautiful girl, Jimmie Lyn. Being tall doesn't take away from your looks."

"Maybe so. It does hurt though when you hear people call you an 'Amazon' behind your back."

"Oh, silly. They're just jealous. They would trade places with you in a minute."

I knew she was just being nice. "Thank you for the compliments. I need to be going now. I'll see you next week." I drove away thinking, what a beautiful dress for the most important event of my life.

The first thing I did at my apartment was to change into my jogging clothes. I ran a three-mile route every afternoon, usually accompanied by my best friend. Piper and I had grown up together, but instead of attending college, she began working for one of the two doctors in town. She ended up marrying him a year ago. She lived down the street, and we met every day around six for our exercise. Piper was beautiful, and maybe that had something to do with the poor image I had of myself. She was small, shapely, blond, and had attracted boys ever since I can remember. Growing up, when we were together, the attention from the boys was always directed at her.

Even with my height I wanted to stay trim, especially for my wedding. I was careful not to put on extra weight. A good fit for me was 130 pounds. Finding clothes was a problem, and I challenged anyone to find a size 30 jean in a length that fit, even in the men's department.

It usually took us about forty minutes to complete our run, and we were back at my apartment by six-thirty. Today was one of the few days I wasn't going to make the trip to Amarillo. I'd spent yesterday with Drake, attending church with him.

Sitting on the small porch and watching the traffic pass, Piper said, "I imagine your wedding dress is beautiful, knowing what a perfectionist Mrs. Proctor is."

"Yes. It might even look good on me."

"There you go again, Jimmie Lyn, running yourself down. What would it take to convince you that you're beautiful? You think being tall is unflattering—well it's not."

"Being tall didn't even make me a good basketball player. You know that. I was clumsy. Everybody expected me to be a star."

"Now you're living in the past. That period of time in your life is over. You're going to marry your dream guy. Celebrate it! Be happy and think positive. I have to be going now. Daniel will be home soon. I'm happy for you, Jimmie Lyn—be happy for yourself."

It was a relief to be left to my own thoughts. I was glad to get out of high school and be done with basketball but reluctant to leave home. I went to Texas Tech and enjoyed my college years. I majored in business, realizing that the High Plains Cattle Auction would be my future. My dad owned the business, and my younger sister had already married and moved away.

My dad also owned a ranch thirty miles west of Dalhart where he ran two hundred mother cows. That was also included in my bookkeeping chores. The ranch had oil and gas production, so the Auction was not the only source of income. I'd never really given it much thought, but my dad would be considered a wealthy man by almost any standard even though he didn't look or act like it.

My parents had a strange relationship. They'd been married for fifteen years before they separated. Most marriages end in confrontation but, thus far, I'd never known of either expressing anger at the other. My dad never said anything negative about my mother and the same was true of her. My mother remarried five years after the divorce, but my dad remained single, never showing an interest in another woman of which I was aware.

I'd learned to ride at an early age and up until my junior year in high school had worked the pens. I still enjoyed being horseback and would occasionally help move cattle from one pen to another. We generally had between 100-200 head of cattle on the grounds at all times. We had six full-time employees and as many as twenty-five on sale day, which was a Wednesday.

I smiled, realizing that Piper was right. I should be happy. Drake had already agreed to move to Dalhart after we were married. He was going to set up his own law practice here, and I could continue to work at the Auction. We would raise a family right here in this wonderful little Panhandle community.

# 5

# DISASTER

 GRACE

"Oliver, you've gone crazy!"

He came out of Lady's stall. "Listen to me, Grace. We can't outrun the doctor's horse. That's for certain. If we can win third or fourth, I'll get a good check. She will not be tested since she won't win. It just makes sense to get everything out of her we can for this race. Henry's name is on the program. That's what you wanted. Now get your pony horse ready, it's about time to take her to the paddock."

I couldn't believe this. I stood and stared at him, at a loss for words.

"Grace! Get moving. Miss Jet belongs to me, and I call the shots." The anger boiled out of him.

As I saddled my pony horse, outrage and indecision accompanied me. Pate handed Lady to me, and we started the quarter mile to the paddock. With every step she became more agitated, and by the time we reached the track she'd broken out in a sweat and, dancing sideways, was difficult to handle. Afraid she'd break away, I tightened my hold.

In the stall of the saddling paddock, she became worse. She was going to get loose! Luke saved the day, appearing out of nowhere to help me.

"What's going on, Mother?" Before I could answer, Wooten, the jockey walked up carrying his gear. "Just help us get her saddled. I'll explain later."

It didn't look like we were going to be able to get it done until two men came to our aid. With the four of us we finally had her ready. By this time, she was lathered. I expected the track vet to intervene at anytime.

I went to my pony horse, and Luke had to circle Lady several times before he brought her to me. When I took the lead rope, I prayed to be able to hold her. I knew, warmup wasn't necessary—it would've only made matters worse. I walked and trotted her the shortest distance possible before heading to the starting gates. I had nothing to say to the jockey, nor he to me.

When the command was given to load, I knew it was going to be hopeless. The man I gave her to couldn't even come close to getting her in the gate. It was only after half a dozen others pitched in to help that they succeeded. They literally pushed her into gate six. She was the last to load and immediately the bell rang and the gates opened. I was behind the gates, still mounted on Gem and could only see the race through the metal bars. I relied on the call of the race to know how Lady was doing.

**"It's a good break for all with Rocket Man on the outside going to the front followed by Top Max on the inside and Three Dots in the middle of the track. It's Three Dots moving up taking the lead and here comes Miss Jet challenging. It's a photo between Three Dots and . . . Miss Jet is down! Miss Jet crossed the finish line and went down!"**

My heart flew into my throat when I heard the announcer. I galloped Gem to the finish line and found Lady struggling to get up. The track vet arrived at the same time I did. Somewhere in the distance, I heard the announcer say that Three Dots had won.

"Hold her down. I need to get a tranquilizer in her." He was going through his bag.

I talked softly to her, holding her head down. "You're going to be okay, baby. Settle down now. Settle down, please. We're going to help you." I continued to hold her head and slowly her frightened eyes relaxed with her body.

The vet spoke softly. "We need to get her in the ambulance. It looks like she has a broken leg."

I stood and watched as they loaded her. I hadn't noticed Oliver who was standing beside me. I didn't scream but spoke in a whisper calling him a name I'd never used before and would never use again.

Luke and Dad accompanied me to the vet barn and watched as they unloaded Lady and took her inside. I felt ashamed for not asking about the jockey, but Luke assured me he was fine. Once inside the barn, they hoisted her into a sling, taking the weight off her legs. I came close to throwing up several times. My dad had been silent up until this time.

"Grace, it looks bad. I don't see how anything can be done for her."

I kept thinking. *I could've stopped this from happening if I'd spoken up and told officials before the race Lady had been drugged. Now, she was going to die because I'd kept silent. What else could happen? I'd lost my husband and now our dream had ended with this.*

The vet was busy taking x-rays with the help of an assistant. We stood in silence as he completed the task and, taking the x-rays, went into another room.

Lady was waking up and even though she was immobilized, started to move around. I went over and held her head in my hands, talking softly to her. I heard him before realizing he was in the room.

"What'd the vet say?"

I looked around, and it was Oliver and his wife. "He took pictures and is developing them now. It shouldn't be long until we know. It's her left leg."

"She won second. She ran a great race," said Oliver's wife.

I stared at her smiling face. I started to reply but knew it wouldn't accomplish anything. Well, maybe it would make me feel better. "Yes. She ran her heart out, and thanks to your husband she's probably going to die!"

The silence that followed was soaked with tension. Oliver refused to meet my gaze, staring at the floor. His wife's stoic expression revealed a lack of empathy.

The vet returned to the room with the x-rays. He pinned them up and turned on a light as we gathered around him. He spoke rapidly as if not wanting any questions until he finished. "The lateral condylar is fractured." He pointed with a pencil. "It runs from the front to the back of the leg and up the lateral or outside. It was fortunate that she went down instead of continuing to run on it." He stopped at this point, giving us an opportunity for questions.

"Do we need to put her down?" Oliver asked.

"That depends on how much money and effort you want to spend repairing the injury. There would be no guarantee it would work."

"How would you go about fixing it?" I asked.

"I couldn't. You would need to take her to a place that specializes in this type of injury. My recommendation would be the Texas A&M Vet Clinic. Their staff and fourth-year vet majors do extensive surgeries on horses. I believe they are the best. Of course, it would be expensive. The fracture is usually repaired through the use of a screw fixation. In other words, the piece of bone is taken and pressed against the parent bone and stabilized with screws."

"How much?" Oliver's wife asked.

"I can't say for sure. On the low end—$5,000. Probably more."

"We have her insured. Can we put her down and collect the insurance?" asked Oliver's wife.

The vet hesitated so long I thought he wasn't going to answer. "Probably. Depends on the insurance company and the amount. The more she's insured for, the harder it gets."

Oliver gave him the answer. "Twenty-five thousand."

"I'll write up my prognosis, and you can submit it to your insurance company if that's the way you want to go. I watched her run. She's a nice filly."

Without giving Oliver a chance to respond, his wife said, "That's what we want done."

"Representatives from our insurance provider are here for the New Mexico Futurity. I can have them over here within an hour to visit with you. We can get this done, so she won't have to suffer." Oliver looked at his wife as a child looks at their mother for approval.

"I guess it's settled then." The vet left without further comment.

When we were alone I asked Dad and Luke to give me a few minutes with Lady. After they left I went over and stroked her head and rubbed her nose. She'd always liked that. I looked into those big, soft, brown eyes and started crying. "I-I'm so s-orry, pretty girl. I sh-ould've t-taken better care of y-you. Henry w-would have n-never let this hap-pen."

Afterwards, I went outside to join Luke and my dad. Blaine was talking with them. I tried to wipe the tears away. "I'm sorry. I love that filly. She doesn't deserve this."

"I'm sorry, Grace. I thought we were going to have a good day after Big Boy won. Is there anything I can do?"

"No, I guess not, Blaine. Thank you for coming by. Oliver went to get his insurance representative. If he approves they'll put her down immediately."

"Let's wait around and see if the insurance is going to pay. Who knows what will happen if they refuse?"

"I appreciate it, Blaine, but I don't see what good that would do," I said. "I'm going to the barn and feed. We'll need to be moving to Albuquerque tomorrow. I have to make arrangements to hire someone to haul the horses. The Fair opens next weekend."

"Granddad, if you'll go help Mom feed, I'll stay with Mr. Waddell to see what the verdict is on the insurance settlement."

"Sure. We'll probably be at the trailer before you find out anything," my dad said.

I didn't understand Luke and Blaine wanting to hang around here.

"Thank you again, Blaine. I hope we can win another race with Big Boy at the Fair. The purses there are really good."

Dad and I left, with me thinking, *what else could happen to me?*

# 6

# A BIG GAMBLE

 LUKE

"Luke, we might as well go inside and find a place to sit. It could be several hours before Oliver returns with his insurance people."

We found a couple of chairs in a corner of the vet's building. "What do you think is going to happen?" This was all new to me. We'd never had a horse good enough to insure.

Mr. Waddell took out a box of Skoal and put a pinch under his lip, then offered it to me.

"No thanks. I tried it once and got sick."

"I'd be only guessing, Luke, but I doubt if they agree to pay the insurance. A lot of it depends on the vet's presentation."

"Mom is attached to Lady. She'll be devastated if they put her down."

"You haven't been out of the service but a few days. Are you going to be able to adjust okay?" He spit in a cup he'd found on the floor.

It was strange, but I felt comfortable talking with Mr. Waddell about coming home. "No, not really. I haven't slept much at night since getting back. Over there, I was occupied with staying alive and keeping my men alive. I was exhausted when I did get to rest and was able to sleep. When I try to sleep now, my mind returns to the rice paddies and jungle, remembering the death I witnessed. I'm hoping it gets better with time." I didn't reveal using drugs that helped me to relax over there, which were absent now.

For the next half-hour he told me about his experience in the second World War. I knew nothing of his past and was surprised to find on D-Day he'd been in the first wave that landed on the beaches of Normandy. The longer he spoke the softer his voice became until I had to strain to hear him. I felt sure he'd not revealed the fear and horror he'd seen to anyone. It's like he'd finally found someone who would understand what he'd been through. He never once made eye contact, staring at nothing as he relived memories that went back twenty-four years. When he stopped, I noticed moisture in his eyes.

"How long did it take you to be able to deal with the memories?" I was almost afraid to hear his answer.

"I don't want to discourage you, but they still return occasionally. I had a friend die in my arms the second day of the invasion, and I still hear his pleas for help sometimes at night.

"My advice would be to keep as busy as possible. I found that physical work was the best way to keep my mind off the war. I'd work twelve to fourteen hours a day and be totally spent in the evening. It became better with time."

I then told him about some of my worst experiences, including the boy who I allowed to take the point who was killed. I knew that would be the guilt hardest to deal with. I shared the anger and frustration of seeing signs condemning the war.

"Every war is horrible, Luke. The difference in the war I fought was that we were defending our freedom. People understood and could see that. You fought in a war that people don't understand. We are in a faraway land fighting for the freedom of someone else. Of course, our leaders portray it as fighting Communism, which will threaten us someday— someday is the key word. People can't see the immediate threat; hence the reluctance, which is turning to anger.

"We came home to a hero's welcome. I feel sorry for you boys that return from Vietnam. You fought and gave just as much as we did. You are just as much heroes as we were. The circumstances are just different."

"Mr. Waddell, I don't believe we can win the war. There is one instance that stands out in my mind like no other. I watched a group of North Vietnamese soldiers stand out in the open and fire their rifles at a plane that dropped Napalm on them. It was unbelievable to see such courage—commitment or whatever you want to call it. The generals keep saying we can win. The politicians believe them. To me it's like someone putting their arm in a meat grinder and thinking the only way to get relief is put it in farther. Maybe I'm wrong. I hope so."

"One thing for sure, Luke—it was good for both of us to be able to talk about it."

✳✳✳

Several hours later, Oliver and his wife returned with two representatives from the insurance company. Oliver knocked on the office door of the vet, and he joined them.

For the next half-hour the vet explained Lady's injuries, showing them the x-rays and possibilities of being able to repair them. He was thorough and gave them almost verbatim the same presentation he gave us. Frequently, one of the men would interrupt him and ask a question. The vet was patient and didn't indicate his opinion one way or the other about what to do with Lady.

The two men asked to have a few minutes to converse among themselves, going outside.

"What'd you think, Doc?" asked Oliver.

"I don't know. This is one of the most difficult parts of my job. I don't like to put an animal down unless it's absolutely necessary."

"Not many people are fortunate enough to have the income that you do though," Oliver's wife announced in a sarcastic tone.

Instead of responding, the vet stared at her until she turned away.

We seemed to have gone unnoticed until now when she addressed us. "What're y'all still doing here? You have no interest in Miss Jet."

Mr. Waddell looked at me to provide an answer. "This filly is special to Mom. We want to see the outcome."

"I still don't see where it's any of your business what we do with our horse," she said, lifting her nose in the air, like she smelled something.

After the two men returned, we waited for their decision. The older of the two spoke. "It's tough, but we understand the possibility that this filly will never recover to even produce a foal, therefore we will honor your insurance claim."

The two men left, and the vet went over and took a vial out of his refrigerator. He produced a needle and syringe. He placed the needle in the vial and began filling it. He went over to Lady and began tapping her neck to find the vein.

"Just a minute!" I said.

The vet stopped, looking at me. "What is it, son?"

"What will you take for Lady?" I looked at Oliver.

Oliver seemed confused. "What do you mean? We're going to get $25,000 for the insurance when we put her down."

"How much will you take for her? Mother has over $6,000 for her share of the purse. Will you take that for Lady and let her live? Your share of the purse is over $67,000."

Oliver might have been confused but his wife wasn't. "We're puttin' this horse down and collecting our insurance, which is $25,000."

"You mean you would kill this beautiful animal, when I'm willing to give you $6,000 to keep her alive?"

"We're not losing $19,000, young man. That's absurd."

I looked at Oliver, who evidently had lost something on the floor, the way he was examining it. "Oliver, what do you say about this?"

He glanced at his wife and resumed searching for whatever it was he'd lost.

"What would you take for her?" I asked. "I have a little money saved." This time I didn't bother addressing Oliver, looking at her.

"We'll give you $25,000 for the filly, and the vet can put his syringe up," said Mr. Waddell.

"No. We're putting this horse down and collecting our insurance. You probably don't even have that kind of money," his wife responded in an angry tone.

Evidently, Oliver found what he was searching for on the floor—his head came up. "We'll accept that."

The vet smiled and put his syringe in the trash can. "Well, that was interesting."

"When can we get our money?" demanded the wife.

Mr. Waddell reached in his pocket and took out his checkbook. "Is right now okay with you?"

This was unreal. He wrote the check out and presented it to Oliver, who looked at it and then promptly gave it to his wife.

They left immediately, leaving us alone with the vet, who was smiling. "I like happy endings. This is a nice filly. I dreaded ending her life. Now we need to make plans for her. We need to rig up a trailer with a sling and transport her to College Station. I'll call a friend of mine at the clinic to be expecting you."

"We need to talk with my mom and decide how to proceed," I said. "We'll be back early in the morning."

Outside the vet clinic, I asked Mr. Waddell, "Are you sure you want to do this?"

He burst out laughing. "I've never been more sure of anything in my life. Now I'm going back to my motel and have a strong drink. I now own half of a stakes horse instead of cheap claimers."

"Don't you want to go with me to tell my mother the good news?"

"No. You deserve to do that by yourself. I'll meet you here in the morning at seven to make plans for Lady."

When I told my mom what had happened—she cried and cried some more. She couldn't believe it.

"Why did he do it, Luke? That was a lot of money. He's a nice man, but I would've never figured that he'd do such a thing."

"I don't know, Mom. It may be a good investment. After all she's a really nice filly. Who knows, she could make a full recovery."

Granddad said, "You deserve something good to happen, Grace. Just accept it and be thankful. After all that has happened, the Lord knows you need something positive."

✳✳✳

I returned to my motel room just before midnight but not before stopping at a liquor store and getting a fifth of bourbon and a Coke. I'd consumed very little alcohol, but I was hoping it would replace the drugs that had allowed me to relax.

I sat on the edge of the bed thinking of the last several days. I'd begun to dread the nights. It wasn't that I dreamed. If I was able to go to sleep, I'd awake suddenly with images of the war. This would happen over and over during the night. Each time, waking up, I would look at the clock and find only fifteen or twenty minutes had passed. After my third drink, I felt drowsy and saw it was almost two o'clock. I lay down on the bed fully clothed and didn't wake up for three hours. I lay there hoping to go back to sleep but gave up after half an hour.

I showered and shaved, studying the image in the mirror. Two years in Vietnam had changed me, putting a permanent wrinkle in my forehead. I seldom smiled and my eyes were different. The color was the same—brown. They were darker, however, and sad. I'd lost weight, from 170 when I went to basic, to 152 when I weighed two days ago. The size 32 jeans I bought when I put away my uniform were loose and needed a belt to keep them up. I was voted most handsome my senior year in high school. I couldn't see that today.

I drove Mom's pickup to a convenience store for coffee and then to the track. There were no lights on in the trailer, so I didn't disturb her. She'd been through so much and needed all the rest she could get.

Sitting in the pickup, sipping my coffee, I thought of my future. Should I go to college? Mr. Waddell had said that long days of physical work had helped him after coming home from the war. Attending college would be the opposite of that. I didn't have long to make a decision since college would be starting within days. The pickup door opened, and I jumped.

"What're you doing sitting out here in the dark? Let's go in and get your mother up." Granddad climbed in and shut the door. "We've got a big day. Decisions to be made about Lady."

"How're you this morning, Granddad?"

"Couldn't be better. Read my Bible lesson and had two cups of coffee."

A light appeared in the trailer. "Let's go. I'm hungry." He was out of the pickup before I could respond.

The three hour's sleep had helped. I was hungry and the eggs and bacon tasted better than in a long time. By the time I'd helped Mom clear the table it was seven and time for the meeting with the vet.

# 7
# THE PARTNERSHIP

 GRACE

Now what? I was pleased beyond words that Lady wasn't going to be put down, but the expense of the vet bill was now the problem. My part had been invested in purchasing Lady, and I had no savings. We'd lived from month to month and struggled to make ends meet. Blaine's investment in Lady was already three times mine, and I couldn't expect him to put more money into her.

On the drive to the vet's for our meeting, I expressed my concern to Luke. "I have no idea how we're going to pay the vet bill."

"I have a little money saved, Mom. It might be enough to pay for half of the bill. Let's not worry until we visit with Blaine and the vet. We'll work something out."

We let Dad out at the barn to feed and were at the vet's a few minutes after seven. Blaine and the vet were visiting when we entered.

Blaine came to meet us, extending his hand to Luke. "Morning, Luke." He turned to me, smiling. "What'd you think, Grace? You ready to take ownership of Lady?"

"I could never thank you enough, Blaine. It was very kind of you."

"I consider it a good investment. Of course, we're taking a chance, but I feel good about it. I see no reason to draw up any kind of legal document. What do you say about a handshake for a 50-50 partnership?"

"That's generous, Blaine. You put up a lot more money than I did."

"Yeah, but I don't have your knowledge of Lady. Also, I don't have the time to give her the care she'll require. It'll work out in the long run."

We visited with the vet for the next half hour about how to proceed. He suggested again that we take her to the Texas A&M Clinic. We agreed, but the decision would be how to get her there. He had a recommendation to address that, also. "I know a guy who transports injured horses. I can get in touch with him and make arrangements for him to deliver her if you'd like. It would be a challenge for you to do it yourselves."

"Do you have any idea what it would cost?" I asked.

"I can find out and get back to you," he said. "You need to get her there as soon as possible."

"When you talk with him, Doc, just go ahead and make arrangements for him to pick her up." Blaine turned to me. "Grace, we really don't have a choice. I can take care of the bill. We'll work it out later."

We thanked the vet and left, and Blaine suggested we go to the track café. It was crowded, but we found a booth at the back and ordered coffee.

"I can't remember being this excited, Grace. At my age it's important to look forward to something. My daughter's getting married next month, and I've been a little depressed. I should be happy for her and looking forward to having a son-in-law, but something doesn't seem quite right. Probably just being an overprotective dad.

"Luke, you're quiet today. Do you think we're making a mistake?"

Luke fiddled with his coffee cup. "No, not at all. I know how much this filly means to Mom."

Blaine took out his Skoal can and tapped it against the table and laughed. "I know this is a bad habit, but I enjoy it. My ex hated it. Maybe that's why the marriage didn't last. Well, anyway, we're probably both happier with the outcome—me with my dip and her with a guy that has zero faults.

"Luke, I've got a proposition for you. You don't have to give me an answer now. Just think it over. I'd like for you to come to work for me.

I have a feeling you're pretty good horseback. I'm short-handed at the Auction, plus I need someone to go back and forth to my ranch. We have an older gentleman who lives on the ranch but is limited as to how much he can do. I'll pay you well, and there's a small house at the Auction that's vacant. It's not much but could be fixed up to be livable."

Shocked, I looked at Luke. He continued to concentrate on his cup. I began to think he wasn't going to answer.

"That's an offer worth considering. I'd planned on starting to college. I'm twenty-one and have no idea what I want to do for the next forty years. I'll consider your offer. How much time before you need an answer?"

"No hurry. Take your time. To tell you the truth, your mom is not going to have time to take care of the filly after her surgery. I thought we could set up a place at the Auction for her. If you were there, we would have someone we trusted to look after her. I know it'll take time for her to heal, and she'll need a great deal of care. I don't want you to feel pressured. I was just thinking of the convenience it would provide."

"Like I said, I'll think about it and let you know, one way or the other. I'm going to help Mom and Granddad move to the Albuquerque Fair. That's going to take several days. She may need me longer. We haven't talked about it yet. I should be able to give you an answer in a week."

"Sounds good to me. I need to be headed toward Dalhart." He took a check book out of his shirt pocket, tore out a check, and signed it. "Here, Luke. The hauler will probably want his money up front."

I thought, *what kind of a man would trust you with a blank check?* I answered my own question . . . a good one.

Luke was quiet on the drive to the barn. I knew better than to question him at this time. When we stopped, he didn't open his door to get out.

"I never expected anything like this. Home five days and a job offer. I'd about made up my mind to start college and maybe decide what I wanted to do for a career."

My heart went out to him. He was such a good boy, and obviously the war had done terrible things to him. I still hadn't seen him smile. He'd always been handsome with a grin that would melt your heart—which it did to many of the girls in high school. Now, he was faced with a decision that he wasn't ready to make. "You have some time, Luke. Just think it over and do what you feel is best for you."

✷ ✷ ✷

We had our trailer and horses moved to Albuquerque by Friday, the sixth. I'd hired a hauler to take the horses since it would've taken too many trips with my two-horse trailer.

The races didn't start until the tenth and ran for seventeen days consecutively. Dad and Luke took this opportunity to go back home to get Luke's car. Henry and I had bought him a 1960 Chevrolet Impala when he was a senior in high school. The car hadn't been driven in months so the battery would be down. It would also give them a chance to check on everything at home. We had no livestock, but it was always a concern that someone would break into our house, knowing we were gone. It always depressed Dad to return to his place. The memories of all the years spent with my mom came back fresh and reminded him again how much he missed her.

I stayed busy. With the nine horses plus Gem it was a daylight-to-dusk job to feed, water, clean their stalls, and get them exercised.

The day after they left the man transporting Lady was there to pick her up. I met him at the vet's and was surprised that Lady was able to walk, hobbled was more like it, but she was able to get to the trailer and up the ramp. The trailer was equipped with a support strap which would keep most of her weight off her feet. When I went to pay the hauler with Blaine's check that Luke had left for me, I received a surprise.

"I always get cash in advance for my service," he said with a frown.

"All I have is a check. It will be good, I assure you."

He shook his head. "I want cash for this job."

"Look, mister, I don't know you from Adam. I'm trusting you with a $25,000 filly, and you should trust me for a $650 check. You either take the check, or I'll find someone else to haul my filly."

For a minute I thought he was going to refuse, but he finally reached for the check.

✳✳✳

Dad returned the eighth of September, but Luke had decided to stay a couple of days longer. I asked Dad if Luke had told him the reason for the delay.

"No, he didn't tell me, and I didn't ask. I have a feeling he was going to stop in Amarillo to see his sister. That would make sense."

"Did he talk much on the trip home?" I was hoping that he'd opened up to his granddad.

"We talked some of when he was growing up and the fishing and hunting trips. He mentioned nothing about the war. He did talk some of Blaine's offer of the job at his Auction in Dalhart. He feels some pressure to take the job because of what Blaine has done. He understands it would help Blaine to have someone to care for Lady during her recovery."

I'd been afraid of that when Blaine made the offer. "What do you think he'll do, Dad?"

"I don't know. I sort of hope he takes the job. I know that Blaine would take care of him and treat him right. It might be the best thing for him at this time in his life. How'd you do while we were gone?"

"Okay. I stayed so busy, I was exhausted by bedtime. We're going to have our hands full with nine horses. It wouldn't bother me if we got several claimed during the meet. The purses are so good, I entered two of ours in $1500 claiming races on Wednesday. We had been running them for $2,000 but, with purses amounting to more than the claim, we'd still come out if we won.

"Without the money from the New Mexico Futurity purse we're going to be on a tight budget. Sometimes, I think it might be best to sell out and go home. I could get a job and probably be better off financially."

"Daughter, I hope you don't go that route. Going home brought back the memories. I miss your mother so much, and it's worse at the house we lived in for over fifty years. If you decide to continue training, I'm going to lease my place out and put that money into good use. That may be selfish of me, but I can't help it."

I knew all along that Dad dreaded returning to his place. It'd only been two years, and hopefully in time he'd be able to handle Mom's passing better. Now was not a good time to make a decision. Maybe in the future everything would become clearer.

# 8
# ENCOUNTERING SURPRISES

 JIMMIE LYN

It was a Saturday, September seventh. Just twenty more days until my wedding. On the way to meet my mother and try on my dress, I was amazed that everything was going so smoothly. Much better than when my younger sister got married. Her future mother-in-law had been difficult. No, a better word would be impossible. She'd wanted everything her way and didn't know the meaning of compromise. Finally, we had given in and let her make all the plans.

I parked at the Sunlight Café, where we were meeting to have breakfast and noticed my mom's car was already here. She was early which wasn't a surprise. She was never late and always dressed immaculately. She was forty-eight and looked ten years younger.

She was waiting for me inside the door. We hugged briefly, and I was reminded again how much taller I was than her.

"You're early. Been here long?"

"No, just a few minutes. You hungry?" She didn't wait for an answer, turning and starting toward a table. She never chose a booth.

Seated, I expressed what I was thinking. "Mother, you look nice. You don't look old enough to have a daughter my age. A stranger would think you're my sister if you weren't so short."

She smiled. "Jimmie Lyn, you're too kind. I don't feel so young today.

We'd better order. We're due at Mrs. Proctor's in half an hour to try on your dress. I don't guess it'd matter if we were late."

"We need to be considerate of her time."

A waitress took our order and, while we waited, I sensed something was wrong. "All right, Mother, what's bothering you?"

"Is it that obvious? I'm just experiencing some nostalgia thinking of your wedding. It brings back memories of mine and your dad's. It's hard to believe, but it's been almost thirty years. We went all the way to Raton for our honeymoon." She laughed out loud, which was unusual. "We had little money and stayed in a roach infested motel that cost six dollars a night. We only stayed three nights since he'd been drafted and was to report the next week. We didn't leave the room except to eat. We were young and in love, and he was going to war." She gazed off, being in a time and place far removed.

I'd never seen her like this or heard her speak this way. I searched for something to say. I tried to sound positive. "You're healthy and have a comfortable life. Sterling is a good husband and makes a good living. You don't have to worry about holding a job. Many women your age would trade places with you."

"I know, Jimmie Lyn. All that is true. I feel guilty for not being grateful and happier."

Our food arrived, and I started buttering my biscuit, but Mother just stared at her food. She picked up her napkin and dabbed at her eyes. "I'm sorry. Food doesn't look good to me this morning."

"Mother, is there more? Have you told me everything that's bothering you?"

"I've kept it inside me for years, and it's about to suffocate me. Maybe, it'll help if I tell someone. I miss Blaine. We've been apart for fifteen years, and I wish it was to do over again. You know what bothered me the most about your dad? Putting that filthy stuff in his mouth. A close second—his boots always smelled terrible. He couldn't get the stench off them."

I was shocked. I'd have never guessed she would admit something like this to anyone. "Sterling doesn't have either of these problems, does he?"

"No. He shines his shoes at least once a week. He brushes his teeth three times a day. Can you believe that? He showers twice a day. He uses Old Spice aftershave. I hate the smell of it. He sleeps in silk pajamas."

Listening to her, I assumed she wasn't happy with Sterling and his cleanliness. "I don't care for Old Spice either, but what's wrong with silk pajamas?"

"Silk is for women. Your daddy didn't even wear pajamas."

I needed to change the subject . . . immediately. "I'm hungry. Let's eat so we can get to Mrs. Proctor's." Where in the world did this come from?

✳✳✳

The dress was beautiful and fit perfectly. Looking in the mirror, I was pleased beyond words. "Mrs. Proctor, I love it. You did a fabulous job. Thank you."

"The dress is okay, but you make it beautiful. I love to sew for attractive clients. They make me look good. The groom is going to be blown away when he sees you coming down the aisle."

Could that be true? "Thank you, Mrs. Proctor. I hope you're right."

Mother seemed to have come out of her depressed state. "Drake is six-foot-five, Mrs. Proctor, and handsome. He's a lawyer and is going to open a practice here after they're married."

Mother paid Mrs. Proctor, and I took my wedding dress and we left. I'd driven my car and Mother had come in hers, so we would go our separate ways. I was hoping the subject of my dad wouldn't come up again. Not so.

"Jimmie Lyn, please don't say anything about what I told you today. I'm ashamed of myself for even telling you."

"Have you said anything to Dad that would let him know how you feel?" I asked.

"Heavens no. Over the years, I kept thinking he might express his feelings to me. It never happened."

It was hard to believe what I was hearing. "Mother, you're married! My dad would never interfere with that. You know him better than anyone. He's not the kind of person who would break up a marriage." Now I was losing patience with her.

"Well, anyway. Don't tell anyone what we talked about. Are you going to Amarillo today to see Drake?"

"Yes. We're going shopping for some furniture. I'm excited."

My mother was full of surprises today, and her next statement caught me off guard. "Jimmie Lyn, I probably shouldn't tell you this . . ."

"Tell me what? Go ahead, let's hear it."

"Your dad doesn't care for Drake. It's probably just a Dad thing. Nobody's good enough for his little girl."

What was my mother trying to do, ruin my day or maybe my life? "Why are you telling me this today? What has he told you? Why doesn't he like Drake?"

"Oh, Jimmie Lyn, it's nothing. I probably shouldn't have even told you. Tell Drake hello for me." She got in her car and drove away, leaving me distraught.

On the drive to Amarillo my mind was spinning like a merry-go-round. My mother had lost it. Maybe she was going through the mid-life crisis. Why today? Three weeks until my wedding and she lays this before me. I could do nothing about her problem. I'd have never thought she still had feelings for Dad. I thought Sterling was the perfect fit for her taste, but evidently she'd been comparing Mr. Clean to my dad for some time. She must've decided the nasty stuff Dad put in his mouth and the smelly boots weren't so bad.

Now, the information she'd laid on me about Dad not approving of Drake. He'd done a remarkable job of hiding it. Should I approach him about it? What good could it do? Whatever he told me wouldn't change my mind about Drake. He was my dream—all six-foot-five of him. What if Drake knew how my dad felt?

✳✳✳

We had a great time shopping and, for the time being at least, I forgot about my mother. Walking into a store with Drake, with my arm in his, I knew from the looks people gave us that we were a sight to see. I wore heels which put me over six feet but that was no problem. Drake was such a gentleman, always opening the door for me and allowing me to choose the eating place.

We bought a bedroom and dining room suite. We had to purchase an extra-long mattress. Drake insisted on paying for all of it, saying we'd soon put our resources together.

We'd planned almost everything except our honeymoon. Drake asked me while we were eating lunch where I would like to go.

"How long can you take off from work?" I asked.

"I have a week's vacation coming. I could probably extend that if necessary." He reached over and touched me on the arm. "I want to do whatever I can to make it special."

"Have you notified your firm that you'll be leaving them soon?" I was hoping for a positive answer.

"Not yet. They're not going to be happy about it. I thought it might be best to wait until after we're married. Are you sure it's all right with you if we move into your apartment until we can buy a house?"

"That's no problem. If we can't find something we like, it might be necessary to build our own house. What would you think about that,

Drake?"

"Sounds good to me. You mentioned that your dad had a ranch. How many acres are there in the property?"

"I believe there are about 12,000 acres. Maybe a little more." Strange, I didn't remember telling him anything about my dad owning a ranch. I probably did and just forgot with everything else on my mind.

I moved the subject back to the wedding. "Do you have a best man chosen?"

"Not yet. It's difficult because I don't know any of the guys in the office that well. I might just have to hire someone," he laughed.

"What about groomsmen?" Surely he'd gotten someone.

"Same thing. Don't worry, Jimmie—it'll all come together. We still have three weeks."

Maybe I was just being a worrier. I wanted everything to be perfect, but Drake didn't seem to be concerned so I shouldn't be either.

"What about going to my apartment and watching the game this afternoon? Notre Dame is playing USC at three."

"I really need to get back to Dalhart. I'm behind on my bookkeeping at the Auction. I've been spending too much time on the wedding." What was wrong with me? I never said no to Drake.

✷✷✷

I was at my office by four in the afternoon. I was the only one there, and it was a good time to get some uninterrupted work done. Try as I could to get my mind on my task at hand, I kept being distracted thinking of what my mother had told me.

I heard the front door open and a few seconds later Dad appeared in my doorway. "What're you doing working on your day off?"

"Just trying to catch up. Sit down and visit with me a few minutes. I just got back from a shopping spree in Amarillo."

"Did you find what you were looking for?" he asked.

"Yes, Drake and I found nice bedroom and dining room suites." Should I ask him? "Dad, can I ask you a personal question?"

"Sure. Go ahead."

"Did you ever think about getting married again? I know you must get lonesome." There, I did it.

He laughed. "Not really. I never met anyone that interested me. That doesn't mean the opportunity wasn't there. I had to quit going to the grocery store. Women would come up and grab my arm under any pretense to start a conversation. I even received a number of phone calls from single women inviting me for dinner."

"You and mother get along so well. I'm surprised you aren't still together." Was I saying too much?

"I don't know, Jimmie Lyn. It's hard to explain. She wanted me to be something I wasn't, and I was probably guilty of feeling the same way about her. She married someone who met her qualifications much better than I did."

"I'm sorry, Dad. I'm just being nosey."

Dad left, saying he had to check on one of the pens. He probably didn't want any more questions.

# 9

# THE OFFER

After replacing the battery on my car, it kicked right off. I decided to stay a few days after Granddad left. I needed some time to think about Mr. Waddell's offer.

The house was musty from being shut up, so I opened up all the windows to allow it to air out. I sat down on the worn couch and thought about how much change had occurred in my life the last two years. I wasn't the same boy who'd left home to be inducted into the Marines. Could I ever return to that innocence of two years ago? No. I answered my own question. I'd seen too much suffering, death, and fear.

I thought about what the Captain had said upon informing me I could go home. "Your service here has been exemplary and your leadership deserves recognition." What about LeBlanc, who I'd placed on point? I'd watched as they picked up what was left of him and put it in a body bag. He deserved much more recognition than I did. Why did I give in and let him take the point? I knew better. There's so much to look for on the point, and he was only eighteen without experience. A savvier man might've seen the mine. I'd looked up his hometown. I desperately wanted to see his family and confess that I was responsible for his death. However, I was afraid to see their reaction—feel the wrath—see the suffering. I thought that confessing might relieve some of the guilt, but I didn't have the courage to do it.

It was important to get my mind off the war and on the decision that was needed about my future. With a steady job, I could help my mother financially. I'd always been aware that they struggled to get by. The choice should've been clear. Why did I hesitate to commit to a job at the Auction? "Because you aren't emotionally able to make a decision about anything," I mumbled.

✳✳✳

I stayed two miserable nights before deciding to leave and go by Dalhart on the way back to New Mexico since it wouldn't be that much out of the way. I left on Monday, the ninth of September, and stopped at a small café in Clarendon to eat. I ordered the lunch which was cheap but delicious. Sitting in the booth eating my dinner, the memories of my dad and me stopping here on the way to Amarillo years ago flowed like water going downhill. We sat in this same booth and ordered the lunch special. I visualized my dad sitting across from me.

The final time I saw Dad was last Christmas when I had a two-week leave. I remembered looking back at him and Mom waving as I stood on the ramp of the plane taking me back to Vietnam. I would like to have just five minutes to tell him how much I loved him. Now it was too late. I ate half my dessert and left.

It was midafternoon when I drove into Dalhart and stopped at a gas station and asked directions to the Auction, which was no problem to locate. It was five miles north of town and visible from the highway. I parked in front of what appeared to be the office and went inside.

"Is Mr. Waddell in?" I asked the lady behind the counter.

"It depends. If you're selling something—no. He doesn't like salesmen."

"I'm not a salesman. My mom trains his racehorse."

She smiled. "Yes, he's in. Let me tell him he has a visitor. Your name?"

"Luke."

Mr. Waddell came in seconds later with a warm greeting. "Luke. It's good to see you. I hope you're here to take me up on my offer. Come into my office."

"I was hoping you might show me around if you have time," I said.

"Of course. I need to move around anyway."

For the next hour we drove around while he explained the workings of the business. Even though there was only one sale a week, cattle were coming in and leaving daily. I was surprised to find that the hay he fed came off his ranch which had several hundred acres of cultivated land. It was a much larger operation than I'd imagined. The pens must've stretched for a quarter of a mile.

We stopped at a small house several hundred yards west of the pens. "This is the house that's available for you. It's nothing fancy but is furnished with appliances. It has a propane tank out back that provides fuel for the space heaters. It gets plenty cold up here in the winter. It has a little over 900 square feet in it. Of course, the smell is noticeable but, being west of the pens, we seldom have an east wind, which helps.

"I think you coming to work for me would be good for both of us, Luke. I need someone I can depend on, and you need a job that will keep you busy. You'd work here at the Auction moving and feeding cattle, but a great deal of your time would be going back and forth to my ranch. We're constantly having to move cattle from here to the ranch and turn them out for a while. They stop doing well in the pens, and it helps to turn them out on pasture. Also, I often need someone at the ranch to work there for several days.

"I haven't given you any particulars, Luke. I'll pay you $300 a month plus free rent with all the bills paid. I have a pickup that you can use on your trips to and from the ranch. I put enough beef up each year to supply my full-time employees, so your meat will be furnished. I also provide health insurance for my employees who work at least a forty-hour week.

"What do you think about that deal?"

I spoke before even thinking. "It's more than generous. When do you want me to start?"

"Just as soon as possible," he said.

"I need to check with Mom and see if she needs me to do anything. If everything goes well, I'll be here next Sunday. That'll be the fifteenth of the month."

"That's great, Luke." He extended his hand, and I took it. "Now, let's get you signed up. You need to meet the payroll clerk and head bookkeeper."

We drove back to the office, and I followed him into another room down the hall from his. The door was open, but he knocked. "Got some more work for you, Honey." He turned to me. "This is Luke. Luke, this is my daughter, Jimmie Lyn. She'll need some information from you."

A voice from the front office announced, "Blaine, you have a call on line one."

He left, leaving me standing in the door. "I'm glad to meet you," I said. She stood, and I was surprised that we were eye level with one another.

"Come in and have a seat. This shouldn't take long. What's your full name?"

"Luke Emerson Ranker. I go by Luke." I couldn't decide if she was pretty or not. She was pale like she seldom spent time outside. Her nose was narrow but longer than most. She had high cheekbones and her blonde hair was in a pony tail. She had the greenest eyes I'd ever seen.

"When were you born?"

"August 21, 1947."

"I need your social security number."

I took out my billfold, found my card, and read the numbers off to her. She smiled, stretching her full lips, thanking me. She was a pretty lady— the smile did it.

"Who was your last employer?"

"United States Marines for the past two years. Before that, I day worked for area ranchers while I was in high school and the summer after

I graduated."

She looked up in surprise. "That explains why my dad liked you. You've been in the military. Who's your closest living relative?" she asked.

"My mom, Grace Ranker."

She hesitated. "That's my dad's trainer, which means your dad just passed. Oh, I'm so sorry. I didn't realize who you were. Dad didn't tell me."

I didn't know how to respond to her sympathy. "That's okay. Your dad offered me a job. I hope he needed someone and didn't just feel sorry for me."

"No, we stay short-handed. My dad is thrifty to say the least. Between the Auction and the ranch, we always need more help. That's all the information I need. We pay our employees each Friday. Do you have a place to live?"

"Your dad offered me the house west of the pens."

She wrinkled up her nose and frowned. "The smell is terrible. You might want to reconsider."

"I'll give it a try. If it's too much I'll look for something in town." The way I'd been living the last two years, I could take a little offensive smell.

"That's all I need," she repeated. "Welcome to the High Plains Cattle Auction."

I wasn't sure what to do next, so I offered my hand. "Thank you." She accepted my hand with a firm grip and another smile. No doubt about it—she was a pretty lady.

I stopped at Mr. Waddell's office on the way out. "I'm finished. I guess it's official now."

"Did the bookkeeper treat you right? She can be ornery sometimes."

"She was nice."

"She's about to get married." He frowned. "To a lawyer."

Evidently, he wasn't fond of lawyers. I stated the obvious. "You're going to have a new son-in-law."

"Yeah. Unless she backs out. Slim chance of that, but miracles do happen. Have you talked with your mother lately, Luke?"

"No. I've been back to our home place the last several days."

"I've talked with her a couple of times. Lady made it through surgery, and the vets are optimistic. Your mother has asked to take care of Lady herself. That doesn't surprise me. She loves that filly. It might work out for the best since you'll be going back and forth to the ranch. She did indicate that she wants you to pick up Lady. Does she know you're going to work for me?"

"No. I didn't know myself until an hour ago?"

"It's no problem. When Lady is ready to pick up you can go after her. It may even be before you start here. If not, you can take off. I'm excited about owning half interest. That helps get my mind off the wedding."

I declined an invitation to stay overnight with Mr. Waddell and left for New Mexico. It was already five o'clock, but I should be there by nine.

I'd made a decision. Why? It seemed that something just took over and the words were out of my mouth before I realized it. Maybe it was the $300 a month, which was a good salary. It could be because Mr. Waddell was anxious for me to say yes, and I wanted to please him.

Driving gives you time to think, and I did a lot of it for the next four hours. I made an effort to concentrate on the good in my life. I was home—safe. I had a job with good pay which would enable me to help my mom. I had a house to live in that wouldn't cost me anything. Lady had come through the surgery well, and the prognosis was good.

All the positive thoughts were eventually interrupted by troubling ones. My dad was gone. I would never see him again. The image of that day in the jungle, hearing the explosion and witnessing my point man's death. I pulled over to the side of the road and cried.

# 10

# NEW MEXICO FAIR

 GRACE

After looking at my bank statement and trying to determine where I could cut costs without being overdrawn, I had a headache. I had to reduce expenditures and the only way to do it was to start exercising my own horses. I'd quit riding ten years ago at Henry's insistence. Now at forty-five, was it possible?

Three owners had picked up their horses before I left Ruidoso. None had said as much, but I knew the reason—woman trainer. That left me with three outside horses plus the three I owned. I received eight dollars a day for the outside horses which only came to about $700 a month. If I had to pay to have all six ridden every other day or even every third day, that would amount to over $200 a month. The feed bill would take up much of what was left. Even after exercising my own horses, I would need purse money.

I kept thinking of the $6,000 I'd given up for my share of Lady. With that money, it would've been so much easier. I shuddered at that thought. They'd have put that beautiful creature down. Anyway, the news from the vet was encouraging.

It was already seven o'clock, and I expected Luke to be here by now. He'd come in last night but refused to stay with me, saying he'd get a motel room. I was relieved that he had taken the job at the Auction. Blaine would look after him—I was sure of that. I insisted that he let me wash his clothes before he returned to start work next Sunday.

It's hard to imagine what coming home from war and your dad not being here would be like for anyone. He'd always shared more with his dad growing up than he had me. I knew he'd never speak to me of the horror he experienced.

My dad was able to do less and less. He couldn't handle the horses, to even put them on the walker. He was able to feed and water, but after cleaning a stall or two he would be exhausted.

I was about to give up and go to the barn to get my day started when Luke arrived. "Morning, Mom. I'm running late. I expected you to be gone."

"I was about to leave. Would you like some breakfast?"

"No, thanks. I'll take Granddad for coffee and get something to eat." He got up to leave.

"Just a minute, Luke." He sat back down. "I wanted to tell you that I've decided to go back to exercising our horses. It'll save money, and it's not that big of a deal."

"Mom, that's not a good idea! I have a job and can help out now. You're not as young as you used to be."

"Luke, I've made up my mind. Besides, it'll be good for me. I miss your dad terribly and staying busy helps me. I'll wear a helmet and be careful. All of our horses are gentle. Please don't argue with me."

"Just the same, I'm going to send you some money occasionally. I can get by on less than $300 a month, especially with free housing."

"That's not necessary, Luke." I almost started crying right there.

"Okay, my turn. Please don't argue with me, Mom."

I went over and hugged him. "We're going to make it."

✳✳✳

The next several days went well with Luke helping. I would work three horses each morning and be on the track at daylight to beat the crowd. I still had my exercise saddle, helmet, and chaps from my riding days. The first couple of mornings it was difficult to get out of bed, but by the third day it was better and I was actually enjoying riding. There were a couple of other girls on the track, but they were years younger.

We had one of our own horses in on Wednesday going seven furlongs in a $1,500 claiming race. The purse was $2,000 which made the race tough. People were willing to drop their horses a class or two for that kind of purse. I'd been able to get our regular jockey to ride him. No one could get more out of a horse than Kenneth Hallmark. Candy Man was not our best horse, but on certain days he would run well. I was hoping this would be one of those days.

When I looked at the program that morning it was not a surprise to find that one owner had dropped his horse from $3,000 to this $1,500 claiming race. I had a sinking feeling after getting my hopes up. Besides the horse which had been dropped down, there were several that had been running for $2,000 claim.

On the way with Candy Man to the saddling paddock, I'd convinced myself we'd probably run last with these horses who didn't even belong in this race. Candy Man was calm; after all, this was the time of day he usually took his nap.

Kenneth was waiting on me in the paddock, since I was the last one to arrive. "Is The Man ready, Grace?"

"Have you seen the field? Candy Man doesn't belong with these horses." I reached and grabbed the cinch pushing it underneath to Kenneth who pulled it tight.

"We'll make a run at'em. Lots of speed in the race. I may hang back and let them fight it out for the first half. Be fresh for the stretch run."

"You've ridden him enough times to know, Kenneth. You ride him the way you want to." I gave Kenneth a leg up and went to join Dad and Luke in the owners' section. Candy Man, who was number 6, didn't need a pony horse. I wasn't optimistic enough to stand at the finish line, close to the Winner's Circle. I noticed the six horse was 25-1 on the tote board.

"How much did you bet?" asked Dad when I sat down beside them.

"Nothing. He can't compete with these horses. I shouldn't have even entered him."

"O ye of little faith," he said, handing me a $5 across ticket, in other words—$5 to win, place, and show.

"Dad, that was a waste of money." I couldn't believe it.

"Luke wasted more money than I did. He bet $10 across."

"Y'all are betting with your heart and not your mind." That was forty-five dollars down the drain, which would buy several bales of hay, I thought.

Ten horses broke from the gates, and when they came by the stands the first time Candy Man was dead last. At the quarter pole he was still last, but at the half-mile pole he'd moved up to sixth, and when they came into the stretch, he'd moved to fourth. With a quarter mile to go Kenneth started asking him for more. I was up screaming by now. Coming to the wire he finished second by a length. I couldn't believe it. Quick math revealed a $600 check.

"Well, Daughter, you want me to cash your ticket?"

"I can't believe it. Kenneth is amazing." I made my way out of the stands down to the track to take my horse.

Kenneth was smiling as he gave him to me. "Another furlong, and we win the race."

I hugged him. "You're something else. Thank you so much. I can use that money."

"Do you have Big Time Boy in this week?" he asked.

"Friday. Going six furlongs for $3,000 claim. It'll be tough."

"I wouldn't have it any other way," he said, walking off.

Dad presented me with $51.75 when I walked up to the barn leading Candy Man. I tried to give him part of it but he refused, saying I could buy his supper. That meant Luke's ticket was worth over $100. As I thought of how much Henry would've enjoyed today, my spirits sank.

❊❊❊

On Friday, I received my first indication of the obstacles awaiting me as a woman trainer. Big Boy had a perfect trip gaining the lead at the eight pole and winning by two lengths. Waiting at the Winner's Circle for Kenneth and Big Boy, the inquiry sign appeared on the tote board. The announcement came that a foul had been lodged against the 2 horse which was Big Boy by the jockey on number 5.

Kenneth rode up on Big Boy. "What ta hell is going on, Grace? We didn't touch anybody."

The wait seemed to go on forever until finally, the decision was announced. "Ladies and gentleman the 2 horse has been moved to second place due to interference in the stretch. The winner is the number 5 horse, Salty Dan."

Kenneth went ballistic, shouting and carrying on until one of his friends took his arm and guided him off the track. He looked back at me as he left. "Grace, they cheated us! We won fair and square. We didn't interfere with anyone."

It so happened that Salty Dan had the leading trainer in New Mexico. I left the track, leading Big Boy, knowing that if Henry had been here this would've never happened.

Luke and Dad were waiting for me at the barn. Of course, both were livid. Dad seemed to be more upset than Luke. "Daughter, we won that race. Luke and I looked at the replay and Big Boy didn't foul that horse. He never touched him. When he went around Salty Dan, there was no interference. I didn't know people would cheat so openly. The Bible says—I believe it's the fourth chapter of James— '**So whosoever knows the right thing to do and fails to do it, for him it is sin.**'"

Of course, instead of cursing when he was upset, Dad always quoted the Bible. I wished my faith was that strong.

"Mom, they were bold enough to do that because you're a woman. If Dad had been here, they wouldn't have attempted it. That's what makes me so mad."

"I know, Luke. I knew it would happen but not this quickly."

I put Big Boy on the walker, and each of us found a chair and sat in silence as he made the circle. Now, I had to call Blaine and tell him the news. His horse was taken down because he had a woman trainer, which cost him $1,200. The three owners who picked up their horses in Ruidoso were right.

I heard a whine and looking behind us saw a dog. He was a mess with cuts and abrasions on his face and ears.

Luke saw him also. "Come here, boy. What happened to you?" The dog whined again, walking with a limp toward Luke. When the dog reached him he put his head between Luke's legs, as if trying to hide. "You been in a fight?" He continued to whine. Luke gently rubbed his head, being careful not to touch the cuts.

Dad warned him. "Be careful, Luke. That's a Pit Bull. They can be dangerous."

"He's hurt, Granddad, and not just physically. Mom, do you have any ointment to put on the cuts?"

"I think so. It'll be in the medicine bag." I returned a few minutes later with Scarlet Oil and some salve. He was still trying to hide between Luke's legs.

Luke lifted his head speaking softly. "You're all right, boy. Let's put some medicine on those cuts."

It moved me to tears watching him doctor that poor dog. He was so gentle and easy. When he finished the dog licked his hand and then put his head back between Luke's legs.

We sat there for another half hour while Luke talked quietly to the stray. I asked Luke what we were going to do with him. It was obvious that he'd been abandoned.

"I'll take him with me. He needs doctoring for several days before we try to find someone to take him."

"The motel won't let him stay. Why don't we take him to the trailer, and you can stay with me tonight?"

"That might be best," he said. When he got up and started toward his car, the dog was right behind him, limping along.

# 11

# WAITING

♪§ JIMMIE LYN ♪⟩

I didn't see Drake the day after we went furniture shopping. I went to church and spent the remainder of the day at the Auction working. I was excited about our plans . . . to buy a house or build one if we couldn't find what we wanted. Drake never disagreed, which I guess was good, but I found myself wanting him to be more assertive at times. I would even occasionally welcome a friendly difference of opinion, which would probably come later.

The next day I signed up the guy that Dad had hired. I was embarrassed when he revealed that his mom was Dad's trainer, which meant his dad had passed recently. Dad was a good judge of character, and I imagine he'd be a good employee. He was young, only twenty-one, but he seemed older. He had the saddest look about him, not smiling once during his time in my office.

Time seemed to drag by on Monday. Drake was coming over tonight for a homemade dinner, and even though I wasn't the best cook, I had everything planned. I was going to cook a chicken casserole dish that usually turned out good, plus a salad. I'd attempted a chocolate pie last night, and I hoped it was as good as it looked. He wasn't coming until seven, so I'd have two hours after work to get everything ready.

A little before five a truck arrived with a load of cattle. Just my bad fortune, I thought. I'm going to be late getting home by the time they're unloaded and I processed the paperwork. I went outside to see they got busy unloading. Sometimes the driver and whoever was working would stand around and shoot the bull before even starting to get the cattle off the truck.

"Are you going to supervise?" Dad asked, smiling. "Expanding your job description?"

"Drake's coming tonight for dinner. I'm anxious to get home."

"Take off. I can handle this. It'd do me good to take over for you." He took out his box of Skoal and tapped it against his other hand. "You take your job too seriously, Honey. Now be off with you. I can handle this."

I reached and kissed him on the cheek. "Thank you. Love you, Dad." I left quickly before my conscience insisted I stay.

✳✳✳

If there was such a thing as a perfect evening—this had to be it. The casserole was good, and I outdid myself on the pie. Drake had two pieces, and his praise was lavish. I soaked it all up like a drought riddled pasture.

"Jimmie, that was delicious. I'm marrying a beautiful woman and a great cook. How could a man be so fortunate?"

"That works both ways, Drake. I never thought anyone would come along like you. I've waited a long time, and believe me it was worth the wait."

"I need to tell you something. I've put it off thinking the situation would correct itself, but that hasn't happened. It's going to be necessary to return to England for a few days. A case is being settled in which I was involved, and they need me to testify. I shouldn't be gone more than a week at the most."

The news caught me completely off guard. "When are you leaving?"

"I have a plane ticket to leave Wednesday. I hate to go, but there's no other choice. I'll be back before you know it."

"But, Drake, it's less than three weeks until our wedding. Is there no way you can get out of it?" For the first time I wasn't happy with him. Evidently, he could see that.

"Jimmie, please understand—I tried to change it until after the wedding. You could've gone with me as part of our honeymoon. My efforts were useless. This is a huge case involving important people."

On the verge of tears, my perfect evening was ruined. "It'll only be eight days until the wedding when you get back. What if there is a delay in whatever business you have over there?"

"I'll leave if there's a delay. Nothing can make me miss the wedding." He came over and took me in his arms, towering above me.

It'll be all right, I thought. You're being silly. Nothing is going to get in the way of our wedding.

❊❊❊

The remainder of the week, I tried to stay as busy as possible to keep my mind off Drake being out of the country. I confided in Piper on Tuesday after we'd completed our three-mile jog but received little sympathy.

"I don't understand why you're worried, Jimmie Lyn. He'll be back in a few days, in plenty of time for the wedding. You have no reason to be concerned. Just think, in a month you'll be happily married."

"I can't help it, Piper. It's too soon before our wedding for him to be out of the country."

"I don't understand. What're you afraid of? He won't return of his own accord—his plane will crash—he'll just disappear into thin air?"

"I don't know. You're my best friend. I was expecting a little sympathy."

She laughed. "I love you, Jimmie Lyn. We've been friends since first grade. I prefer encouragement over sympathy."

She was right, I thought, after she'd left. She knew me better than anyone. All those years we'd been friends and only once had we had a disagreement, which came close to ending our friendship. The doctor she went to work for out of high school was married. Two years later he divorced his wife to marry Piper. It was wrong, and I told her so. We didn't speak for three months, but our past was too strong to keep us apart. I finally went to her, saying I would accept her decision to marry Daniel.

✸✸✸

When I went to work on Wednesday, Dad realized something was wrong. He could always read my moods much better than my mother, probably because she was usually thinking about herself.

"Honey, what's bothering you? You're down in the dumps, that's evident to your daddy."

"I'm trying to deal with it but not being successful. Drake is leaving today for England. Something about a case he worked on before he came to Amarillo. It's so close to our wedding. It's not supposed to take long—a week at the most."

"Is that all? I thought y'all might have broken up. I wouldn't worry about it. You're going to have a lifetime with him."

"You're right. Being depressed doesn't help anything. Do you have a nice suit for the wedding?" I hadn't seen him in anything but jeans for years.

"Certainly. You don't think I'd embarrass my daughter, do you? I tried it on a couple of nights ago, and it still fits. I'll take it to the cleaner's tomorrow, and you'll be proud of your daddy when he walks you down the aisle. However, I may back out of giving you away."

"Oh, Dad. I'll still be around. You'll just be gaining a son." The smile didn't appear as I'd expected.

"I've always been proud of you, Jimmie Lyn. It doesn't seem possible that you're grown and getting married. It didn't affect me when your sister married and moved off." His voice cracked a little. "I've always been a little partial to you."

Now, he had me in tears. I hugged him. "I love you, Dad. I've always been partial to you, too."

✳✳✳

Drake called Friday night, saying everything was on schedule, and he was due to testify on Tuesday and should be home late Wednesday night. He sounded good, and after ending the call I chastised myself for being upset. Like Dad said, we'd have a lifetime together.

The next morning, I met my mother again for breakfast at the nicest restaurant in town. Afterwards, we were going to plan the rehearsal dinner being held in their party room, which was large enough to seat everyone comfortably.

She started in immediately with suggestions for the rehearsal menu. "I think we should have seafood. Shrimp and lobster would be perfect. For dessert, three types of cheese cake would be nice. A white wine would go well with seafood. What do you think?"

What an irrelevant question. She didn't really care what I thought. I might as well upset her. "Mother, most of the people in the wedding have never eaten lobster. We'd have to have it and the shrimp flown in and that would be expensive. Most of them don't even drink wine. I think that rib eye steak and a baked potato would be more appropriate with iced tea, soft drinks, or even beer for those that would prefer it. Your dessert sounds good. But just one choice."

The frown appeared immediately. "Jimmie Lyn, that's what everyone in this town has at their rehearsal dinners. I wanted this to be special."

"It will be special. It's my wedding rehearsal. Besides, Dad can furnish the steaks, and they'll be delicious."

"Do we have to serve beer? That is so—so country. Couldn't we serve wine instead? It would implement a little culture anyway."

"We can do both. Remember, Dad likes beer with his steak." I knew immediately it was a mistake to bring up Dad.

"Does he ever talk about me, Jimmie Lyn—about when we were together?"

How was I going to address this? "Ever so often he will mention something that happened when you were still together."

"That's not what I mean. Does he ever mention me specifically? Has he ever indicated that he was sorry we divorced. I know he must be lonely."

There was no way out of this without disappointing her. "He respects you. I have never heard him say anything negative about y'all's marriage. He's never said anything to the effect that he was sorry it worked out the way it did."

She ducked her head. "Oh."

"Let's see if we can talk with the owner about the rehearsal dinner." Anything to get off the subject of my dad.

✳✳✳

I talked with Drake again Sunday. He said his flight schedule would have him back in Amarillo at nine-thirty Wednesday night. We didn't talk long because the reception was poor, but the words "I miss you and love you" came through distinctly.

We usually didn't jog on Sunday, but after talking with Drake I was anxious and decided to make an exception. For some reason exercise cleared my mind. As I approached the halfway mark in my route, I started thinking about the meeting with my mother. She was preparing herself to approach my dad about getting back together. She'd always been a little flaky, and now she was approaching, if not going off, the deep end. Surely, she'd wait until after the wedding. Should I warn Dad? What if I was wrong? I knew my mother well enough to be right about her most of the time. I'd been so caught up in my wedding, I'd missed the obvious— she would do it.

Drake would be home Wednesday, and I'd talk with him about it. I was going to surprise him and be at the airport when he arrived. This was the first time we'd been apart, and the reunion would be movie-like. I saw a vision of myself running into his arms when we saw one another.

✳✳✳

I thought Tuesday would last forever and the same Wednesday. I took special care to wear my favorite pant suit Wednesday to meet Drake. The black bellbottoms fit my long waist and longer legs, and a crocheted black wool vest topped the white tapered mock turtleneck sweater, which seemed to draw attention. Even though I favored my dad in mannerisms, attitudes, and beliefs, I inherited my mother's hair. Thick as a horse's tail and blond, but that worked to advantage in being able to put it up and out of the way. Today I pulled it into a high bun which covered the back of my head. A black and white silk scarf hid the pins holding it in place. I spent extra time with my makeup but still arrived an hour early. I found a seat at the exit for his flight and waited as the minutes dragged by. My scattered thoughts sifted through the reason I would wear black today since my closet contained many happy-colored items. Oh well, too much analyzing. I should've brought a book to read or even a magazine.

At 9:45, I went to the window and watched his plane land. It would only be a matter of minutes now, and I stood at a place where he couldn't miss seeing me when he entered the terminal.

A short time later people started arriving from his flight. I smiled, thinking it wouldn't be hard to spot him. I waited as the crowd entered. Several more minutes passed and now only one or two at a time were coming in. Then there was no one. Fear ran through me like something from a horrible nightmare. Where was he?

# 12

# A NEW JOB

I woke up with the dog staring at me inches from my face. He immediately licked me from my chin up to my forehead with one swipe of his tongue. "You need to potty?" Another sloppy kiss before I could dodge it. "Okay, let me get dressed."

It was only the fifteenth of September, but the jacket felt good when we went outside. Bull did his business, and we were back inside in minutes. Even though I'd only had him a short time, giving him a name meant he'd be permanent. He was short and stocky like most Pit Bulls. His grayish body with its white face had a perpetual smile, which I thought was unusual for any breed. I'd already discovered that people gave him distance when we came close.

I stayed as quiet as possible since Mom wasn't up. I put the coffee on and sat down at the table. I was leaving today for Dalhart and a new future. I'd grown up with cattle and horses, so the work at the Auction would be familiar. However, I knew that events of the past two years would be hard to put aside. Hopefully, staying busy would keep my mind off the memories, which thus far would not go away.

Mom was doing better, despite the setback Friday with Big Boy being taken down after winning. We'd talked late the last two nights about her plans, yet Dad kept coming back into the conversation, but at least she could talk about him without breaking down.

She'd decided to go on to Sunland Park for the fall meet without going home, feeling like it would be too difficult to return this soon. She was probably right. The few nights I'd spent there were miserable. Everywhere I looked, there were Dad's memories. I'd just poured my first cup of coffee when Mom came in. "Morning. I tried to be quiet and not disturb you," I said.

"I slept late for me. It's already five-thirty. What time are you leaving?" She sat down with her coffee.

"Around noon, I guess. No hurry. It's only about four hours." Bull whined and put his head against my leg.

"You've only had that dog a day and a half, and he already adores you. From the looks of him he was abused. His cuts already look better."

I reached down and rubbed him on the back, avoiding the wounds. "They fight Pit Bulls. I imagine that's part of his history. Evidently, after his injuries he'd been abandoned."

She smiled. "Finding you was the best day of his life. Is he going to ride in the front seat with you?"

"Probably. I hope he's welcomed at the Auction."

"I have a feeling that Blaine likes dogs. Which reminds me, Luke—Lady's going to be ready to pick up in a few days. It'd help if you could keep her until I get moved to Sunland. That would prevent us from having to trailer her from here."

"That shouldn't be a problem. Are you sure you can take care of her?" With Granddad not being able to help much, it was a legitimate concern.

"I think so. I talked with the vet at A&M a few days ago. He said she was able to walk and stand longer periods of time. He was amazed that she was so gentle. He thought it was going to be an advantage for her in healing. According to him, she actually lays down when she becomes tired or starts hurting. He said she was the most sensible racehorse he'd ever had in his clinic."

I still wasn't convinced. "Just the same, if it proves to be too much for you, I can come get her."

She didn't respond, so I knew what that meant.

✳✳✳

I drove up to the Auction that afternoon. I'd been late getting off, spending time with Granddad. The office was closed, but a man approached me, introducing himself as Bronc, which I assumed was a nickname. He was older than me, probably in his mid-twenties.

"Blaine told me to expect you this afternoon. I have your house key. The electricity and water have been turned on. I didn't light the water heater, though. The phone hasn't been connected yet. It'll probably take a few days to get someone out here to do that. If you need anything, I'll be around until dark."

"Thanks. Do you have a few minutes to visit?" I asked.

"Sure." He took out a package of cigarettes. "I need a smoke break anyway. There're some chairs around back."

I was glad to have an opportunity to ask some specifics about my work. "Have you worked here long?"

"Three years." He'd leaned back in his chair and propped his feet up on a five-gallon bucket. "I rodeo on weekends. I'd like to do it full time but don't have the money. It's not a bad job. Blaine's a good guy."

Hence, the name Bronc, I thought. "How many workers are there?"

He thought for a moment. "Six full-time, an additional twenty-five or so on sale day."

"Can you give me an idea of a typical day?"

"I assume you'll be full-time. We start at seven-thirty—have an hour for lunch—and get off at five. Of course, it varies with the weather or trucks coming in. Winters here are cold, and when we get snow, feeding takes more time. I hope you have plenty of warm clothes.

"I generally spend most of my day putting out feed and loading or unloading cattle. Even though we only sell cattle one day a week, there's plenty to do on the other days. They furnish us horses to ride. Some are okay—others not so good."

"Thanks for the information. I'll let you get back to work," I said.

"What'd you do before taking this job?" he asked.

"Marines. In Vietnam for the past two years. Just got home a little over two weeks ago." Silence followed, and I thought *he must be against the war.* I got up to leave, wondering if this was going to be a common reaction.

"Sorry." He looked off in the distance as if searching for something. "Your answer surprised me. I have a younger brother over there. He left a couple of months ago. He's only nineteen. I worry about him. Is it as bad over there as he says? I get a letter from him every ten days or so."

How could I answer and still be truthful? "It's been a terrible year for us. The Tet Offensive was our worst defeat and hurt morale among our troops. We retook Saigon and the fighting has tapered off some since then. As I'm sure you are aware, Nixon is campaigning on ending the war. I imagine he's going to be the next president.

"I'm not going to lie and say not to worry, your brother will be fine. Hopefully, he'll get a platoon leader who's wise and takes care of his men. Where is your brother stationed?"

"He wasn't specific. Just said he was outside Saigon." Bronc continued to stare off in another direction.

"I'm sorry. I'll help with any information I can. I'm trying to forget about the war but it's impossible."

"I should be over there rather than my little brother," he said, rising and leaving.

I drove down to my new home. The odor hit me full in the face. There was a slight wind out of the east, and it was almost unbearable. I let Bull out, and he immediately put his paws between his legs and began rubbing his nose.

"We'll get used to it." He looked up, shaking his head, like he understood and didn't agree. The smell wasn't as bad inside. The house was actually better than I expected. It was small with a living room, two cracker-box bedrooms, a bath, and a tiny kitchen with a table and four chairs. I looked in the fridge, and it was empty but working. There was a two-burner stove with an oven.

I unloaded my car and made a trip back to town for groceries, and by the time we returned it was getting dark. The temperature must've dropped twenty degrees when the sun went down. After lighting the space heater, I made myself a sandwich and put out a pan of dog food. Bull looked at the dog food and then looked up at me several times.

"Okay. I get it." I made him a sandwich which he ate in three bites. "That's all. Eat your dog food now or go hungry."

There was a black-and-white television in the den that only received two channels out of Amarillo. After watching several shows and the news, I went to bed with Bull on the floor beside me on an old blanket I'd found.

*It was steamy hot and we were on a search and destroy. I was on point and uneasy as we advanced through an open area. It was quiet—too quiet. The silence ended with the all too familiar blast of the K-50 machine gun and the scream of the man to my right.*

I bolted upright, shaking with fear. This was the first time since coming home that I'd dreamed. I lay there for some time attempting to get the war out of my thoughts. Finally calm again, I kept smelling something, thinking it was the pens but decided it was Bull.

"No more sandwiches for you, buddy." I got out of bed and took him outside hoping a BM might help. Going back inside, I took the bottle out of the cabinet I'd placed there earlier. Three drinks later, I crawled back into bed.

✳✳✳

My first several days were busy with one truck after another coming in to unload or pick up a pen of cattle. The only time I sat down was for lunch. There were three of us working together—Bronc and an old man named Spoon were the other two.

On Wednesday, sale day, I worked in the loading area. People who'd purchased cattle brought their paperwork to me with the pen number on it. I'd drive the cattle to the loading chute and get them into the owner's trailer.

Benny was yard foreman and was available to help with any problems. He'd been at the Auction for years, and I heard Blaine say that he couldn't do without him. He had the ability to find cattle put in the wrong pen, cattle which had just disappeared, or calm down a disgruntled seller or buyer. Everyone knew and respected him.

I didn't see Mr. Waddell until Wednesday when Benny sent me to the office with paperwork. "Luke, how's everything going? You finding your way around?"

"Yeah. Staying busy," I nodded.

"I'm going to the ranch tomorrow. I'd like you to go with me. I'll pick you up at 7:00."

"No problem." A day out of the dusty pens would be welcomed.

When I returned to the loading dock, I told Bronc about being gone tomorrow. "We'll probably be back by noon."

"Don't count on it. The few times I went with him we were gone most of the day. I always enjoy the trip. The ranch is a neat place. You'll probably see deer."

We didn't have time to talk further because another truck was backing up to the loading dock.

✳✳✳

When Mr. Waddell picked me up the next morning there was a

change of plans. His daughter's future husband was due to arrive back in Amarillo last night from a business trip to England but wasn't on the plane.

"Jimmie Lyn is in a panic. She waited on the next flight thinking he might have missed his scheduled one, but he wasn't on it either. She checked his apartment, thinking he might have caught an earlier one, but he wasn't there. We're going to her apartment and try to get her calmed down before we go to the ranch."

I wasn't comfortable with this situation. Hopefully, I could stay in the pickup and not be a part of this family drama. It was none of my business.

When we arrived at her apartment Blaine didn't give me a choice. "Let's go in and see what we can do." He was out before I could object.

He knocked and opened the door without an invitation. I hesitated and then followed. She was sitting on the couch with her head in her hands.

"Have you heard anything, Honey?" He went over and sat down beside her, putting his arm around her.

"Nothing."

"When was the last time you talked to him?"

"Sunday."

"Are you sure he was coming home last night?" he asked.

"Positive. He was supposed to be in Amarillo at 9:30. I was going to surprise him and be at the airport when he arrived." Her voice quivered. "I-I'm afraid something has happened."

"Have you called the law firm in Amarillo where he works?" he asked.

"They won't be open until nine." She'd paid no attention to my presence.

"Have you called your mother?"

"No. She's the last person I need right now. Maybe I can find out something when I call his law firm."

"Luke and I were on the way to the ranch." He waited for a response but none came.

Mr. Waddell got up and motioned for me to go with him. I followed him outside, and he turned to me. "I can't leave her this upset. Take my pickup and go on back to the Auction. When we find out something, she can bring me to my office. We'll go to the ranch tomorrow."

I left, wondering why she didn't want her mother to be with her.

# 13

# A CHANGE OF PLANS

 GRACE

I knew when I hit the ground my leg was broken, and I lay there in pain until a man ran up and asked, "Are you okay?"

"I think my leg's broken." By then several people were crowded around me. I was going to faint.

"Get a vehicle so we can get her to the hospital." I didn't see where the voice came from.

"Could someone catch my horse and get it back to Barn Twelve. My dad will be there." The next thing I knew several guys were lifting me up and placing me in the backseat of a car, causing excruciating pain. I awoke when pushed into the emergency room on a gurney.

A nurse cut my jeans off with scissors, and then I was placed on an x-ray table, again causing terrible pain. When I was moved back onto the gurney, I passed out again. This time a doctor was standing over me when I opened my eyes.

"You have a fracture. I'm going to give you a sedative and set it. We'll get you in a room where you'll need to stay at least a couple of days. We won't put a cast on you until tomorrow to make sure the swelling is minimal."

A nurse gave me a shot and told me to count to ten. I made it to eight before going out.

My dad's wrinkled frown greeted me. "Luke didn't want you to exercise the horses. He was afraid this would happen."

"I know. I dread telling him. It shouldn't have happened. A rider came up behind me flying and spooked my horse. He jumped sideways, and I lost my balance. I wouldn't have fallen ten years ago. Luke was right."

"A man brought Sunny Time back to the barn. He was fine. I've already called Luke, and he's on his way. He should be here late this afternoon."

I cringed, wishing he hadn't called Luke. Now, he was going to miss work because of me. What else could he do? Dad wasn't able to take care of the horses.

A nurse took my vitals and gave me a pill. Dad leaned closer assuring me everything was going to be all right as my consciousness faded. I'm sure there was a Bible verse, but I didn't hear it.

***

I woke up wondering what I was going to do. Seven horses to care for and on crutches for the next six weeks at least. Dad could do very little to help, and I didn't have the money to hire someone. I couldn't continue training. The owners could find another trainer, but what about the horses I owned? I'd have to sell them and move back to the farm. Then it came to me—it was my right leg. I couldn't drive.

The next thought frightened me, sitting at home, not being able to do anything. I'd never been into self-pity, but the situation that I was facing moved me in that direction. I didn't have anyone to blame but myself for what I was about to endure. I should've never started back to exercising my horses instead of hiring someone.

A knock on the door and Luke walked in. I expected the worst, but he was kind and sweet not saying, "I told you so."

"How're you feeling, Mom? You look better than I expected."

"The pain's not too bad. Of course, they're giving me medicine." I might as well tell him my plans. I told him what I'd been thinking—selling the horses and going home—giving up.

"Mom, I thought about it on the four-hour drive. Now listen and don't interrupt me until I'm finished. You can stay with me until you get well. I have plenty of room. We can keep your horses and Lady at the Auction. Granddad can stay with us or go back home. When you recover, the horses will have rested, and you can return to the track. What do you think?"

"Dad won't go with us."

"It's not a perfect plan, Mom. It's the best we can do for the time being."

"I'd like to decline the offer, but the prospect of going home and sitting alone in that house scares me."

"Then it's settled. Mr. Waddell told me to take off as much time as I needed. We'll see what Granddad wants to do. Regardless, we need to take your trailer home. Wait a minute! Maybe that solves a problem. Granddad might be willing to stay in your trailer at the Auction. I could encourage him by saying we needed him to help you while I was working."

"You've got it all figured out, don't you?" I asked. "Why don't I stay in the trailer at the Auction? That way I wouldn't be an intruder."

"Steps. You couldn't navigate the steps. You'd probably fall and break the other leg."

"Where's your dog?"

"In the car. They wouldn't let me bring him in."

"I don't know what else could go wrong, Luke. It's just one thing after another. After your dad passed, I knew it would be hard, but nothing like this."

"I miss Dad, and it saddens me to think we'll never see him again.

After that, the rest of our problems are nothing compared to what I've been through the last two years. Some of these problems are welcome—it gets my mind off the memories that haunt me. I better check on Bull. Rest and I'll be back later to visit with you."

✳ ✳ ✳

Three days later, we were ready to leave Albuquerque. Luke was driving my pickup pulling the trailer, and Dad followed us in his pickup. Another trainer had taken two of the horses, but Blaine wanted to bring Big Boy back home. We hired someone to haul my three racehorses, the pony horse, and Big Boy to Dalhart. There were two guys hired to haul our horses, and one agreed to drive Luke's car and save us a trip back to Albuquerque.

I needed help getting into the pickup and was clumsy moving around on the crutches. It was going to be a long, slow process to recovery. With Bull between us, his head in Luke's lap, we headed toward Dalhart, Texas. I made the first two hours pretty good but the last two were a different story. By the time we stopped in front of the little frame house, I was miserable. I'd been determined not to take the pain pills until it was absolutely necessary, but as soon as Luke got me into the house, I downed a couple.

"Let's get you to the living room, and you can lay down on the couch. We only get two stations on the TV. At least the smell is not too bad today."

If it's not bad today, I dread the days it is bad, I thought. "Luke, I'm going to be a lot of trouble. I should've gone home."

"I don't mind, Mom, and it'll be good to have company. Bull stays in the house. I need to warn you he's a little gassy sometimes, but you hardly notice it with the smell from the Auction pens."

I smiled. "It's your home, Luke. I can handle whatever comes along.

I appreciate you caring for me."

"The horses should be arriving any time. I need to wait for the haulers at the front to show them where to go. After I get the horses taken care of, I'll get the trailer parked and hooked up to electricity and water. We don't have a sewer hook up, but Granddad can use the bathroom in the house."

When he left to get the horses taken care of, Bull came in and stood next to me, his face close to mine. He was smiling, as if saying, "Welcome to our home." I reached out and petted him, and he licked my hand with a wet kiss. I imagined that's the only kind he gave.

I began to feel the effects of the pills as the pain decreased. Wondering if things were going to get better in my new residence, I relaxed.

✳✳✳

I woke up the next morning confused, at first, about where I was. I'd slept on the couch, and someone had put a blanket on me, but I was still cold. The pills had knocked me out, and when I moved my leg, I immediately was wide awake with the pain. I smelled bacon cooking, so someone was up and around, but it was still dark.

Dad came into the room. "Morning. We didn't want to move you last night you were sleeping so good. Can I get you some coffee? Breakfast will be ready in a few minutes. Luke went to feed the horses."

I had the blanket pulled up to my chin. "I'm freezing. Could you light that heater over there?" I was literally shaking. "How cold is it anyway?"

"Probably freezing. The wind blowing out of the north makes it seem colder. This house doesn't have the best insulation. How about that coffee?"

"Let me warm up first. I couldn't hold the cup now. If you'll hand me my crutches and help me up, I need to go to the bathroom."

Once in the bathroom it was a challenge. Since the cast only came to my knee I was able to succeed. At least, I wasn't completely helpless, but taking a bath was going to be out of the question. For the time being, I'd have to be content with a sponge bath. I hobbled back to the kitchen on my crutches and sat down, with Dad providing me with a cup of coffee. "How long has Luke been gone?"

"Half-hour. The horses are penned close to the house. It'll still take some time to get them fed. I believe Luke is a little better, Daughter. Staying busy is good for him."

Dad and I went ahead and ate breakfast and had finished when Luke came in with Bull right on his heels. "That bacon smells good. Got the horses fed. We need to get them in a pen with a shelter of some kind. They warned me about how cold it gets up here, and after this morning I believe it." He sat down and Dad put a plate piled high with scrambled eggs and bacon in front of him.

"Luke, does Blaine know about me and your granddad coming to stay with you?"

"Sure. I talked with him several days ago. He said it would be fine. He's occupied with another problem that's consuming most of his time." He then told us about the disappearance of his daughter's future husband.

"That poor girl must be going through a horrible time. When was the wedding scheduled?"

"Tomorrow, the twenty-eighth."

I'd been dwelling so much on my problems that I'd forgotten other people were facing difficulties also. I noticed that Luke cleaned his plate. Maybe Dad was right, and Luke was getting better.

# 14

# UNEXPECTED VISIT

 JIMMIE LYN

I kept hoping and praying that Drake would contact me or even show up at my apartment. Piper made a point to come see me every day, attempting to cheer me up. She repeated over and over that I was better off finding out about him before we married. She was convinced that nothing kept him from coming back except the desire to stay in England. I'd called the law firm in Amarillo every day to ask if they'd received any information as to his whereabouts. They were as confused as I was.

My mother was another problem. All she could talk about when she was around was how embarrassing it was that the groom had disappeared. She kept showing up at the office every few days dressed in a mini skirt and some type of top that was more appropriate for a sixteen-year-old.

After the first week, I wanted to go to England, but my dad talked me out of it. He asked me to wait another week, and I agreed. In three more days it would be two full weeks and I was going—nothing could stop me. My emotions had gone from grief and anger to fear. Something must've happened to him or he would've come back. The wedding had been scheduled for tomorrow, but of course, it'd been postponed. I still hoped my prayers would be answered, and he'd suddenly appear at my door.

It was Friday, September twenty-seventh, and I'd been going to work for the past week, attempting to stay busy. Occasionally I would close my door, break down, and cry for long periods of time. I was in the middle of one of these episodes when someone knocked.

"Honey, there's someone here that wants to talk with you."

"Tell them to come back later, Dad. I don't want any visitors now."

"They said it was important. I'll give you a few minutes, then you better see what they want."

Suddenly, a thought. Maybe they had information about Drake. I jumped up and opened the door. "Who is it?"

"I have no idea. Two guys in suits. They look important. Do you want me to tell them to come in?"

I was trying to dry my eyes and make myself presentable. "Yes. Show them in."

My dad left and returned with two men. The older one had a crew cut and was probably in his fifties, but the other one was much younger. The older spoke first. "Ms. Waddell, we need to talk with you. I'm Agent Fitzgerald and this is Agent Donnelly."

My heart was racing. They must have information about Drake. "Yes. Sit down." I motioned to the chairs in the room. "I'd like for my dad to stay."

Fitzgerald frowned but nodded. "Both of you need to understand this is confidential and cannot leave this room."

It was about Drake! I took a deep breath, trying to stay calm. "Do you have information about Drake?" I tried to speak normally but blurted it out.

"Yes." Both sat down in the two chairs facing my desk, and my dad took a chair in the corner. "I want to emphasize again that you cannot share this information with anyone. Drake is okay. It's a long story and quite complicated."

I was overwhelmed with joy. I choked back a sob trying to hold on to my emotions. "Where is he?"

Fitzgerald raised his hand as if to stop any questions. "He's safe, that's all I can tell you. Drake was part of a sting operation in one of the largest law firms in London. They were involved in money laundering, drugs, and weapon sales. Drake was a plant in the firm for three years and gathered enough information on them to send most of the partners in the firm to prison. After we had the information, we assumed that Drake would not be needed, so he left the country. After presenting our evidence, we were informed by the court that he would have to testify.

"We received word that he was going to be in grave danger before he appeared in court. A day before he testified, we moved him to a secluded place to film his testimony. They convinced the judge to postpone the trial for thirty days. We knew they would try to get to him before the trial. The judge has agreed to accept the film of his testimony, so he'll not have to appear in court. The accused doesn't know this. This is what we're counting on to ensure Drake's safety. We'll keep him in protection until after the trial and these guys are convicted and in prison."

I couldn't contain myself any longer. "But that might take months."

"Probably not. With the amount of evidence, the trial should be over in thirty days at which time Drake should be able to leave protection. Do you have any other questions?"

"Why Drake? Why was he a spy in this law firm?" I asked.

"Drake had a career in law enforcement before he became a lawyer. He came to us with this idea. He has a gift for this type of work. I would've never thought anyone could gain the confidence of this group of criminals."

"Why did you wait so long to tell us?" I was becoming angrier with each passing minute.

Fitzgerald looked at his partner as if passing the question to him. "We became afraid you might be in danger. These men are desperate enough at this time to try anything. We know they're aware of yours and Drake's relationship. Since they can't locate him, they may come after you." Donnelly leaned forward in his chair. "We're offering you protection because we believe it may be necessary."

My dad jumped up. "Are you saying these thugs may come after my daughter to keep Drake from testifying?"

Fitzgerald turned toward my dad. "It's a possibility."

"What do you mean by protection?" Dad asked.

"Take her to a remote location and keep her until after these men are convicted and in prison."

My dad looked at me for an answer. I froze. I couldn't find the pieces much less put them together in this puzzle. "I need some time to think about it."

"No problem. I'll give you my card, and you can contact us when you make a decision."

"I'll let you know something in a few days. This is more than I can handle. Did Drake insist that you get in touch with me? We were to be married tomorrow." I noticed a look of surprise on Fitzgerald's face.

"I didn't realize that the relationship was that far along. Drake, as far as we know, is still married to a woman in Spain. He has a four-year-old son. I assumed you were aware of that."

I couldn't speak. I opened my mouth but nothing came out. Dad came to my rescue. "We'll be in touch with you. I'll show you out."

When my dad returned, I couldn't talk. He tried to make conversation, but I just sat there and stared at the wall. Finally, I said, "Dad, I need to be alone."

For the next hour, I hardly moved, trying to comprehend what had just happened. Drake had lied to me. No, that's not correct. He never said anything about having a family in Spain. I didn't ask and he didn't tell. He was pretending to be something that he wasn't—a single man. He wasn't even divorced. He was going to marry me, having a wife and son in Spain. He'd convinced the law firm that he was one of them. He'd made me believe that I was the one he loved and wanted to marry.

Now what? I was in danger. Should I go into hiding? No way. I wanted no part of this. I'd go back to being a twenty-three-year-old, soon to be known as an old-maid. When I opened my door, Dad was standing outside. He followed me back inside.

"Honey, we need to talk. I know this is a shock to you, but you may be in danger."

"Dad, I'm not going anywhere. I don't want to be around strangers. I've been made a fool of, and it's humiliating. I should've known he was too good to be true. I don't know whether to cry or laugh for being so stupid.

"What I don't understand is what his purpose was of marrying me when he already had a wife and child? Was he just going to abandon them forever? What kind of man would do that?"

He came around my desk and hugged me. "What can I do?"

With tears flowing, I said, "Just be here for me. That's all I know."

✳✳✳

I didn't leave my apartment over the weekend. The more I thought, the angrier and more bitter I became. I dealt with my anger by rehearsing what I was going to say if Drake ever had the nerve to show up again. I hated him!

My mom came over Saturday and I didn't let her in—speaking to her through the door. "Mom, I don't want to see anyone. Please leave me alone."

She left angry, but she'd get over it. I wasn't going to listen to her feel sorry for herself because her daughter had been left at the altar.

The weekend was long, and by Monday morning I was ready to go to work and get my mind on something else. I could hide from the world in my office. When I got into my car and started it, the windshield wipers came on. That's strange I thought, it hadn't rained in a month. I'd been so out of it I probably turned them on by mistake.

*I should be on my honeymoon,* I thought on the ten-minute drive to the Auction. *What had I done to deserve this? How was I going to explain this to my friends? I couldn't—it was confidential information. Should I just make up a lie?*

I went straight to my office, avoiding the two other women who were already there. I closed my door and dived into my work.

At mid-morning Dad knocked and came in. "How're you doing today? I worried about you all weekend."

"I don't know, Dad. It's all I've thought about. I'm tired of going over it and not discovering any answers. He had me completely fooled. Did you suspect anything? Mother told me you didn't care for him."

He frowned, shaking his head. "Your mother—she's something else. I should've known better than to say anything to her. All I said was 'I didn't think he was good enough for you.' I imagine she added to that."

"Yes, she did. But you had an idea something wasn't right with him, didn't you?"

"Like most fathers, I doubt if anyone would be good enough for you. Yes, to answer your question. I just had a strange feeling when I was around him. I can't put my finger on it. Maybe he was too perfect. I wish my feeling would've been wrong."

He moved to another issue telling me about the new hire bringing his mother and granddad to live with him. "I feel sorry for his mother. She's lost her husband and now has broken her leg. I'd suggest that you meet her. She's a nice lady and has been going through some hard times. I've found that providing comfort to others is good medicine for one's own suffering."

My dad was so different from my mom. No wonder their marriage didn't last. "I'll make a point to go see her today. How's her son doing? Is he going to be a good employee?"

"He'll be fine. My heart goes out to him, also. He spent two years in Vietnam and has been through hell over there. Right now, he needs understanding and time to adjust to civilian life. I can tell you—he's a good boy that I can trust. I plan on using him at the ranch a great deal."

"He seems older than twenty-one. I haven't seen him smile. He has the saddest eyes I've ever seen."

"That's what war does to you. He was a platoon leader, which places a terrible burden on anyone, much less a young man. You're responsible for others. Can you imagine having one of your men killed under your leadership. Anyway, please go out of your way to be nice to him."

He continued. "I need to get to work. We have three truck loads of cattle shipping out this morning."

"Thank you for checking on me. I don't know what I would do without you." Nothing could be truer.

❊❊❊

At noon, I walked down to meet the nice lady. Dad didn't tell me her name. The granddad came to the door and invited me in. Introductions were made, and Grace was nothing like I'd expected. She was younger and prettier than I'd anticipated. I liked her immediately, and talking with her my mood lightened. Dad was right.

# 15

# THE TRIP

If anybody doubts the size of Texas, they should drive from Dalhart to College Station in one day. I left at seven o'clock Saturday morning, October fifth, to pick up the filly at the Texas A&M Vet Center. I left Bull with my mom and granddad. My route took me to Amarillo, then to Abilene, where I took Highway 36 to Temple and on to College Station. I arrived at the university at seven in the evening.

Mr. Waddell had given me a check to pay the vet bill and money for expenses. However, I decided to sleep in the pickup rather than get a motel room. He'd made arrangements for the vet to meet me the next morning even though it was a Sunday. I took his pickup and a covered stock trailer with plenty of bedding. I'd asked my mom about taking another horse to haul with her, but she didn't think it would be necessary. We discussed whether or not I should come back in one day or stop for a layover. We decided to ask the vet and go with his recommendation. I was nervous about hauling her for that distance, but her disposition should make it possible without any problems.

Of course, no one was present at the clinic when I arrived, so I parked under a street light, and after the long drive I spent the next two hours walking over the campus. I'd heard so much about the university and the rich traditions that accompanied it. I saw a number of students, and it seemed strange not to see any girls.

The long drive and walk had taken its toll, and I actually slept pretty good in the pickup. I was surprised when someone knocked on my window the next morning before daylight.

"You here to pick up a filly?" he asked.

"Yes sir. I didn't expect you this early," I said, getting out and introducing myself.

"Jeff Rogers," he said, extending his hand. "I thought you'd want to get an early start. I'm a graduate student in my final year. If you'll pull around to the back, we'll get you loaded."

I was impressed with the inside of the clinic and the adjoining stalls. After paying the bill, I asked him about Lady.

"I've been part of her treatment, beginning with the surgery. She's a remarkable animal. She has a lot of sense, especially coming off the track. We get some doozies. Of course, I don't have the experience that my supervisors have, but they are optimistic about her recovery."

"Do you think I should make it a two-day trip back to Dalhart? It's about a twelve-hour drive. I do have bedding in the trailer."

"Definitely. I asked my supervisor yesterday and that was his recommendation."

I followed him to her stall and was surprised to see her looking so good. She'd lost weight but not as much as I expected. It was obvious that she'd had good care and had even been groomed.

"I'm going to give her a mild tranquilizer. She probably doesn't need it but just to be on the safe side. I'll also send a couple of syringes and a bottle of Ace if she becomes agitated. Can you give her an injection?"

"In the muscle. I'd be afraid of giving it in the vein," I said.

"No problem. It just takes a little longer for her to feel the effect."

She walked with a slight limp but didn't seem to be in any pain. Mr. Waddell had included a ramp, knowing she didn't need to jump into the trailer. She walked right up the ramp.

"Let us know how she does. Call us if you have any questions."

I thanked him and drove off with my valuable cargo. Traffic was light, and driving gave me time to think. The previous week our family had settled into a routine that seemed to work for us. Granddad would get up first and fix breakfast since he was a much better cook than I was. I'd grab a cup of coffee and go feed the horses, and by the time I returned Mom was up and breakfast was ready. Days when I was able, I would eat lunch with them. Sometimes I had to eat when I could take off, due to loading or unloading cattle.

Mr. Waddell had asked me if my granddad would like a job. I explained that he wasn't able to do much because of his health. He came up with the perfect solution—driving the truck for the guys putting out feed. It gave him something to do, which worked out great.

I stayed busy during the day, but the nights were long, and I always welcomed the mornings. I had dreams of actual events that had occurred in Vietnam, but sometimes they could just be called nightmares—imaginary fears I'd experienced over there.

Overall, I was pleased with my decision to accept the job. The money was sufficient to get by on, and there couldn't be a better man to work for than Mr. Waddell.

✳✳✳

At two o'clock in the afternoon I pulled into the gate of the B & K Cattle Company in Trent, a small town about twenty miles west of Abilene. Mr. Waddell knew the owner and operator of the feed lot and had called and informed him I might need a place to stop on my way back to Dalhart. When I entered the office a lady came forward and asked me what I needed. I introduced myself and told her my purpose.

"Certainly. Blaine called, and we were expecting you. R.L. is around somewhere. I'm Rosemary. My daughter, Diltizie is here. She can show you where to put your horse." She left and came back a few minutes later with a girl that resembled her mother. "This is my daughter, Diltizie."

Diltizie rode with me and directed me to the area at the back of the pens where there were a number of covered lots. "This is where we keep our horses, but we have a vacant stall."

While we were putting Lady in her stall, watering and feeding her, Diltizie told me about her family. It was obvious she was proud of her three brothers and sister who, along with her, were involved in rodeo. She also mentioned that she had just recently married, and her husband was a calf roper who hoped to go professional.

I felt a tinge of disappointment with the information she was married. She was very attractive and had this little crooked smile that was captivating. Strange—the first time I have any interest in a girl after coming home, and she's married.

When we went back to the office, Mrs. Bland invited me to supper. I declined, saying I wanted to stay close to Lady.

"We have a night watchman who comes at six, so the office will be open. You're welcome to the couch in the back. Just make yourself at home.

"Your filly raced, didn't she?" she asked.

"Yes, until she fractured a leg."

"We have horse racing here. There's a brush track, about ten miles north. In fact, they're running today. If you're interested I can give you directions. It'd be a way to kill some time."

I did need something to do for the next several hours. "Sure."

After giving me directions they left, and I went back to check on Lady. She was munching on hay and as calm as any of the other horses in the adjoining stalls. She looked amazingly well with what she'd gone through.

It was still early, so I decided to visit the brush track. I unhooked my trailer and found FM 1085 and drove north. I needed to go ten miles and turn off into a cotton field, and a sign on the road would point the way.

I crossed a creek and sure enough the sign appeared on the left side of the road. I wound my way through the field, passed some starting gates, and came to a place where a number of pickups were parked with horses tied to their trailers. Men and a few women were standing around, many holding a beer.

I hung back, feeling uncomfortable, since everyone was a stranger. A man approached me and introduced himself. He was thin and had a three-day growth of grey whiskers.

"I haven't seen you before," he stated.

"No. First time here. In fact, my first visit to a brush track." I went on to explain my presence, including my stopover at the feed lot on my way back to Dalhart.

He looked me directly in the eye. "You're a soldier, aren't you? Probably a Marine."

Surprised, I said, "That's right. Just returned from Vietnam a little over a month ago. How did you know?"

"I was in the war myself. It's been twenty-five years. The way you carry yourself—the sadness. It took me a long time to get over it. That's not a correct statement. Too deal with it is more accurate."

"I didn't realize it showed."

"It doesn't for most people. You have to have been there and gone through it to recognize it."

I was uncomfortable and a little embarrassed that someone could read me, so I changed the subject. "Tell me about what is happening here."

He took a drink of his beer. "It's pretty simple. You try to match a horse that you can outrun. There's some really good horses here and some average ones. Some people resort to insults to make a guy angry enough to put up money that he has the better horse."

For the next several minutes he pointed out horses, describing their abilities. He would also comment on the owner. He was most critical of the owners he portrayed as not taking good care of their horses.

I stayed the rest of the afternoon, watching half a dozen match races. It was a very enlightening experience since I had no idea this type of racing existed. Before leaving, I located Mack and told him how much I enjoyed the afternoon. A small petite lady was standing by him, who he introduced as his wife, Wanda.

"Luke, we're glad to have met you. Come visit us again and bring a horse with you."

***

Early the next morning, I left a note at the office thanking the Blands for their hospitality before getting back on the road. I'd met some nice people on my trip, and I was thankful for that. Who knows? I might bring a horse to this little brush track in Trent, Texas, in the future.

# 16

# LADY'S COMING HOME

*Luke will be here with Lady today*, was my first thought on waking. I pulled the covers up to my chin and shuddered. How could it be this cold so early in October? I moved my right leg, jolting into pain. It'd been two weeks since my spill, but my leg was healing. I had a follow-up appointment with a doctor in Amarillo next week.

So much had changed in my life the last five weeks. Henry had passed, Luke had returned home, and Lady had finished second in the New Mexico Futurity and fractured her leg. I'd made a poor decision, deciding to gallop my own horses, and here I lay with a broken leg. Too much of my time had been spent wondering why so much sorrow had come my way. I was determined to make an effort to dwell more on my blessings. Luke was home and healthy, at least physically. My dad was doing better and enjoying his new job. He received a check Friday, which was a surprise.

I was anxious to see Lady and begin taking care of her. Blaine had a stall built for her with a small pen, and the vet had instructed him not to allow her much room to move around until she was completely healed. He was afraid, when she was free of pain, she might become too rambunctious. I tried not to think about how much money Blaine had spent on her with the hauling and the vet bill, plus the $19,000 he paid Oliver.

I missed Henry, and when anything good happened it was squashed with the thought that I'd never be with him again. What hurt so much,

I could remember very little of when he had not been a part of my life. Nothing seemed important until we were together.

I struggled up and dressed myself, even though it took some time. Dad had coffee made but had gone to feed the horses. I could actually stand long enough to put the bacon on and butter the toast and was scrambling the eggs when he returned.

"Well, what do you know? I've got my cook back. You probably shouldn't be doing that, Daughter."

"I'm kinda proud of myself, Dad." I hobbled over to a chair and sat down. "I'll let you finish up. I wanted to have breakfast for you, so you could do your Bible reading before going to work."

He opened the oven and removed the toast. "I appreciate that. My day just seems to go better if I have time with my Bible.

"I like being useful and making a little money. Blaine's a good guy. Not many men would've given an old man a job." He put the bacon and eggs on the table.

"I know, Dad. I'm grateful for what Blaine's done for us. Maybe Lady will be a good investment for him. I certainly hope so."

"I feel sorry for his daughter. Her future husband just disappeared, and she must be devastated. She's a really sweet girl."

We finished our breakfast, and Dad settled into the recliner with his Bible.

✳✳✳

In the early afternoon, Luke drove up honking. I made it outside before he was able to come to the door. "You made it. How'd she do?"

"Good, no problems. I didn't have to give her a tranquilizer. She's something else. Let me unload her, and you can see for yourself." He went around to the back of the trailer, opened the tailgate and backed her out.

Tears came when I saw her. I hobbled over to her and rubbed her forehead, speaking softly. "You're home, beautiful Lady. I'm going to take good care of you." She nickered like she understood, then nudged me with her nose, affirming that we, the two cripples, would overcome.

"I had no idea she would look this good, Luke. It's amazing."

"That is some clinic, Mom. We couldn't have taken her to a better place. She can walk pretty good, and the vet was optimistic. The bill was $4,200, but I expected it to be more."

Quick math brought the total cost to almost $24,000 for Blaine. I moved back and looked at her. She was worth it! Somehow, I would make it right with him.

"I need to get her stalled. I didn't give her any water on the trip, and she's been in the trailer for over five hours."

"Did you stop at the office and show her to Blaine?" I asked.

"No. Come go with me, and we'll do that now." Luke reloaded Lady.

I managed to climb into the pickup without assistance. I couldn't wait to get rid of these crutches.

The entire office staff came out with Blaine to inspect Lady. Blaine was as surprised as I was about how she looked. "I can't believe it, Grace. She looks like she could step on the track today."

We all stood around for several minutes before Blaine invited me to come into his office while Luke took care of Lady.

"We did good, Grace," were his first words when we were alone in his office. "I am beyond excited about this adventure."

I expressed my concern about how much money he'd invested in Lady. "You may never get that back. She looks good, but who knows what she'll be like a year from now."

He laughed. "Don't you see, Grace? It's only money. I'm purchasing hope and excitement for the future instead of living in the doom and gloom of today. My life right now is stressful. It's devastating to see my little girl suffer the way she is. Anything that can get my mind off that misery is worth the cost."

We were interrupted by one of his office workers. "Mr. Waddell, your wife is here to see you."

He looked up in surprise. "Tell her I'm busy."

She hesitated. "I don't believe that will work, Mr. Waddell." Before she could continue, we heard the clip-clop of heels coming down the short hallway.

She didn't slow down coming through the door, nudging the messenger out of the way. She was dressed to the hilt and not for church. I stared in disbelief as she addressed Blaine.

"What's going on Blaine? I need to talk with you, and it's important." She turned and stared at me. "Who're you?"

"Grace Ranker." I spoke as meekly as possible.

"I need to speak privately with my hus . . . my ex-husband." She turned her attention back to Blaine. "Is she the reason I have to ask to see you?"

My crutches were against the wall. I pushed myself up on the chair arms but before I could reach for them, Blaine was handing them to me. I was out of there as fast as a cripple could be.

The woman who was the messenger stopped me before I reached the outside door. "I'm so sorry. When she's like this there's no stopping her. Poor Blaine. He'll catch it now. Please have a seat, and let me get you some coffee. Luke is not back yet."

I thought about an attempt to crutch my way back to the house but decided that would be too much. I sat down in the closest chair. The lady, who introduced herself as Eve, brought me a cup of coffee. I could hear some of the conversation from Blaine's office—his ex-wife's part. It wasn't nice. I kept thinking I'd seen her somewhere before today.

I'd finished half my coffee when I heard her coming from Blaine's office—clip-clop, clip-clop. She stopped in front of me, stood there a few seconds and left, slamming the door. Then it occurred to me why she looked familiar. Coming through Amarillo, I'd seen her likeness walking the streets. Of course, she wasn't who I saw. She was only dressed the way they were.

Luke came in soon after she'd left. "You ready to go?"

"Definitely." I took my crutches from him, but before we left, Blaine appeared.

"Grace, I'm terribly sorry. Gwendolyn is upset about Drake not being here for the wedding. All her plans have gone down the drain. She's generally not that rude."

"No problem. I understand how disappointing it must be." I'd like to see her on a good day, I thought. "Don't worry about Lady. I'll be able to take care of her soon."

When we left, Blaine followed us out. He kept apologizing for his ex-wife. I continued to assure him it was okay. He opened the pickup door for me. "Do y'all need anything? Are the appliances working in the house? Has Luke checked the propane tank to make sure it has plenty of fuel? It's going to be winter soon."

We finally got away from him. On the ride back to the house, Luke expressed confusion about what had happened. I explained the incident with Gwendolyn.

"She must be something. I've heard the guys I work with talk about her. I imagine she's jealous of you."

I was caught off guard by his observation. "Why would she be jealous of me?"

"Because you are a beautiful and classy lady, Mother. Word's out that she's trying to get Blaine back. I don't think he realizes it, but that's what's going around."

How absurd, I thought. I'd just lost my husband. "That's ludicrous. She must be insane."

"Whatever you say, Mother."

✳✳✳

The next several days I spent as much time as possible with Lady. I could hobble around and brush her, even braiding her mane. By the third day, I'd overdone it and had to stay in the house with my leg elevated. At least to some extent, I'd gotten use to the smell of the pens, and Bull was actually a bigger problem. I finally suggested that Luke ask a vet what we could do. If he was going to stay in the house and keep me company something had to be done. He would let go of a big one and look up at me with that grin like he'd done something special. With the small living room where I stayed and the space heater on, it was almost unbearable.

A couple of days later Luke spoke to a vet that called on the Auction, and his recommendation was to change his dog food and stop feeding him from the table. The special dog food was more expensive, but it would definitely be worth it. He'd just have to get used to not getting a piece of bacon every morning at breakfast.

I continued to worry about Luke. I'd hear him up at all times of the night. When I questioned him, all he would say was, "I have trouble sleeping." I wanted so badly to do something to help but felt useless. I knew if his dad had been here he'd have talked to him. He was letting his hair grow longer. I thought about suggesting a haircut but decided against it.

We hadn't gone to church since moving to Dalhart. I looked through the yellow pages in the phone book and found a Presbyterian church. Before Luke graduated from high school, and we were at home, we hardly missed a Sunday morning service. Of course, we were at the track much of the time where we seldom attended a service. I felt a need for myself and Luke to get involved. When I asked Dad about it, he agreed. "I've thought about it, Grace, and started to mention it several times. If you'll find us a house of worship, I'll go with you and Luke. Luke needs help, and I don't know of a better place to find it."

It was settled. I felt better already.

# 17

# PANIC

✦ JIMMIE LYN ✦

It was Wednesday, October ninth, and I was getting ready to go to work. I'd missed yesterday, trying to get myself together for another week. Today was sale day, and I needed to get back on the job. I only wanted to stay home and hide, convinced that people were laughing behind my back.

The phone rang. *Please don't let it be my mother,* I thought. When I picked up a muffled voice spoke. "Drake knows we're coming after you. Tell him to back off." Click. I sat down—my legs so weak I couldn't stand. Since the visit from the FBI, I suspected someone was watching me. Strange things happened—the windshield wipers were on when I started my car one morning—the next day my emergency brake was on—then my car was unlocked with all the windows down. I kept telling myself I was paranoid, that I was only imagining things. Now I knew their purpose. They wanted to let me know they could get to me and wanted to frighten me into convincing Drake not to testify.

I felt my pulse, and my heart was racing. I took several deep breaths trying to calm myself. I had to get out of the house and around people! I finished dressing and looking through a window, could see nothing outside. I hurried to my car, opened the door, and screamed. A dead cat was in my seat! I ran back in the house and locked the door. Gasping for breath, I went to the phone, called the Auction, and asked for my dad. I was informed that he was outside, but they'd try and locate him.

Then another person took the phone. "Jimmie, your dad took a couple of cattle buyers to breakfast in town. Is there anything I can do?"

My mind was spinning like a tilt-a-whirl. "My car won't start. Can you send someone to help me?"

"Sure. I'll get someone right away."

I put the phone down and went to the kitchen, taking a butcher knife out of a drawer. I would defend myself if they came after me. I wasn't thinking straight. What good would a knife be against professionals with guns? The minutes dragged by, and several times I heard something or someone outside. Why wasn't my help here? It didn't take but six or seven minutes to drive into town from the Auction. I was about to call again when I heard a car. Looking through the window, it was a pickup, and someone was coming up the walk. Finally, a knock and I opened the door.

"Ma'am. You're having car trouble?"

It was the young man who'd come with my dad to the house earlier. "Come in and let me explain."

He came in taking off his dusty hat. "It took me longer than it should have. I had to get my pickup. I was already at work. Let's have a look at your car."

I motioned to a chair. "Sit down. I'll explain." I sat on the couch and attempted to remain calm. "It's not my car. There's a dead cat in my front seat."

"What?"

I raised my voice. "I said there's a dead cat in the front seat of my car."

"That shouldn't be a problem. I'll go remove it, and put it in the back of my pickup." He spoke like it was an everyday occurrence to find a dead cat in your car.

"Don't you want to know how it got there?"

"I guess someone must've put it there, ma'am. I doubt if it crawled in and died."

What was the matter with this boy? He didn't seem the least bit concerned. He didn't know the whole story. Should I tell him, so he'd take it seriously? We'd pledged confidentiality. I couldn't explain why I was terrified. "Would you take the dead cat out of my car?"

"Yes ma'am. I'll get right on it."

That did it! "And stop calling me ma'am! I'm not a hundred years old."

"I'm sorry, m- Miss Waddell." He left quickly.

Why did they send a boy instead of one of the older men who knew me? "They didn't know I was terrified for my safety," I mumbled my answer.

He opened the door and stuck his head in. "You're good to go, Miss Waddell. I brushed off the seat for you."

"Would you follow me to work?" I asked.

"Sure."

He stayed right on my bumper for the five-mile drive. He'd gone from ma'am to Miss. I guess that was an improvement.

I stumbled to my office and locked the door. When would Dad return? What was I going to do? More questions came. Would Drake care if they took me? Would he testify knowing I was in danger? He wasn't honest with me from the beginning. He already had a family. Were they in danger, also? Would I ever see him again?

One thing for certain. People were laughing at me because they didn't know the whole story. They thought he'd just run away from the marriage. I could see the look they gave me. I wasn't fooled. Probably some of them felt sorry for me. I hated myself for being so stupid.

Now, I was scared—not concerned but scared. I kept hearing the voice on the phone. It was evil. A knock brought me back to the present. "Who is it?"

"Me."

"Who's me?"

"Luke. The guy who fixed your car."

I unlocked the door, and he was standing there with his hat in his hand. "Mom told me to come invite you to lunch."

I looked at my watch, and it was twelve. "Thank you, but I'm not hungry. Maybe some other time." I closed the door and returned to my desk.

Another knock. "Who is it?"

"Me. Luke."

Why couldn't people leave me alone? I opened the door again.

He hadn't moved. "You sure. Mom doesn't like to eat by herself. Me and Granddad can't get off for dinner today."

This was ridiculous. "Okay. You win. I'll have lunch with your mom."

"Thank you, Miss Waddell."

"My name is Jimmie. Drop the Miss stuff. How old do you think I am anyway?"

He stood and stared like he was giving it a lot of thought. "I don't know, but you're the boss's daughter, and I want to be polite."

"Well, I'm just twenty-three, so quit addressing me like I'm old."

He frowned. "I'm sorry if I offended you. I need to get back to work," and he disappeared.

✵✵✵

Mrs. Ranker or Grace, as she insisted I call her, had a salad and homemade soup for lunch, and even though I wasn't hungry it was very good. After we finished, I felt obligated to stay and visit for awhile.

"Luke told me about your problem this morning. Are you okay?"

I didn't think he'd even given it a second thought. "Yes. I appreciate him coming to help me. I'm surprised he even mentioned it."

"He came back immediately and told me he was worried. To be truthful, he suggested I invite you to lunch. He knew your dad would be busy."

"I'm totally confused. He didn't seem to be aware that I was upset or concerned about me."

"Well, anyway, Jimmie, since it's sale day, I'm pleased that you came and had lunch with me. I hope you feel better, and I'm sorry for your experience this morning. I can't imagine anyone doing such a thing."

I thanked her for lunch and left, glad to get my mind off my problems for a little while at least. I kept thinking of Luke and how I'd misread him. Evidently, I was easy to fool, by older men and young boys. And he was just a boy—who needed a haircut.

Dad came into my office as I was gathering up some work to take home. "How was your day?" he asked.

I sat down and started crying. He closed the door. "What is it?"

It took me a few minutes to start telling him about what had happened, beginning with the phone call. I tried to stay as calm as possible but broke down several times before finishing.

My dad didn't say anything for several minutes. "This is serious, Jimmie Lyn. I should've seen it coming. We need to get in touch with the authorities. You still have their card, don't you?"

I went through my purse until I found it. "I don't want to go into hiding with them, Dad. That's the last thing I want to do."

"What other choice do we have? You're in danger."

"I could stay with you. I'd feel safer. Anything but going with strangers."

"Okay. We'll give it a try, but if I feel the danger is too great, you're going into protection."

❖❖❖

I moved in with my dad and everything seemed to go well for a few days until we received another visit from the two Federal agents. They showed up on Monday, October fourteenth, with the meeting being held in my dad's office.

Fitzgerald did most of the talking again, and there'd been a change in plans. The judge reversed his decision about accepting Drake's testimony via film and insisted he was going to be required to testify in person. They had information indicating that if they couldn't get to Drake they were coming after me. They suggested that I go into protection until the trial was over.

"These guys are dangerous. Please let us protect you until this is over. Consider this—a couple of our agents have been killed protecting Drake. I'm telling you this to convince you to do what we recommend."

I had to ask the question. "Does Drake know you're talking to me? Has he said anything about me?"

Fitzgerald looked at Donnelly, his partner, passing the ball to him. "Drake knows you're in danger. I don't know if he's said anything about you. He does understand how serious the situation is."

I no longer cared. I had to know. "Are his wife and son in protection?"

Donnelly looked at Fitzgerald and he received no help. "Yes."

"Does Drake express concern about them?" I couldn't help it. I knew it wasn't an appropriate question.

"I'm sorry. I can't answer personal questions," Donnelly said, squirming in his seat.

My dad looked at me to answer their question about protection. I hesitated but knew the answer. "No. I do not want protection. Thank you for trying to keep me safe, but I'm not interested."

After they left, we stayed in Dad's office. He threw up his hands. "What're we going to do, Honey?"

"I don't know, Dad. I do know that strangers protecting me in a strange place is not acceptable to me and never will be. Let them protect his wife and son."

# 18

# DOUBLE DUTY

 LUKE

I'd just come in from work and was sitting on the couch with Bull, who considered this his family time with me, watching the six o'clock news. The phone rang, which was in the kitchen, and Mom answered.

She came into the living room saying that Mr. Waddell would like to see me in his office. That's strange, I thought. When I got up Bull whined like he was objecting. "All right, you can go with me." He followed me out and didn't have any trouble jumping into the pickup. His wounds had completely healed, and the change in his diet had helped his problem with excessive gas. He minded most of the time, and when I told him to stay, he didn't try to follow me out of the pickup.

Mr. Waddell was waiting for me just inside the door when I entered. "Sorry to interrupt your evening, Luke, but it's important."

Inside his office, with the door closed, he went right to the point. "We have a problem, Luke. It's a long story, and it's supposed to be confidential, but I'm desperate and have no choice but to share it with you."

For the next several minutes he told me about their situation involving Drake, the trial in London, and the Federal agents. His desperation stemmed from the fact that his daughter was in danger and would not accept the offer of protection from the FBI, who were working with the authorities in London.

"She's stubborn, Luke. I can't make her accept protection. She insists that going with strangers into hiding is not an option. I'd like to ask you for a big favor. Would you take her to the ranch, and stay with her until this is over? I know it's asking a lot, but it'd be safer than living with me.

"The house is at the back of the ranch. I've had a man living there, but he's in his mid-80s and needs to retire. I'll move him to town and set him up with a comfortable pension."

I would've never guessed this was why he wanted to talk with me. I tried to think of something worse than being in a remote house with the purpose of protecting someone. I'd failed at protecting my men in Vietnam and now he was asking me to do the same for his daughter—the most important person in his life. "Is she aware of your plan?"

"No. I was going to wait until I had your consent. I believe she'll accept it. Her objection was going with strangers to a strange place. I feel sure I can talk her into it. You need to understand. She's devastated about this whole situation. She's hurt and angry. Imagine discovering the person you were going to marry already had a wife and child. I don't know if she'll ever be the same after this. If we can just keep her safe until after the trial is over, I'll feel better about her other problems.

"I'll double your salary. Of course, you'll need to look after the cattle on the ranch. Winter is a busy time, and usually I have to send hands out to help feed. That won't be possible this year. You'd stay busy, but of course, you'd need to have Jimmie Lyn in your sight at all times."

"Mr. Waddell, I've lived with fear and death for the past two years. This would almost be like going back to war. I failed at protecting my men. Why would you choose me to protect your daughter?"

He leaned back in his chair and took out his box of Skoal. "I trust you, Luke. I know you'll take care of my daughter. I'd not consider anyone else that I know to take on the job." He opened the box and took out a pinch putting it under his lip.

"Could I have some time to think it over?" I asked.

"I'll say it again, Luke—I'm desperate. I need to know something right away."

"Could it wait until in the morning? I'll need to tell my mother."

"I've thought about that. Only tell her that you're protecting Jimmie Lyn. You can't go into detail. I've already broken my word to keep it confidential."

I left, frustrated and angry to be forced to make such a decision. This was crazy! She should've gone with the Feds into their protection program.

***

We spent two hours talking about the offer when I returned home. My mother kept asking me if it was dangerous. The best I could do was tell her there might be some risk, but it would be minimal. I finally had to tell her the details were confidential to avoid answering specific questions.

"Mom, he's done so much for us it's hard to say no to him." That'd been going through my mind over and over.

"Would he think less of you if you declined?"

"I don't know. He'd be very disappointed. He's convinced that I can protect his daughter. I've racked my brain trying to think of ways to get out of accepting the request. With all he's done for us, it's hopeless."

"What about doing it on a trial basis—say for two weeks," she suggested. "At least you'd have an out. Would he accept that?"

"Probably. Maybe he'd have more information by that time about how long this is going to last." It wasn't the best solution, but at least it'd give me an option. "That's what I'll do."

After the discussion, I went for a walk, taking Bull with me. The night was clear and cold with millions of stars. The sky seemed bigger in the Texas Panhandle. We returned, and I went to bed with Bull in his usual spot on the floor beside me, and I lay wide awake before finally drifting off sometime in the early hours.

❉ ❉ ❉

I was in the front office first thing the next morning, anxious to inform Mr. Waddell of my decision. He and his daughter were the last ones to come in, and I could tell something was wrong.

Not a word was spoken until after he walked by me. "Come on back, Luke."

He didn't sit down but stood behind his desk. "She got another call at three this morning. This time they were specific, telling her that Drake had better not testify, or she would die. I begged her again to go into protection with the FBI, but she refused. Have you decided anything?"

I told him my decision to take the job on a two-week trial basis. It was the best I could do. "If I see that it's something I can't handle she'll have to look elsewhere, hopefully the Federal guys."

"Thank you, Luke. Now, we need to get moving. I'll talk to her immediately. After last night, I believe she'll be agreeable. I'll let you know something as soon as I talk with her. She's in her office with the door locked, I'm sure. I'm confident enough that you can start getting your things together you'll need to take."

I went back to my house and packed my clothes. Two hours later I still hadn't heard from Mr. Waddell. His daughter was probably not as agreeable as he'd anticipated. I hated waiting around with nothing to do but was afraid to leave and miss his call.

After lunch, I gave up and walked over to Lady's pen. She was gaining weight and looked as good as she ever had. It was a beautiful fall day, and she was out of her stall walking around the pen without a limp. It gave me an opportunity to clean out her stall.

I'd just finished when Mr. Waddell drove up. I got in with him, and he told me how it went with his daughter. "It was a hard sell, Luke. She finally agreed after I told her it was only for a two-week trial basis. She doesn't want to leave until in the morning. It'll take her that long to get everything together.

"I'm moving Griffin into town today. He was ready to retire. I found him a nice little house in town, close to the grocery store. I need to warn you though—he's an old bachelor, and the house at the ranch will be a mess. Get ready to do some cleaning. The house has a cook stove and refrigerator, but the only heat is from a wood burning stove. I have a couple of cords of wood cut each year for him. There's a bathroom with a tub."

I listened without questions as he explained that everyone, including her mother, would be told Jimmie Lyn had gone to England. They'd assume she was looking for Drake. He'd tell anyone who asked about me that I went back to the track to train horses. Neither of us could be seen. He would send Bronc out every week to bring us groceries and whatever else we needed. He trusted Bronc, but he'd be the only one who knew where we were besides my mother and granddad.

"Luke, if you'll make me a list of what you need, I'll get it for you. I'm rushing everything, but we need to get Jimmie Lyn out of here as quickly as possible. She'd promised she's be ready to leave early. I'll have her at the office in the morning at six."

While he'd explained the plan, I wrote out what I needed on the back of an envelope and gave it to him. He looked at it and said, "This should be no problem."

"Have you informed Bronc?" I asked.

"No. I haven't had time. I'd like you to do that this afternoon. He's going to be at some risk."

Mr. Waddell thanked me again and left—a man on a mission.

✳✳✳

I found Bronc on the flatbed truck putting out hay with two other men. We sat down on the edge of a cement water trough while the truck moved on down the alley. I started from the beginning and told him everything. When I finished he just sat there looking confused.

"Are you sure you're not just making this up—joking or something?"

"No. Everything I told you is the truth. I know it sounds crazy. Are you willing to help?"

"It sounds like a James Bond movie. Bad guys are after the girl who is being protected by the good guys. And we're the good guys. Sure, I'm in!"

"Do you think it has a chance to work?" I asked.

"I guarantee it's a remote place. The ranch is about halfway between Dalhart and Clayton, New Mexico. When you turn off the highway it's seven miles to the house. The country is open, and you can see anyone coming. Nobody is going to sneak up on you. The house is close to some hills that make it inaccessible from the south.

"If you're replacing old Griffith, you're going to work your butt off, especially in the winter. You'll be feeding most days and it ain't easy. I don't know how the old man did it by himself. That, plus looking after Jimmie Lyn is more than I'd want to take on."

"Thanks for the encouragement. Maybe I should reconsider."

He laughed, reached over and pushed me. "You're up to it. I haven't had this much excitement in—I don't know when."

I joined the feeding group, putting out hay.

# 19

# PROTECTION

JIMMIE LYN

I was on the way to the Auction with my dad to meet Luke and sneak off in the dark. I'd finally given in, agreeing to go into hiding with a guy I hardly knew. I'd been about to marry a thirty-year-old man, and now I was being protected by a boy. I'd objected, but my dad was persistent. He'd never talked to me the way he did when I expressed myself about being in exile with a boy.

"I trust this boy. Tell me how your trust in this man you were going to marry turned out? I know people better than you do. That's been proven beyond doubt. You need to do what I ask and get over your self-pity and anger."

I suddenly became a little girl again, wanting to please my daddy who'd hurt my feelings, so I agreed to go to the ranch with Luke.

He was waiting on us when we arrived. Dad put my suitcases in Luke's pickup. Little was said but, before we left, my dad hugged me saying, "I love you, Honey."

"I'm counting on you, Luke," my dad said, as we got in.

I closed my door and turned, receiving a wet tongue that covered my entire face. "Ugg. What is that?"

"Bull, my dog. I've never been to the ranch. You'll need to tell me where to turn off."

"It's about twenty-five miles. I want you to know this is not my idea.

I'm doing it because of my dad. I can take anything for two weeks. After that, I'm coming back to civilization. What is that smell?"

"Bull. He likes you. He thinks that farting in your presence is a compliment. He is somewhat restricted by the change in his diet. You might want to roll your window down a little. It has a tendency to linger."

I rolled my window down and put my head out, remaining that way until I told him to turn off at the ranch road. I gladly got out and opened the gate, closing and locking it after he'd driven through.

The sun was just coming up when we drove up to the house. I got out quickly, sucking in the fresh air. The little cabin was not locked and going inside I was surprised at how clean it was. It'd been years since I stepped foot in it and hadn't realized how small it was. The living area occupied the front. An old western couch and rocking chair hugged two walls and a cabinet with a radio sat next to it. A set of deer antlers hung above the couch. A wood burning stove stood against the other wall. The combined dining and kitchen area contained a small white drop-leaf table with four cane-seated chairs. On the other side of the cabin a hallway led to a bathroom and a small bedroom. My exile was going to be confined to a 600-square-foot house.

Luke crossed the back porch carrying my suitcases. "Where do you want your stuff?"

I pointed to the back and followed him. "This is the only bedroom."

"No problem. I can sleep on the couch. Can we talk about this situation we're facing?"

I had no idea what he was going to say. "Sure."

We returned to the den, and he sat on the couch, and I took the chair. "Okay, let's hear it." I'd not paid attention to his face before now. It was narrow and thin. His mouth was wide with lips that were flat. I'd never seen his teeth since he didn't smile. He would have been handsome—his personality didn't allow it.

"I didn't volunteer for this job. Your dad asked me to do it. He's been so good to my family, I had no choice but to accept. It's obvious that you don't want to be here either. We can make the most of a bad situation, or we can make one another miserable. I'm going to choose the former. I hope you do also.

"You've got to do what I ask of you. The most important is being with me at all times. That means going with me to feed and whatever else I need to do on the ranch. Do you understand?"

It didn't look like he was giving me any choice. "Yeah, I understand. Can I ask you a question?"

"Sure. Ask away."

"Why don't you ever smile?"

He looked surprised. "I wasn't aware of it. It's probably not any one thing in particular—just the last two years. Any other questions?"

"What's in the long box that my dad put in the back of your pickup?"

He hesitated before responding. "Something I hope not to need."

"A gun?" I asked.

"Yeah. Just as a precaution. Anything else?"

"What about the case of Jack Daniels? That's a lot of liquor."

"Something I'm probably going to need."

"So, I'm being protected by an alcoholic? That's just great."

"It's not too late to change your mind. You'd be better off with the Feds anyway. You ask too many questions. I need to finish unloading. You might want to put the groceries up." He got up and left.

He was a strange character. Why would my dad have such great trust in him? He must see something that I don't. I began putting up the two sacks of groceries that was supposed to last a week. The fridge was practically empty except some stuff that needed throwing away.

After we had everything unloaded and in place, he said he had a job to do outside that would take awhile. I watched from the porch as he went up the road, the dog right on his heels, and began digging a hole with a shovel he'd found somewhere. Why would he dig a hole in the middle of the road? He returned to the house carrying the shovel over his shoulder.

"I haven't eaten this morning. If you'll cook us some eggs, I'll wash the dishes. We can switch at the next meal." He didn't wait for an answer, walking on by me.

I hadn't eaten either and cooked enough for both of us. As we sat down, I asked him if he wanted to say the blessing.

"No. I don't pray anymore."

"Is it all right if I do?" I asked.

"Suit yourself."

I said a short blessing, and he actually waited until I finished to begin eating. The dog stayed beside him, looking up and begging, but received no food.

"Why don't you pray?"

He continued to eat. "You ask too many questions."

✳✳✳

The next several days we stayed busy putting out hay. There was an old flatbed truck that was kept on the ranch for that purpose. The barn west of the house which had a top but no sides held several thousand bales of hay. During the winter months the hay was supplemented with range cubes, but being confined to the ranch made that impossible. Hopefully, by the time extreme cold arrived, the trial would be over and someone could replace us to feed, allowing our return to civilization.

Most of the ranch was open country except the south part which held some hills covered with cedars and pinions. The cattle came to the horn of the truck since the grass had already turned, due to several freezes. I'd help load the hay, but when putting it out I drove and Luke would push bales off the truck. The dog rode in the front with me but looked occasionally in the back to check on his master. His digestive system was better, or maybe I'd gotten used to the smell. We also would check each of the windmills which provided water.

We talked very little except about the work involved, avoiding our personal thoughts and feelings. I kept thinking that he would loosen up and become more social. I'd never paid that much attention to the way he looked until we were together night and day. He was small, but he had unusually broad shoulders with narrow hips. He was constantly having to pull his jeans up, I assume, because he used to be heavier. I was taller than he was by probably an inch. His dark hair came below his ears and was over his collar. I wondered why he hadn't got it cut. His eyes were dark brown, almost black, and when he didn't like what I did or said they seemed to look right through me, becoming darker.

I would wake up during the night, and the house was so small I could hear him moving around. Eventually, I would hear the clink of ice hitting the bottom of a glass. He was always up before me and had the coffee made. He never left me alone in the house or left the house without me.

As he had suggested, we took turns cooking and washing dishes. He wasn't a bad cook, but most of our meals consisted of simple dishes that didn't require much detail. Evenings were the most difficult for me since there was no TV, but we did have a radio. I'd brought several books. Most of the time, after dinner, I would go to my room and read. I could hear the country music coming from the kitchen, which I had no choice but to tolerate.

On the fourth morning I woke up shaking. I could hear the wind blowing and rain hitting the house. I dressed quickly and went to the kitchen welcoming the warmth from the wood burning stove. "It's freezing."

"Norther. Heard the forecast last night on the Clayton radio station. I went ahead and brought in wood and built a fire so it would be warm this morning. We have butane. I don't understand why we don't have a space heater.

"Bronc is coming today with our supplies. It hasn't been a week, but he's going to come every Sunday. If there's something you'd like from home, you can tell him."

"I want some more reading material. More desserts in the groceries would be nice."

"Make him a list so he'll remember," he said.

The dog came over to me. I petted him and was rewarded with a wet lick of my hand. "Your dog has the longest tongue I've ever seen."

"His name is Bull. He likes you. He's had a tough time, give him a break. It's your time to cook this morning. Can you make pancakes?"

"Sure. Are we going to feed this morning?"

"No. Bronc will be here at ten. We put out feed yesterday, which should hold them until tomorrow. We'll sit by the fire this morning and wait on Bronc."

I cooked pancakes and they were good, but I received no compliment. I couldn't believe it. I didn't go back to my cold bedroom to read, instead I took my book to the western wagon-wheeled couch and covered myself with a crazy patchwork quilt. He brought in wood, keeping the fire burning.

At a few minutes until ten, he took the long box out from behind the couch. "I'll be out in my pickup, waiting on Bronc." He left taking the box with him.

A half hour later he and Bronc came in carrying several sacks of groceries. I started putting them up while they sat by the fire and visited. I joined them after I'd finished.

"How's Dad doing?"

"Surviving. Your mom has been out every day harassing him. She suspects something and is determined to find out what's going on. Everyone else has bought the story of you going to England. Nobody seems to be interested in Luke except, of course, his mother and granddad.

How are y'all doing?"

Luke glanced at me for a response. "All right, I guess. We're staying busy."

"So far, so good. She's been a real trooper," he said, looking at me.

Did I hear what he said, correctly? He said something good about me! What was going on? I thought he was incapable of being positive about anything.

"Luke, that's some chug hole in the road. I hit it and turned over all the groceries. I'll be careful next time. I need to be going. Do y'all have any requests?"

I gave him my list, which had grown longer the more I thought about it. He left and Luke followed him out. The dog came over to me. "Well, Bull, we may need to be friends, after all." He moved up against me.

# 20

# NEW CHALLENGES

It was Wednesday, and Luke had been gone a week. I'd begun to regret not discouraging him from going to the ranch with Jimmie. He'd ignored my questions as to the danger involved, which was proof that it was real.

It'd been a month since I fractured my leg. On my visit to the doctor in Amarillo he'd replaced my original cast with a walking cast. I wasn't using my crutches now but was still slow getting around and had at least two more weeks before the doctor said he'd consider removing the cast.

Bronc had come to the house Sunday after returning from the ranch, assuring me that Luke and Jimmie were doing well. When I questioned him about the danger involved, he was as evasive as Luke. I was pleased that Luke had found a friend in Bronc.

My dad continued to do well. The job was a godsend since it made him feel useful and kept him occupied. Not an hour went by that something didn't remind me of Henry, especially when I was with Lady. Two months had passed, and I wondered if I would ever stop grieving. I'd still wake up during the night and reach for him. The phone rang, bringing me back to the present. It was Blaine.

"Grace, could you come up to the office. I need to talk with you."

"Yes." I was able to drive since getting my walking cast. Luke had taken Dad's pickup, so I was driving his car.

"Good, it shouldn't take long."

For a second, I panicked. Could something have happened at the ranch? No, Blaine was too calm. I'd been wearing jeans most days and had ruined most of them by splitting the leg to allow them to fit over the cast. I put on one of my few dresses and was at the office in a few minutes. When I told one of the ladies I'd been summoned by Blaine, she told me to go on back to his office.

I hesitated at his doorway until he looked up. "Come in, Grace. Have a seat. How're you doing?"

"Good, I guess. It frightened me at first when you called."

"I should've told you when I called—this is not about Luke. They're fine. I'm in a bind and was hoping you might be able to help me. We're lost without Jimmie Lyn. I have Madge, a young girl that has some experience working with Jimmie Lyn, but she's behind. Would you be interested in filling in until she returns? With both of you, maybe we can get caught up. I thought about going to a two-week payroll, but our employees wouldn't like that."

"Blaine, I have no experience in bookkeeping."

"Don't worry about that. You can learn as you go. Mostly it's going to be working with payroll. I don't require my employees to punch a time clock. They just keep track of their overtime, so it gets a little confusing."

"Sure. I'll do the best I can. I'm limited on mobility with this cast."

He laughed. "We won't have you working in the pens. Can you start in the morning?"

"Yes. I need to go shopping. I don't have appropriate clothes to work in the office."

He laughed again. "You look fine to me, Grace."

After meeting with Blaine, I found a dry goods store which had a good selection of women's clothes. Junior sizes fit my small waist and the rest of me better than the miss sizes. I wanted to look nice, but happy colors only made me sadder. Almost hidden by the cheerful miniskirts and bellbottoms, I found an old-gold straight skirt with a matching pull-over sweater. I added a black and gold plaid blouse to stretch the wardrobe. The skirt had large fabric buttons closing on the right side. It would make it easier getting over my gimpy leg. The next purchase was a dark-brown corduroy fitted jumper with a slightly flared skirt. My new blouse and several tops at home would match. My last purchase . . . a little black dress. Yes, I couldn't help it. I just felt like black. Not only the color but the softness of the velveteen appealed to me. The bonus was that the simple coat-dress, with buttons all the way down the front, fit like a glove. Walking to the counter, I tried to sweep the cost of the purchases out of my practical mind. But it appeared, nagging like a glop of mud on a shiny floor—probably wasted a week's salary. I got up the gumption to lay the pile down and shut the door on my doubts. I had to have something presentable.

Could I do this? It was exciting to have a new challenge. I had too much time to think staying at home all day by myself. This would be good for me, if I wasn't in over my head.

✳✳✳

I woke up early the next morning after a restless night's sleep. I took my bath, washed my hair, and was drinking coffee when Dad came in at six.

He poured a cup of coffee and sat down. "You're up early. Excited about your new job? The whole family is now working for Blaine."

"I know, Dad. Can you feed the horses this morning? I don't want to dress twice. I can do the afternoon feeding."

"Yeah. That'll be fine. Lady's really looking good. I wouldn't be surprised if she made a full recovery."

"Dad, do you think Luke is in danger? I regret not discouraging him from taking on this job of protecting Jimmie."

He got up and poured himself coffee and refilled my cup. "I imagine so. Not as much though as when he was in Vietnam. Daughter, you still see Luke as he was growing up. I worry about him, but I have no doubt but what he can take care of himself. Blaine realized how capable he is and trusted his daughter with him. I can't even imagine what he went through over there but whatever it was—he's well prepared for this job."

I hoped my dad was right. "I'll have breakfast ready by the time you finish feeding."

Dad left and my thoughts returned to Lady. Was it possible that she could make a full recovery as my dad had said? It was almost too much to hope that she could race again. She would be eligible for the New Mexico Derby, which was still ten months away.

After breakfast and getting dressed it was past seven o'clock. I put on my makeup and still arrived early for my first day. Madge, the woman I was to work with, was already there. After a brief visit, we went right to work.

She gave me the task of going through the bills and making out checks for them while she worked on the payroll. Time went fast, and the only interruption we had was Blaine coming in at mid-morning.

"How's it going? You look busy to me. Remember now, it's about time for a coffee break."

"We're getting so much done, Mr. Waddell, it's hard to find a stopping place," Madge said.

"I wish all my employees were so conscientious," he said, laughing.

As he left, Madge put down her pencil. "We better follow the boss's orders. I don't drink coffee, but I have a Diet Coke in the fridge. How about it?"

We returned a few minutes later with our coffee and Diet Coke. I was glad to be working with someone so nice. Madge was young— probably about the same age as Luke. She was a pretty girl, with beautiful red hair, a few freckles, and a peaches-and-cream complexion.

"How long have you been working here?" I asked.

"I started part-time in high school and went full-time after I graduated. My parents wanted me to attend college, but I wasn't interested. I'd had all the school I wanted. I like it here. Mr. Waddell is a great boss, and the other ladies I work with are wonderful. Tell me about Luke. Is he married or involved with someone?"

"Neither. He just got back from Vietnam. He had a girlfriend when he left, but she married while he was gone."

She blushed. "I'm not married either. I kept hoping he'd notice me. He's so cute. Every time he came around I tried to talk with him, but he didn't seem interested. Finally, I just gave up and now he's gone for good. I wish I'd tried harder."

"Luke had a difficult time in Vietnam. He's not the same as when he left. He left a fun-loving, always smiling boy, and returned a sad young man. I hope he's able to overcome that and can find happiness."

Madge smiled. "I'd be very willing to help him find happiness again." She took a long drink of her Coke and deposited it in the trash. "Well, it's back to work."

We didn't take off for lunch until one and were back at work by two. We stayed so busy time just flew by. A few minutes until quitting time I heard someone coming down the hall—clip-clop, clip-clop. It sounded like . . .

She was in the office before I could finish my thought. "What're you doing here?" she glared.

I was caught by surprise, and Madge answered. "She's helping me with the books since Jimmie Lyn is gone. We're getting a lot done."

"I'll bet." And then she was gone.

We could hear every word she said from Blaine's office but couldn't make out a response from him. "Why didn't you ask me to help? Why did you get her? I would've been glad to take Jimmie Lyn's place. She's not in London, is she? You lied to me!"

It went on and on until we heard one of the ladies from the office loudly proclaim, "Mr. Waddell, there's an emergency at pen 38! You're needed immediately!"

I looked at Madge who was trying to muffle her laughter. "The front office takes care of Mr. Waddell. There's no emergency, but you can bet he won't return to the office today."

I didn't realize how tired I was until I got home. It'd been a good day, but I was exhausted, and now it was time to feed the horses. I changed clothes and drove to the pens. It took me half an hour to feed and water. Then I sat down in a chair at Lady's barn. Watching her eat, I tried to concentrate on the blessings in my life. Luke was home, Dad was doing well, and I had a job that hopefully would keep me from dwelling on my grief. We owed so much to Blaine, beginning with saving this beautiful filly.

What was going on with his ex-wife? Today she was livid. I was afraid she'd eventually find out Jimmie Lyn's whereabouts and reveal it to everyone.

Madge reminded me about how attractive Luke had been to the girls. I'd not given it any thought since he returned. In high school they chased him to the point of embarrassment. I smiled, thinking that he and Madge would make a nice couple.

✻✻✻

The next two days went much like the first day. We stayed busy and time went fast. Blaine's wife didn't show up again, thank goodness, and we were able to get the payroll completed, so everyone received their checks on time.

Bronc came to the house late Friday afternoon. We had a nice visit. He said he was going to the ranch Sunday morning, and if I wanted to send anything to Luke, he would take it.

"That is so thoughtful, Bronc. I'll bake some cookies to send. I also want to write a letter telling him about my new job. Please ask him if there's anything in particular he would like me to cook for them. Also, tell Jimmie that Madge and I are doing our best, but we're looking forward to her coming back."

He left, and again I was thankful that Luke had found a friend.

# 21

# WINTER ARRIVES

 LUKE

The first week at the ranch was busy. Mr. Waddell was right about physical work being good for me and getting my mind off memories of the war. The nights were still bad, and I usually ended up having several drinks to help me relax and sleep a few hours. I was truthful to Bronc about Jimmie. She'd done well thus far and did whatever was asked of her, and I hoped that continued. I wasn't naive about the situation. The closer it came to the trial the greater the chance we would have visitors. I had to think ahead and be ready.

The seventh day we'd been at the ranch, after we finished putting out hay and were back at the house eating lunch, I asked Jimmie if she was familiar with the ranch.

"Sure. I've been coming out here since I was a little girl. I helped with rounding up cattle from the time I was six years old until I graduated from high school. Why?"

"We need a place to go that would offer shelter and be difficult to locate. Of course, it would need to be in the hills. This country is so wide open you can see over much of the ranch."

She didn't hesitate. "I know a place that would be perfect."

"How far is it from the house? Can we drive close to it?"

"It's several miles from the house. We can drive to within a half-hour walk—uphill."

We finished our meal and, with her directing, we drove to the area she had in mind. We stopped at the bottom of some hills unable to go further. We left Bull in the truck.

"You ready to climb?" she asked.

"Lead the way." The trees, mostly large cedar, were thick, and we had to weave our way through them. I had to hurry to keep up and realized she must be in good shape to move that fast.

She stopped and turned around, smiling. "You need to rest?"

I swallowed my pride. "Yeah. I think so." I plopped down.

She sat down across from me. Her face was flushed, and her blouse had sweat stains under the arms. She smiled. "I thought you'd be in better shape."

I realized it'd been a game—outdo me. She'd been successful. I didn't respond until several minutes later. "I'm ready to go." I'd drop dead before telling her I needed to rest again. We continued to climb, and I found myself looking up at her backside too often. I lied to myself by thinking, *I don't want to lose sight of her.* We dropped off into a ravine and the climb became steeper. We came to several large rocks and weaved our way through them. As we rounded the last huge one, I saw a shelf extending out from the mountain and darkness underneath it.

"We're here. What do you think?"

"Is it a cave?" I couldn't see inside.

"You might call it that. It goes back about thirty feet. I discovered it with a friend when we were in junior high. Follow me." She took a small flashlight out of her pocket.

It was damp inside, and the light revealed it was about twenty feet wide. The walls were rock, and I wondered if some people had lived here hundreds of years ago.

"What do you think?"

"It's better than good. It'll serve our purpose. We can stock it with supplies, and if we ever have to leave the house and hole up, we'll have a place."

The trip back down was much easier, but the scenery wasn't nearly as good.

✱✱✱

For the next three days, after feeding, we took canned goods, eating utensils, jugs of water, and other necessities which would allow us to survive for an extended time. We were fortunate that the former occupant of the house had hoarded so much canned food. We'd need to replenish our supplies on Bronc's next trip. The last afternoon we gathered firewood from dead trees and stacked it in the shelter. We had perfect fall weather to stock our hideaway.

Late Saturday afternoon when we returned to the house, we were exhausted. "Whose time is it to cook tonight?" I asked.

She moaned. "You know it's my time. How's Vienna sausage and crackers sound? My feet are killing me. How many trips did we make up that mountain the last three days?"

"Eight or nine. I'll fry some potatoes to go with your presentation. How's that sound?"

"With plenty of ketchup it'll be wonderful. Now, I'm going to take a hot bath while you cook. Would you fix me one of those drinks you have late at night after I've gone to bed?"

Surprised, I did as she asked, giving it to her before she left for her bath. She was a strange character—calling me an alcoholic and then asking me to make her a drink.

While the potatoes were cooking, I went outside to bring in some firewood, bracing against a north wind that had gotten up and was much colder. I finished the potatoes and built a fire, realizing it was getting colder by the minute. I turned on the radio hoping to get a weather report.

I opened the Vienna sausage and put it, along with the crackers and potatoes, on the table. I was so hungry it even looked good. With my plate piled high, I was about to start eating when she came into the kitchen in her housecoat.

She held up her glass. "I need a refill."

"You sure?"

"Pos-itive," she slurred.

I mixed her another drink. "Are you ready to eat?"

"Not quite. I wanna sit by the fire and rewax—I mean relax."

While she kicked back with her drink, I ate. I trudged outside for more wood, being welcomed with sleet stinging my face. When I returned, she was leaned back against the chair with her mouth open, snoring. She must've guzzled the second drink—if I just had a camera. I turned up the volume on the radio, hoping it would wake her up.

The weather forecast was finally given for Eastern New Mexico and Northwestern Texas. Sleet turning to snow later tonight with up to three inches. Bronc was coming tomorrow. Would he be able to get here?

I sat by the fire for the next two hours listening to country music and finally decided she wasn't going to wake up. She was out, but if she slept in that position with her neck twisted, she could be permanently injured, giving me no choice. I put my blankets and pillow on the couch. We'd have to change places tonight. Was I up to this challenge? I put one arm under her legs and the other under her neck and lifted her up, turning and placing her on the couch. She moaned softly, opening her eyes. "Shank you," and closed her eyes again. I covered her with a quilt.

While I was distracted, Bull had climbed up in a chair with his front feet on the table, helping himself to the rest of the fried potatoes.

✲✲✲

I slept in the bedroom with blankets piled high. I woke up several times but was able to go back to sleep. At five I went to the kitchen and put the last of the wood on the fire, so it was back to the woodshed. When I stepped outside the ground was covered with ice, and it was snowing. I carried as much wood as possible back inside. I had to move Bull from the foot of the stove to put in more wood. I'd started the coffee when she moaned and sat up, putting her head in her hands.

"The coffee will be ready in a few minutes."

Another moan. Then she was up and moving quickly toward the bathroom. Gagging sounds came from that direction. I actually felt sorry for her. Evidently, Bull thought so too because he left his warm place and walked quickly to the bathroom.

More gagging. I followed Bull and found her leaned over the commode. "Are you all right?"

She shook her head. "Go away." More gagging.

"Come on, Bull. She wants to be left alone." I left, but Bull stayed.

At a few minutes past seven she came into the kitchen. She poured herself a cup of coffee and sat down.

"You better?"

She nodded. "I don't understand why I became so sick. I've drunk liquor before and this didn't happen."

"Empty stomach and exhaustion. It hit you twice as hard. Your system's not used to it. After you finish your coffee, we have work to do. It snowed last night, and we need to get hay out. I'd recommend some dry toast to get something on your stomach."

"Bull stayed with me. He wouldn't leave. Why?" she asked.

"He was worried about you. He knew you were hurting. In the Marines we call that 'having your back.' After that pile of fried potatoes he had last night I'm surprised you could tolerate him."

She looked toward Bull. "Come here, boy." He walked over to her. She took his huge head in her hands. "Thank you."

My estimation of her went up considerably.

After breakfast we braved the snow and the cold to load the truck with thirty bales of hay. We'd have to make a trip back to get another thirty after we put this out. We didn't have time before Bronc got here to even put out this load, so we went back to the warmth to wait.

At fifteen minutes until ten, I took my box out to the pickup to wait for him. He was probably going to be late due to the weather. I opened the box and pulled the gun out. Two months ago I didn't have any idea I'd be holding this familiar weapon.

The snow was falling heavily now, and she walked briskly to the pickup with her head down. Once inside, she shuddered. "I can't believe it's this cold and not even November." She looked down at the gun beside me. "That looks like a shotgun. I thought you had a rifle."

"It's a 12-gauge Remington pump with a 20-inch barrel. This is what I asked your dad to get me. It's all I need."

"I thought shotguns were used to hunt dove and quail. Is it a special gun? It's really short."

"You ask more questions than anyone I've ever known."

"Shouldn't I have a right to ask questions. You're supposed to protect me. You have a gun used to hunt birds. What am I expected to think?"

Now she'd made me mad. "I didn't ask for this job. I told you that. I'll protect you the best way I know how. We can call this off any time you want. You'd be better off with the Feds anyway." That shut her up, and we sat in awkward silence until we saw Bronc coming. He slowed down and went around the hole in the road.

I helped him carry our groceries inside, then Bronc shared information from outside of our little world. "Blaine received news that the trial date was set for November nineteenth. They still have Drake in protection, but he's going to be required to appear in person." He looked at Jimmie. "Those guys from the FBI came back again yesterday and encouraged Blaine to have you placed in protection."

She remained silent long enough that I asked, "What about it? Is that what you want?"

She shook her head and muttered. "No. I'll stay here."

"Your mother is still showing up every day or so demanding to know where you are," Bronc said. "She's irate that Luke's mother is working in the office. Everyone feels sorry for your dad."

"How's my mother doing? Is she getting around without the crutches," I asked.

"Yeah. She seems to enjoy her job and everyone in the office really likes her. I need to be going. Is there anything else you need?"

"We depleted our stock of canned goods this week. Double up on those. Also, we need two sleeping bags—heavy duty."

"Will do. Jimmie Lyn?"

"I need to send some of my clothes back to be washed. You better give them to Grace. That's all."

Bronc left, and we spent the snowy afternoon in silence, putting out hay to hungry cows.

# 22

# OLD WOUNDS SURFACE

 JIMMIE LYN

I was sorry to have upset Luke by questioning him about his ability to protect me. I know now that it was wrong. My problem was I honestly didn't think he was qualified or capable of keeping me safe in case the thugs came for me. Why didn't I agree to go under Federal protection? I kept asking myself that question. All I could come up with was I'd been humiliated and made a fool out of by Drake and wanted to hide from everybody. The closest I could come to that was staying out here with Luke. For some reason I didn't believe that he gave a hoot about me being jilted by Drake; in fact, I don't think he'd ever given it a thought.

I'd never known anyone as strange. He seemed to be in misery, never laughing or even smiling. I saw the empty bottles and, by my calculation, he was downing a fifth of whiskey every three days, always drinking at night after I'd gone to bed. My dad knew he drank and still furnished him with a whole case of liquor.

It was still over three weeks until the trial where Drake would testify. I wondered if he'd return to the states after the trial. In one way I wanted to see him again and tell him how I felt about what he'd done to me. In another way I hoped to never see him again.

I went from being on top of the world to total disgrace. Why couldn't I, at least, suspect something was not right—after all, he was too perfect and never disagreed with me until he told me he was going to England to testify. Why couldn't I see through some of this? That was easy. I was twenty-three years old and desperate to find someone. My younger sister was already married, and there were no prospects in sight. Suddenly, there he was—all six-feet-five inches.

It was Monday, and since Bronc left, we'd only spoken when it was absolutely necessary. I could apologize, but it wouldn't be honest. I woke up several times last night, and the noise coming from the kitchen indicated that he hadn't slept.

The weather was nice today, so predictable for Texas—unpredictable. By the time we came in from lunch the snow had melted, and we had shed our heavy coats. I was miserable with the current situation and determined to do something about it. "This weather is something else, isn't it?" Maybe this would start a dialogue.

"Yeah."

I went about putting a bag of chips on the table and bringing the sandwich makings out of the fridge. "Would you like coffee for lunch or a Coke?"

"Coke."

This was going nowhere. Maybe I should just give up. No way. "All right, I shouldn't have said what I did about you protecting me. You've chosen the best way to punish me. I need social interaction—communication. I can't talk to myself. We're out here alone, just the two of us. Please don't pout for the next three weeks. I'll go nuts."

"You were right. I probably can't protect you. I failed the last time and men died because of it. You'd be safer with the Feds, and they'd probably be more social."

Stunned—I didn't know what to say.

"I can't figure out why you're so determined not to go under the protection of Federal agents. You want to tell me?" He was looking right through me with those piercing eyes which had turned black.

It was my turn to be honest with him. "I was stupid, and Drake made a fool out of me. I was humiliated, and people were laughing at me. I just wanted to hide, and you could care less about my situation. This was a good place to be secluded from the world." I told him the entire story of Drake and how I thought he was perfect before he disappeared and I discovered he had another family.

He sat in silence for a full minute as if in deep thought. "I'm ready for my sandwich and Coke now."

✵✵✵

The next two weeks were without incident. The fall weather returned with sunshine and beautiful days. Nothing was said about protection or Drake, and civility returned. Bull served as a catalyst in our relationship since we could always talk about him and his antics. He'd started sleeping on top of my bed. His body provided warmth, and as long as we kept him away from the table food his system behaved.

Bronc brought enough canned foods to refurbish our supplies and delivered two heavy duty sleeping bags which we put in our hideout. Luke's mother sent us delicious chocolate chip cookies and several pies. The routine that we followed kept us busy most of the day. I discovered that Luke was quite the handyman when one of the windmills broke. He seldom talked of himself and when he did it was about growing up in a small town. I found out that he'd played football and had a scholarship offer at a junior college. He mentioned several high school friends but no girls, and the one time I mentioned Vietnam he let me know quickly it was off limits.

We were waiting in the pickup when Bronc circled the chug hole and drove up on Sunday, November tenth. We both were surprised that Dad was with him. I dove out and hugged him. "What a nice surprise!"

Inside, he explained the reason for coming with Bronc. "I received another visit this week from Fitzgerald and Donnelly. You remember them, I'm sure. They scared me, Honey. They have information that the bankers who've been charged are desperate. They've hired some guys from the Russian Mafia to locate Drake. Which means they may come after you. It's only nine days until the trial. Would you consider going back with me and joining the Federal protection program?"

"No, Dad. It's only a few more days. I don't want to leave the ranch and go with strangers."

"Well, I wanted to give you one more chance. How're y'all getting along?"

"Not bad. Feeding keeps us busy. The weather's been beautiful. What about you, Dad? Is everything going all right at the Auction?"

"Except for your mom, everything is great. She's a royal pain. Grace, Luke's mom, has really stepped up and filled the void that you left.

"That reminds me, Luke. Lady is doing amazingly well. When you're able to return, I'd like for you to take her back to A&M for an exam. I never thought she would come back this quickly."

We talked for another half hour before Dad produced a letter from his jacket pocket and gave it to Luke. "Your mother asked me to give this to you. It's from Washington." He chuckled. "Maybe they're sending you some back pay."

After we walked them to their pickup, Dad hugged me—longer than I ever remembered. It was so good to see him. He actually looked great for all the stress I'd caused in his life. It should be no surprise that my mom wanted him back. He was a handsome man. I wish I'd inherited his dark complexion instead of my mother's. He was taller than me, but not by much. He had a little gray in his dark hair, and his face was rugged but gentle at the same time. He'd gained weight over the years and it showed in his midsection, but he wouldn't be called overweight. It struck me how silly it was of my mother not to be willing to tolerate his tobacco and smelly boots.

✳✳✳

The weather changed the afternoon my dad and Bronc left, becoming colder. The next few days were dreary with little sunshine and a north wind that made being outside miserable. We made another trip to our cave, making sure everything was undisturbed. While there, we built a fire ring out of rocks several feet inside the shelter.

By mid-week I was getting nervous. It was only a few days until the trial. Was it possible we were going to escape the danger and all this hiding was going to be for nothing? I was ready to return and face the consequences—whatever that would be. It's been almost two months since the planned wedding; maybe most people would've forgotten. I'd go back to work and resign myself to a life as an old maid. That thought disgusted me. If I was going to wallow in self-pity, maybe I deserved whatever was in my future.

By Friday, Luke had stopped talking. It seemed that his mind was in another universe. When I asked him about it, he shrugged and said, "I'm just reminded of another time and place."

Saturday morning, I woke up in the dark, freezing. Bull was gone, and there was no light in the kitchen. Luke was always up before me with a fire going. I put my housecoat on and went to the kitchen and turned on the light. His head was on the table beside an empty bottle, and Bull was lying at his feet. I went back to my room and dressed.

After I'd got the fire started, I put the coffee on. He still wasn't awake. Did he drink the entire bottle? When the coffee started perking, I poured a cup and placed it down beside him. I put my hand on his shoulder and shook him gently. He mumbled something I couldn't understand, so I shook him again, harder this time.

"Wake up, Luke. Here's some coffee."

He mumbled again, and this time I understood. "Sor-ry, sho-uldn't have, no, no." He sat up quickly—tears streaming down his face. When he saw me, he tried to stand, falling back in his chair. He put his head down in his hands, as if trying to hide. I left him like that, taking my coffee back to the bedroom.

An hour later he appeared in my doorway. "Breakfast is ready."

Nothing was said the remainder of the day about the episode. He was quiet but that wasn't unusual. I couldn't help but wonder if I'd made a mistake by not accepting my dad's offer for Federal protection.

✳✳✳

Sunday morning, I woke up warm, with Bull's heat adding to my comfort. A light was on. I dressed and went to the kitchen, leaving Bull in bed.

"What about pancakes this morning?" Luke asked.

What a difference between yesterday morning. "Sure. Sounds good. I think we have some sausage left. Coffee smells good."

He poured me a cup. "We need to celebrate. Just three more days until the trial. We may just get out of this without any problems. If they were coming, surely it would've happened by now."

My pancakes were even better than usual, and we savored our breakfast together. We had more coffee in front of the warm fire until it was time for Bronc to arrive. Outside, we waited for him fifteen minutes until ten.

Bronc was punctual. At exactly ten o'clock his pickup appeared. When he reached the chug hole there was no effort to avoid it.

# 23

# GOOD NEWS

Seventy-five. I needed to stop counting how long Henry had been gone. Every morning I'd wake up and think how many days I'd been without him. My life was moving along, but sometimes I'd experience a good feeling about something and immediately feel guilty and then correct myself. Henry would want me to be happy. He'd never been a selfish person.

I was enjoying my job in the office. Madge was a fun co-worker and time went fast. Several times last week Madge had been summoned to the front office to help out, and I was left alone working on the books.

It was Sunday morning, November tenth, and Blaine had gone to the ranch with Bronc. I'd sent chocolate chip cookies, one of Luke's favorites. I was curious about the letter he received from Washington.

I needed to get ready if I was going to be on time for Sunday School. The week after Luke left, I started going to church, and I was approached after the first service by a couple who invited me to join their Sunday School group. I took them up on their offer and had enjoyed it more than I could've imagined. Anywhere from twelve to sixteen attended each Sunday, and I was one of the younger participants. Everyone was friendly in the class and made me feel welcomed immediately. I hadn't realized how much I needed the spiritual guidance and social interaction that was provided. The first ten minutes or so of the class was spent visiting and naming people who needed prayer and also sharing blessings that had occurred the previous week.

One thing I appreciated about the class was the avoidance of political discussion. Richard Nixon had been elected president the previous week, and like any election year there was no absence of opinions. He had campaigned on ending the Vietnam War and that was enough for me to vote for him. Dad didn't tell me, but I'm sure he voted for Humphrey. He always said, "The Republicans liked to have starved me to death during the Depression."

I didn't follow politics closely, but I know what the war did to my son. Anytime someone began discussing the merits of the war, I got as far away as possible. I was thankful to have Luke home, but was he safe now? When I questioned Blaine, all he would say was, "Luke can take care of himself." I didn't understand how he could be so sure when he didn't know Luke that well. However, he felt strongly, else he wouldn't have trusted him to protect his daughter.

❊❊❊

Monday morning the first thing I did when I arrived at the office was to ask Blaine about his visit to the ranch. He closed his door and motioned me to sit down. "They're doing fine, Grace. I know you're worried about Luke. I understand that, and it'll be a relief when it's over. I've thought a great deal about how Jimmie Lyn got herself involved in this situation. Everything just came together—timing was perfect. She was desperate for a relationship and along comes Drake. She was blind to anything but seeing the good in him. He was a con and convincing. It will take her a long time to get over it. As you know, we want to protect our children from any kind of hurt."

"Blaine, I'm still confused why you would trust Luke to protect Jimmie. You know so little about him. Even when she wouldn't go into protection with the Federal agents, you could've found someone who was more qualified and experienced. I just don't understand."

"I'm going to share something with you that I probably shouldn't. Luke and I talked the night we waited for information about Lady. I'm a veteran as well, with some terrible memories. We traded some of our horrible experiences. It was the first time I'd talked about mine to anyone. That's strange since it's been twenty-four years since the Normandy Invasion. I doubt if he ever talks with you about what he's been through. Luke was a platoon leader and led about two dozen men. He lost several of those men, and he's struggling with that and probably will the rest of his life. I guarantee you it wasn't his fault they died, but he blames himself.

"I admit of thinking first about my little girl. However, Luke is going to get another chance to protect someone. It's a long shot, but he might come out of this feeling better about himself.

"You also questioned Luke's qualifications to protect Jimmie Lyn. I have absolutely no doubt about that. You see him as your son, as he was before he left for Vietnam. I did some research through a friend of mine who has made a career out of the military. It's a small world when it comes to the military. I wish you could've heard what he said about Luke. One statement stands out. "Luke was one of our best platoon leaders, risking his life time and time again to protect his men. His men would've followed him into hell."

I knew Luke was suffering, now I understood why. "Thank you for telling me. I won't speak with Luke about any of what you've said." I left Blaine's office with a better understanding of my son and his behavior.

Madge was already in our office. We went to work and didn't stop until our break at ten o'clock. Drinking my coffee as she sipped on her Diet Coke, I asked about her weekend. "Boring. I had a date with this guy who I couldn't stand. I thought it would be better than staying home—it wasn't."

She put her Coke down on the table. "I'd like to look like you at your age."

"Why, thank you." I was surprised at the compliment.

"You look so clean and wholesome. I don't mean washed clean—just clean and healthy. You're so trim and fit. When I'm your age, as much as I like to eat, I'll be fat. You wear so little makeup, but you don't need it."

"You're too kind," I said.

"No, just honest. Time to get back to work."

✽✽✽

After changing into my jeans, I fed in the afternoon, and Lady's pen was my first stop. Anytime I was feeling down I would think of her. I kept waiting for her to have a setback from the injury and surgery, but so far so good. I was looking forward to a report from the vet at A&M. Would it be possible to put her back in training this spring?

The other horses we'd brought from the track were doing well, also. They should be since they were getting grain twice a day and generous helpings of alfalfa. Blaine had said we might turn them out on wheat this spring.

I wasn't anxious to return to the track. I liked my job and, with my dad working, we were making more money than we ever had at the track. I'd feel different if Lady was able to resume racing.

When I returned to the house, Angie's car was there. My oldest daughter had been out a couple of times from Amarillo. The last time I felt bad lying to her about Luke's whereabouts, saying he'd gone back to the track. She and Dad were in the living room, and she got up to hug me when I came in. She seemed upset. She started crying and my dad left, saying he needed to check on something in his trailer.

"What is it, Angie?"

"It's Evert," she said, sniffing. "I don't know what to do. He won't get a job. He just lies around the house all day watching television."

"Have you talked to him about it?"

"Mom, I've begged him to get a job—any job. His reply is the same every time. 'I can't find anything that interests me.'"

"Y'all have been married for two years, Angie. He's never held a job."

"I know but—but now it's different. I'm three months pregnant. The most I could work would be three more months. Standing on my feet all day at the salon is already becoming difficult."

Suddenly, an involuntary smile appeared. I took her in my arms and held her, the thought flashing through my mind: *I'm going to be a grandmother.* Holding a crying adult daughter, whose life was falling apart, I couldn't get rid of the smile. I kept assuring her everything was going to be all right. We could help her financially. I was working, her granddad also had a job, and Luke was getting a weekly pay check. The second the words left my mouth, I realized the mistake.

"You told me Luke was at the track training horses," she said.

Now, what was I going to do? "Angie, listen carefully to me. I can't tell you where Luke is and what he's doing. In a few days, he'll be back here working at the Auction. Please trust me, and don't ask any questions."

She wiped away a tear. "I want to see Luke when he gets back. He always makes me feel good. He reminds me of Dad." She seemed to be satisfied with my explanation.

"I promise—the first day he's back I'll call you. You can see him then. Okay?"

She nodded. "I'm sorry for bringing my problems to you."

"No, don't be. I'll always be here for you." We talked well into the night, and I insisted she stay until morning.

In better spirits, Angie left early, declining breakfast. It appeared that our long talk had been successful. Over coffee, Dad took the opportunity to express his opinion.

"How can anyone be that lazy? Sitting at home all day would drive me crazy. She needs to run him off."

"What do you think about being a great-granddad?" I thought that might soften him up a little.

He took out his package of Camels and smiled. "Psalms 127 Verse 3—**Children are a gift from the Lord: they are a reward from Him.** Don't you think we need a reward, after this year, Daughter?"

"Definitely. I'm going to be a grandmother. The thought of holding a baby fills my heart with joy." I wasn't exaggerating—new life in our family was something that brought unexpected happiness and hope for our future. Now, if we could just get the "Leaner" off his rear and into the job force.

# 24

# CHAOS

LUKE

"Get out and walk to the house. Don't run, just move normal." When I was sure she was in the house, I took the 12 gauge, pumped a shell in the barrel and opened the door, staying behind it. I made sure the gun was not visible. Time seemed to slow down, and a calmness came over me as Bronc's pickup stopped, and the passenger door opened. A burly man wearing a round fur hat stepped out, remaining behind the open door.

"I have something for you," he said with a thick accent. He pulled Bronc out, shoving him forward, holding a gun to his head.

The driver's side door opened, and a taller man with the same type hat stepped out, pointing a pistol in my direction. "We will make a trade, and nobody gets hurt," he said with a similar accent. "We know the girl is here. We saw her go in the house."

According to my calculations they were about twenty yards from me. I looked directly into Bronc's eyes and saw the fear. Suddenly, he screamed, "No, Luke! They're going to kill us anyway." He then dived forward.

The man on the passenger side shot and broke the window on the door. I dropped to the ground at the same time slamming the door. At twenty steps the 12 gauge impregnated with number 4 buckshot spoke three times and was just as deadly as it was in the jungles of Vietnam.

Bronc was lying face down with his hands covering his head. "It's okay, Bronc. It's okay."

He got up slowly looking at the two men on the ground. The first time he tried to talk nothing came out. He tried again and was successful. "They were going to kill us, Luke."

"Are there anymore of them?" I asked.

He continued to stare at the bodies. "Yeah. A guy stayed at the car. They came out of nowhere and jumped me when I got out to open the gate. What're we going to do, now?"

I put my gun on the hood of the pickup. "Help me put these guys in the back of your pickup." We removed their coats and hats before putting them in the back. It was no easy task. Both of us got blood on our clothes during the process.

"Now, go in the house and tell Jimmie what happened, and then bring her with you when you return." After he left, I picked the pistols up off the ground. Anger rose up in me as I recognized the same make weapon we'd taken off North Vietnamese regulars. I couldn't pronounce the Russian name—we just called it a PM. I put both in Bronc's pickup.

Bronc came out of the house with Jimmie whose face was drained of color. She avoided looking at the blood on the ground. "Where are they?"

I made a head motion toward Bronc's pickup. "In the back."

"What're you going to do with them?" she whispered.

"We're going to send them back where they came from." I then told Bronc what we had to do. "You and I will put on the coats and hats of the two guys, and with Jimmie riding in the middle, we'll return in your pickup to the awaiting driver. Thinking it was a successful venture, he won't be cautious when we arrive.

"Why don't we just wait here until the driver comes to see what happened?" Bronc asked.

"He would come expecting trouble. It'd be impossible to surprise him. If possible, I want to take him alive."

A few minutes later, with Bronc and me wearing the hat and coats of the Russians, we left with Jimmie riding between us. I'd given Bronc one of the pistols and showed him where the safety was. Nothing was said until we came within sight of the car parked in the gate.

"Both of you stay inside."

I drove, at what would be a normal speed on a ranch road, right up beside the passenger side of the car. Before he recognized it wasn't his men, I jumped out, placing the barrel of the shotgun up against his window. "Get out!" I shouted.

He opened the door and climbed out slowly. He was larger than either of the other two men. "Put your hands behind your head. Now!" I pushed the gun against his stomach.

"Bronc! I need you to help me."

He was standing beside me in seconds. "Reach inside his coat and get his gun."

"Bronc took a pistol out that was identical to the others."

"Now, look in the car and see if there's a gun."

He opened the passenger door and reappeared with a Soviet SKS carbine, the most common weapon of the Viet Cong. My anger came close to the breaking point.

I jabbed him in the stomach again. "Now, get your comrades out of the back of the truck, and put them in your car. One in the back—one in the front to keep you company."

He made an animal sound and lunged for me. I swung my gun around and sunk the butt of it into his stomach knocking the wind out of him. He bent over gasping for air, and I brought the butt of the gun up catching him under the chin. He fell against his car, sliding to the ground, then struggled to get to his knees, placing his hands on the ground for support.

I put the barrel of my gun on the back of his thick neck. "Now you listen to me. I'm going to give you a choice. Nod your head if you're going to do what I tell you. If I don't see you nod in five seconds, I'm sending you straight to hell."

The head began nodding immediately. He struggled to his feet and did as he was told—putting the two bodies in the car. I noticed that Jimmie had gotten out and was watching.

After completing the task, the Russian stood by the door of his car. "Are you going to kill me?"

"No. Take your dead friends back to whoever sent you. Show them what will happen if they try this again."

He got in his car, backed around and headed in the direction of town. I turned to Bronc. "Take us back to the house. We need to pick up a few things, then you can take us to a place we're going to hole up for the next several days. They may come back. I doubt it, but it's possible."

Less than an hour later, with Bull riding in my lap, we stopped in front of the area leading up the mountain to where we had stored our supplies. We bailed out, grabbing hiking packs we'd filled with additional clothes. I then instructed Bronc what to do. "Tell Blaine what happened. I see no point in contacting the authorities. Don't come back until you have information that we're out of danger. When you return, park here and give three long blasts on your horn."

"Do you want to keep the pistols?" he asked.

"Just one and the rifle. You keep the other two. And thanks, Bronc— you did good."

The climb seemed easier today probably because of the adrenaline. Jimmie hadn't said a word since we left the house. After we put our clothes down in the shelter, I poured some dog food in a plate for Bull. We'd made sure to stock the shelter with plenty of food for him. I asked her if she wanted something to eat.

"No. I couldn't eat anything. I feel like throwing up. How can you be so calm after what you did?"

I didn't respond, instead going to a corner of the cave and taking a bottle out of a bag. I also produced a cup, pouring it half full of whiskey and filling it to the rim with water. I stirred it with my index finger before sitting down on a stool we'd brought on one of our earlier trips. "It's going to get cold tonight. We need to start a fire. The only time we can have a fire is after dark. They definitely won't be back today. The heat will reflect off the walls, and it should be warm by dark."

She was still standing. "You didn't answer my question."

I took a sip of my drink. "How do you know I'm calm? All you can see is the outside. Today was not an unusual day for me the last two years of my life. I had a responsibility for the lives of others, and I had to portray assurance and confidence. What would my men have thought if I went around wringing my hands, excited and agitated? I have a responsibility for you. Would you feel better if I was emotional about what happened and distraught over what I had to do?" I took another sip of my drink and waited for a reply. Instead, she started crying, which turned to sobbing. Bull went over and rubbed against her.

I sat my drink down, walked over to her, and held her by the shoulders. "It's okay. We're going to be fine. Now, help me get a fire going. Go outside and gather some small twigs." I needed to get her mind on doing something besides just thinking of the last two hours.

She did as I asked and, within a short time, we had a nice fire going. She'd calmed down and, as the sun slid slowly behind the western hills, I asked her about growing up and visiting this ranch. She loosened up and talked freely about time spent with her sister and her dad. She didn't try to hide the fact that her mother's conduct angered her.

She began asking me questions about my hometown and my high school days. Uncharacteristically, I talked freely about my teachers, friends, and family. I described fishing trips with my granddad and day-working on ranches in the summer. I replayed football games and even talked of social events such as banquets and proms.

"It's time for a bathroom break," she said, interrupting me.

We'd brought a five-gallon bucket and filled a third of it with dirt. It was placed at the back of the shelter. I'd made it known that the outside would serve me better. I went outside to give her some privacy. The night was cold and clear with a sky that could only be viewed in the Texas Panhandle. I stayed out longer than necessary to give her plenty of time.

It was amazing how much warmer it was in the cave. She actually ate some cheese and crackers before we bedded down in our sleeping bags. Bull went over and lay down as close to her as possible. I thought of how much more comfortable this was than the damp jungle.

❖ ❖ ❖

The next morning when I went outside to take my bathroom break, Bull joined me, dousing several tree stumps. It was bitter cold, but the sun was shining. Back inside, there were some coals which, stirred, were hot enough to make coffee. I put the coffee pot on a small grate at the edge of the fire. In a few minutes the water was boiling. I took it off the fire and let it set for thirty seconds or so and stirred two tablespoons of coffee in it. I let it sit for a couple of minutes and poured a cup. I took a sip, grimacing. It'd have to do.

Bull went over to Jimmie's bed roll and gave her a quick cheek wash. She rolled over, and he had a clear target of her entire face and took advantage of it.

"Uggggg." She sat upright. "Oh, Bull, you're drowning me."

"Coffee's ready. It's not great, but it'll wake you up," I announced.

"I'll take some. Lots of sugar and some canned milk."

I fixed her coffee, gave it to her and asked, "Could you eat something this morning?"

"Maybe, a little later."

"How do you feel?" I asked.

She took a sip of coffee, making a face. "That's the worst coffee I've ever drunk. I don't know how I feel. I woke up during the night thinking it was all a dream. After a few seconds, I realized it wasn't. I lay there for an hour before going back to sleep. Strange—but I wasn't afraid. What are the plans for today?"

"Can we get a view of the ranch if we climb to the top?" I asked.

"If we walk uphill for another hundred yards or so we can be on top. When we go to the right for several hundred yards, we'll come to a point. From there you can see much of the ranch, including the house. If it's a clear day you can see as far as the entrance to our gate."

"Then we have a plan. We'll spend the day looking for visitors. I don't expect any, but I might be wrong. Better not to take a chance. We'll let the fire go out during the day because of the smoke. We can start it again after dark. It looks like a nice day to be outside. If you'll put us something together for lunch, we'll take our guard duty."

# 25
# LOOKOUT

I lay awake in my sleeping bag while trying to get the episode out of my mind. After Luke told me to go into the house, I'd witnessed it all from the kitchen window. The man pulling Bronc out of his pickup with the gun to his head, and then the other guy appeared, pointing his pistol at Luke. Hearing Bronc scream, and dive forward. Seconds later it was over, with the two men lying motionless on the ground. It happened so quickly, I couldn't look away soon enough to avoid the scene. The three blasts from Luke's gun sounding almost like one. The men were lifted off the ground and thrown backward when they were hit. They had no chance, caught by surprise and having no idea what they were up against. I turned from the window, unable to look at the bodies of the men who'd come for me. A few minutes later Bronc came into the house to get me. "Jimmie Lyn, Luke wants you outside."

"I saw it. He killed them so quickly. How did he do it, Bronc?"

"My brother is in Vietnam. In a letter he told me that the Viet Cong feared a Marine with a shotgun. You just got to witness why they feel that way. Now we need to go."

These recent memories kept going over and over in my mind. I was finally able to concentrate on the stories that Luke had told last night about growing up in a small town. He'd talked more in a couple of hours than he had in the month we'd spent at the ranch. I know he did it to get my mind off the morning's events. The last thing I remembered before dropping off to sleep was him describing his junior senior prom.

*✻✻✻*

I was supposed to get something together for lunch. The choices were limited, but I finally settled on a block of cheese, crackers, and a can of Spam. I also included two cans of Coke in the small lunch bag. From out of nowhere came the menu for my reception dinner—rib eye steak, baked potato, and cheese cake for dessert. I quickly dismissed the thought.

I led the way and Bull and Luke followed as we left the shelter. It was not a difficult climb, and coming out on top the terrain was flat with very few trees. A few minutes later we were standing on the point overlooking the ranch. It'd been years since I'd been here, and the view was even more amazing than I remembered. The house could be seen plainly and the main entrance to the ranch, even though miles away and minuscule, was in view. I sat down on a large flat rock. "What do you think?"

"Perfect. You must've been quite an explorer in your younger days." He sat down on the rock beside me. "Look," he said, pointing. "What're those dots between here and the gate?"

"That's a herd of antelope. There used to be more but the drought in the '50s reduced the numbers."

The sun was warm, and I moved down to the ground and leaned back against the rock. I'd slept little last night, and in a matter of minutes I was dozing. We passed the morning with me napping, while Bull lay against my leg. Luke served as lookout. We had our lunch, which actually wasn't as bad as it sounded. Bull looked so pitiful watching us eat that we gave him the left-over Spam.

The afternoon dragged by, interrupted once when a car pulled into the entrance to our gate only to use it as a turnaround. After that alert, which turned out to be nothing, Luke sat down and leaned back against the rock, closing his eyes. I'd never studied him this close and saw that he had a small scar on his chin. After yesterday, I had an altogether different vision of him. He'd seemed so young, just a boy, and then he saved my life as well as Bronc's against two professional killers.

He looked so innocent leaned back against the rock with his eyes closed. I wished my skin was as dark as his. His hair had gotten longer and now was to his shoulders. It was thick and dark. His eyebrows were narrow and his eyelashes were long, more like a woman's. I'd never seen his teeth because he never smiled.

He opened his eyes and saw I was looking at him. He turned away and quickly rose. "We can go back now, it's getting late."

The sun was setting. As we reached a point where our shelter was directly below us, a loud boom shook the ground. Suddenly, I was lying flat, with him on top of me. "What are you doing? It was only a jet breaking the sound barrier. You're squashing me."

"Sorry." He rolled off me. "I'm sorry," he repeated, getting up and dusting off his jeans. He offered me his hand and pulled me up. "It sounded like a mortar round."

"No problem," I said, amazed at how quickly it had happened. Then I realized—he'd been protecting me, with no concern for himself.

It was already getting cold, and I started building a fire when we reached the shelter. "What would you like for supper?" I asked.

He was occupied making himself a drink. "We have plenty of potatoes. What about French fries to go with a can of beans. I'm hungry after that Spam."

"If you'll peel them, I'll get the grease hot," I suggested.

The fried potatoes with ketchup and beans were better than I ever remembered. We'd actually put in some cookies which we had for dessert. Bull's anxious looks didn't get him any of our food so, looking disappointed, he went over and began nibbling on his dog food.

We spent the two hours after supper, resuming our talk about the past, staying away from current happenings. Tonight, I talked more about my high school and college days. I was comfortable telling him about my basketball career and how I'd disappointed everyone, not living up to their expectations, but I was more positive in describing my college experience and friendships that were established.

When it was his turn, he talked about his dad and their relationship. It was sad hearing him describe the special bond that existed between them. I thought, what a terrible tragedy for him not to be here for his dad's funeral. The light from the fire was enough to see the tears when he talked about the last time he'd seen his dad. I'm sure he wouldn't have opened up and expressed his feelings if not for the liquor. My heart went out to this boy-man as I tried to imagine going through the horror of war and returning home without my dad.

After a bathroom break, we crawled into our sleeping bags. Bull took his place—as close to my side as possible. I was drowsy from sitting by the fire but couldn't sleep. Drake entered my thoughts and wouldn't leave, with images of him appearing as my anger grew. He was the reason all this was happening, and I shared the blame for being so stupid. What was his purpose? Did he plan on deserting his other family and living here from now on, never seeing them again, or was I just a stopover on the way to something else?

The trial started tomorrow. Hopefully, he would testify during the first day or two, and we'd be out of danger and could return to civilization. However, it could drag on for days or even weeks.

I'd made the right decision coming to the ranch rather than going into Federal protection, and it hadn't been as bad as I anticipated. I'd learned more about Luke the last twenty-four hours than the previous thirty days. I was ashamed for not thinking he was capable of protecting me and questioning his capabilities. Dad had been right, which was no surprise.

I began to get drowsy and was on the verge of sleep. I heard it first but still was not ready for the result. It filled the warm air in the cave, becoming stronger every second until I turned over and buried my head in my sleeping bag. Today was the last time Bull would get any Spam.

**❋❋❋**

I woke up freezing the next morning. The fire had gone out, and we couldn't rebuild it until tonight. The wind was howling and could be felt coming into the shelter. I snuggled down further in my bed, covering up my head, deciding to wait as long as possible before getting up. When I heard Luke moving around, I peeped my head out. "I don't think we have any fire."

"Nope. Looks like you won't get coffee this morning."

"Darn. I was so looking forward to a cup of your steaming hot gourmet coffee."

"You're being ugly now. It's already daylight. We need to get a move on. This may be their last chance to get to you."

I moaned and crawled out of bed. I'd slept in my clothes which I'd planned to change today. "It's potty time."

He left with Bull following and stayed out longer than necessary. I finally went to the entrance and called him. "Luke, you can come back in." The wind hit me in the face and I thought, *we'll freeze sitting out in this.*

We'd downed cookies and water for breakfast. I put together a lunch of crackers, Vienna sausage, and cheese, including two canned Cokes to go with our feast. We left immediately and were at our lookout a short time later. Out on the point, we took the full force of the north wind.

"You need to move around on the other side of the rocks, so you'll be out of the wind. It's going to be a miserable day, but we have to stay here. The trial is starting, and your friend will probably testify either today or tomorrow."

"He's not my friend! Don't say that."

He ignored me, taking his seat and looking toward the house. I moved around to the other side and huddled down between two large rocks. Bull went with me, and we spent the next several hours with him lying across my lap until we were interrupted by a summons from Luke.

"What is it?" I asked, when he came into view.

"Look," he pointed toward the house that we'd deserted.

I could see nothing, but expanding my view, saw a car parked several hundred yards from the house. I then saw four men spread out walking toward it.

"They still think we're there. Our pickup is parked in the back, and I doubt if they've even considered that we would be hiding out on the ranch."

We stayed sitting, which would make it impossible to see us. They surrounded the house and closed in, with two of them disappearing inside and staying at least fifteen minutes. After coming out, all four approached the hay barn. It didn't take long until they could see we weren't there. They moved together and were probably discussing what to do. The consensus must've been that we'd gone somewhere else, because they returned to their car and left.

I hadn't noticed Luke until now. His lips were blue and he was shaking. "Can we go back now?"

"No. It's not probable, but they might return. We can't take a chance." His teeth were chattering.

I had to do something. I moved over, turned my back to him and sat down between his legs, leaning against him, taking his hands and pulling them around me. Bull lay down across my lap and that's the way we spent the remainder of the day, not bothering to eat lunch.

# 26

# THANKSGIVING

 GRACE

I'd worried for Luke's safety for two years and thought when he returned home it would be over. Now, this Wednesday morning November twentieth, while getting ready for work, I was frightened for his safety more than ever.

I'd learned from Blaine on Monday what had happened at the ranch on Sunday. He left out the details, but it wasn't difficult to fill them in. An attempt had been made and thwarted to take Jimmie, but he assured me that Luke and his daughter were fine. I didn't ask, and he didn't volunteer that violence was involved, but it must've been present. Maybe I didn't want to know for sure. I wanted Luke back here as soon as possible.

I arrived at the office early and two men in suits were waiting to see Blaine, but he wasn't there. I went to my office and began work immediately, even before Madge arrived. When she did come in, I asked her about the two men.

"They've been here a couple of times. Something to do with the law. That's all I know," she said.

*It must have something to do with Luke and Jimmie,* I thought. I had trouble concentrating, anxious for Blaine to arrive. Finally, I heard him come in and invite the men into his office. Waiting to learn what was happening, I was a nervous wreck.

Madge realized something was bothering me. "You all right, Grace?"

"I'm sorry. Maybe I can tell you later. I need a cup of coffee. Would you like something?"

She declined, and I went to the front to get my coffee. On the way back, Blaine opened his door and asked me in. I was afraid of spilling my coffee as I entered. Blaine motioned to a vacant chair. He introduced the two men as Federal agents. "Grace, they have information about Drake. They received word last night that Drake testified and is going to be held in protection for several weeks just as a precautionary measure. I'll let Agent Fitzgerald explain what this means for Jimmie Lyn."

He turned to me. "For all practical purposes, the case against the law firm has been successful. Our lead witness has testified and should be safe now. It wasn't without cost. An attempt was made to get to Drake and two agents were killed. There were a dozen agents protecting him, and thank goodness they were successful. I have informed Mr. Waddell that his daughter should not be in any danger now. Do either of you have any questions?"

I shook my head when Blaine looked at me. He then focused his attention on the agents. "Will there be any attempt at Drake's life?"

"No, I think not. Drake Davis has done his job. The men he testified against are going to jail for a long time. I know it's been stressful on you, with your daughter in danger. You are fortunate that no attempt was made to take her as a hostage. Those Russians are vicious.

I stiffened, meeting Blaine's gaze, who quickly looked away. "Yes, we are. We appreciate your help and keeping us informed."

They left and Blaine explained. "I didn't tell them, Grace. Maybe I should've. I didn't see what good it would do. She and Luke were safe and that's what mattered.

"I can't express in words how much I appreciate Luke for what he's done. It was selfish of me to put him in danger. I was worried about Jimmie Lyn and took advantage of having Luke to protect her. I apologize for putting him in harm's way, especially after what he went through in

Vietnam. I might add—he's a remarkable young man, and my faith in him was proven to be justified."

"I just want him back with us. I worried for two years and this last month was as bad or worse." I wasn't ready to accept his apology. That might come later after talking with Luke.

"The first thing we need to do is go to the ranch and tell them the news, so they can return to civilization. I don't know how Jimmie Lyn will take it. She's angry with Drake and has been hurt greatly. I hope he stays in Europe." He rose from his chair. "Would you like to go with me?"

"Yes. I'd like that."

We took Blaine's and Bronc's pickups to the ranch. From the house we drove to the site where Luke and Jimmie had gone up the mountain to their hideout. Bronc gave three long blasts on the horn, and we got out and stood by the pickup. It was cold, but the sun was shining. I kept looking at my watch, and after twenty minutes I was getting anxious. I couldn't stand still—pacing up and down a twenty-yard path. Finally, I saw them coming with Bull in the lead. I was determined not to cry but wasn't successful.

Luke hadn't shaved in several days and looked different as he came and hugged me. If possible, he'd lost more weight.

"Mom, dry the tears. I'm fine. Nothing a bath, shave, and hot meal won't take care of."

Jimmie hugged me, also, saying, "Thank you for taking over my job."

Luke, with Bull in his lap, and I rode back with Bronc, and Jimmie rode with her dad. I'm sure he wanted to give her the news of Drake in private. I told Luke what we'd learned from the Federal agents.

"So, they think Drake is safe?" he asked.

"Yes. How will Jimmie take the news?"

"I'm not sure. She thinks she hates him, but who knows? She's a strong person. I respect her for how she's been able to handle this."

I told Luke about his sister and the problems she was having. I did tell him the positive news that he was going to be an uncle, and he seemed pleased. I noticed a change in Luke—for the better. He was not back to his old self, but he was definitely moving in the right direction. Maybe I shouldn't be too hard on Blaine; after all, he'd done so much for us.

※ ※ ※

A week after Luke was able to return home was Thanksgiving. I'd always heard how difficult holidays were after losing a loved one but was not prepared for the sadness. It started the day before, with memories flooding me. Henry loved dressing, and I always cooked two large pans. His favorite dessert was apple pie with ice cream. As these memories came back, I would just sit in silence trying to keep from breaking down.

Jimmie hadn't come back to work yet, and Madge seemed to understand, not questioning my moods. I'd told her about Luke and Jimmie staying at the ranch because of the threat against her.

Blaine came in my office the afternoon before Thanksgiving and invited us to have Thanksgiving dinner with him and Jimmie at a restaurant in town. I tried to think of a way to decline but couldn't come up with anything. It was nice of him to invite us and it would've been rude to decline.

When I informed Luke about the invitation, he was more positive than I'd been, knowing that preparing a Thanksgiving meal would've been difficult.

Thanksgiving morning was beautiful with sunshine and little wind, unusual for the Texas Panhandle. I noticed that Luke had bought new jeans, which actually fit him, and a red flannel shirt. He was a handsome man, and if Madge could've seen him this morning it would've sent her heart fluttering.

I'd decided to be who I was but up it a notch. As a cowgirl I chose to wear the soft suede camel western suit that Henry had given me several years ago for my birthday. It was paired with my brown turtle neck sweater and the brown dress boots that Henry had given me the first Christmas after we were married. The dark brown Stetson hat was left on the closet shelf . . . a little much.

My dad refused to go, saying he would work instead, allowing someone else the day off. "Someone has to drive the feed truck, and if it isn't me, he will miss spending Thanksgiving with his family."

We met Blaine and Jimmie at eleven-thirty to beat the crowd. Jimmie looked nice, and it struck me that she was a very attractive young lady. We selected a table at the far end of the restaurant, allowing us some privacy. We ordered the Thanksgiving special and had time to visit before it arrived.

"Luke, are your ready to take Lady back to the A&M clinic for an evaluation?" Blaine asked.

"Anytime. She's doing so well I expect a good report. I'm wondering if I could make it a three-day trip. They'd need one day to complete the evaluation. I'd stop several times going and coming and unload her to rest. What do you think?"

"I think that would work. You might ask the vet," Blaine said. "What would you think about a passenger?"

Luke looked confused. "A passenger?"

Blaine chuckled and nodded at Jimmie. "She'd like to go."

"I've always wanted to see the campus at Texas A&M. I've heard so much about it. Of course, if Luke doesn't want me to go . . ."

"I don't mind. It'd be good to have company on a long trip. In fact, we can trade out driving. I'd planned on taking Bull. That might change your mind."

She laughed. "No, not at all. I'll bring some spray deodorant. I've grown attached to him. Nobody's perfect—and it's our fault, anyway, for giving him table food."

Watching the back and forth between them, it struck me. *She's not just grown attached to Bull.* I smiled. *And Luke doesn't have a clue.*

### ✳ ✳ ✳

I made it through Thanksgiving and went back to work Friday, even though Blaine had told me to take a long weekend. The busier I stayed the better. Luke had decided to wait until Monday to make the trip to College Station.

Saturday was a bad day for me with nothing to do but reminisce. I'd kept a scrapbook since Henry and I'd married in 1943. It included some of our first win pictures at the New Mexico tracks, and I was inundated with memories of the joys we'd experienced in our early years. I stopped and cried awhile until I'd leafed through the entire book.

I finished and returned the story of our marriage to its resting place in one of the dresser drawers. I forced myself back to happier thoughts. I was going to be a grandmother. I had to pick out a name that she/he would call me. I found a piece of paper and began writing down possible selections. Grandma—no, that made me sound ancient. Ma Ma—no. Mia—that was better. Gracie—I like it!

# 27

# HIS PROTECTOR

 JIMMIE LYN

The first thing I did when we arrived in town from the ranch Wednesday was to pay my mother a visit. She was glad to see me—at first. When she began questioning me as to where I'd been, it went from bad to worse. The longer I tried to explain, the angrier she became until I threatened to leave if she didn't settle down. What upset her the most was not being informed about what was going on. I didn't dare tell her she wasn't told because we couldn't trust her. I imagined that she'd already guessed that. After an hour of trying to reason with her, I left. By that time, I was an emotional wreck. Her parting reply was, "Just wait until I get hold of your dad."

I didn't know how to take the news about Drake. I hated him but was glad he survived the trial. I tried to put him out of my mind completely, but it was impossible. I wasn't working and the days were long. I'd continued to stay with my dad after coming home. I wasn't ready to be alone at night after the experience of the last month. I still had thoughts occasionally that would frighten me about what could've happened.

The Friday morning after Thanksgiving, I went to the office just to have something to do. As I entered, the women were gathered in a corner taking their break. Madge, who had her back to me, commented to the others quietly, "He's got the cutest little butt I ever saw," and giggled.

I smiled, wondering who she was talking about. I continued on to my office where Grace was working. "Aren't you taking a break?"

She looked up from her work. "I usually stay in my office. The others are a little young for me to fit in. I bring my coffee back here and let them visit."

"I understand. When I came by Madge was describing someone who had the cutest little rear. I didn't stop to inquire who she was talking about."

Grace burst out laughing. "I agree with her. Ever since I started changing his diapers, I thought the same thing."

I must've turned red from my toes up. Madge was talking about Luke. "I'm sorry. I had no idea who she meant."

She continued to smile. "No problem. She's had a crush on Luke from the time he came to work, and he has no idea. She's been trying to get him to notice her. Luke can be a little dense about these things."

She continued to talk about the job, but my mind was going in another direction. Madge shouldn't be speaking about Luke that way. It just wasn't respectful. He wouldn't approve of it. Besides, Luke was my protector, and he wouldn't be interested in Madge. Suddenly, it was like someone threw a bucket of ice water on me, and I came to my senses. How would I know what Luke liked or disliked? What right did I have to even think he wouldn't be interested in Madge. The truth was, he wasn't my personal protector any longer.

There was a pause in Grace's talking, and I told her to have a good day and left. I met Madge coming down the hall. I greeted her but didn't stop to visit. She needed to get back to work.

Since it was a beautiful late fall day, I walked out to the loading dock. Bronc and Luke were pushing a pen of heifers onto a truck. They were not aware of me as they struggled to load the last bunch, which kept trying to turn back. Both were dust covered, and Luke's hat was about ready for the garbage. I'd noticed he had on a new pair of jeans yesterday at the restaurant that actually fit. He was wearing the jeans again today, and I realized where Madge's observation came from.

They walked over to where I was when the last heifer went up the ramp into the truck. "You ready to go to work?" asked Bronc. "We can always use another hand."

"You know, I've done plenty of that. I've kinda outgrown it, you might say."

"You ready for a long trip on Monday?" Luke asked.

"Sure. What time do we need to leave?"

"Early. It's about 600 miles. Leaving at five, we should make it easily by dark if we don't have any trouble."

"It'll be cold that early," I said.

"We're taking the stock trailer to give her more room. Bronc and I are going to enclose the trailer with some panels to make it a more comfortable ride. I checked the weather, and it looks good for Monday and Tuesday."

"I'll see you Monday morning, early. I'll let y'all get back to work." Walking off, I wondered, *would he rather Madge be going with him?*

I decided to go by Piper's house on the way into town. She didn't work after marrying the doctor and was involved in all kinds of civic activities. She told me recently that in a few years she was going to run for mayor. If I looked like her, Drake would never have left and gone to England. Here I go again, I thought, *wallowing in self- pity.*

What was the deal with Madge, anyway? What did she see in Luke? What would she think if she'd seen him kill those two men and act like it was nothing? He was a different person when he had the gun on the back of the guy's neck. His words were chilling and seemed to come from another person. If the man had shaken his head rather than nodded would he have killed him right there in front of me and Bronc? I answered my own question. "Without a doubt."

Why was I going with him to College Station? That was easy—I felt safe with him. Also, I was bored sitting at home. The main reason for not returning to work was Grace would be out of a job. I would talk to my dad about finding another place in the office for her when I returned.

✳ ✳ ✳

I didn't sleep well Sunday night, and didn't hear my alarm go off at four. I woke up at five in a panic, realizing that I should be at the Auction. I dressed quickly and was out of the house with a small suitcase fifteen minutes later. When I arrived Luke was sitting in my dad's pickup with the horse loaded in the trailer. I looked at my watch, and it was 5:25.

"You're late. If you were in the service, you'd be on latrine duty for a week."

"Well, I'm not in the service, and I'm just twenty-five minutes late," I said. It was not a good start to a long day. We left in silence with Bull laying down with his head in my lap.

We drove to Amarillo before I broke the silence. "I'd like a cup of coffee."

He pulled into a convenience store and gave me a dollar. "Just black for me. We're not stopping again for 200 miles."

We only stopped two times on the 600-mile trip and arrived at Texas A&M in College Station at five in the afternoon. Arrangements had been made for a vet to meet us. After we had Lady unloaded, in a stall and fed, we unhooked the trailer and went to find a place to eat. It hadn't been a bad trip. Luke got over his anger at me being late and was actually civil.

As we drove through town, we approached a crowd gathered with signs denouncing the war. Suddenly, a number of them blocked the road. One held a sign which said, "Child Killers."

Luke bailed out and attacked the man. I was stunned momentarily, but when several others jumped on Luke, I was out and rushed to his aid. I saw someone hit him over the head with something and he went down. I pushed one of them aside and grabbed another one's hair. I heard one of the men scream, "Get him off me. Help me!" I glanced to where the sound came from and saw that Bull had one by the leg. The man continued to scream and beg. The others stopped and tried to pry Bull loose. He finally released the man and the crowd backed off leaving us. Luke was lying face down, and it was obvious he was hurt. Bull had his front feet on Luke's back as if inviting someone else to touch him.

When I approached him, Bull growled. "It's me, Bull." He whined, lowering his head, as if apologizing. I noticed that Luke had blood coming from a cut on the back of his head. I turned him over and he wasn't conscious. What should I do? I was afraid to move him. I heard a siren and within seconds an ambulance drove up with a man and woman approaching. I grabbed Bull whose hair was already standing up on the back of his neck and he was growling so low it was barely audible. I pulled him back toward the pickup. "Load, Bull." I opened the door and he jumped in.

They bent down, examined the cut and checked Luke's blood pressure and pulse. "What happened?"

I explained in a few words Luke's response to the sign and the fight which occurred, saying that someone hit him over the head. I left out Bull's part.

Luke opened his eyes and mumbled, "My head."

"You took a blow to your head. We're going to take you to the hospital for an evaluation. Just lay quietly, and we'll get a stretcher," the girl said.

I knelt down while they went for the stretcher and took his hand. "You're going to be okay."

He didn't speak, only looking confused, as they returned. They loaded him and drove off toward the hospital, sirens blaring. The crowd of protesters were nowhere in sight. I managed to follow the ambulance to the hospital, which was only a few blocks. They entered under a sign which read Emergency. Inside, I followed them to a room which was enclosed with curtains. By this time, Luke was able to get off the gurney onto a bed without assistance.

A doctor came in a few minutes later. He introduced himself and began his examination. "How do you feel?" He shined a light into each of Luke's eyes.

"Dizzy—head throbs."

"What happened?" The doctor continued with his attention focused on Luke from the neck up.

"Can't remember exactly. Everything's kind of hazy."

I spoke for Luke. "We were detained on our way to dinner by a protest group. One had a sign which said, 'Child Killers,' and Luke jumped him. He's a veteran and has only been home a few months from Vietnam. Somebody hit him over the head with something."

He turned to me. "Did he hurt any of them?"

"His dog bit one. He may need stitches."

The doctor smiled. "Good. I hope he comes to the emergency, so I can tell him my opinion of his demonstrations."

He turned back to Luke. "You have a concussion. I don't believe it's severe, but we need to keep you overnight. If everything checks out in the morning you should be good to go—if you take it easy and don't get into any more fights." He put his hand on Luke's shoulder. "And thank you for your service."

I stayed with Luke until they came to take him to a regular room and then went looking for a motel. I tried two but neither allowed pets, so I secured a room in a third one, without asking about pets, and sneaked Bull in. I sat down on the edge of the bed and he put his head between my legs and whined.

# 28

# TRAVESTY AND TRIBUTE

 LUKE

*"Please, Sergeant Ranker, let me take the point today. I'm not pulling my load, and the rest of the guys know it. I don't want any special privileges. I promise you I can handle it. It's not right for me to sit back and watch others take my duty. You know that."*

*"I've told you, Louis, your time will come. Right now, you don't have the experience. You could put the entire platoon in danger. Just be patient, it'll happen soon enough."*

*"Sarge, I've been patient. I tell you, I'm ready. Just let me take the point one time, and I'll leave you alone. At least the men will know I'm doing my part. Please, I'm begging you."*

*"One hour—that's all. If you promise, you'll be patient after that and let me decide when you're ready."*

*A boyish grin appeared. "Thanks. You'll be proud of me. I guarantee you."*

The deafening blast shook the room. I bolted upright in bed. Seconds later, I realized where I was. The hospital room was dark except for a small light over my bed. The dream seemed so real. The conversation was accurate—word for word. The image of Louis flying through the air was as clear as if it was happening now. I lay there until morning regretting my decision to give in, knowing it cost the boy his life.

My memory was gradually returning. I recalled the anger upon seeing the sign. These people had no idea. My platoon did everything possible to protect civilians and especially children. It was difficult to tell the ages of the Vietnamese. Most were small, and what appeared to be a twelve-year-old boy might be a thirty-year old man aiming to kill you. The "Child Killer" sign was referring to an incident several months earlier that made the national news.

Jimmie entered the foray to help me. That was a change since I was supposed to be the one protecting her. Bull turned out to be the decisive factor in stopping the fight. She told me about the guy screaming, "Git him off me." I smiled, surprised that he would bite someone, as kind and sweet as he was.

A nurse came in to check my vitals around six o'clock. "How're you feeling, soldier?"

"Head still hurts a little?" How'd you know I was in the service?"

"Everybody around here knows it. The guy your dog bit came in last night to get his leg sewed up. Let me tell you—the doctor gave him a tongue-lashing like you've never heard. I imagine he was glad to get out of here. The doctor has a nephew in Vietnam."

"What time does the doctor make his rounds?" I was ready to start the trip back to Dalhart.

"Oh, the doctor is consistent in making his rounds. It varies from seven in the morning to nine in the evening.

"Who was that pretty lady that came in with you?"

"Just a friend. We brought a horse to the vet clinic at the university."

"You sure she's only a friend? She seemed awfully concerned about you."

"You ask a lot of questions."

She smiled and patted my arm. "That's how I know so much, sweetie. Now, your breakfast will be here shortly. Would you like me to get you some coffee?"

"I would appreciate that."

The doctor came in at midmorning. I told him I felt fine and was ready to leave. He seemed to have a fixation on my eyes, spending time shining his little flashlight in each. He asked me three times if my head still hurt. I finally admitted it did a little but not much.

"I want you to stay one more day. Concussions are strange creatures, and you can never be too careful. I know you're anxious to be on your way, but bear with me." He left quickly, probably knowing I was going to object.

Jimmie had been in the room and heard what the doctor said. "I'd better go out to the clinic and tell them we won't be picking up Lady today. I called my dad early this morning and told him what happened.

"Tell the vet we'll be there tomorrow to get her. I'm not staying any longer than that. I should be leaving today."

"Have you looked at yourself in the mirror? You look like warmed-over death. The doctor's right."

"Thanks. That makes me feel better. Why'd you help me yesterday when those guys were flogging me? You could've been hurt, then what would I have told your dad?"

"You were outnumbered. I was afraid for you. Besides, my dad would've approved of what I did. I'm leaving now. Try to be in a better mood when I get back."

She hadn't been gone more than five minutes when a knock announced the arrival of another guest. He was wearing a suit and tie. I immediately identified him as one of those hospital preachers that make the rounds praying for everyone.

"Luke Ranker?"

"Yeah, that's me." I hoped he didn't stay long.

"James Rudder. How're you doing?"

"I've been better. I was hoping to get out of here today." Come on get the praying over with and leave.

"Is there anything I can do for you?" he asked.

"No. I just want to get as far away from this place as possible." What's the deal anyway?

"I want you to know, Sergeant Ranker, that we appreciate your service to our country, and we are sorry for this unfortunate incident."

"Thanks. I kind of lost it yesterday."

"I understand." He put his hand on my arm and squeezed it. "I'll be going now. If you need anything just let us know."

That was strange. He didn't even pray over me. I closed my eyes and thought of the long trip back to Dalhart. We wouldn't get off early, and it'd probably be after dark when we arrived. That was my last thought before sleep blanked out everything.

Still half asleep, I felt something close to my face. Opening my eyes all I saw was, what looked like, an ear within an inch of me. "What're you doing?" I blurted out.

"Oh, I'm sorry. I was checking to see if you were breathing. You were so still." She quickly stood up and backed away.

"I was sleeping. How long have you been gone?"

"Two hours. I stopped and got us some burgers for lunch. Are you hungry?"

"Yeah. Thanks. It'll beat whatever they bring me," I said. "Are they okay with us picking up Lady tomorrow?"

"They were unbelievably nice. It was like I was special or something. I told them it'd probably be midmorning before we got out there." She unwrapped a burger and gave it to me.

She had her hair up in a bun and was wearing jeans and a blue long-sleeved shirt. She looked good, or maybe it was the effect of the hamburger, which was delicious.

The pills they'd given me for pain had a familiar effect on me—relaxed and drowsy. I tried to concentrate after finishing the meal, but went to sleep while Jimmie was talking.

The nurse woke me up putting a cuff on my arm to take my blood pressure. "Do you work all the time?" I asked. "You were here last night, this morning, and now this afternoon."

She laughed. "It seems like it. How do you feel?"

"Better. I've been asleep for awhile."

"Awhile. I'd say about four hours. I checked on you several times, not wanting to wake you but gave up," she said. "Where'd the pretty girl go?"

"Don't know. I guess she left when I went to sleep."

She finished taking my blood pressure and wrapped up the cuff. "I noticed you had a visitor this morning."

"Yeah. The preacher came, but it was strange. He didn't even pray over me."

"Man, you must've been out of it. That was General Rudder the president of the university. I hope you were nice to him."

How totally embarrassing I thought. Was I rude to him? My mind went back to our conversation, which I vaguely remembered. How was I to know who he was? Why would he come to see me? My head began hurting again.

"I have a headache. Could you give me something for it?" I asked.

"Sure. I'll be back in a few minutes."

She left, and I settled back down in the bed. I'd actually slept without dreaming or waking up. Another couple of those pills, and I could stay relaxed.

✳✳✳

The doctor came by earlier the next morning. I lied to him, telling him that my head felt normal. Actually, the slight ache was still there and, when I stood up, the dizziness returned for a short time. Being truthful would've been rewarded with another day in the hospital. The result was that he released me, and I was out of the hospital by nine o'clock with Jimmie driving us to the university. We arrived and found a line of cars being turned away. The gate was blocked by members of the Corps in full uniform. "Now what?"

"Who knows, probably some kind of emergency. We'll stay in line and find out. We may not be going home today. And I thought we were going to get an early start. Are you feeling any better? I know you lied to the doctor."

"I'm good. Just a little dizzy when I first stand. My headache comes and goes. I should be able to drive later in the day," I said, hoping that would end her questions.

We were next in line, but the car ahead of us was taking a long time. Evidently, he was arguing with them. He finally turned around, and we were motioned forward.

A Corps member looked in the window, came to full attention, saluted and said, "Good morning, Sergeant Ranker! Welcome to Texas A&M University." He then stepped back and motioned us forward, with the Corps members blocking the gate, stepping aside.

Jimmie drove slowly through the gate but stopped once inside. The scene before us was beyond description. Corps members about ten yards apart lined both sides of the road for the entire distance to the vet clinic. There must've been three hundred at least.

"What in the world is going on, Luke?" she mumbled.

I didn't answer—struck silent by the scene before me.

She drove slowly and each of the Corps came to attention and saluted as we passed. I noticed that Jimmie had tears streaming down her cheeks. When we reached the clinic four men in uniform were waiting. One came to my window, which I had kept down, stood at full attention and saluted. "Sergeant Ranker, sir. If the young lady will back up to the trailer, we'll get you connected. There is no need for you to exit. Your horse will be brought out and loaded." He saluted again and returned to the others.

Within minutes we were hooked on to the trailer and Lady was loaded. A vet appeared at my window. "Sergeant Ranker, your mare has had a thorough examination. She is about as I expected, doing well but needing more time. I'd recommend giving her two more months of rest. After that, go with light exercise, even riding her. If she shows any sign of soreness, take off her for another month. If she does well after riding her, use your judgment. I believe, with patience, she could be fully recovered by midsummer. Do you have any questions?"

I still hadn't recovered from the reception but was able to get out a few words. "I need to pay the bill. How much is it?"

He gestured with his hand. "No charge, this one's on us."

"I don't understand. This reception and then no charge. I'm sorry, it's confusing."

"General Rudder, our president, maintains close ties with the military. He developed an interest in you when hearing what happened with the demonstrators. He contacted some friends in Vietnam, and it seems he learned quite a lot about you. You may not be respected in town; however, you are a hero to this university. Have a safe trip home, Sergeant Ranker." He stepped away from the pickup and saluted.

I glanced toward Jimmie and she was still wiping at her eyes. "Can you drive?"

She nodded and drove slowly back through the two lines of uniformed men who stood at attention and saluted as we passed. By the time we reached the gate my eyes were blurred.

# 29

# HEALING

When Blaine told me about Luke being in the hospital, I panicked. He assured me Luke was fine and would soon be released. I kept praying that Luke would return to normal, or the boy he'd been before he was drafted into the Marines. I realized that might never happen.

I tried to concentrate on the positive. My dad was doing great and was better than he'd been since my mother passed. The news that Blaine gave me about Lady was encouraging. I enjoyed my job and, financially, we were better off than we'd been in years. However, it was obvious to me that I was not going to recover from losing Henry. I was kidding myself to think otherwise. I needed him and kept thinking—why? I was hoping that going to church might provide some answers but, even though I looked forward to Sundays, it hadn't happened.

I wanted to go home, at least for a few days. I would stay in the house we'd shared for twenty-five years and visit Henry's grave. Maybe that would help the healing. I needed to do something that might allow me to move forward with my life.

After the information from Blaine, I talked with my dad about Luke and my concern about him. He was calm and deliberate with his response. "Grace, Luke will be okay. It might take several years, but he will return to his self. The way he was raised will make the difference. Just be patient and give him time. I believe that God will look after Luke and help him with what he's been through. I have faith in that."

"Dad, Luke's been drinking. He tries to hide it, but I found the bottle in his bedroom. I'm worried that he's dealing with his past by using this crutch."

He took out a cigarette, lighting it before he responded. "I know, Grace. I was hoping you wouldn't find out. Luke has been through something that we can't comprehend. This is his way of dealing with it—temporarily. It won't last. Let's just love him and give him support."

"I wish my faith was as strong as yours, Dad. Regretfully, it's not."

He lay his Camel in an ash tray. "Healing takes time, Grace. I'm still not over your mother. But life moves on. I'm doing better than this time last year. Be patient, Luke will get better. The same goes for you. I know you continue to suffer the loss of Henry. You need to pray every day for strength, and I will pray for all of us. God hears our prayers. I believe that. He often takes his time in answering them, but that's why we must have faith. I need to get to work. That's enough preaching for today."

I was already dressed for work but had some time before leaving. I went into my bedroom and took my Bible off the table by my bed.

✳✳✳

Luke and Jimmie didn't get home until late Tuesday. It was already dark, and I went with them to put Lady in her stall. She was driving and neither one had much to say. I asked several questions and received one or two word answers, so I gave up.

After unhooking the trailer, I told Luke that I wanted to visit with Jimmie. He didn't argue as he left. I wasted no time. "What's bothering Luke?"

"I think he's still hurting. He tried driving but couldn't handle it, running off the road several times. I had to insist that he let me behind the wheel. His head still hurts. He lied to the doctor in order to be released, which was a mistake. He should still be in the hospital. You can't tell him anything, though."

She told me what happened when they went to pick up Lady. Reliving the drive through the Corps, her voice broke as she described it. "It was the most awesome thing I've ever experienced. To have that happen after seeing the horrible signs and the confrontation with the demonstrators restored my belief in America and what we stand for."

"How did his dog handle all this?" I asked.

She laughed. "We were fortunate he was along." She then told me about his role in the ruckus.

"You should've seen him when we drove through the line at the university. He sat up straight between us like he was at attention and hardly moved. He knew something special was happening."

I knew she was anxious to get home, so I thanked her for looking after Luke and got out.

"I'd like to be able to do more to help him. I don't know how," she said.

*That is my sentiment, exactly*, I thought, as I walked away.

❊❊❊

Wednesday morning, Luke wasn't up at his usual time. When I checked on him, he was still asleep. I noticed a bottle of pills on his night table labeled Hydrocodone. I left without waking him, thinking he needed rest.

At work I stopped by Blaine's office. He stood. "Grace, thank goodness the kids got home safe." He sat down and motioned for me to do the same. "Jimmie Lyn is worried about Luke. She thinks he needs additional medical care."

"He's still in bed this morning. Maybe the rest will do him good. I'll try to get him to the doctor if he's not better this afternoon.

"Have you seen Lady this morning?" I asked.

He smiled. "First thing I did when I got here. I'm excited, Grace. Do you think we might have her ready by late summer for the big race?"

I was hoping he wouldn't be this excited and disappointed if she didn't come back full strength. "Maybe. It's a long shot after going through surgery. But we can hope."

He then gave me the news I'd been dreading. Jimmie was coming back to work, but he said I could work in the front, since one of the ladies had given notice she was leaving. I'd enjoyed working with Madge and the seclusion of our own office. However, I accepted the offer, glad to keep earning a salary.

I asked him about the possibility of me and my dad taking off for several days to go home. I didn't dwell on the reason. He said it would be no problem and to take as long as we liked.

We visited a few more minutes about my new position, and I went to the temporary office where Madge greeted me. "Morning, Grace. I guess you've heard you're being transferred to the front."

"Yes. We'll still be working together—just not as close. I've enjoyed the last several weeks back here in our own office."

She perked up. "Guess what?"

"From your expression it must be good. Let's hear it."

"Bronc stopped me on the way to my car yesterday and didn't greet me, inquire about my day, or anything. He just asked, 'Would you like to go with me to Guymon Saturday?'"

"Rodeo? I imagine you told him that it would be necessary to check your calendar and you'd get back to him. Right?" I knew the answer but wanted to hear what she said.

"Are you kidding? Of course, I said yes. I'd ride in the back of his pickup to attend a rodeo with him. I love cowboys. He's been my second choice behind you-know-who."

"That's wonderful, Madge. He's a nice young man, and you'll have a great time. He and Luke have become really good friends."

✱✱✱

Luke assured me he was better the next morning, and promised he'd tell me if his head started hurting again. We actually had a nice visit after Dad left to feed the horses. I told him we planned on heading home on Saturday to spend a few days. I asked him if he'd like to go, but he declined.

He contributed more details about his trip to College Station. When he left the house for work, I felt more at ease.

I was surprised to find Jimmie already at work. One of the ladies tutored me on my new responsibilities, which consisted mostly of paperwork on cattle being brought in and those being shipped out.

The next two days I managed to stay busy, but the work was not nearly as demanding as Jimmie's job. The other women in the office were nice and made me feel welcome. Madge did her part, coming over and visiting at every opportunity.

After feeding the horses Saturday morning, we left for home, which was located between Childress and Wellington. We took Luke's car and four hours later were in Childress where we turned left onto Highway 83. We crossed the Red River and ten miles later turned right onto a dirt road. Another half mile and I stopped at Dad's house. I went in with him to check if everything was in tact.

I drove another quarter of a mile to our house. Sitting in the car I kept repeating to myself, "I can do this." My plan was to go through Henry's clothes and personal items, selecting some of them for Luke and Angie. If I could get through it, I was hoping this would be a movement toward closure.

I opened the door and encountered darkness and a musty odor. I flipped on a light switch, thankful I'd decided not to have the electricity turned off. I spent a few minutes going through the house. The most difficult part was looking at the pictures on the wall. Several were of the kids when they were in school, ranging from elementary to high school. The ones lining the hallway racked my emotions and froze me in time. They were win pictures at racetracks in Texas and New Mexico beginning at one end when Henry and I were in our mid-twenties and concluding at the entrance to our bedroom with ones taken the last few years. All smiles—happy times when the future was bright, if only for a short while. I finally moved into the bedroom.

*Now begins the tough part,* I thought. I opened the closet and there were his clothes. Henry and Luke were about the same size. I started going through shirts, mostly long-sleeved, because that's about all he'd wear. I sorted out the better ones from the older, more worn. Occasionally, I'd have to stop as an image of him wearing the shirt flashed across my mind. I finished the shirts and congratulated myself for not breaking down. The jeans were worn out, for the most part. He'd used them for work during the times we were home. I put them in the throw-away pile.

Maybe I deserved a break—a walk outside to the barn. Then I saw them toward the back of the closet. I'd been too quick with the congratulations. I lay down on the floor and sobbed, thinking of the old boots that I tried to throw away so many times, only to have him talk me into letting him keep them. I refused to let him take them to the track, and many times I'd insisted he change them before we went to town. He loved those old boots. He should've been buried in them.

✳✳✳

We stayed three days and each one became a little easier. I divided Henry's personal items between the two kids. A railroad watch he'd inherited from his granddad, a buckle he'd been awarded as part of a prize for the feature race, and various other keepsakes were to be Luke's. Angie's were, for the most part, old pictures that I'd put in an album for her. I'd also included his senior ring from Childress High School, class of 1935.

As we drove away Tuesday morning, I knew it'd been a beneficial trip for me. I couldn't speak for my dad. I felt a sense of calmness and tranquility that had not been present. Visiting the cemetery each day and facing reality was good for me. I felt Henry's presence and knew that his message for me would be to move on with my life and welcome happiness when it came my way. I wasn't there yet, but my journey to healing had begun.

# 30

# CHRISTMAS IN RED RIVER

One thing you could say. There was never a dull moment around Luke Ranker. I was delighted to get back to work and a normal life. I was pleased that Grace was still working, and the thought crossed my mind again—my dad's interest in her exceeded that of his other employees.

A week after returning to work, I moved back into my apartment. I wasn't comfortable living with Dad, and he probably felt the same way. I fell back into a routine similar to what was present before Drake came into my life. My sister had just announced that she was pregnant and was due the first of July; of course, my dad could hardly contain himself with the news, but my mother expressed shock at becoming a grandmother.

I'd be twenty-four my next birthday which wasn't that far away. I'd probably be prematurely gray and look much older within a few years. That's what happened to old maids. I'd shrivel up and walk bent over and people would say, "She was never the same after being left at the altar."

\*\*\*

Two weeks before Christmas Dad came into my office and sat down, something he seldom did. I could tell by the look on his face he had something on his mind.

"How're you doing, Daughter?"

"Good, I guess. What's going on?"

"I have an idea. It may be crazy." He took a deep breath. "Christmas is coming up, and it would be nice to do something special. It's been a tough couple of months." He hesitated. "I've been thinking about it for some time." Silence.

"Well, Dad, let's hear it. It can't be that hard to get out." I'd never seen him so unsure of himself.

"A trip. I'd like to go somewhere Christmas." He finally got it out.

I wanted to hear more about this trip. "Where do you want to go?"

"Maybe, Red River . . . skiing." He sighed, slumping down, as if relieved.

"It's been years since we've been skiing, Dad. Just you and me?"

He looked more uncertain. "I thought we might invite some guests. It was just a thought, maybe I should forget it?"

"No. I want to hear this idea of yours." Now, it was all coming together.

"Well, you know." He looked at the floor. "I thought, with all that's gone on, it might be good to invite Grace and Luke to go with us as our guests. Luke saved your life. This would be our way of showing appreciation. I should probably forget it."

"Dad! That's a wonderful idea. I haven't been skiing since my first year in college. We'd have a white Christmas! Do you think they might accept the invitation?"

"I think so. Would you issue the invitation? It would be more appropriate for you to do so."

I tried not to smile. "Yes. I'll be glad to do that. When are we leaving? More important—how do you think Mom will take this?"

"I thought we could leave on the twenty-second and return the day after Christmas on the twenty-sixth. I have a friend who has a cabin which I've already spoken for. I need to accept the fact that this Auction can run itself without me."

"You didn't answer my other question about Mom."

"I'm tired of this game, Jimmie Lyn. We didn't get along. I'm sorry. It was as much my fault as hers. She may think it might work again. I don't. She has a good husband who cares for her. Let's just leave it at that."

I rose and hugged him. "I love you, Daddy."

He left, looking relieved. My dad was something else. If there was a better man, I would challenge anyone to find him. He was smitten with Grace but was embarrassed because it was so soon after losing her husband. I smiled, wondering what I'd do with Luke for four days.

I didn't waste any time, talking with Grace the day she returned from visiting her home. She was confused at first, but when I explained this was my dad's way of thanking Luke for saving my life, she understood. I went on to explain that my dad felt badly for putting her through the stress of worrying about Luke and that was the reason he wanted her to be included. She seemed to buy my explanation and accepted the invitation but didn't know about Luke.

I had Luke paged over the outside speaker, and he was in my office a short time later. His hair was below his shoulders now, and I wondered if he was ever going to get a haircut. I'd thought about my presentation before he arrived.

"What is it?" he asked.

"Is there some way I could get you to smile?"

"You called me in here to ask me that?"

"No, I have something else to ask you. My dad wants to invite you and your mom to spend Christmas in Red River with us. He has a cabin on loan from a friend for a few days. We could go skiing. What do you think?" He was stone-faced as usual and showed no reaction.

"I haven't been skiing since junior high school. We couldn't leave Granddad by himself over Christmas. Holidays are hard enough for him anyway."

"We could invite him, also. I'm sure Dad would be agreeable to that."

"He wouldn't accept the offer." He had that look I'd seen so often.

"So, that means you won't go?" I wasn't surprised at his refusal.

"I didn't say that. Have you talked with my mother?"

"Yes. She accepted the invitation when I told her it was our way of showing appreciation for what you did for me."

He looked confused. He just stared at me with those dark eyes like I'd done something wrong.

"Would you like some time to talk with your mother? You don't have to give me an answer today. We wouldn't be leaving until the twenty-second. It could be a fun trip. Who knows, you might even enjoy it."

"Okay. I'll get back with you after talking with Mom and Granddad." He rose and started to leave.

"Would you wait a minute, please?" He stopped but remained standing.

"This trip is important to my dad. He's never left the Auction for this length of time. He wants to do something special for you and your mom. Think about someone other than yourself."

I received the look. "I told you, I'll let you know." And he was gone.

Luke Ranker was a challenge. He was probably going to refuse, which meant his mom wouldn't go, and my dad would be disappointed. I tried.

The next morning Luke came into my office and said he and his mom would go with us. His granddad would stay here and look after the horses. He wanted to take Bull, also. I told him that would be fine. It didn't surprise me that he wouldn't leave his dog for that long.

✳✳✳

The morning of December twenty-second we picked them up in my dad's 1968 Jeep Cherokee, which he seldom drove. It was a four-wheel drive which we would need in the mountains. There was ample room for the four of us and the dog. I'd already thought about the seating arrangements. My dad and I would ride in the front and our guests, along with Bull, would be in the back seat. I was hoping that Bull's digestive system would behave on the four-hour drive. An awkward silence existed for the first hour until Grace brought up the subject of Lady. From then on, the conversation was lively with talk of her potential future.

We stopped one time for a restroom break and were in Red River by noon, then parked in front of an A-frame cabin within walking distance of the ski area. The weather was beautiful and our housing was the perfect set-up. Dad and I took the upstairs and our guests the downstairs. There were plenty of beds, a connected kitchen and den together, with a large fireplace.

I knew that my job would be to provide social activities to supplement the skiing. After we unpacked, I suggested we get our ski equipment and be ready to hit the slopes the next morning. We drove to a rental place in town.

An hour later, we were fitted out, and my dad and Grace were signed up for lessons. The next thing on my list was shopping for me and Grace. Luke and Dad's job was to go grocery shopping and then build a fire. That should keep us busy for several hours.

The weather had turned colder and a few snowflakes floated down as Grace and I walked to the downtown area.

"It's beautiful, Jimmie," Grace said. "It was a great idea to go shopping. I haven't had an opportunity to buy any gifts. You can help me select something for Luke."

"He loosened up some while we were together at the ranch. After the trip to College Station, he's regressed into silent mode. I keep thinking I must've done something wrong."

"No. He's been the same way with us most of the time. He did talk to me one morning after the trip, but besides that he's had very little to say. My dad insists he'll be fine, just to be patient. I hope he's right. I think he's still in pain. He continues to take the pills and had them refilled when he ran out."

We arrived at the row of shops lining Main Street, and for the next three hours we looked for Christmas gifts. By the time we finished, both of us had all we could carry. The more I was around Grace the more beautiful she became. I could see now why my dad was enamored with her. To my knowledge he hadn't been interested in a woman since he and my mom divorced.

"Do you think we can make it back with all this?" I asked as we came out of the last store at the end of Main Street. "We could ask to leave it here in this store and come back in the car."

Her face was flushed with excitement and the cold. "I'm feeling strong today. Let's go for it. We can stop and rest along the way."

We crossed the street to the side our cabin was on and started east. We hadn't gone but a short way when a pickup pulled over to the curb, and a woman lowered her window. "Looks like y'all could use a lift. Just lower the tailgate and put your stuff in the back. We're kind of crowded up here, so you can sit on the tailgate. It beats walking."

I breathed a sigh of relief. "Thank you. We appreciate it. We're staying next to the ski area."

They stopped within a hundred yards of our A-Frame. We thanked them profusely and struggled up the hill with our loot. We'd have never made it walking from town.

Dad and Luke had the fire going, and Bull was lying as close as he could get to it. "We made it," I said, dumping everything on the couch. "Is dinner ready?"

My dad and Luke were at the table having a drink. I don't remember ever seeing my dad so relaxed. "It's only five o'clock," Dad said.

"We're starved. It seems later. Shopping always makes me hungry. Are y'all solving the problems of the world?" I asked.

My dad lifted his glass in a toast. "We're trying."

I opened the fridge, and my dad had bought enough food for a month. I guess we could leave what we didn't eat for the next occupant. "What would y'all like?"

"I thought me and Luke would cook some steaks on the outside grill. It won't take long if y'all can wait," Dad said.

"Sure. Steaks sound great. I'm going to fix me one of those drinks your having. High altitude causes alcohol to have more effect on you, but I can hold my liquor." After all this time, the private joke did it. I looked at Luke, and he was smiling!

# 31

## CONFESSION

LUKE

I woke up slowly, unaware of where I was—disoriented. I'd been that way since I started taking the pain pills. The good thing was being able to relax and sleep throughout the night. The doctor in College Station gave me a prescription that allowed for several refills. The pills were just as effective or more so than the liquor and much cheaper. I'd lost more weight, not having much of an appetite.

It would've been easy for me to go back to sleep, but my mom was already in the kitchen. Jimmie and her dad would be down any minute, and I needed to get up and get dressed but kept telling myself—in a few minutes. I woke up again with mom gently shaking my arm. "Time to get up, sleepy head. Breakfast will be ready shortly. Everyone else is up."

I struggled to the downstairs bathroom, took a shower and dressed. I kept wondering if I could handle the skis. It'd been seven or eight years since I'd gone skiing with a church group. This would only be the third time I'd been. To my knowledge Mom had only been skiing one time when she was a chaperone for a church trip.

So far this had not been as bad as I'd expected. I found myself even enjoying it. It was easier to talk with Blaine than anyone else, and I was even comfortable sharing my feelings about Vietnam.

When I went to the kitchen, they were already eating. The pancakes and sausage looked good. "Who did the cooking this morning?"

Mom motioned toward Jimmie. "She knew you liked pancakes."

"We didn't wait on you," she said. "It'll take us awhile to get ready. We don't have any of those fancy ski outfits, so we'll have to Scotch Guard our jeans. It's going to be really cold today. I checked the outside thermometer and it's right on zero. What about it, Luke? Think you're tough enough to handle it?"

I stopped with the fork halfway to my mouth. "Is it as cold as that day on the mountain at our lookout spot?"

Jimmie laughed. "No. I don't think so. Your teeth were chattering, and your lips turned blue."

✳✳✳

The first day wasn't bad. The clear sky and the sunshine made it bearable. We both fell several times but, as the day progressed, we improved to the point that by the afternoon we were even contemplating trying one of the intermediate or Blue slopes. However, we decided that could wait until tomorrow. We called it quits at three-thirty, found a bench to sit on, and waited for Mom and Blaine.

"Okay, Luke Ranker, tell me you didn't have fun today." She bumped up against me.

"I did enjoy it. I'm as tired as I've been in a long time."

She stretched out her long legs and leaned back against the wall. "We're going to be sore tomorrow. Did you bring your swim suit?"

"Of course not. What would I need a swim suit for?"

"Hot tub. Didn't you see it on the west side of the cabin? The hot water will help the soreness. It feels so good and relaxing after skiing all day."

"You mean go outside and get in a tub of hot water? That doesn't make sense."

"Don't knock it until you've tried it. How do you think your mom did today?"

"I imagine she did very well. Mom's athletic and fearless as well. She's an amazing rider." I saw them coming just as I finished the compliment. Mom looked like she was in better shape than Blaine.

"How'd it go?" asked Jimmie.

"I'm beat. I can't go another step." Blaine sat down on the bench. "I overdid it trying to keep up with Grace. Jimmie Lyn will y'all go bring the Jeep, and we'll wait right here?"

We had the Jeep back in a few minutes and were in the cabin shortly. Blaine collapsed onto the couch, saying he wasn't going to move until he had recovered.

"Who's ready for the hot tub?" Jimmie asked. "I reminded Grace to bring a swimsuit."

"I'll take your word that it helps with the soreness, which I'll have a lot of in the morning. What about you, Luke?" asked my mom.

"Nope. I'm going to work on getting the fire going. I'm not as tough as you and Jimmie."

"Don't even ask me. You already know the answer." Blaine had leaned back and had his feet propped up on a hassock. "Y'all can tell me how great it was."

I didn't notice when they left because I was gathering wood from a bin at the back of the cabin. By the time I had a fire going they came back in dripping and shivering. Jimmie dropped her towel and came over to the fire. I'd spent weeks with her, night and day, but had not seen so much of her. Never would I have thought she looked so stunning in a bathing suit. I caught myself staring and quickly looked away.

"Luke, you want to help me cook dinner tonight?" she asked.

"Sure. What're we going to have?"

She turned toward me. "I thought take-out pizza might be appropriate to end our day."

"Sounds good to me."

She changed, and half an hour later we were sitting in the Pizza Hut waiting on our take-out. Two men at a table next to ours were talking loudly, using profanity, and making conversation impossible. I avoided looking at them, hoping our pizza would arrive so we could leave. They rose, but instead of leaving came to our table accompanied by an overwhelming odor of liquor. One was tall and muscular, the other was overweight. They were probably in their mid-twenties.

The tall one spoke to Jimmie. "I see you're not wearing a ring." He shifted his gaze to me. "This hippie must be your little brother." He shifted his attention again to Jimmie. "This is a dull town, but we're on our way to a party. Why don't you go with us? Junior here can go home to y'all's parents."

"No thank you. I'm not interested." She looked at me. "Let's go, Luke."

The other one stepped forward. "What's your hurry. You don't have your order."

"We're leaving. Come on, Luke."

She tried to rise, but the taller one laid his hand on her shoulder pushing her back down. "We're not through talking with you."

I stood up. "Take your hands off her."

"Well, the hippie can talk." He came around the table within a few feet of me. "Just what're you going to do about it, junior?"

I looked past him toward the door. "That cop might have something to say."

He turned his head to look, and I kicked him between the legs. He bent over, letting out a groan. I picked up the sugar jar and hit him over the head, shattering the glass. He went down.

I turned to the other one. "What about it, fat boy? You want in on it?"

He stood, looking at his friend on the floor, as if he couldn't believe it.

At that moment, the waitress arrived with our pizza, staring at the guy on the floor. Another man followed her. He introduced himself as the manager. "I saw what happened, from the beginning. I'm sorry. These guys are nothing but trouble. I called the police, and they should be here anytime. There's no need for you to stay. I'll explain what happened. I'm going to file charges against these guys. This isn't the first time there's been an incident." He smiled. "They picked on the wrong man this time."

On the drive back I asked Jimmie not to say anything about the episode to her dad or my mom.

"You don't fight fair. That man didn't have a chance."

"Where I've been the last two years there was no such thing as fair. I did what I had to do."

"I'm not complaining. That's the second time you've rescued me. I'm beginning to believe you're a dangerous man."

"No. I just want to be left alone."

"I'm still amazed at how calm you are after violence. I know what you told me but it's hard to believe. The guy really thought there was a policeman when you pointed toward the door. You fooled him good."

The incident wasn't mentioned when we delivered the pizza. After eating, Jimmie had the night time activity planned—Blackjack. She had the chips and everything. After the table was cleaned off, she explained the rules. "I'll be the dealer. Y'all will get $500 worth of chips. Dealer has to stay on seventeen. You can double down with aces. We're going to play again the next two nights. You'll keep track of how much you have left after we finish tonight. At the end of three nights whoever has the most money gets a prize. Any questions?"

I'd played before, but mom needed help and Blaine volunteered. We played for three hours before Blaine said it was time for him to retire. It was a good time, and I enjoyed watching Mom's excitement when she won. And she won more than her share of the time. She had a pile of chips left while Blaine and I had considerably less than when we started.

Blaine went upstairs, and we stayed at the table and visited, nursing cups of hot chocolate that Mom had made.

"That was fun," Mom said. "I feel bad, though, that y'all didn't win as much as I did. I'll share my chips if you run low."

"You are so nice. How many people would share their winnings with the losers?" Jimmie shook her head. "Did you enjoy skiing today, Grace?"

"Yes, of course. I did better than I expected, it'd been so long since the last time I skied. I worried about your dad though. He was so exhausted."

"Dad's not in very good shape. He spends a lot of time behind his desk and doesn't eat right. I worry about him, too."

We talked for another hour, going over the day and the evening activity before Mom said it was time for her to go to bed. She left us at the table alone.

There was an awkward silence for several minutes. "It's weird, Luke, how we've been thrown together these past several months. I still don't understand why you're so sad. You're home safe from the war and should be thankful. It's like you won't allow yourself to be happy. Would you like to talk about your problem?"

"You wouldn't understand."

"Try me. At least help me understand why you refuse to allow yourself happiness."

I began by telling her how useless the war was. How territory taken from the enemy at the cost of lives would be right back in the hands of the Viet Cong the next week. There was no progress being made. The generals wouldn't admit it, and the information passed on to the politicians was not accurate. I eventually got around to telling her about Louis, the eighteen-year-old who'd been killed while in my platoon.

She questioned me about Louis, saying it wasn't my fault the boy was killed—and didn't I lose other men as well.

"Five. That's how many died under my leadership. Louis was different. He'd be alive today if I'd made the right decision. I couldn't control my emotions. She gave me some tissue she had in her pocket.

She moved to another topic. "I'm curious about the letter you received from Washington that my dad delivered while we were at the ranch. You want to tell me about it?"

"They want to give me a medal. I don't want it. I don't deserve it."

"Why would they give you a medal if it wasn't deserved? Who nominated you for recognition?"

"I guess it was men in my platoon."

"What medal is it?"

"The Distinguished Service Cross. I'm not accepting a medal of any kind. I threw the letter away." I'd gone from grief to anger. "I'm going to bed now. I've already told you too much."

"Would you do something for me?" she asked.

"Probably not. But you can ask." I was standing now.

"Please let me hug you." She came to me. We stayed in each other's embrace longer than I expected.

# 32

# COFFEE AND DONUTS

GRACE

It was the evening after Christmas Day and we were home. I was sitting on a bale of hay watching Lady eat her grain, thinking of the trip. The five days we spent in Red River was a contrast of enjoyment and guilt. Try as I might, the feeling that it was too soon for me to have fun wouldn't go away, even after the trip home had moved me closer to healing. And the time spent at Red River was enjoyable. Equally important was seeing Luke become closer to the way he was before the war. He couldn't hide the fact that he was having a good time.

It'd only been five months since Henry passed—too soon for happiness of any kind, especially at Christmas. If I was so riddled with guilt, why did I accept the invitation? I did feel an obligation to Blaine even though any debt should've been repaid with Luke's protection of his daughter. My dad insisted it was the right decision. Maybe that made it okay. My dad's moral sense of right and wrong was infallible.

And then there was Blaine. I kept trying to deny he had an interest in me. But, I wasn't being truthful. Of course, he was attracted to me, but he'd been a perfect gentleman, hiding his feelings. How long would that last?

A solution would be for me to return to the track and train horses. Lady wouldn't be ready for months, but I had my three claimers and Blaine's horse. The reality was that I couldn't make a living with four horses. What chance would a woman trainer have of attracting more outside horses? I might as well bide my time and then, when Lady was sound, return to the track.

✳✳✳

Angie and her husband came to our house that evening to have our family Christmas. Angie had insisted on bringing dinner since we'd just returned and wouldn't have time to cook.

We had a short family meeting before they arrived and agreed to be nice to Evert, whom we all detested.

Angie's specialty was Mexican food, and she brought enchiladas, refried beans, guacamole, cole slaw, and pralines. It was a delicious meal, and she glowed as we heaped praise on her.

Evert's comment challenged us. "It'd be nice if we had this kind of meal occasionally. Most of our meals consist of Hamburger Helper or bologna sandwiches."

I glanced at Luke, hoping he'd live up to our agreement, but I was looking in the wrong direction.

"That's my granddaughter you're talking about. You're fortunate to have her. A lot of men would be glad to eat her bologna sandwiches. While you're in my presence, don't speak badly of her."

Evert was surprised at Dad's rebuke and said nothing. Conversation after that was sparse, and they left a short time later. I was hoping that Angie's pregnancy would have a positive effect on Evert, but evidently that wasn't going to happen.

✳✳✳

When I woke up on New Year's Day, something was different. The wind rattling the windows alerted us to the bitter cold, and when I reached over to turn on my lamp nothing happened—no electricity. I had no idea what time it was as I felt my way to the kitchen, and lit two burners on the stove. With the glimmer of light, I found a flashlight in a kitchen drawer. The clock read 5:35.

I lit the space heater in the kitchen and with the additional light was able to start the coffee. My dad appeared with a flashlight. "Daughter, it's here on us. The weather report said it would be bad, but I didn't expect anything like this. I imagine the wind is blowing forty miles an hour. The temperature has to be in the single digits. Is Luke up yet?"

"No. You might check on him." Luke had been sleeping later recently, which was unusual.

He returned a few minutes later. "He's awake. Said he'd be here shortly. Everyone is going to be needed today. It's going to take a lot of feed. The water's going to be frozen, also."

I was hoping Dad would stay in but knew that was his way of telling me he'd be working. I lit several candles and had enough light to cook breakfast.

Luke came in just as I'd finished. "Looks like 1969 isn't starting out very good. I'm not hungry this morning. Just coffee will be fine."

I'd given up nagging him to eat more. He'd lost weight, and none of his clothes fit, even the jeans he bought last month. I'd asked him, more than once, if he still had headaches from the concussion. He always assured me the pain was gone, yet he was still taking the pills. I didn't press the issue, but it worried me.

When we were ready to eat, I asked Luke if he would like to say the blessing. He declined again, but I wasn't giving up. Before going into the service, he never refused. My dad kept telling me to have patience.

Dad and Luke left after breakfast to get an early start to a tough day. I'd told them I'd feed the horses. I put on the warmest clothes available. I wasn't having the problem Luke did with losing weight. I'd put on ten pounds since leaving the track. Most of it could be attributed to sitting in the office and not doing enough physical activity. I waited until daylight to venture outside. The door opened to the south, but as soon as I was away from the house the north wind pushed me forward. Sleet stung my face, making the journey to Lady's pen miserable. Her stall faced the south and, with the heavy blanket we kept on her, she wasn't suffering. She nickered when she saw me.

"Yeah, it's me. I bet you're hungry this morning." Her feed was in a small room attached to her stall. We kept it there for the other horses, too.

I'd just finished feeding and was dreading facing the north wind on my return, when Blaine drove up. I hurried to his pickup, and the warmth welcomed me when I opened the door. "I'm glad to see you. I'm frozen."

"We've had a relatively mild winter. We're due some cold. This is more like what we usually have up here in the top of the Texas Panhandle. I have a thermos of coffee and an extra cup."

"That sounds great. How long is this cold supposed to last?"

"It looks like about three days. Snow's coming later this afternoon. We've got our work cut out for us."

"Is there anything I can do to help?" I asked.

"I have no one in the office, since it's a holiday. You could answer the phone and keep the coffee going for everyone. I brought donuts out this morning. It's tough to stay out for extended periods of time. The men can come in for coffee, donuts, and a few minutes of warmth."

"I'll be glad to do that. Just take me to my house, and I can change clothes."

"What's wrong with what you're wearing?" he asked.

"It's not appropriate for the office."

He laughed. "Grace, this is not an ordinary day. You look fine, believe me. In fact, you look appropriate for this situation."

✳✳✳

I spent the day making coffee and acting as a hostess for cold men who came in for a break. I enjoyed being able to help. The men were appreciative, and it turned out to be one of my best days since Henry passed.

Blaine was correct in his weather forecast. Wednesday, Thursday, and Friday were terrible with blowing snow and freezing temperatures. My dad and Luke came in exhausted each evening. Dad had developed a terrible cough, and by Friday at noon, I convinced him to go to the doctor. The doctor took x-rays and put him in the hospital immediately. He diagnosed it as pneumonia.

The doctor spoke to me out in the hall. "Your dad is very sick. He should've never been out in this kind of weather at his age. I'm not blaming you. My dad is in his 80s, and you can't tell him anything either. I guess we'll be that way when we get older. You work for Blaine at the cattle auction?"

"Yes. My dad and son do, too."

"Blaine is a good man. He's paid many a hospital bill for people who weren't able. Very few are aware of it and that's the way he wants it. He wouldn't approve of me telling you."

I wasn't surprised. Blaine was a generous and caring person. I thanked the doctor and told him I'd be back to check on my dad later.

Dad improved the next two days, and when I went to see him Sunday morning he wasn't in his room. It was early and I waited, thinking they might've taken him for x-rays. When the nurse came in she was surprised to find him gone.

"I checked on him half an hour ago, and he was asleep. I can't imagine where he could've gone," she said.

"I have an idea where he might be. Where is your smoking area?" Dad couldn't go long without a cigarette.

"Just go to the end of the hall and turn left."

Sure enough, I smelled the smoke before I turned the corner. He was sitting with his back to me in his pajamas, looking out the window. I tried to sound angry, but it was no use. "Just what you need with pneumonia—a Camel."

"Caught me red-handed, Daughter. I woke up feeling so good I thought a celebration was in order. This is the first one I've had in three days. I got off the oxygen last night."

I hugged him and sat down. "You look better. Ready to go home?"

"Definitely. The doctor usually comes by in the morning. Maybe he'll release me today. I shouldn't have stayed out in the weather until I ended up in the hospital. I wanted to do my part. It's hard to admit being old and not able to do what you used to do. Pride is the sin. I admit to that. My greatest fear is being a burden to you and Luke. Before that happens, I want to live in a nursing home."

I'd never heard him talk this way. "Oh, Dad. You've been a big help to me, especially these last few months. I couldn't have done without you. What's with this talk of being old? You just have to take care of yourself. Luke and I still depend on you."

He rose, steadying himself on the arm of the chair. "That's nice to hear. I'm going to do better at taking care of myself. No more being out in blizzards. Of course, I probably have the lungs of an eighteen-year-old." He smiled and started off toward his room.

# 33

# SWITCHING ROLES

My mother was going to drive me crazy. When we returned from Red River, she was at my apartment within an hour. I had no idea how she found out so quickly. When I opened the door, she looked like an escapee from an insane asylum. She burst in, hammering me with questions. "What happened at Red River? Whose idea was this? Why wasn't I told?" Then she started sobbing and speaking incoherently.

I sat and watched her have a nervous breakdown. This went on for what seemed like an hour but was only ten minutes. She finally calmed down enough to speak. "What's going on, Jimmie Lyn? Is he going to marry this woman?" She glared at me. "You've put me out of your life. You're treating me like a stranger. I'm your mother! How could you do this to me?" She broke down again.

As she sobbed and gasped for breath I thought, *will this never end?* A knock at the door gave me hope of an interruption. When I opened it, there stood Sterling. Now, it was going to get interesting. "Come in, Sterling."

He was calm and dressed immaculately. "I need to speak with Gwendolyn." He came into the room and stood before his wife. "What's going on, Gwendolyn?"

I waited for a response from my mom who buried her head in her hands and continued to sob. It was up to me to do something. I asked

Sterling to wait outside, to let me speak with her. "Mother, get hold of yourself! What's the matter with you? Talk to me!"

She raised her head and gulped several times. "Y-your dad is—a-another wom-an. Y-you don't l-love me." She covered her face with her hands and started crying again.

I went to the kitchen and brought her a glass of water. "Here, Mother, drink this and calm down. Get control of yourself. Sterling is waiting outside."

She sipped the water, staring straight ahead. She didn't say a word for several minutes, as if she was in some kind of trance before speaking in a whisper. "My life is miserable. I never expected Blaine to find someone else. I never stopped loving him. Now, he's taken up with this—this woman."

"Mother, listen to me. This woman is a nice lady who recently lost her husband, and they are not involved in a relationship. Her son saved my life. The trip was an attempt by Dad to repay them."

"Why didn't you tell me about the trip? It's like you were hiding something."

Now, I had to be honest with her. "I was afraid you would react exactly this way. I'm sorry. I should've told you, but Mother, you have Sterling and his family. You were able to spend Christmas with them. It's obvious Sterling loves you. Why can't you be happy with him?"

She started sniffing again—probably another breakdown coming. She sat up straight as if determined to answer my question. "Sterling is not like Blaine. He's not able to do—what Blaine did. I feel old, Jimmie Lyn. I need Blaine to make me feel young and alive again."

I couldn't believe this was coming from my mother. "Stop it, Mother! I don't want to hear about that part of your life."

"See, I knew you wouldn't understand. Nobody understands."

"What're you going to tell Sterling?" This should be interesting.

"I'm leaving him. I'm not telling him anything. I never really loved him. I was enthralled with his cleanliness and the way he dressed. I would rather live by myself."

I kept telling myself that she was not herself. That she would come to her senses and see how unreasonable she was being. I needed to be honest with her and maybe that would help her accept reality. "Mother, please listen to me. I can't speak for Dad, but he appears to be happy with his life. It might be good for you to address him directly about your feelings and see how he responds. Would you be willing to do that?"

She perked up. "Do you think if I expressed my feelings for Blaine we might get back together? Of course, I'd have to leave Sterling first."

I wasn't going to tell her, in my opinion, the chance of them getting back together would be slim to none. She needed to hear it from Dad. Maybe that would put an end to this fiasco. "You need to speak to Dad directly. Make your feelings known to him."

She stood. "I'm going to do it." She strolled out—a woman with a plan.

I wondered what she was going to say to Sterling who was waiting for her.

***

It was January fourth, a Saturday, which gave me too much time to think. It'd been almost four months since Drake left for England. He'd been out of my life longer than I'd known him. Of course, I'd never really known the true Drake. I tried not to think about him but couldn't get past the fact I'd been so stupid. Evidently, he wasn't going to come back. What if he did?

The weather was improving since the snowstorm that arrived on New Year's Day. The ground was still covered, but the sun was shining, and I took the opportunity to resume my three-mile run. Piper declined my invitation, saying she would wait a day or two longer.

When I returned, feeling better after the exercise and fresh air, my phone was ringing. I picked it up. A voice asked if this was Jimmie Lyn Waddell.

"Yes, this is she."

"This is Officer Mondale with the Amarillo Police Department. We have a Luke Ranker in custody. He requested that we call you. He was in an accident and was under the influence of drugs. The drugs were prescription and no charges have been filed. However, we can't release him in his present condition. Can you pick him up?"

"Yes. I'm in Dalhart, so it'll be about an hour and a half."

"That's no problem. He's not going anywhere."

I wasn't surprised at the situation. After his injuries at College Station, Luke continued to take the pain killers. The doctor had made a mistake by giving him a number of refills. I knew from the time spent with him at the ranch that he used the liquor to deal with his memories of the war. Now he was using the pills.

We continued to depend on each other. On my drive to Amarillo, I wasn't angry with him. He blamed himself for the death of the young man in his platoon and probably the others who were killed, also. I'd like to help him but had no idea how to do it. It concerned me that violence didn't seem to bother him. I'd seen him kill two men without hesitating and go about the day as if nothing happened. His action saved our lives, but I expected at least some remorse. He seemed so young and innocent until his mood turned dark.

My dad understood him better than anyone—that much I knew. Why else would he provide him with a case of whiskey while we were at the ranch? They shared a common experience, even though it was different wars.

He was a good-looking boy. Why did I keep calling him a boy? I immediately became angry at myself because I was comparing his small stature with Drake. Luke was more of a man than anyone I knew besides my dad. Did he consider me attractive? Of course not. The only time he'd touched me was when the jet broke the sound barrier, and he threw me to the ground, protecting me. He did put me to bed when I'd had too much to drink. However, I wasn't conscious then. He'd protected me on more than one occasion, but he considered that part of his job. He stayed mad at me at least half of the time we were together. Occasionally, it was justified. He seldom complimented my conduct, but when he did it pleased me more than it should.

***

When I arrived at the police station, I found him sitting in the lobby with his head in his hands. "You ready to go?"

He looked up. "I rear ended a car at a red light. A little boy was taken to the hospital." The fear in his eyes was evident. "I'm so sorry."

My heart went out to him. "Is the boy seriously injured?"

"Don't know. They took him in an ambulance."

I reached and touched him on the shoulder. "Come on. We'll go to the hospital and check on him."

He was quiet on the way. We parked in the emergency room parking lot. More than likely, we could find out information here. He wanted to wait in the car, but I insisted he go in with me. He stood behind me when I addressed the man admitting patients. "We're here to inquire about an accident that happened several hours ago. The patient was transported to the hospital by ambulance. We'd like to know if he was admitted to the hospital."

"Are you related to the patient?" he asked.

"No. We'd just like to know about his condition." I turned back toward Luke. "My friend witnessed the accident."

He shuffled some papers on the counter and didn't answer for several seconds. "I'm sorry to say he didn't make it. He died on the operating table."

I heard Luke whimper. He'd fallen to his knees and was repeating "Oh, God . . ."

The man came from behind the counter. "Is he going to be okay?"

"Just give us a few minutes. He was involved in the accident."

I tried to get him up but he refused, continuing to say, "Oh no."

"How was he involved? The man who died was in a one-car rollover on the loop."

I whirled around. "You mean it was a man who died in the accident and not a boy?"

"Of course not. The man was in his fifties."

"What about a small boy that was brought in this afternoon?" I asked.

"Oh, that. He had a cut that required several stiches and was sent home with his mother."

Evidently, Luke had blocked out everything and didn't hear the good news. He was still on his knees. I reached down, grabbed him by the shoulders and shook him. "Listen to me, Luke. It wasn't the boy in the car you hit that died." I went on to explain what I'd heard from the receptionist.

He rose, and we left the room with me supporting him. In the car, I asked him if he was okay. He didn't answer and I repeated the question.

"Yeah," he whispered. "I thought I'd killed the little boy. I came to Amarillo to get my prescription for the pain pills filled. The pharmacy in Dalhart was closed today. I usually take a pill in the morning and one at night. For whatever reason, I took two when the prescription was filled. It hit me hard and much quicker than it ever had. I came to the red light and my reaction was slow. I hit the car ahead of me. I saw them put the little boy in the ambulance and could see he was bleeding. I was stupid! Since I wasn't drinking the police didn't blame me."

"Would you like something to eat?"

"No. I'm not hungry."

"Well I am. Stress makes me want to eat. We'll go to the Big Texan

Steak Ranch on Amarillo Boulevard. It's one of my dad's favorite places to eat. It's early, so they shouldn't be busy. I hear they're moving out on Route 66 next year."

Once seated and looking at a menu, Luke decided to eat. I was mesmerized by his eyes which were a distinct brown. How could a mood be reflected in the color of someone's eyes? When I approached him at the police station, they were black.

I enjoyed the meal and he relaxed somewhat, but I still did most of the talking. "Did you see your granddad this morning before you left? I heard they put him in the hospital."

"Yeah. He was already doing better. He should've never been out in that weather."

"Are you still having pain from the injuries you received in College Station?" I asked.

"Not much."

I thought now was a good time to change topics. "Have you given any more thought to accepting the medal that's been awarded to you?"

"No. I don't deserve a medal."

"Because of the boy in your platoon who was killed? I believe you said Louis was his name."

"Yeah, that's right. He was from a little town in South Louisiana. He was always saying he would take me fishing after we got home."

"Have you considered visiting his parents?" I might be pushing this too far.

He turned and looked at me. "Yeah, I'm afraid of facing them. Can you imagine what they think of me?"

"They might surprise you. I believe it would be good for you to go see them. Would you consider it if I went with you?"

He went silent, drawing back into his shell and saying nothing the remainder of the way.

# 34

# WILD COW

LUKE

Winter in the Texas Panhandle is not a good time to work at a cattle auction. The month of January we experienced one storm after another. Most days ice and snow covered the ground. When the snow melted your boots would sink up in mud, making it difficult to even walk. One consistency was a relentless north wind that was raw and brutal. The cattle had to have feed and water, which made for twelve-hour days.

Granddad wasn't able to return to work after his bout with pneumonia. The doctor had given strict instructions for him to stay out of the weather. The trailer was impossible to heat, and he moved into the house. He objected, but Mom and I insisted that he sleep in my room. After a twelve-hour day the couch looked good at bedtime.

Blaine was right about physical work being a benefit in healing. I was exhausted at the end of each day and able to sleep. I flushed the pills down the toilet after my accident in Amarillo. What if the car I'd rammed into had killed the little boy?

The last week in January Blaine summoned Bronc and me into his office. He said a number of the cattle were not doing well. "We need to get at least fifty to the ranch on wheat. They'll do better out of the muck and in the open. I want y'all to haul the ones we cut, out to the ranch. You can get about twenty head in the goose-neck. It'll take several trips, but if we don't do something they'll probably not recover.

"I'm not happy with the guy I hired to stay at the ranch. I'm going to give him one more chance, then he's gone. Griffin spoiled me. He'd been out at the ranch for twenty-five years and never had a problem. All this new man does is complain and ask for more help. Do you have any questions?"

Blaine asked me to stay when we rose to leave. After Bronc was gone, he inquired, "How're you doing, Luke?"

"Better. You were right about the physical work. It keeps my thoughts from going elsewhere. I wouldn't say that everything is normal, but I seem to be dealing with it."

"Good. I'm glad to hear that. How is your granddad?"

"He's fine. He doesn't like staying inside and not working. Health wise—he's doing good."

"Great. How's your mom?"

"She's good. She enjoys her job. My mother is a strong person."

"I know. I admire her greatly," he said. "I know she misses your dad."

"Yeah. But she's getting on with her life. It helped her to return home. She came back feeling better about moving on."

"I'm glad to have your family here, Luke. You've been an asset to me and this company. Now if you need anything, let me know."

❋❋❋

For the next several days we hauled trailer loads of sick cattle to the ranch. They were weak and wobbly when we unloaded them but went right to grazing on the ankle high wheat. It was a good feeling to know that we were saving many of them.

I enjoyed the time with Bronc. One particular morning, he questioned me about Vietnam, worried about his younger brother. I didn't like to talk about it but understood him being concerned about his brother.

"I should be the one over there. He's so young and won't see the danger."

"Bronc, that's the thing about it. The military likes the young men because they are not as cautious and aware of their immortality. The younger the better."

"It's not right, Luke—it's just not right."

"I know that. I saw it first-hand. When's your brother coming home?" I asked.

"Five more months. It seems like a lifetime."

I wanted to talk about something else. "What about Madge? You've been seeing a lot of her."

"I enjoy her company. I'm several years older than she is, but it doesn't bother us. We have fun, and she likes rodeo, which is a plus. I've never been seriously involved with anyone. I'm going to take this slow and see how it plays out."

I counted Bronc as one of my few friends, and I hoped everything worked out for him and Madge. I had a feeling it would, if left up to her.

It was easy to see why Blaine was put out with Swartz, the man who had replaced Griffin at the ranch. He came down to the wheat field several times when we were unloading. He never had anything positive to say, complaining that one man couldn't handle the work load. I could testify that the work was demanding, but he should've been able to see that when he accepted the position.

The last day we hauled cattle to the ranch the weather turned much warmer, and it appeared that spring had arrived. When we went back to work in the pens, they had even dried up somewhat. For the first time in weeks, a long-sleeved shirt was sufficient to be comfortable.

On Tuesday, February fourth, we were at the back of the pens when we heard an ambulance. Fearing that someone had been injured in an accident we made our way back to the front. The ambulance was leaving as we arrived.

My mother met us outside the office. "Luke, it's Blaine! He was in the alley talking with one of the hands, and he was run over by a cow. He wasn't conscious when they took him in the ambulance. Jimmie was hysterical and asking for you. She rode in the ambulance. You better go to the hospital to be with her."

My car was at the house, so I took Blaine's pickup and was at the hospital soon after the ambulance. I went to the emergency entrance and Jimmie was immediately in my arms, crying softly.

"They w-won't let me be with him. I'm s-scared, Luke. H-he's n-not c-con-scious. I-it was crazy. A cow just ran over him. They were pushing a pen down the alley and one turned back, running full speed. My dad was talking to someone and never saw it.

I gently pushed her away, and we moved to chairs as far from the others as possible. She stopped crying but leaned against my shoulder. I put my arm around her. We stayed that way for an hour until a nurse came in, saying the doctor would see her now.

She rose and took my hand. "Please go with me, Luke."

We followed the nurse back to a hallway where we met the doctor, who evidently knew the family. "Jimmie Lyn, we need to send him to Amarillo. He may have internal injuries, and we know he has several broken ribs. He's awake. You can see him for a few minutes. I've made arrangements for transportation to Amarillo. The doctor he will be seeing is one of the best. I'd like to be able to tell you more but that's all the information available at this time."

"Thank you, Doctor Nolan. I'd like to see him, now." She grabbed my arm and we followed the doctor.

Blaine was lying on a bed with an oxygen mask on. When he saw us, he managed a smile. He whispered, "I never saw what hit me."

Jimmie held up well but never let go of my arm until she leaned over and kissed him on the cheek. "That's okay. I'm just glad you're awake. You're going to Amarillo where they'll take good care of you. Luke and I will follow you."

He turned his head in my direction. "Thank you, Luke, for looking after my little girl."

A nurse said it was time to get him ready to leave. Jimmie kissed her dad again and we left, going to Blaine's pickup. She talked non-stop while we waited to follow the ambulance to Amarillo. I think she was dealing with her fear by endless chatter.

"I dread my mom finding out. She's threatening to leave her husband and is a basket case. She'll go ballistic when she hears about Dad. I appreciate you going with me. I just feel better when you're close. I need to notify Piper. You haven't met her, have you? She's my best friend. She's married to a doctor and runs with me most days." She stopped and took a breath and then went on and on about topics that avoided her dad. She didn't stop until the ambulance drove away.

We stayed at the hospital the rest of the day and throughout the night. Jimmie stayed in the room with her dad, and I went to the lounge area. The next day, which was a Wednesday, more tests were run and a doctor finally met with us at two o'clock in the afternoon. The doctor came to Blaine's room so he was included. The news was not encouraging.

He spoke directly to the patient. "You have internal bleeding, and we're having trouble locating the source. You do have fractured ribs, but that's not the problem. All we can do is continue with the tests and hopefully we can find where it's originating. I'll let you know as soon as we have more information. Right now, the best thing for you is rest. Do you have any questions?" He turned and looked at Jimmie.

"Will you have to do surgery?" Like anytime I was close to her, she had hold of my arm.

"That's a possibility. It just depends on the location of the injury and how severe it is. Sometimes, rest and medication is all that's needed. I'm sorry for being so vague, but at the time we just don't know." There were no more questions, so he left.

Blaine asked us to raise the bed. "I need to talk with you and not lying flat on my back."

It took me several tries, but I finally was able to master the controls and raised him to a sitting position. His dark complexion had paled and his voice was weak. "Listen to me, Jimmie Lyn, and don't interrupt. I may be here days until they decide what to do. You need to get back to Dalhart and run the business. There is no one else, and it won't run itself, effectively anyway. Decisions have to be made daily, and you're going to have to make them. The ranch is another problem. I want Swartz off the place. Sitting around and doing nothing—hoping he'll improve his attitude—is not going to solve anything. If issues come up, you can call me. I have a phone right here at my bedside. Lastly—don't argue with me. Do you have any questions?"

She moved closer to the bed, pulling me with her. "Who's going to be at the ranch? Somebody has to replace Swartz."

"That's up to you to find someone. Now, lower the bed. I'm tired from all that talking." He closed his eyes as if to signal that the instructions were over.

A few minutes later we were on our way back to Dalhart. I was surprised she was willing to leave her dad without an argument. "Looks like you're the boss now. What're you going to do first?"

"Replace Swartz. That was my dad's orders. The ranch is important to him, and he wants someone out there who will take care of the operation. After all the years Griffin was there, we came to take him for granted. Dad should've known replacing him was going to be difficult."

"Who're you going to get?"

She reached over and poked me in the ribs. "You—for the time being. I can't worry about the ranch and run the Auction. You're the only person I totally trust."

"What if I don't want the job?"

"I'm the boss, remember? You don't have a choice. It'll only be temporary until my dad returns, and we can find someone permanent." She moved over next to me, took hold of my arm, and put her head on my shoulder. "I need you, Luke. You're my protector, and I'm your boss."

I drove the rest of the way to Dalhart with the boss sitting next to me, with her head on my shoulder, asleep.

# 35

# EXPECTING THE
# EXPECTED

GRACE

The month of January went by fast. I was becoming accustomed to my new job and enjoying it. Dad had recovered from his bout with pneumonia but was not going back to work until the weather was warmer. Angie was five months pregnant and still working. I'd been to see her several times and insisted she quit, but she refused, saying she didn't want to depend on anyone. Evert continued to be without a job, lying around the house all day while she worked. I'd given up on him ever providing a living.

Lady had improved to the point she was kicking up in her small pen. It would only be a few weeks until the two months were up, and she could be ridden. I'd already decided to be the first to ride her. There was a small field joining the pens that would be perfect, but I hadn't told anyone my plans.

The injury to Blaine on February fourth was frightening. When Luke returned the next day and told me what the doctor had said, I suspected the worst. He went on to tell me about Blaine's request that his daughter take over the responsibilities of running the business. It surprised me that he was going to the ranch and replacing Swartz, at least temporarily. Jimmie's dependence on Luke hadn't decreased as evidenced by her reaction to Blaine's injury when she insisted that he be with her. I would've thought she needed him, now more than ever. It was a strange relationship, and I had no idea where it was headed. Luke seemed to be okay with taking over the ranching operation.

✳✳✳

When I went to work on Thursday, the sixth of February, Jimmie was already in her dad's office. When she asked to see me, I suspected it was to inform me that I would be moving back to payroll.

She rose when I entered. "Grace, please sit down. I have a huge favor to ask of you."

"I'll be glad to do what I can. I've been praying for your dad. I know you must be worried."

"Yes, but he wants me here rather than at the hospital. When I talked to him this morning, he sounded a little better. I need your help, Grace. I can't do the work here unless I know my dad is being cared for. I'd like to ask you to go stay with him, at least, until we know what's going on. Hopefully, that won't be for too long. There's a hotel across the street from the hospital. You can get a room and stay there at night. I know staying around a hospital all day is tiring, but you can come and go as you please. The main thing is that someone is close by to see about him and report to me. Also, I know that he'd appreciate your company." She hesitated, waiting for a response.

I was surprised to say the least. "I'd like to help anyway I can, but what about your mother? Wouldn't she want to stay with him?"

"Yes, but that would be the worst possible solution. She's anything but rational now, and he'd never forgive me if I sent her to stay with him."

I didn't know what to say. It would create an awkward situation if I agreed, yet if I didn't it would be declining to help someone that needed me, which wouldn't be a Christian thing to do. "Would you make sure your dad understood that you asked me to stay with him. You would need to make that plain to your mother, also."

"Certainly, I'll do both. You'll continue to be paid, and the hotel room will be taken care of." She smiled, "It'll be a little easier to inform my dad.

"Grace, I'll have someone look in on your dad while you're away. On cold days when he can't feed, Bronc will take care of that for you. I'm sure Luke told you that he's going to be at the ranch for the time being."

"Yes. I was surprised he was going back to the ranch."

"I know. In a time of crisis, I look to Luke. That's probably natural since he saved my life. I can send someone for him if he's needed, which I will do."

"Your mother's not going to like this." The understatement of all time.

"I know, but Dad comes first. She'll just have to deal with it." She rose, seeming to be taller than I remembered. I took this as a cue the meeting was over.

"If you could be in Amarillo tomorrow that'll give me time to speak with my dad and try to reason with my mom."

"Okay. Let me know your dad's feelings about my staying with him. I already know what your mom will think."

I left the meeting, dreading what was to come. I didn't mind staying with Blaine, but his ex was going to explode when she heard the news. She'd view this as her opportunity to be his nursemaid and get them back together. I returned to work, but my mind was elsewhere the rest of the day.

✳✳✳

On my way to Amarillo, I was deep in thought as how to handle this challenge. My dad had insisted I was doing the right thing—what any good Christian would do. He assured me he'd be fine staying by himself and seemed pleased about the responsibility of looking after himself and the horses on days he could get out. Maybe some good was going to come out of this besides Blaine having company and being looked after.

My life had been so much simpler when Henry was alive, and we were at the racetrack. The scheduled day-to-day activity, always knowing what the day would bring and what was expected of you. Now this life— full of constant surprise and change. I'd developed a certain amount of resilience which, I assumed, should be considered positive. Maybe God was going to use me in a different way, and I should accept that. My dad was constantly reminding me to have faith and everything would work itself out.

I arrived at Blaine's hospital room, knocked, the door opened and I was face-to-face with Gwendolyn, his ex-wife. She glared at me. "He doesn't need you. I'm going to take care of him!" And she closed the door, leaving me standing in the hall.

Back outside, I got in my pickup and sat there thinking. I wasn't going to confront her. Jimmie's talk did no good. It's just what I thought would happen, and Jimmie should've realized it. I had no choice except to go back to Dalhart and my job.

An hour and a half later I walked into the office of the High Plains Cattle Auction. I went directly to Jimmie's office and informed her what had happened.

Her reaction was calmer than I'd expected. She rubbed her temples. "I should've known. She didn't hear anything I told her yesterday. I'll go to Amarillo this evening and get this worked out. Dad's going to need to help me.

"I'm sorry, Grace. You did the right thing by not getting into it with her. She's beyond reason. You can help Madge out today, and Lord knows, she needs it."

Madge was glad to see me. "Grace, you are a godsend. I'm just getting started, and I'm behind already."

I didn't look up the rest of the day which lasted an hour longer than usual. I was able to help her catch up.

My dad was surprised to see me. I explained what'd happened before changing and going to feed Lady and the other horses. After the day I'd had, it was nice to be around horses, especially Lady. She looked even better than before her fracture. If I started riding her the last of this month it would still be a good five months until the stakes races in Ruidoso. I could go slow with her for a month, and if she stayed sound I could gradually increase her work. By the first of May, she might be able to go into full-time training. That would still give her three months to be ready for a race. The big question was how would she come back from that long a layoff. She might remember the pain of the injury and be hesitant when asked to run. Only time would tell.

Today, sitting here looking at this beautiful filly, I wished I was at the racetrack instead of involved in this family feud. I almost felt sorry for Gwendolyn. She was convinced she wanted to get back with Blaine. Too late, she'd realized that it was a mistake to not accept him as he was. Now she realized that the tobacco and smelly boots were minor items. From all indications, Blaine didn't want to get back together.

From out of nowhere, came the next thought. *I was going to be a grandmother in four months.* I smiled, just like every time the thought came to mind. I was going to be 'Gracie' to some little boy or girl, it made no difference to me. They would never know their granddad, but I would tell them about him.

The positive thoughts were extinguished like water poured on a fire when the "leaner" entered the picture. Evert, with his attitude, put a damper on everything. Angie must love him or she'd have run him off a long time ago. I smiled, thinking of what Henry had said about him. "He's so lazy he wouldn't holler 'sooey' if the hogs were eatin' him."

# 36

# A STRESSFUL DAY

JIMMIE LYN

On the drive to Amarillo, I was fuming. My mother hadn't said anything when I told her about Grace staying with Dad. How naïve could you get? Of course, she wasn't going to accept that, and why should I have ever thought she would? It was just another of my stupid blunders.

Was sending Luke to the ranch a mistake? With any type of bad news, I clung to him like a person hanging to a life raft. At least I admitted it, even though it wasn't easy. He had an inner strength that I lacked and had taken on the role of my protector. I depended on him to be there for me when needed, much like a bodyguard. I realized it was more than just physical but emotional as well. He could care less that I'd been humiliated by Drake, probably never even thinking about it. Maybe he was the brother that I never had.

The few hours I'd spent in my dad's chair was an awakening to what he went through each day. I had at least two dozen calls ranging from clients who were not satisfied with the sale of their cattle, to people inquiring about the market. I understood now why he insisted on me replacing him while he was away.

When I arrived at the hospital, I sat in my car, lecturing myself. "You have to stay calm—no shouting match with your mother, no matter how frustrated you are. Try to understand her position. She's a desperate woman who's willing to give up everything to reunite with Dad." I walked toward the hospital, doubting if the lecture to myself had done any good.

I reached his room, knocking and entering without waiting for an invitation. My mother was sitting on the side of his bed. Her look let me know I wasn't welcomed. "I've been expecting you. Don't start in on me! I'm not going anywhere. He needs me, not some stranger who isn't part of this family."

I took a long deep breath. "Would you let me talk to Dad alone for a few minutes?" It was a long shot, but maybe if I asked her, she might consent.

She turned to my dad and then back to me. "Why can't I stay and hear what you say?"

My dad came to the rescue. "Gwendolyn, we have some business we need to discuss. It would only bore you. Give us a few minutes alone, please."

She slid off the bed. "Okay, but I'm coming back in five minutes." She left but was probably standing outside the door listening.

"Dad, what're we going to do? She sees an opportunity to force herself back into your life. She's determined that y'all get back together."

He looked tired, and his voice was weak. "That's not going to happen. We tried it for fifteen years, and it didn't work. I'm not going there again. I haven't been able to rest. She's been sitting on the bed most of the day. If you'll stay in here with us, I'll try to convince her we have no future. Maybe she'll leave after that; if not, I don't know what to do."

"She's angry with me. I'll stay, but it may do more harm than good."

The door opened, and she was back in the room. "That should've been long enough to get your business taken care of." She sat on the bed ignoring me and spoke sweetly to Dad. "Can I get you anything, Blaine?"

"No, thank you. We need to talk, Gwendolyn." He commenced to tell her what he'd rehearsed with me. When he came to the part where they had no future, she started crying. By the time he finished with, "Sterling is a nice guy and really loves you—go back to him."

She broke down and began sobbing. She looked at me and screamed, "I-It's y-your fa-ult!" and ran out of the room.

"You did good, Dad. I know it wasn't easy."

"I feel bad, Honey. She's confused and angry. I did the only thing I could do. Now, I'm so tired. Maybe I can rest with her gone."

I leaned over and kissed him on the forehead before sitting down in the only chair in the room, a recliner. I'd brought a book that I'd started several days ago. For the next two hours I buried my head in Dr. Zhivago, a love story set during the Revolutionary War in Russia. If I couldn't find love, I could at least read about it.

My dad slept three hours after my mother left. He asked for a glass of water and then went back to sleep. A nurse came in several times and took his blood pressure, but he didn't wake up. He must've been exhausted. I left around midnight, deciding to get a room at a motel since tomorrow was Saturday, and I could stay with him during the weekend.

✳✳✳

I left Amarillo early Monday morning in time to go by my apartment, shower and, dress for work. My mom hadn't shown up again at the hospital, so maybe Dad had convinced her they weren't getting back together. My first stop was at Grace's, and I caught her coming out of the house on the way to work. I told her about the episode with my mother, and it should be fine for her to return to the hospital. She didn't seem too happy but agreed.

At work a few minutes early, I found a stack of unopened mail on my desk. On top of the stack was a letter from the U.S. government. It went right to the point, saying a representative would be here Wednesday, which was sale day, to conduct an inspection to determine if we were complying with the environmental laws pertaining to waste disposal. Just what I needed, a visit from the government. I remembered Dad dreading these inspections, saying it all depended on the guy that came. Some were good, others not so good, and some impossible.

The number one concern would be the manure piles and the effect it was having on water and air pollution. We offered it to farmers for fertilizer, and we used it on our ranch also. Of course, during the dead of winter the piles were at their highest of anytime during the year.

I didn't have time to worry about the government visitor for the next two days. Our feed truck broke down and had to be towed to town, leaving us in a bind. Several calves escaped while unloading a trailer, and it took two cowboys half a day to get them back in the pens. Thankfully, none reached the highway.

By Wednesday morning, I was already a nervous wreck, and I thought about hiding out until this was over. Today was sale day and we only had a run of about 400 head. The sale didn't start until eleven o'clock, and a few more would come in before the day was over.

One of my biggest concerns involved Dad, who wasn't going to be here to set the opening bid on the cattle. He was so knowledgeable about cattle and their value, which was important, since if he started a cow at a certain price and nobody bid then the Auction would buy the cow. It was called catching, and very seldom did this happen with Dad starting cattle as they came into the ring. Harold Dawson relieved him for breaks but wasn't nearly as good. Harold generally would catch more cattle in an hour than Dad did for the entire sale. Now he was going to replace my dad for the day. I couldn't remember another sale that Dad had missed.

The inspector arrived an hour before the sale started. He was a thin little man with thick glasses. He looked unhappy. The timing couldn't have been worse. He introduced himself and immediately wanted to inspect the pens. We had catwalks running the length of the pens with several branching off, so it was possible to see most of the pens from the ten-foot elevated walkway.

He immediately called my attention to the manure piles, especially those toward the back where we kept cattle for more than a day. I tried to explain that they were harder to dispose of during the winter, but he wasn't impressed with my explanation.

He left after an hour, evidently pleased that he'd found something unsatisfactory which he could write us up on. Goodbye and good riddance, I thought, as he left with the parting words, "You'll be hearing from me."

I decided to watch some of the sale, which was a mistake. During the fifteen minutes I sat there, Harold caught five head. I drew the attention of the auctioneer who glanced at Harold and shook his head. It was obvious what was happening. The market was not as good due to being winter and ranchers had nowhere to go with their cattle—hence the price of livestock was down. Harold was starting cattle like spring was already here, and we had plenty of grazing. I left, deciding not to punish myself by sitting there any longer. The Auction was just going to buy a lot of cattle today. We would keep them awhile and sell them. We might be able to put some on wheat.

I met Benny in the hallway on the way to my office. I knew from his look something was wrong. "Problem, Missy. Paperwork got messed up and the boys loaded a truck with the wrong pen of cattle. He left about half an hour ago, headed toward a feedlot in Kansas. He's hauling a load of stockers, weighing about 300 pounds each. It'll be the lightest cattle ever sent to a feed lot."

"Who would make such a stupid mistake?" I asked, angrily.

"Doesn't matter now. What do you want to do?" He took out a cigarette, lit it, and inhaled deeply.

Maybe I needed to start smoking. It looked relaxing. "I'll call the highway patrol and see if they can stop him and get him turned around."

"Sounds like a plan," he said, walking away like this was an everyday occurrence.

My dad had a friend who was a trooper. I called the office and asked if they could get a message to Trooper Crawford. I gave them a description of the truck and the license plate number, explained what'd happened and asked if they could help us out. They said if they were successful, they'd let us know.

I asked one of the girls in the outer office to check the catch pen and see how many head there were. She reported that there were thirty-one.

We're here to sell people's cattle, not buy them. I made my way to the back of the sale ring and stood behind Harold. I tapped him on the shoulder, motioning for him to follow me.

"What do you need?" he asked.

"I have to talk with you."

Dewayne, the auctioneer, understood what was happening, and as the next cow and calf was let into the sale ring, he said, "That's a nice pair and she's bred back—175 and she'll make you money," and the bidding started.

Thank goodness for Dewayne. He should've been starting cattle all day. Harold followed me back to my office.

"What's going on?" he asked.

"You're catching too many cattle, Harold. I'm sorry, but we're not here to buy cattle."

"The market's just off today. I'm trying to help out our customers. I think the buyers just want to buy cattle cheaper than their value. It may be because Blaine isn't here."

"Right now, the problem is that you're catching too many cattle. Let Dewayne have it awhile. Go eat lunch, and come back in an hour." Maybe he'd have time to think about what I said. I didn't like being the bad guy.

I went back to the sale, and everything was better. I watched for twenty minutes, and Dewayne didn't catch a head. I breathed a sigh of relief and returned to my office, where I had a call waiting.

"Jimmie Lyn—Crawford here. We got your truck pointed in the

right direction."

"Thank you so much. That's a huge relief."

"I heard about Blaine. How's he doing?"

"They're running tests and haven't reached any conclusions. He's resting and is not in any pain. Maybe we'll know something soon. Thank you again for your help."

"No problem. Be safe."

The call ended and I thought, *another problem solved.*

One of the ladies who worked out front, relayed a message from Harold. "He said to tell you he was leaving and not returning until Blaine was back at work."

Harold had his feelings hurt. A woman told him what to do and he couldn't handle that. Too bad. I was raised around this auction barn, and I knew as much as anyone about it, with the exception of my dad.

The sale ended and Dewayne came by my office. "Jimmie Lyn, you did the right thing. Your dad would be proud of you. The market was off today, and Harold wouldn't accept that."

"Thank you. I needed to hear something positive."

"Tell Blaine we're thinking about him." He left, but the warm feeling remained.

Benny came in next with a big smile. "Well, the truck is back and we're loading it with the right cattle. You did good, Missy." He'd been calling me Missy as long as I remember and was the only one who did.

*** *** ***

By six that evening everything had calmed down and most everyone had left. I was drained—physically and emotionally. I went out, got in my car, and headed toward the ranch and my protector.

# 37

# BULL

On February the seventh I went to the ranch to replace Swartz. Benny had gone to the ranch the day before and told him the news—he wasn't working for the High Plains Cattle Auction any longer.

I took enough food to last a week and several changes of clothes. After giving it some thought, it was probably for the best. I had Bull for company, and some peace and quiet—along with hard work—would be good for me.

After two days of feeding by myself, I found it hard to believe that Griffin could have done this by himself up until he was eighty-five years old. I'd put out fifty bales of hay two days and the third day range cubes. The cubes were like a day off, since the spreader on the back of the truck made it easy.

The weather for February wasn't bad the first few days, but Monday morning I was greeted with a north wind and blowing snow. I built up the fire and moved Bull over, so I could drink my coffee in comfort. Bull had established a permanent residence on a blanket as close to the wood burning stove as he could without singeing his hair.

For the first time since coming home, I'd thought little of the war the last three days. I'd been so tired at the end of the day that sleep came easy. I was eating more and had gained a few pounds. My clothes fit better.

Bull moved his legs and gave a muffled bark which meant he was having a dream, probably chasing a rabbit. I reached and poked him with my foot. "Wake up. It's time for us to get to work."

He struggled to his feet and moved over, turning his rear toward me. That was his favorite place to receive attention. He would stand there all day if I'd scratch his butt.

"You want your jacket on this morning?" I'd made him a coat out of an old sweatshirt. I pulled it over his head and put his feet through the arms pulling it over his body. It actually worked pretty well, and he didn't object to wearing it.

We went outside and made it to the truck, but I had to give Bull a lift. I thought for a minute that the truck wasn't going to start. I was about to give up when it kicked off. I backed into the hay barn and got out, but Bull made no effort to follow me. The barn had no sides so it offered little shelter from the cold and blowing snow. After loading twenty-five bales, I froze out and got back in the truck, which by now was warm. Bull had gone back to sleep.

I drove along the side of the hills, honking until cattle began appearing with snow-covered backs. I stopped every fifty yards or so and threw off five bales, cut the wire and continued on, repeating the procedure until I'd put out the twenty-five bales.

I stopped at the house on the way back to get another cup of coffee and warm up by the stove. Bull followed this time, but when I opened the door to go in the house, I looked around and he wasn't behind me. It'd quit snowing and visibility was better. I saw Bull checking out the area around the woodshed and thought he was just marking his territory. Then I saw it! A coyote was standing less than a hundred yards from him. When he spotted it, he took off, running all out. I ran after him shouting, "Bull, come back! Bull stop!"

It was no use. I'd witnessed this before, years ago while I was at home. A female shows up and leaves her scent. A male dog sees an opportunity and goes after her. She leads him off where a pack is waiting to attack and kill him for food. Winter, when game is scare, is a prime time for this to happen.

I ran to the truck and within seconds was going in the direction Bull had taken, but he was already out of sight. When I'd gone half a mile, I knew he couldn't run that far. I turned around and drove slow enough to look for tracks. I found them going into the hills. The coyote had turned, leading Bull to an ambush. I stopped and got out, following the tracks as fast as possible. Halfway to the top, I heard the sounds of the battle— snarling, growling, and yelping off to my right—and I followed the sound. The scene was suddenly before me. Four coyotes had Bull down and were tearing at him. He was fighting back but losing.

I hollered, picked up a rock and threw it at them. They slinked away, reluctantly. Bull's coat was torn to pieces, and he was bleeding from wounds on his neck and throat. He whined as I picked him up and started back toward my truck. I prayed all the way down the hill. "Please God, I need this dog. Let him live."

By the time, we were back at the house, blood was flowing from the wound in the neck. I didn't stop, driving as fast as possible toward the highway. I thought it might be closer to Clayton and the vet clinic there, so that's where I headed.

I arrived carrying Bull and rushed into the clinic. The receptionist directed me to a room, and a vet appeared immediately. "What happened?" he asked.

"Coyotes."

He examined Bull's wounds. "He's lost a lot of blood. We need to do a transfusion immediately." He picked him up and was gone, leaving me without any further explanation. I returned to the waiting room and sat down with several others in line to see the vet. I couldn't believe this was happening. I'd saved this dog and now he might die.

A woman sitting beside me asked, "What happened to your dog?"

"Coyotes."

"I'm sorry. Is it bad?'

"Yeah. I don't know if he'll make it." I didn't want to talk about it. Maybe that would satisfy her.

I waited two hours before the vet came out and motioned me to follow him. I was afraid that the news would be bad. He took me to the room where Bull was laid out on a table.

"I stopped the bleeding, and gave him a transfusion since he's lost a lot of blood. I sewed up his wounds, and now we just have to wait and see if he's able to recover. We should know something in a couple of days. If you'll leave your phone number, I'll call you if there's a change."

"I don't have a phone, but I'll check back with you. Please do everything you can for him. He's a special friend, and I need him."

He smiled. "I'll do everything I can."

I thanked him and left, going back to the ranch and a lonesome house.

❊❊❊

The next two days, I made four trips back to the vet clinic to check on Bull, but the vet was not able to give me any hope. On my fifth trip, Wednesday evening, the vet had given up.

"He's not making progress. I believe that we should euthanize him and end his suffering. I'm sorry—we did everything we could."

My heart sank. "I want to see him."

He motioned me to a room. I went in and he was lying on his side with his eyes open. I rubbed him on the rear. "Hello, big boy. You need to be careful with the ladies that you chase."

I bent down close to him. He reached out with that long tongue and gave me one of his wet kisses. With tears in my eyes, I went back to the vet. "No. I don't want to put him down. We'll wait a few more days."

"Okay, it's your choice, but I believe you're making the wrong decision."

I left, as depressed as I'd been since coming home from Vietnam. I didn't understand why this had to happen. I was doing better and had quit the pills. Why did this happen?

I didn't feel like doing anything when I arrived at the ranch house. I made myself a drink and sat down in front of the fire. I'd continued to pray for Bull. It hadn't done any good and here I was, waiting for him to die. I heard a car drive up. There was a knock at the door. Jimmie was standing there.

I had trouble talking. I retreated back and sat down. I was embarrassed and tried to hide my emotions.

"What's wrong, Luke? Talk to me."

"It's Bull. He's dying. Coyotes got him. He's at the vet clinic in Clayton. They want to put him down."

"Oh, Luke. I'm so sorry. When did it happen?"

"Two days ago, after we came in from feeding. They trapped him."

"Is the clinic still open?" she asked.

"I don't know."

"I want to see him. Let's go."

The vet clinic was closed, but there was a sign on the door in case of an emergency. I called the number and told the person who answered that I needed to get in to the clinic to see about my dog. It wasn't the vet who'd treated Bull, but he agreed to come.

The vet, who appeared a few minutes later, was a young man. He opened the door, and we followed him in. They had moved Bull to a cage, and he lay motionless with his eyes closed. For a brief moment I thought he was dead, but when I called his name, his eyes opened. I unlocked the cage and rubbed him on his head.

When Jimmie called his name, he raised his head slightly. She moved closer to the cage talking to him. "How you doing, big boy. I've missed you the last several days." He whined and tried to raise his head but was too weak.

"Let's take him home, Luke. If he's going to die, it doesn't need to be in a strange place with people he doesn't know looking after him." She turned to the vet. "Would you look up the bill so we can pay you?"

"I have no idea where they keep the paperwork. Just leave your address, and we'll mail you a bill." He left and returned with an old blanket. "Here, wrap him in this."

I picked him up gently and we left. Jimmie drove and I cradled him in my arms. He whined softly, and I didn't know whether it was from the pain or just because he was happy leaving that place.

We stopped at a grocery store and Jimmie bought several bottles of Gatorade and a half dozen cans of chicken noodle soup. "We're going to try and get something down him. He's weak and probably dehydrated," she said.

At the ranch we made him a soft bed in front of the stove, his favorite place. Throughout the night we gave him small portions of Gatorade with a large syringe, kept at the ranch for vaccinations. We took turns staying awake for a couple of hours. We followed this schedule until morning at which time we substituted the chicken noodle soup for the Gatorade. He was actually able to raise his head for longer periods of time.

"He's a little better, Luke. I have to get to work. I'm going to be late as it is. Keep giving him the Gatorade and the soup. I'll see you this evening."

"Thank you. He was going to die last night in that clinic. You should've been a vet."

"He still may die, but I believe he has a chance now. Don't worry about feeding cattle today. Look after our dog," she said, going out the door.

I went ahead, against her advice, and put out hay after she'd left. When I returned to the house, Bull had taken a turn for the worse. Was it going to be true that people and animals got much better before they died?

# 38

# STAND UP - STAND BACK

 GRACE

I wasn't looking forward to going back to stay with Blaine. The last thing I wanted was to get involved in family business. If Gwendolyn showed up again at the hospital, I was leaving and this time for good.

When I arrived, Blaine was sitting up in bed attempting to eat. I was struck by how poorly he looked. "How's your lunch?"

He made a face. "Ugh. Not good. I'm doing my best. I need to eat to keep up my strength. Army K-rations would even look good compared to this."

"I'll go to the cafeteria and see what they have that looks good." I moved his tray away from the bed before leaving.

I selected a ham and cheese sandwich with chips and a piece of apple pie. When I returned, Blaine had gone to sleep. I tried to determine what was so different. It was his color, which had been a deep tan but now was chalky. His lunch would keep until he woke up, and then, hopefully, he could eat.

I'd brought several Quarter Horse Racing Magazines, which I subscribed to, and for the next two hours I thumbed through them looking at races Lady would've been in had she not been injured. Several horses she'd defeated had won stakes races, making me even more anxious to get her back on the track.

When Blaine woke up, he ate most of his lunch, and I spent the next hour showing him the magazines and encouraging news. He was more alert and anxious to talk about Lady. The subject eventually strayed away from Lady and went to more personal issues. He talked about Drake and how he'd hurt Jimmie Lyn. I noticed that people who'd known her during her lifetime always referred to her as Jimmie Lyn; whereas Luke and I called her Jimmie. It was obvious, listening to him, that she was the most important thing in his life.

It occurred to me that both of us were going to be grandparents in the near future, and I pointed that out to him. He was pleased and was sorry that Gwendolyn didn't feel the same way. She dreaded being called grandmother. I asked him what he was going to be called by his grandson or granddaughter.

"You know, I haven't thought about it. Help me select a name."

"Would you like it to be formal, like Grandpa or Granddad? Maybe you'd like something unique and different."

"Definitely unique. I don't want to be just Granddad or Grandpa."

"What do you think about Boss. It fits you and is different yet easy to say. It could be one of the first words your grandson or granddaughter says."

"Perfect! Boss it will be. Now that's out of the way. What would you like to be called?"

"Gracie. It took me awhile but that's what I settled on."

Later, he asked about Henry and our life together. I told him about my late husband and his dream of owning a great horse. I described our life with it's ups-and-downs at the racetrack. It was the first time I'd been able to talk openly about Henry without becoming emotional.

I moved from Henry to Luke, describing him as a child and later a teenager. "Luke is better but still a long way from the boy who left home and went into the service. Do you think he'll ever return to the way he was before the war?"

"I doubt it, Grace. He's gone through too much to ever be the boy you remember. I expect he'll move toward that but never reach the level of innocence and carefree happiness he once possessed. He's a fine young man, Grace. You have a right to be proud of him. I catch myself comparing him to Drake, and you can imagine how that comes out." He went on to explain his reluctance to accept Drake as being good enough for Jimmie. "I never liked him, from the first time we met. He was too perfect. He needed some kind of flaw to make him genuine. I never bought a horse with perfect conformation. I wanted his head to be too large or better yet that his feet be too big. I love horses with big feet—that's what attracted me to Big Time Boy.

"Now, Lady is a different story. She has great conformation, but when I bought her she had a fractured leg, so she was flawed. Isn't it strange how, as we get older, we come up with all this philosophy? Most horsemen would laugh at me for judging horses the way I do."

We talked until late in the evening, and I learned a great deal about Blaine Waddell. Nothing made me have any less respect for him—in fact the opposite was true.

The longer I stayed with Blaine the more concerned I became. He had trouble keeping food down and slept much of the day. I talked with Jimmie in the morning and evening and expressed my concern to her each time. The third day I was there, the doctor came in. I didn't know whether to leave or stay, but Blaine asked me to remain.

"Blaine, we've decided your problem is not a result of your injury but something else. We'd suspected this for some time. We need to do more tests to locate the source of the bleeding. We're going to put you on a bland diet and see if that helps." The doctor left without further details. I didn't know how Blaine would react.

"He didn't say it, did he? It could be cancer. I'd assumed it was a result of the injury and never considered anything else—now this. My dad and granddad both died of cancer. It's always been a fear." He stared at the wall as if talking to it rather than me.

I just stood there, not knowing what to say. I knew I would need to tell Jimmie. I moved over next to the bed. "I need to call Jimmie and let her know."

He raised his hand to stop me. "Not yet, Grace. Let me think about this awhile. Her knowing will not cause anything but worry. Today's Thursday. She'll be coming tomorrow evening. I'd rather tell her in person."

Within an hour, a nurse appeared with a wheelchair and told him they were going to start the testing. She looked at me. "This is going to take several hours if you have something else to do."

Two hours would allow me plenty of time to visit Angie. She continued to work even though she was six months along. The last time we talked she told me that Evert still wasn't working. It was only three more months, and I'd be holding my grandbaby. And that brought a smile.

I was at the salon in twenty minutes. I was shocked to see how big she'd gotten just within the last several weeks. She had a customer in the chair and didn't see me when I entered. I sat down and watched her. It was difficult for her to move as she cut the lady's hair.

I guess we all have a breaking point and this was mine. I left without her seeing me and drove to her house. I knocked on the door several times before Evert opened it, looking confused. "I need to talk with you, Evert." I didn't wait for an invitation. The room was dark so I flipped the switch. He looked like he'd been asleep, with wrinkled clothes and uncombed hair sticking out in all directions.

"Sure. Is there a problem with Angie? She seemed fine when she left for work."

I sat down, again without an invitation. "Yes, Evert, there is a problem. She's six months pregnant with your child, and she's working. It's obvious that she's miserable and should be home. But you're home while she's having to earn a paycheck, so she can pay the bills. Doesn't that bother you?"

He squirmed uneasily in his chair. "She seems to be okay with it. I haven't been able to find work that suits me."

"Horse sh-manure!" I stopped before it came out, knowing that's what Henry would've said. "You're young and healthy. Get a job! Be a provider! The work doesn't have to suit you. It breaks my heart to see my daughter working while you sit at home doing nothing. You're going to be a father. Assume some responsibility and stop thinking only of yourself.

"You might think I'll leave and that will be the end of it. Wrong! If you don't get a job, I'll be back to tell you what I think, again. The next visit I won't be so nice. Now I'm leaving and the next time I talk with Angie, she'd better tell me you're doing something besides sitting here on your rear." I was out the door before he had a chance to react.

On the drive back to the salon, I tried to calm myself. "Why did I do this?" I asked out loud. The answer came quickly and to the point. You realized that nothing was going to change unless you did something. Waiting around for a situation to get better, without intervention, is useless. It wasn't just the right thing to do—it was the only thing to do in order to take care of my daughter.

This time, when I entered the salon, Angie saw me. She left her customer and came over. We hugged, and I asked her when she took her lunch break.

"After I finish this customer. There's a sandwich shop around the corner."

✳ ✳ ✳

I felt better on my way back to the hospital after lunch with Angie. I'd told her about my talk with Evert, and her response was even better than I expected. She thanked me, saying she was about to give up and leave him. Had it not been for the baby, she'd already have done it. She admitted she couldn't work much longer. In fact, she'd given notice that this was going to be her last week.

She was worried about the doctor bills, since she had no insurance. I assured her that we could help and not to be concerned. When we parted, both of us seemed to feel better, fortified by the love that can only come from family.

When I returned to Blaine's room, he still wasn't back. *That must've been some kind of test,* I thought.

I was thumbing through a magazine when he was wheeled in by the same nurse who came for him. "How was the test?"

He grimaced. "Terrible. They had me drink a gallon of this chalky stuff. Could you get me a soft drink? Surely there's a machine around here. A Pepsi if they have it." He climbed on the bed without assistance.

I left and returned a few minutes later with his Pepsi. "The machine is in the lobby."

"Thanks. Now, a pinch of Skoal would be nice." He sipped his drink.

"Sorry, can't help you there. I'd get in major trouble with the doctor. How long have you been using tobacco?"

"I discovered Skoal Wintergreen Mint when I was a senior in high school. I stayed with it. It was hard to get during the war, and I changed over to chewing tobacco. After the war I went back to Skoal.

"Gwendolyn objected, but I refused to quit. Of course, there were things about her that displeased me. I wanted to move to the ranch. That has always been my dream—to build a nice home and live there in seclusion. She refused to consider it. I wanted her to learn to ride, but she never got on a horse. We had different interests, and the longer we were together the more evident it became."

I felt uncomfortable hearing about his failed marriage, so I moved to another topic. "How long have you owned the auction sale?"

"My dad bought it in the early '30s. When he passed in 1949, I took it over. I'd grown up around it and was familiar with the operation. I purchased the ranch a couple of years later. Everything just worked out. Oil was discovered a year after that, and within five years the ranch was paid for. I love the ranch and hope to eventually turn the Auction over to Jimmie Lyn and spend the rest of my life there."

He seemed to feel better after the test. We talked until I felt it was time for me to leave and allow him to rest.

✻✻✻

The next morning, a Friday, I didn't get to the hospital until nine. Blaine had little to say and his mind seemed far away. "Grace, Jimmie Lyn will be here this afternoon. I dread telling her there's a possibility I have cancer. I don't fear it as much for myself as I do the effect it will have on her. Does that make sense?"

"Sure. You're worried more about Jimmie than you are for yourself. That shows what a good parent you are. Have you eaten breakfast?"

"Not really. They brought me some scrambled eggs that were like rubber and dry toast. I ate a few bites and gave up. What I'd really like is a couple of donuts and some chocolate milk."

I smiled. "That doesn't sound very healthy. I'll see what I can do." I remembered a pastry shop a few blocks from the hospital.

On my way, I said a prayer asking that this kind man received a good report on the test he was given yesterday.

# 39

# A DIFFERENT LUKE

 JIMMIE LYN

With worrying about my dad, the problems on sale day, and then finding Bull seriously injured, I didn't have time to think about Drake.

I was going to see my dad tomorrow afternoon when I could get away from the Auction. The concern in Grace's reports were evident and frightening. I couldn't even think about him not making a full recovery. From what I'd learned, it was an Angus cow that ran over him. They were the most aggressive. Working in the pens, I'd been kicked by them more times than I cared to remember. They just had a bad attitude, especially when riled.

I tried not to think about how Luke would react if Bull died. With all he'd been through, to lose something else he loved would be devastating. And he did love that dog.

I didn't know whether Wednesday was a typical sale day or not. Surely, Dad didn't have to deal with that many problems every week. I did understand why Dad depended so much on Benny, the yard foreman. He'd been at the Auction for so long he was familiar with every inch of it. One of my first memories of the Auction was riding behind him while we moved cattle from one pen to another. I couldn't have been more than three years old.

When I drove up to the Auction Thursday morning, my mom's car was parked in front of the office in a handicapped spot. *How appropriate,*

I thought. She was, at this point in her life, mentally challenged—to put it nicely. I considered turning around and leaving but knew that wasn't possible. I was running a business and had responsibilities. I'd just have to deal with her.

When I entered, Madge rolled her eyes and pointed toward my office. I braced myself and started in that direction.

She was sitting but rose upon seeing me. "You're late. It's already nearly nine o'clock. I wanted to inquire about Blaine since I'm not allowed to see him."

I moved around behind my desk, gathering my response. "Mother, you can see Dad any time you want. Nobody has told you anything different."

She straightened up as if preparing to strike. "Yes, but I'm not welcome since that woman is staying with him."

This was going nowhere. "I'm not going to argue with you, Mother. I'm too busy to spend time trying to change your mind about anything. I'm going to say this one time. I'm concerned about Dad. They don't know what's causing the internal bleeding. Hopefully, in the near future they can locate the source of the problem. You're welcome to visit Dad anytime as long as you don't create a scene. You know what I'm talking about, so it's no use pretending you don't."

She lowered her head, looking pitiful. "I can't believe you're talking to your mother this way. Your sister would never do that."

"So, just when is the last time you talked with my sister?"

"Well, I-I don't exactly remember."

"You can't remember, Mother, because it's been months since she called you." I didn't feel the least bit guilty or ashamed. "Think what you want. I repeat—I'm not going to argue with you. Now, I have a dozen things that need to be done."

She wiped at her eyes. "I'll leave. Nobody cares about me anymore. I may just give up and end it all." She left, without giving me a chance to ask what she meant.

The morning passed quickly. I skipped lunch, anxious to finish and get back to the ranch. I left at five o'clock and stopped at a café to get burgers and fries. When I drove up to the house Luke was coming from the barn carrying a shovel. "Oh no," I muttered. Bull has died, and he's going to bury him. I got out of my car, moving slowly, dreading the news. Luke saw me but didn't stop, leaning the shovel up against the house and going inside.

I reached the house and hesitated, afraid of what I'd find. When I opened the door, I was met with a strong odor. The first thing I saw was Bull sitting up, devouring a can of Spam.

Luke looked up from his seat at the table. "I know. He shouldn't be eating Spam, but he was hungry. This is his second can. We'll just have to deal with the after effects."

Relief flooded me. I went to Luke, bent over and kissed him on the forehead, wiping my eyes on the sleeve of my blouse.

"What was that for?"

"I just felt like it. I brought burgers and fries but forgot to bring them in. Are you hungry?"

"Starved. It's a nice evening. Let's eat outside. Bull can finish his Spam in the house."

"Good idea." We sat in a couple of metal lawn chairs and enjoyed our meal in the fresh air. Luke ate his and finished off my French fries.

"Your appetite is better," I said. "Ranching must agree with you."

"I was worried about Bull. He started improving around lunch today. When you drove up, I was on my way to fill up the hole in the road. We won't be needing it anymore."

It was getting colder, so we put our coats on and stayed outside. I told him about my day, including the episode with my mother. I also revealed the concern about Dad. "Your mother is worried about him. I can tell by the reports that she provides me. I'm going to see him tomorrow afternoon after work. Would you like to go with me? I'm sure your mother will come home for the weekend, and you can ride back with her."

"I won't get through feeding until around four o'clock. Can you wait that long before you leave? I can be at the Auction by four-thirty."

"Sure. That's not a problem." I was surprised and pleased he was going with me.

"It's time for me to be heading back to town. I need to tell Bull good-bye." I found Bull lying on his bed in front of the fire even though it wasn't burning. I reached down and took his head in my hands. "Good-night, Bull. I'm glad you're feeling better."

I stood up, turned around, and was face-to-face with Luke. And then he kissed me—not a long passionate kiss, just a sweet kiss that lasted for two seconds. I must've looked shocked.

He smiled. "I just felt like doing that."

At that instant, I saw a different Luke Ranker. The mischievous smile transformed him into a gorgeous creature who would send any girl's heart racing. I didn't know what to say.

He smiled again. "Have a safe trip back to town. I'll see you around four-thirty tomorrow afternoon."

He walked me to my car, and I managed a, "Bye, see you tomorrow," as I got in to leave.

✳✳✳

When I woke up Friday morning my first thought was it's February fourteenth. I lay there soaked in self-pity. I didn't have a Valentine—no one to present me with candy, flowers, anything. What was Drake doing? Probably visiting his family in Spain. I was out of bed in an instant, regretting even thinking of him. I showered, dressed as quickly as possible, and got out of my apartment.

Friday was actually a calm day. I had an opportunity to exercise my authority in a positive way. Bronc came in and asked if he could get off at noon for a rodeo in Shattuck, Oklahoma. I was glad to grant the request, but afterwards he didn't leave. I knew he had something else to say but seemed to be having a hard time. Finally, he was able to get it out. "Would it be possible for Madge to get off, too? I'd like for her to go with me."

"Of course, Madge can get off. That's no problem."

He left and, for the first time, I realized there were some rewards for sitting in this chair. I was happy for him and Madge. Could it be because of her interest in Luke? Of course not. I had no interest in Luke, romantically anyway. He was younger than me and not tall enough. On the other hand, he did kiss me and was eye level. It really wasn't a kiss—more of a peck. Would I have liked for it to be a real kiss? I quickly put Luke Ranker out of my thoughts.

I met Piper for lunch at a sandwich shop in town. She usually did most of the talking, and today was no exception. She'd been asked to chair a committee for the development of the downtown area and report back to the city council. She'd already begun making plans on how she was going to transform the city.

She stopped talking long enough for me to get in a few words. I began explaining Drake's absence, which I'd kept to myself. There was no reason for it to be a secret now. She actually remained quiet the entire time. I didn't leave out anything, including his wife and child.

"You found out all this information about him when you went to England?" she asked.

Now, I had to tell her the rest of the story. "I didn't go to England. I was at the ranch the entire month."

"What? You lied about going to England?"

I finished telling her about the threats, staying at the ranch with Luke, the abduction attempt, and hiding out in the hills. The longer I spoke, the wider her eyes became, and when I finished her mouth was wide open. For once in her life, she was speechless. "Do you have any questions?"

"I-I don't know w-what to say. You went through all that and didn't tell anyone? Weren't you frightened? Who is this Luke, anyway?"

I went on to describe Luke the best way possible—which wasn't easy. I even included Bull in the story.

"You stayed with this man for a month at the ranch. Did you—you know—did you . . ."

"No. He was strange and didn't want to be there. He didn't even like me. We stayed angry at one another much of the time. We were both glad to get off the ranch and back to town."

"That is so exciting, Jimmie Lyn. Where is Drake now?"

"I don't know and I don't care."

"This makes my life seem so dull. I can't imagine something like this happening in Dalhart. I've got to meet this Luke."

I'd already taken more than my hour for lunch. I asked her not to tell anyone about my ordeal. She continued to ask questions on the way to our cars.

On my drive back to work, I wondered why I'd told her about Drake. Maybe I just wanted her to know that he didn't leave without a reason. Luke was another issue, and I didn't like the way she expressed an interest in him. "Here I go again, thinking Luke belongs to me," I mumbled. He'd only been my protector, and he wasn't even that now. We'd been thrown together by circumstances. However, he did kiss me, if you could call it that. It wasn't the kiss so much as the smile which transformed him into a prince—a younger, shorter-than-me prince.

# 40

# THE KISS

LUKE

Watching her car disappear into the darkness, I wondered about what I'd done. I'd kissed her on impulse. It could be my way of showing appreciation for her helping Bull recover. More likely, I was attracted to her in a way which came suddenly and with surprise. Was it crazy that it took me this long to realize it, after all we'd been through together?

I went back and let Bull out, hoping a potty break might help with his digestive system after two cans of Spam. He moved slowly, still hurting from his wounds. The vet had stitched up the cuts in his neck and throat. He wouldn't have lasted long if I hadn't arrived on the scene. He stayed close to the house, probably remembering the last time he left, chasing the female coyote.

When I let him back in, he gave me that look which said, "I could use another can of that Spam."

"No way, buddy. You've had more than your quota. We're going to bed." I was hoping he'd stay in the living area and out of my room.

I spent a restless night with horrific nightmares of the jungles and rice paddies, culminating with Louis's death. I woke at three o'clock, soaked in sweat, and got up after lying there for half an hour. Something must trigger the dreams, but I had no idea what it was. The last several nights I'd slept pretty good, but now this.

I had to do something. The guilt I was feeling was going to haunt me from now on if it wasn't addressed. I decided then and there to go see his parents. Maybe confessing my mistake would ease my misery.

The few days I'd stayed at the ranch were good with the exception of last night. I stayed away from the pills that caused the accident in Amarillo. I continued to have a couple of drinks occasionally at night. The problem was, after one of these dreams I stayed depressed.

I finished putting out hay in time to bathe and put on clean clothes before meeting Jimmie. On the drive into town, I considered my future for the first time since coming to work at the Auction. I wouldn't be satisfied doing this for years. I needed to be thinking of something permanent with a goal. The first issue would be whether to attend college or not. What good would college do if I didn't have some type of career in mind which required it? It would only be a waste of time and money.

I missed Dad and thought of him often. He would've advised me on a possible career path. It seemed unfair that he died so young without enjoying the success he deserved. Just another example of life being unfair. I'd witnessed it many times in Vietnam and couldn't even begin to understand. I went into the service believing in God and came out doubting if He existed. If He did, why would He allow such needless death and suffering? It made no sense, yet Granddad's faith was strong and unwavering, and I had the utmost respect for him.

I arrived at the Auction on time and found the office empty. Evidently, the boss had let everyone go home early since it was Friday. I met Jimmie in the hall coming out of her office.

She smiled, and it struck me how attractive she was. Her hair was up in a bun, and she was wearing a dark pant suit. "You're on time."

"Yeah, the service will do that to you." When she was close, I reached and pulled her into my arms, hugging her. She didn't resist. "You look good. Of course, Bull is all I have to compare you with."

She shoved me back. "And I thought you were going to say something nice to me. I should've known better." She giggled.

"You ready to go?" I asked.

"Yes. As soon as I lock up. The night watchman doesn't come in until six."

✳✳✳

An hour and a half later we were at the hospital. She'd been unusually quiet, and I discovered why as we were walking from the car. "I'm worried. I can tell your mother is concerned when talking with her. I've had a bad feeling all day about what we're going to find out about Dad."

We reached the room, she knocked briefly and opened the door. We received a warm greeting from both Blaine and Mom. Jimmie went right to the point. "Have you found out anything?" She looked first at her dad and when he didn't answer then my mom. "All right, let's hear it."

Blaine smiled, in an attempt to portray optimism. "They don't believe my problem is a result of the injury. They did more tests, and we should have the results soon."

"What kind of tests?" she asked softly.

"I had to drink this awful stuff. I guess it has to do with my stomach." Another weak smile. "It's probably nothing."

Jimmie had told me that her granddad died of cancer and Blaine had always harbored that fear. Mom quickly changed the subject to Lady. For the next hour we kept the topic away from Blaine's illness, but the concern in Jimmie's eyes never left.

A knock at the door interrupted us. I saw the terror in Jimmie's eyes when the doctor came into the room. No doubt she was anticipating bad news. I moved closer to her, slipping my hand in hers.

"We have finally located the source of your problem. It's not the best of news, but it could be worse. You have a growth on your intestine. It's going to take surgery to determine if it's malignant. I know that's disappointing news, but even if it is malignant the treatments have improved to the point that a chance of recovery is good."

Jimmie let go of my hand and grabbed my arm, choking back a sob. I could see the fear in Blaine's eyes.

"When would you do the surgery?" he asked.

"As soon as possible. I'll need to look at our schedule. Do you have any more questions?"

The doctor left. Blaine attempted some humor. "We need to thank that ole hussy who run me down. Else they might not have discovered the problem. All right, let's lose the long faces. Jimmie Lyn, it looks like you're going to be the boss for a while." His gaze shifted to me. "Luke, I know you'll be there to have her back."

Mom and I stayed another hour, mostly engaging in small talk and staying away from the dreaded topic. When we left, Jimmie followed us out.

Mom hugged her, saying, "Jimmie, we'll continue to pray for your dad." She turned to me. "Luke, I'll wait on you at the car."

The second she turned to leave Jimmie was in my arms, sobbing. I held her for several minutes until she quieted. "He'll get through this. He's a strong man, and you have to be strong also."

She clung to me again before stepping back. "Promise me you'll be there when I need you."

"I give you my word." After another hug, I left.

✵ ✵ ✵

On the ride back to Dalhart with Mom, we talked about Blaine's diagnosis and the challenge that Jimmie faced. I reminded Mom of Blaine's feelings for her and that her support would mean a lot to him.

"I know, Luke. I like Blaine and it won't be hard to do. He's a good man—one of the best I've ever known."

I think the emotion of the evening caused me to talk of my problems.

I told Mom about my decision to visit Louis's parents in Louisiana. For the first time, I told her about my guilt because of his death after allowing him to take the point.

"I believe you're doing the right thing in visiting his parents. Tell me about this young man, Luke. Evidently, he was special to you, but you've never mentioned him before."

"Mom, he was so much fun. He kept correcting us when we called him Louis, insisting it was Loo-ee. None of us had ever been around anyone from South Louisiana. He was Cajun all the way. At first, we couldn't understand what he was saying. It was almost like he wasn't speaking English, with the Cajun dialect. When we did finally understand him, he told stories about catching big fish and wrestling alligators. He described relatives and was always telling us about the food his momma cooked. He would keep us entertained for hours with his tales, which were probably just that. The rest of the men loved him. He was like our mascot.

"He grew up hunting and was the best marksman in the platoon. I've spent hours thinking about why I gave in to him. He so much wanted to be like everyone else and do his share. I guess giving in was a result of wanting to please him. But it could've been just to stop his constant begging. I don't know, Mom. What I do know is that it cost him his life and his parents their son."

She moved to a more positive conversation. "I'm going to start Lady in about three weeks. I'll ride her slowly before even trotting her. It's exciting, thinking about her being able to resume racing.

"Luke, what about Jimmie? I know you like her. Is there anymore to the relationship? It's obvious that she depends on you. She started wanting you immediately when Blaine was injured. I saw her clinging to you when the doctor was talking. It was almost like a child wanting their mother when hurting."

How could I explain it to Mom without understanding it myself? "I don't know. We've been through so much in the last several months. We stay mad at one another at least half the time. It seems as if we've been together for years. It's a strange relationship, to say the least. She helped me nurse Bull back from the brink of death, staying up most of the night. If not for her, he might've died. I'll admit that lately I've found her attractive, which is strange.

"She's going with me to Louisiana. For some reason, I need her to go and might not consider it otherwise.

"Time about is fair play. Tell me about Blaine, and your feelings toward him. It's evident that he's more than interested in you. That's been obvious for some time."

"Oh, Luke. I loved your daddy and still do. I think of him often and have only recently been able to relive some of the memories without losing it. I'm not ready for another relationship and may never be. Blaine has been wonderful to us. I dread the day when it becomes necessary to tell him my feelings. I know it will come, but hopefully not for a long time. Does Jimmie know about this?"

"Of course. Anyone that was around him when you're present would be aware of it. He doesn't hide it well. He's too honest. I want you to know that whatever you decide will be fine with me. I miss Dad terribly, however, he would be the first to insist that you be happy, whatever it takes." I'd been wanting to have this conversation with Mom. It was important that she knew how I felt.

"Back to the subject of Lady. Are you sure you're up to the task of riding her? Remember what happened the last time you exercised a horse?"

She laughed. "I'm older and wiser now, Luke. I'll be careful and go slow—I mean slow. Wouldn't it be something if she was able to come back sound? If she does, I'm going to the track with her. I won't trust anyone else."

"When do you see all this taking place?" I asked.

"I'm shooting for the middle of June. That would give us two months to be ready for the Derby. I'm almost afraid to think it will happen."

If anyone deserved to have a dream fulfilled, it was Mom.

✳✳✳

I returned to the ranch Friday night to check on Bull. He was glad to see me and anxious to get outside. I couldn't believe he'd held it for that long, but I didn't see or smell any evidence to the contrary.

The next two days, Saturday and Sunday, were beautiful as if spring had arrived. I felt better than I had in a long time. I think my decision to visit Louis's parents had something to do with it.

Jimmie came out late Sunday evening, bringing a home cooked meal including a chocolate pie. It was actually very good, and I told her so.

"Wow, a compliment. That makes the cooking worthwhile. I'll admit it does beat the Vienna sausage and crackers.

"Dad is having surgery tomorrow. I've prayed until God is probably tired of listening to me. I can't imagine life without my dad.

"I won't be able to make the Louisiana trip for some time. There's no way to know when Dad will be able to come back to work. It frightens me to think about running the Auction."

I couldn't help staring at her. Her hair was up, which I liked. She was wearing jeans and a pull-over sweater that did nothing to hide her shape.

She caught me. "Why're you looking at me like that?"

Surprised, I didn't know what to say. Maybe I could get by with denying it. "I didn't realize it."

"It's not the first time. At Red River when I came in from the hot tub, you stared at me. Are you going to deny that, too?"

"Well, I-I don't remember."

She smiled. "You're blushing. I can't believe it!"

I was humiliated and embarrassed. She was making fun of me. "Is that how Drake looked at you?" I asked angrily.

She rose. "It's time for me to leave. Since I cooked, you can wash the dishes." She started for the door but turned. "You can be a mean person, Luke Ranker."

And just like that she was gone. I sat there for about fifteen seconds before going after her. She was already in the car when I motioned her to roll the window down. She complied, and I could see the tears. I bent down, reached through the window, put my hand behind her neck and pulled her to me. I kissed her long and deep. I felt her relax and lean into me.

"You're right. I was looking at you. You look good—better than good. Now, be careful going home." I backed away and as she left, her car weaved and went off the road into the shallow ditch. She corrected it and disappeared into the night.

# 41

## WHO'S IN CHARGE

JIMMIE LYN

I straightened my car and was out of the ditch instantly. I hoped he didn't see it. My breath seemed to be hung in my throat. Maybe I was having a heart attack! No, surely I was too young for that. I reached the gate and stopped, got out, and inhaled. I leaned back against my car and thought, *I'll soon be twenty-four and have never been kissed like that.* It was rough, demanding, you don't have a choice—like I wanted a choice. I'd always heard of something taking your breath away but never figured it would be like that.

***

I was at the hospital the next morning at eight. Dad surprised me, asking me how Luke was doing. Instinctively, I blushed. "Good. I took supper out last night. Bull is still sore but is going to be okay."

"I like Luke. I hope he stays with us. What do you think?"

What was going on? Did he have some kind of intuition? "I hope he stays also. Grace will probably take Lady to the track this summer. Luke may want to go with her."

"I've had a lot of time to think, lying in a hospital bed the last two weeks, and especially after the news last night. I'd like to spend more time at the ranch. That would put more responsibility on you at the Auction.

I've seen how you depend on Luke. I was thinking that maybe he would be around to help—you know if something unexpected came up."

I could see where this was heading. "What about Benny? He knows more than Luke will ever know about the Auction."

"Right. But Benny is good where he is. We couldn't replace him, and he enjoys his job. I believe that Luke would be the one to help you."

"Dad, we've only known Luke a few months. Why him?" I was anxious to hear his response.

He cleared his throat. "I trust Luke. It didn't take me long to see what kind of a person he is. Besides, he likes you. I've watched the two of you together." He shifted around in the bed. "Isn't there a cup or something in here. I need a dip. I've been hiding a box of Skoal." He reached under the bed and brought it out, tapping it on his other hand.

"Dad! You're about to have surgery. You don't need any tobacco in your system."

"Hand me that Coke can over there. My system will do better with a little tobacco in it."

I gave him the can. He opened the box and took out a pinch. Maybe the questions would cease if he had tobacco in his mouth. I wasn't surprised about his wanting to spend more time at the ranch. I didn't know whether or not the Auction could run without him. It certainly couldn't operate as effectively with me in charge. Evidently the tobacco worked. He was silent until they came to get him. Thank goodness he'd gotten rid of the tobacco just before they arrived. As they wheeled him out, I kissed him on the forehead and said, "I love you."

I settled down in a chair to wait. The doctor told us the surgery would take at least two hours. I prayed again for a negative result for the cancer and a full recovery. In a panic mode, I thought of having to run the Auction for a long time. I didn't consider myself *boss* material, and the thought of having to make major decisions frightened me to no end.

A knock at the door and my mother came in. Great, I thought. What could be worse than waiting two hours with my mother? I was punished for asking such an ugly question with the answer—spending three hours with my mother. First, she was upset because she wasn't notified immediately of the surgery. She didn't find out until church yesterday when he was on the prayer list. Of course, she was embarrassed and let me know, in detail, how it made her feel. From there she spent an hour criticizing Sterling, raising the question in my mind of how one man could have so many faults. I finally did the best I could to tune her out. It had to be the longest three hours of my life.

The doctor finally appeared and gave us a report. "Blaine did well. He's in recovery and will be there for a couple of hours before he's moved back to his room. It'll be several days before we receive the results. The surgery took longer than expected but went well. Do you have any questions?"

He shouldn't have asked. My mother had a deluge of questions, most of which were unnecessary, but she had a captive audience for a while anyway. The doctor finally looked at me. "Do you have any questions?" I shook my head and he left the room with my mother still talking.

"Well, that was rude," she said. "I wasn't finished."

***

Dad ordered me to go home early Tuesday morning, saying I needed to be at the Auction to get ready for the Wednesday sale. He was doing well and was already complaining about having to remain in the hospital all week. Praise the Lord, my mother had left Monday evening.

All during the day Tuesday, people kept coming in the office asking about Dad. I had to tell the story of his surgery at least a dozen times. It just showed how much his friends and employees thought of him.

***

The Auction has a café that serves burgers, sandwiches, and a lunch special on sale day. I invited Piper to have lunch on Wednesday. It wasn't the greatest place to eat, but I didn't want to leave to eat in town.

She came to my office, and we were on the way to the café when we rounded a corner and came face-to-face with Luke. "I came in to have lunch with you and get a report on your dad." His gaze shifted to Piper.

"Luke, this is my friend, Piper."

She smiled, extending her hand. "So . . . this is Luke. No wonder you've been hiding him, Jimmie Lyn." She held on to his hand longer than necessary.

"I'm having lunch with Piper. We shouldn't be long. Just wait on me in my office. I talked to Dad this morning, and he's doing well. I'll give you a full report later." I should've known that wouldn't work.

"Oh, no, Jimmie Lyn. He can join us. I insist." She reached out and touched him on the arm, looking at him like Bull salivating over a can of Spam.

I could've broken her arm without an ounce of guilt. Until now I'd paid little attention to the way she was dressed. I should've known, since she was coming to a place where there were men, she'd look like a walking invitation.

Luke smiled. Naturally, he would smile. "I'm sorry for interrupting. I want to watch some of the sale. I'll give you plenty of time to eat with your friend—then come by your office."

I could've thrown him to the floor and kissed him right there. "Great. If anything comes through the ring that might fit on the ranch—buy it for us." I was heavy on the us.

Then, of all things to do—he reached and kissed me on the cheek before turning and leaving—not even saying a farewell or glad to meet you to Piper, who looked like she'd just been slapped away from the table.

"Let's eat, I'm starved." I walked through the doorway, not able to contain my smile.

We went through a line, getting sandwiches and a soft drink. Piper recovered quickly with the stares she was receiving from the diners, who were all male.

She started in on Luke when we sat down. "I had no idea he'd look like that, Jimmie Lyn. Are you going to marry him? He's—I don't know a word to describe him. Maybe heavenly would fit." She rolled her eyes and breathed deeply.

I was smug. For one time since we'd become friends, a man paid attention to me. Of course, she saw Luke at his best and not with those dark eyes staring holes through you. The subject throughout the meal seldom strayed from Luke Ranker with her doing most of the talking. I was anxious to return to my office and, immediately after finishing my sandwich, told her I needed to get back to work.

"You mean back to him, don't you?"

I was enjoying this immensely. "Oh, I don't know. He's unpredictable. He may already be gone back to the ranch." I lied without hesitation.

"Yeah, sure. I saw the way he looked at you." She left with many eyes following her to the door.

I found Luke sitting on the top row of bleachers watching cattle sell in the ring. He looked up when I tapped him on the shoulder. "Sit down. You shouldn't have told me I could buy something for the ranch. I've already bought three heifers that are bred. I charged them to you."

After settling in beside him, I put my hand on his leg and squeezed. "Thank you."

He looked at me and smiled—heavenly. "You have strange friends." He turned his attention back to the sale ring and bid on a young cow and calf.

I rose and left, thinking, *he can buy whatever he wants.* I went back to my office, and found we had over 800 head today. Not bad; of course, twice that many would've been better. We received a commission for each head that went through the ring, so the more cattle we sold the better our financial sheet looked. I do remember having as many as 3,000 and the sale lasting for twenty-four hours.

Luke came by before going back to the ranch, and I gave him an update on my dad. He didn't stay long, saying he had to hook on to a trailer and take the five head we'd bought to the ranch. I thanked him again for his reaction to Piper.

***

I was at the hospital early Thursday morning, hoping the doctor would have test results. I assumed Dad was feeling all right since he was complaining about the food.

"When Grace was staying with me, she brought me donuts and chocolate milk for breakfast."

"That wasn't good for you. Eat your oatmeal and dry toast." Little wonder that he liked Grace to stay with him.

"Did everything go okay at the sale yesterday?" he asked. "How many head did Harold catch?"

I made a zero out of my thumb and index finger.

"That's great. How did he manage that?"

I made another zero. "That's how many cattle he started yesterday."

"Was he sick?"

"Nope. He said he wasn't coming back until you did. He caught thirty head last week before we were halfway through selling. I took him out of his chair and had Dewayne start cattle, as well as auctioneer. Harold didn't like to be told what to do by a woman. When you come back to work y'all can work it out."

Dad laughed like no sick man should. "No, we won't work anything out. He's gone. He should've respected the boss. If we owe him any wages send them to him with a note that we won't need his services any longer."

The doctor came in while Dad was still chuckling. "What's so funny?

I seldom have patients that're having such a good time."

"Meet the boss. I'm proud of her, Doc."

"I've met her and if I had a boss as pretty as her, I'd do anything she asked." He turned back to my dad. "I have some results for you. The growth was malignant, but we are confident that we removed all of it. Just to be on the safe side, you need to take some radiation and chemo treatments. You should be able to go home the first of next week after your initial treatment. You'll need to come back once a week."

"When can I go back to work?" Dad asked.

"You're not going to feel like working during the treatments. I'd say it will be at least six weeks and probably eight. These treatments are important, Blaine. I'm optimistic about the surgery, but you can't be too careful."

After the doctor had left, Dad sank down into the bed and looked ten years older. "Well, that's the way it goes, I guess."

I left, then came back with two donuts and a pint of chocolate milk.

# 42

## FIRST RIDE

 GRACE

It was Thursday, February twentieth, and Lady was about to have her first passenger since her injury. I brushed her before putting the light blanket on. The saddle Luke had found in the auction tack room had to be adjusted but that was already done. I lifted and placed it on her back, and she didn't move. "You're going to be ridden today, pretty lady—not fast but slow. What do you think about that?"

I didn't pull the front cinch tight and had taken off the back cinch. The stock saddle was light and hadn't been used in years. The night before, a coat of olive oil had softened it up. We'd always used it rather than the more expensive saddle oils sold in stores since it worked just as well. She accepted the racing bit without fighting me. I led her out to an area a couple of hundred yards from the barn where the ground was soft.

After tightening the cinch, she stood still as my foot found the stirrup, and I was in the saddle. We didn't move for several minutes and then started off at a walk. She was quiet and calm, not dancing sideways as most racehorses that haven't been ridden in months. There'd never been anything like her, and the thought that she might've been destroyed frightened me.

I rode her for an hour, never getting out of a walk, after which I groomed her before putting out feed. It was one of those days that made you think winter is over. However, the weather report was calling for a drastic change Sunday with snow and freezing temperatures. The long-sleeved shirt was comfortable with the temperature around sixty degrees. I sat down on a five-gallon bucket and watched her eat, dreading going back inside.

The New Mexico Derby was still six months away. One thing for sure—I was going to have to be more aggressive. I did nothing when they took Big Boy down at Albuquerque last year. I should've lodged a complaint with the New Mexico Racing Commission. At least it would've gotten their attention. Lying down and letting them run over me was going to stop. I owed it to Blaine and any other owner that was daring enough to allow a woman to train their horse.

While I was still at her pen, Jimmie drove up. I went over to her car and she asked me to get in. I could tell she was upset.

"It was malignant, Grace. The doctor was optimistic, but Dad's going to need chemo treatments and radiation. It would be six weeks at least before he could return to work."

My heart went out to her. "I'll do anything I can to help. I'm so sorry."

"I'm going to need you, Grace. I can't run the Auction and take care of Dad without help. The doctor talked with me without my dad present and explained that he would be sick from the treatments."

"Certainly, I'll be available whenever you need me."

"Words can't express how much I appreciate that, Grace. We're going to have to endure some difficult times. I'm afraid it's going to begin Sunday with the winter storm hitting us."

The spring-like weather continued, and it was hard to believe it would be freezing again on Sunday. I rode Lady the next day after work. I was tempted to trot her but refrained, remembering my promise to walk her the first two weeks. She'd actually grown and gained weight since her injury.

I thought about returning to the track this summer and wondered if

I should insist on Luke going with me. No, I thought, Luke was doing well; he's making progress. I doubted if my dad would accompany me either. He was happy, and since the weather warmed up, was working again even though that would change in a few days. More than likely, I was going to face the challenge of working in a man's world alone.

✳✳✳

Saturday morning, I decided to go see Angie, hoping to discover that Evert had a job. I would visit Blaine afterward. I left after breakfast and was in Amarillo by nine. I arrived at Angie's and knocked. It was several minutes before she opened the door. I could tell right away that she'd been crying. She hugged me before saying a word. "He's gone, Mother. He left yesterday, saying he wouldn't be back. I don't know what to do." She started crying and couldn't talk.

I kept my arms around her. "Angie, Angie. We'll make it. You have me, your granddad, and Luke to help. It might be for the best that he's gone." I thought of the tongue-lashing he'd received from me. Was I the reason he'd left? What if I was? It had to be done or nothing was going to change.

I stayed with her until late afternoon, telling her over and over we'd be there for her. She gradually accepted my assurance and perked up somewhat. I tried to get her to go back to Dalhart with me, but she refused. I gave her a check for $200 to cover her expenses for the next month and left, thankful to be able to help her.

I went directly to the hospital from there, and Blaine was sitting up in a chair when I entered. "Grace. I'm glad to see you. How're you doing?"

"I'm fine. I should be asking you that question."

He was sitting in the only chair and motioned for me to sit on the bed. "I guess you've heard the news. To be truthful, I'm scared, Grace. I wouldn't tell anyone that but you. It's not the first time. I was terrified when we landed on the beaches at Normandy. However, this is a different kind of fear. Twenty-five years ago it was the fear of instant death. Today it's the fear of something which causes suffering and hardships on family and friends. I watched my dad wither away slowly with this horrible disease and suffered with him."

I wanted so badly to say something that would encourage him. "There's nothing wrong with being afraid. We all have our fears. You're going to get well and return to work. Remember you have a grandson or granddaughter on the way who's going to call you 'Boss.' Don't forget this beautiful filly, whose life you saved. I'm moving my timeline up and hope to be in Ruidoso when it opens the middle of May."

I thought sharing information about my daughter might take his mind off his concerns. I told him about Angie, and finding out today that Evert had left, which I believed was for the good.

"Would she move in with you? That way you could look after her, at least until the baby comes. I understand we're going to have some terrible weather beginning tomorrow. She doesn't need to be alone."

"I offered, but she refused. It would've made things much simpler. I worry about her staying by herself. The baby is due in less than three months."

"Tell you what, Grace. Go back by her house on the way home and ask again. Tell her it would make your life easier. I imagine she thought staying with you would be an imposition. She doesn't need to stay by herself with only three months remaining, especially with this storm coming. Anything could happen."

"I'm going to do that. If I present it that way, it just might work." I imagined he was right. She refused, thinking it'd be a hardship on me.

"You know, Grace, some good things are happening. Jimmie Lyn has really stepped up at the Auction. She's made some decisions that took courage, and they were good for the business. I'm proud of her. If not for me being run over and ending up here, she might never have had the opportunity. She has gained some confidence and hopefully that will continue.

"She depends on Luke and that's not a bad thing. If anything happens to me, he'd be there for her. I'm so thankful that Drake is out of her life. I'm talking too much—tell me about your plans for Ruidoso."

"I moved up my timeline because Lady's doing so well. I'm going to give her a test in early May. And if it works out, we're going to the track. I'll still take her slow and probably not enter her until the first of July. I want to make sure she's fit. It's almost unbelievable that she's done so well.

"I'd like to pick up a few more horses, but it'll be difficult. Most owners won't trust a woman trainer. Of course, I'll take Big Boy. He should be good for one more year, and I'll take my two horses."

Before I could continue, there was a knock and Jimmie came in. "How's the patient today?" She hugged him.

"We're making plans for this summer. How's everything at the Auction?"

She frowned and shook her head—problems. "The feed truck broke down again. We had it towed in, and I went back this morning to see what the problem was. I didn't understand much of what he described except the bill to repair it was going to be $1,200. What should I do? We have a storm coming tomorrow, and we need a truck. Do you want me to buy a new one?"

"Honey, I'm not the boss. At the moment I'm laid up in a hospital bed. It's your decision. You'll make the right choice."

I knew it was time for me to leave and let father and daughter work this out. I asked if they needed anything and I left. Blaine's idea about Angie was a good one, and I went back to her house and presented the move to Dalhart in a totally different manner—as something that would help me.

She wasn't difficult to convince, and an hour later we left after loading her clothes and some personal items. I felt good about her coming with me. It would take a load of worry off me.

We stopped in Dalhart at the grocery store and bought a week's worth of food, in case we couldn't get into town for several days

✳✳✳

I went to church Sunday, beginning with my 9:30 class, which I always looked forward to. When my teacher asked for a prayer list, I put Blaine on it. All the members of the class knew Blaine, and I had to give them details of his diagnosis and future treatment.

I always left the class feeling good—like I was part of a church family. Our teacher was knowledgeable and gave everyone the opportunity to become involved in the discussion. The pastor preached on weathering the storm in times of great difficulty. When I left church the black cloud in the north seemed to give credence to his message.

# 43

# NIGHTMARE
# FROM THE PAST

 JIMMIE LYN

When I returned from the hospital Saturday, I stopped at the car dealership in Dalhart and bought a new Ford heavy duty flatbed truck. They agreed to have it ready and delivered by noon the next day. They usually closed on Sunday, but with the storm coming they made an exception.

I went to my apartment, then planned to go see Luke at the ranch. I was changing clothes when the doorbell rang. I groaned, thinking that will be my mother, so I let it ring several times before heading in that direction.

I opened the door and froze—Drake! I slammed the door, turning away and leaning my back against it, as if to shut out what I'd seen. I wasn't prepared and had been able to put him out of my mind for the last month. I'd forgotten the rehearsed speech I'd spent hours preparing for him in the event he returned.

"Jimmie. I need to speak with you—please. I can explain. I beg you to open the door so we can talk."

I pushed harder against the door. Maybe he'd go away if I didn't answer. Why'd he come back? It'd been almost three months since the trial ended.

This time he knocked. "You have to hear me out, Jimmie. I didn't know this would happen to us. I promise—I didn't know. You need to let me explain. You owe that to me."

His last sentence caused me to explode. "I owe you nothing! Go away! I want nothing to do with you, ever!"

Silence followed my outburst. I continued to lean against the door for several minutes before going over and sitting down on the couch. I stayed there for at least half an hour. He must've left, I thought. I went to the door and opened it halfway. He was still standing there. I shut the door quickly but not soon enough to keep his foot from blocking it. I backed away as he came in.

"You have to listen to me. I'm not leaving until you sit down and listen to me. If you'll do that, I'll leave when I'm finished."

I wasn't going to have a choice. I sat down on the couch giving him the evilest look possible.

He pulled several pages out of his sport's jacket pocket. "This is the divorce papers that were being processed before I left the states for England. They're final now. I didn't tell you because I was afraid you wouldn't marry me.

"Being detained in England was the last thing I imagined. It was supposed to be a week's trip and I'd be back here. I never thought these men would've resorted to violence to keep me from testifying. I knew them, worked with them, and just didn't think about them being violent. I'll admit it was a mistake and naive. Thank God, I didn't take you with me since you were safe over here."

I let him continue, which he did non-stop for half an hour, insisting at least a dozen times that he loved me. He'd received a large amount of reward money for breaking up the criminal activity of the law firm and he wanted to be married immediately, leaving on an extended honeymoon in the Caribbean. He said that he was a hero to law enforcement and had been offered a high-level job, which he refused in order to come back.

"I know it was hard on you, Jimmie. I'm sorry for that, but it couldn't be helped. I thought about you every minute I was gone."

I broke my silence. "Why did it take you three months after the trial to return?"

He smiled, evidently because I'd joined the conversation. "I was in grave danger. Law enforcement insisted I stay under protection until the men started serving their prison sentences. If not for them, I would've returned immediately. I want to get on with my life, Jimmie. You're the most important thing in the world to me."

"You humiliated me. People were laughing at me, and I suffered. Why should I believe anything you say now?"

"I never lied to you. Just think about what information you received. I was in Europe for five years working at a law firm. I did insist on coming back to the states. I didn't ever tell you I hadn't been married. I was getting a divorce—it just wasn't final. I was over there doing something good for society. I shouldn't be punished for that."

The longer he talked the more confused I became. Every time I came up with a question—he had an answer for it.

He commenced to plead his case again, going into detail about the undercover work and sacrifices he'd made to bring these criminals to justice. Every few minutes he would repeat how much he missed and loved me, adding that he wanted us to get married immediately.

While he talked, I thought of the respect which I would regain when people found out why he'd left. A hero who'd left to go undercover and break up criminal activity was forced to return to England and testify in order to put the villains in prison. Those people who laughed at me behind my back would be ashamed of their conduct. I heard little of what he was saying, but it didn't matter since he was repeating himself.

He stood, and I was struck again by how tall he was. "I guess that's all. Please think about what I've said. I'd like to come back tomorrow."

"I don't know."

"Please, Jimmie. Think about what I've said and just give me a chance. If I come back and you want me to leave, I will immediately."

I got up and he towered over me. "Okay. I guess it won't hurt anything for you to come back tomorrow."

"Great." He stepped toward me and I held up my hand to stop him. "Fine, I understand. I'll see you tomorrow."

After he left, I went to my bedroom closet and took my wedding dress down, holding it up against me, as I looked into the mirror. It was beautiful. I didn't expect it to be like this. Was I really considering accepting Drake Davis back into my life after what he'd put me through? Three hours ago the answer would've been a resounding "No." Now, here I was, holding my wedding dress. I must be crazy to even consider marrying him, but that was exactly what was happening.

What did he say that made me change my mind? He was a lawyer making a case for the defense. I had no one to represent me as the victim. I was no match for his arguments since he shot down every one of them— maybe with lies.

I sat down on the edge of my bed, holding the dress in my lap. I needed to talk with Piper. I went to my phone in the kitchen and called her. She picked up immediately as if expecting me. I asked her if she could come over—that it was important. She must've dropped everything because she was coming in the door five minutes later.

"What is it, Jimmie Lyn?" She looked frightened.

"Drake's back. I need to talk."

She exhaled deeply. "I thought something had happened to your dad. You scared me. Do you have anything to drink while we hash over your problem?"

"How about a margarita?"

"How about a pitcher of margaritas? We're probably going to need them."

While mixing the drinks, I poured out my story to her. Of course, I didn't finish until we were on our second drink. Piper usually wasn't a good listener, but tonight was an exception. I had to stop completely before she said anything.

"You told me several times that you hated him and hoped never to see him again. It sounds like you've changed your mind. Are you trying to get me to say 'take him back and marry him?'"

I drained my glass. "I don't know, Piper. I'll be twenty-four next month, and he's begging me to marry him."

"What about Luke?"

I'd tried not to think about Luke. "He's unpredictable. There's no way of knowing what he'll do. He's over two years younger and probably shorter than me if I stand up straight." I immediately felt stupid for mentioning his age and height.

"What else is wrong with Luke besides his age and height? I mean—that's not very important if you love him."

"I'm a little bit afraid of Luke, sometimes. He has this look—you'd have to see it to understand. Violence doesn't appear to bother him in the least. I saw him kill two men without hesitating."

"You told me about that. What would've happened if he had hesitated?"

I should've seen this coming. I wasn't thinking clearly. "I might've been killed."

"At this moment, my dear friend, you aren't even thinking rationally. You'd better get hold of yourself before you make a huge mistake. My advice is not to do anything now. Just let Drake wonder. See how he reacts. Spend more time with Luke. If I were you, it'd be an easy decision."

The margaritas had begun to take effect. "You're right, of course. I'm confused and angry at myself for listening to Drake. I thought he was my dream guy, and we'd live happily ever after. Then he left, and now he's back again igniting that dream.

"Thank you for coming over and for being such a good friend. You'd better get home. Daniel will be worried about you."

"Are you kidding. He had a long day at the office and is probably already asleep." She paused and smiled. "Marrying a younger man might have some advantages."

She left. The drinks had made me relaxed and sleepy. I went to bed early but was wide awake at midnight. I lay there for an hour going over Drake's visit and Piper's reaction. I'd wanted her to tell me to give him another chance, but that didn't happen. Her advice was probably good—not to do anything and let Drake wonder. What if he gave up and left the country again? I'd return to old-maid status and people would still be laughing at me.

I finally gave up going back to sleep and finished reading <u>Dr. Zhivago</u>, which ended poorly and depressed me further, convincing me that love never worked out the way it was supposed to.

✷✷✷

I headed to the ranch by noon the next day. I'd taken my dad's Cherokee to ensure I could get back if the storm caught me. I was trying to decide if confiding in Luke would help, but as I drove up to the house, I still hadn't come to any conclusion. I wore my work clothes, intending to help him feed, hoping some physical work would make me think clearly.

He was already at the barn loading hay and, as I walked up, he stopped. "Good afternoon. You ready to go to work? I could use some help. A storm's coming."

"Sure. That was my plan. I'll stack if you'll throw me the hay." He didn't even ask me why I didn't come out last night. Why should I expect him to? He had his dog.

For the next two hours we finished loading and putting out hay for the cattle. Back at the house, I asked him if he'd driven the calves out of the wheat field into the pasture."

"No. Why should I?"

"They'll need shelter, at least whatever they can find. They might not survive out in the open. I'll help you move the calves."

I could tell he didn't like me telling him what to do. "I can do that by myself. Besides these weather people always exaggerate."

"Maybe they are exaggerating. But if they're not, you've never been in a storm like this." I immediately saw that stubborn look.

"I'm going to eat lunch before I do anything else. The calves can wait. It shouldn't be that bad anyway, until later tonight. You want something to eat?"

"No. I'm really not that hungry. You go ahead, though. I can take Bull for a walk while you eat." Luke had gained weight, but I couldn't help but notice how short he was compared to Drake.

"He'll like that. Don't let him go running off after any females. That always get's you in trouble."

I didn't have to ask Bull but once if he wanted to go for a walk. He was right under me when we went out the door. I couldn't believe the weather for February. Having shed my coat, it was comfortable. Looking in the north, though, the warning signs were visible. We started back up the road toward the gate since I didn't trust him in the wooded areas close to the hills. What did Luke mean when he said, "Running after females always gets you in trouble?" Was he talking about himself or Bull?

Occasionally, Bull would bump up against me and smile as if saying, "This is the best part of my day—being with you." Why couldn't his owner smile at me like that. In Luke Ranker's mind, I was no part of his future. We walked toward the gate and was back at the house an hour later.

Luke molded into one of those ancient curvy metal chairs and asked, "Have a nice walk?"

"Yeah. It's a beautiful day but that's about to change. I've grown to love this ranch. The wide-open spaces and the big sky gives me a spiritual feeling—tells me there is something much bigger than myself out there."

"You've got something on your mind. I've spent enough time with you to know that." He leaned forward in his chair with that mischievous look.

I lied. "My dad won't be back at work for weeks. Do you still want to visit the people in Louisiana?"

"I'm doing better, Jimmie. I like living out here and working hard. However, the thoughts and dreams still come too often. It always depresses me when they do. The answer to your question is 'Yes.' I've waited this long. I can wait several more weeks until your dad is able to return to work."

I might as well ask him. "Is that where we are, Luke—you're my protector and I'm your helper?"

For one of the only times since I'd known him, he looked confused. "I don't understand. What do you mean?"

I started this and might as well finish it. "The way you kissed me the other night made me think it might be more than that. Remember?"

He presented that heavenly smile with those brown eyes sparkling. "That was nice, wasn't it?"

"I don't know. Was it nice for you?" Maybe this was going somewhere.

"Yeah. First girl I kissed like that in a long time—maybe ever."

There it was. "Luke, I'm not a girl! I'll be twenty-four years old next month." Maybe that would wake him up.

"I'm still confused. You're becoming angry, and I don't understand."

Well, here goes. "Drake's back. He wants to marry me."

The transformation occurred immediately. His eyes turned black.

# 44

# RENEWED FAITH

 LUKE

I had little to say to her after she told me Drake was back. I told her she could go back to town, but she said I needed help moving the calves. "You don't have a horse so we can use the Cherokee to drive them out. Don't argue with me."

It looked like I didn't have a choice. It was about two miles to the wheat field. When we got there, I noticed at least two dozen deer grazing at the far end of the field. That's strange, I thought, it was mid-afternoon and they usually didn't come out until sundown.

Herding the calves toward the gate in the Jeep was not easy. I have to admit, Jimmie was a big help, and without her it would've been difficult if not impossible. I just couldn't get over my anger when I heard about her even considering allowing Drake back into her life. I kept telling myself it was her decision and none of my business, but that didn't work.

The black cloud in the north kept creeping closer, and by four o'clock there was little daylight left. A dust storm struck just as we were getting the last of the calves out of the wheat field. She drove through the gate and the Jeep died. For several minutes she tried starting it, but finally gave up.

"What's wrong with it?"

"I have no idea. It's never done this. I can't believe it just died. Dad bought it new less than a year ago. Do you know anything about cars?"

she tripped the latch that opened the hood.

"Not much. Do you have a flashlight?"

"Look in the glove compartment."

I found it, walked to the front of the jeep and looked under the hood. I didn't see anything out of place. I did know where the coil wire was and it was intact, eliminating the one thing I thought might be the problem. By now the wind was blowing a gale, and it was becoming colder by the second, so I got back in, having trouble closing the door.

She tried it again and still—nothing. "It's a long walk to the house. We're not dressed for the cold, but we have no choice." She started to get out and the wind caught her door, jerking it from her hand, blowing it open.

I got out, but the wind was so strong it moved me forward. It was actually hard to stand. We started toward the house, which was east, with the north wind making it difficult to walk in a straight line. For the first time, I was uneasy, similar to the fear of walking into a Viet Cong ambush. By the time we'd gone a couple of hundred yards, sleet began to fall, stinging our faces. I was glad we'd left Bull at the house. I moved to the left of Jimmie, trying to block as much wind as possible. She grabbed my arm and leaned against me as we trudged on toward the house.

The cold was numbing, and after about half an hour Jimmie stopped and gasped, "I've got to rest. My legs won't go any further." She collapsed to the ground.

I reached down and grabbed under her arms. "Get up! We can't stop! We have to keep moving toward the house." I struggled to get her up, and finally did. We were able to walk slowly with me supporting her for a while before she went limp. I kept her from sliding to the ground.

"Jimmie. We have to keep moving. Help me. We can't stop!"

There was no response and she remained limp. She'd fainted from cold, fatigue, or both. My mind went back to another time on another continent, and I swung her around, picked her up and put her over my shoulder, continuing toward the house. I was numb and was now focused on putting one foot in front of the other. If I ever went to the ground, I wouldn't be able to get her up on my shoulders again. How much farther? "Keep moving," I muttered. "You've been in worse situations than this and you survived. Please God—give me strength."

When I realized I couldn't go any further, three feet to my right I saw the hay barn. Only fifty more yards to the house. I started counting my steps and sixty steps later came to the back door. Out of the wind, I felt much better. I opened the door and placed her on the couch.

Bull commenced to cover her face with slobbery kisses. It was effective as she moaned and turned over. I found a rag, soaked it in warm water and bathed her face. She moaned again and slapped at my hand. "Stop it, Bull. Leave me alone."

I shook her gently. "Jimmie, it's not Bull. It's me. We're at the house."

She opened her eyes, looking confused. "W-We made it. I-I don't remember."

"Just lie there and relax. I'll build a fire." I went to the bedroom, returning with a blanket to put over her. I had the fire going shortly and by then she was fully conscious.

She sat up with the blanket wrapped around her. "You carried me, didn't you?"

"A little way. You're not that heavy."

"How'd you do it? The cold and wind were horrible."

I hesitated, then mumbled, "I prayed for strength."

"I thought you didn't pray?"

"I needed help. I couldn't make it on my own. Would you like to move closer to the stove?"

She moved over and sat down in front of the fire. "Thank you and thank God."

"You can take my pickup if you want to try getting to town," I volunteered, thinking she wouldn't want to stay.

She looked back at me. "Are you kidding? No way. You're stuck with me for the duration of this storm."

✳ ✳ ✳

The next morning, we felt the full force of the storm with winds rattling the windows. When I stepped outside the snow was piercing the cold air. I couldn't see my pickup which was only about twenty feet from the door. I'd gotten up several times during the night, from the recliner, and built up the fire, but it was still cold. I was thankful that she had insisted we bring several loads of wood into the house before we left for the field. Jimmie was bundled up on the couch covered by several blankets, and Bull was as close to the fire as possible.

The electricity was still on, but Jimmie had assured me that wouldn't last. She'd had me fill up water jugs because the pipes would freeze. The cook stove was gas, so that wasn't a problem. It made no sense that the house didn't have space heaters.

Jimmie, wrapped in her blankets, came to the table for breakfast. "Do you realize that we could've died yesterday? If we hadn't made it to the house, there's no way we could've survived. Have you thought about that? They wouldn't have found us until this storm was over, and we didn't show up in town."

"I haven't given it much thought." I didn't tell her, but many of my days the last two years had been spent wondering if I was going to die.

I put our plates on the table, piled high with scrambled eggs. "Would you say the blessing?"

She looked surprised. "I'd be glad too. **Thank you, God, for life and for giving Luke the strength to get us home. Amen.**"

We had the radio on the Amarillo station, and every few minutes they would give blizzard warnings. Interstate 40 was already closed, as were most roads in the area including Highway 87 going from Amarillo to Dalhart. The temperature was 2 below 0 with a wind chill of 40 below. They kept emphasizing that the storm would continue for the next several days.

After one of these updates, I asked Jimmie how anything could survive in these conditions. "Animals have a way of adjusting, especially those raised in this country. However, this is unusual, even for us. I expect to lose cattle, especially some of the calves we turned out. I never cease to be amazed at the weather here in the top of the Texas Panhandle. It looks like this could be one of the worst storms we've ever had, and it's almost the first of March. You saw the deer grazing yesterday afternoon. That was a sure sign of how bad the storm was going to be.

"I never expected anything like this. I'm glad you came out to help. It was kind of you."

"Thank you for admitting it. You were so angry with me because of Drake it kind of surprised me." More than a little, I thought.

That seemed to be a cue for the lights to go out. It was already nine o'clock, but the room was pitch black. Jimmie lit a burner on the stove to enable her to light candles to place on the table and around the room. The light was dim and somewhat eerie, casting strange shadows. She sat back down at the table. "You didn't have a chance to comment on being mad at me." The lighting emphasized the profile of her facial features, and she was even more beautiful than I'd ever realized.

"I didn't understand after what . . ."

She interrupted me. "He did to me. I know. That's what everyone except my mother will think. Is that all you were upset about?" She almost looked supernatural with the reflection of light making her eyes resemble green emeralds.

I had to be honest. "No. I was jealous. I thought we were . . ."

Another interruption. "Girl friend—boy friend—like high school sweethearts? I know what you thought. There would be more kissing and fondling like teenagers do. This might go on for months or even years.

Did you ever think about marriage, Luke?"

"Well, I-I—no. W-We-uh . . ."

Interrupted again. "We would just go on doing what we're doing, until someone else comes along that you fall head over hills for and want to marry. Right?"

I found my voice. "And Drake wants to marry you immediately? One in the hand is better than two in the bush? Why do you think Drake is anxious to marry you?"

"Maybe he loves me and wants to spend the rest of his life with me," she retorted.

"Will your dad ever accept him as a son-in-law?"

She didn't answer the question but went right on making her case. "Luke, I'll be twenty-four in a few weeks. The average age for a woman to marry today is twenty. I'm on the verge of being a spinster, or that's the way I feel. Before I met Drake there were no prospects."

Maybe it was the dark that gave me the confidence for my next statement. "I need more time, Jimmie. With what I've been through the last two years, it's just not possible to make life-altering decisions. I have trouble with small choices, but it's possible, even probable, that'll change in the future. I care about you, and we've been through more experiences than most couples who've been together for twenty years. Drake is not what you're looking for to spend a lifetime with. Trust your dad's judgment and don't marry him—at least not now."

"Are you only thinking of my welfare or your personal feelings, too? It seems you and my dad are wanting to keep me from making what you consider a bad decision."

"Both. I'm not good at this. You're right about the girlfriend analysis. I was moving along at that rate." I smiled. "But I was about to move on from the kissing to the fondling stage. That's not bad considering you're the first g-woman I'd kissed in over two years."

She smiled and reached out to touch my arm. "I'm losing this debate.

Which I should to a guy who saved my life again."

*** 

We stayed at the ranch for four days. The snow stopped Thursday morning and the drift at the front of the house allowed me to walk up on the roof. We found six calves that had died, but all the cows survived. We put out four loads of hay before we drove to the Cherokee with the intention of towing it to town. When she got in and turned the starter—it kicked right off! I guess stranger things have happened but that would've ranked up toward the top. It was almost as if it was destiny for us to spend four days together in order to better understand one another.

# 45

# HEADLINES

Monday morning it took me fifteen minutes to drive the quarter of a mile to the office. I couldn't see the front of Luke's car as I crept toward the Auction. I would stop every few yards, afraid I was going to run into something. A security light informed me I'd arrived. I struggled into the office, which was open but vacant, and went into the small room where a gas two-burner stove was located. I put the coffee pot on and went back into the outer office and lit the two space heaters. It was only seven, so I was early.

I was worried about Luke and had thought of little else since getting up at five this morning. I'd never seen anything like this storm and neither had my dad. He tried to assure me that Luke would be fine.

Benny came in just as the coffee was ready. "Grace, isn't this something? I talked with Jimmie Lyn yesterday before she went to the ranch to help Luke. There's no way she could've gotten back to town. It may be for the best."

"Oh, Benny. I'm relieved that she's with Luke. I've been worried about him."

"No need to worry, Grace. Missy will know what to do. I couldn't get to the donut shop. It was probably closed anyway. I'm hoping our hands will get here, but I'm not counting on it. We have to make sure 200 head have water and feed. There's no way I can do that by myself if no one else shows."

The door opened and Bronc burst in. "I made it! It took me an hour to go five miles. I've lived here all my life and have never seen anything like this. Where's the coffee and donuts?"

"Coffee's ready but no donuts," Benny said.

At eight o'clock no one else had shown up. "Benny, I can drive the truck for you and Bronc. Maybe that'll help a little."

"It'll be more than a little help, Grace. Are you sure? We do have a new truck, and the heater should be good."

"I can do it."

We went out into the blizzard, and stayed as long as possible without getting frost bite, putting out feed. Benny and Bronc broke ice on the water troughs. When we were back at the office two hours later, they were covered in snow and ice. I brought them two cups of steaming coffee.

Two other men showed up, and I was able to stay in the office when they left to continue feeding. I was so thankful that Angie had decided to stay with me. I'd have been worried sick if she was in Amarillo alone during this storm.

❄❄❄

I did what I could for three days to provide some comfort for the men working in the bitter cold. They were kind enough to feed my horses. I brought egg sandwiches from home to go with the gallons of coffee.

The storm was gone Thursday morning when the sun broke through for the first time since last Sunday.

When I arrived at the office, Benny opened the door. "Mornin', Grace. You're just in time. Blaine's on the phone."

"I'm going crazy in this hospital. I should be home. I feel good. I'm anxious to hear from our kids. Benny said they're at the ranch. Jimmie

Lyn should be able to get in by noon since the county will have snowplows out this morning.

"Have you seen Lady?" he asked.

"No. That's going to be my first stop today after making the coffee."

"Grace, I feel good. You know, people should get sick occasionally to make them appreciate their health. I love this country. Can you believe this storm? Just when you think winter is over, here it comes again. Makes you feel small.

"I've only got one problem—Drake Davis. I'm afraid Jimmie Lyn is going to marry him after all. She called me Sunday before going to the ranch and told me he was back. She wasn't as angry as she should've been."

"Is he that bad?"

"Worse. No one could convince me otherwise. He's smart, manipulative, and a con—a terrible combination. He attempted to convince Jimmie Lyn that he cares for her, and I'm afraid she's buying it."

I didn't know what Luke would think about her getting married. I still hadn't figured out their relationship.

"It's going to be muddy to start back riding Lady, Grace. I have a friend who has an indoor arena. He wouldn't mind you using it. It's not over ten or twelve miles, and the hauling would probably do her good."

"I plan to start trotting and even galloping her soon," I said. "The indoor arena would be a good idea." We talked longer about Lady and her future. Before we ended the call, I told him about Angie coming to stay with us and thanked him for his suggestion.

I went to check on Lady, and she was feeling good. I took the blanket off and brushed her before putting out feed. It was still cold, but the sun was shining, and the reflection off the snow was beautiful. When it warmed up, the pens were going to be a mess. The wind had blown hard and, with the huge snowfall, the drifts were as high as the fence.

I thought of my decision to move up Lady's training, wondering if it was the right thing to do. One thing for sure, I couldn't leave until the baby came, and it wasn't due until the middle of May. My dad was pleased that she'd agreed to come stay with us. The few days with us she'd seemed content and was a big help to me with the cooking. She didn't speak of Evert, which was fine with me, and I couldn't help but hope he was gone for good.

When I got back to the office, most of the coffee was gone and the men had eaten all of the donuts before going to feed. Someone had left an Amarillo Globe-News on the counter of the lounge. I poured myself what was left of the coffee, put another pot on, and sat down to read the paper. Nothing interested me on the first page, but opening the second was a quarter page picture of a man dressed in a suit with the headlines— **DRAKE DAVIS LOCAL ATTORNEY GOES UNDERCOVER TO BREAK UP CRIME RING.** Unbelievable! I read the headlines several times. The article, which took up the rest of the page, went into detail about Drake's role in bringing the law firm in England to justice. Toward the end of the article, the senior partner in the Amarillo firm was quoted. "We are extremely proud of Drake and consider him a hero for putting his life in danger to destroy this crime organization posing as a reputable law firm. We are very pleased to have him back with us."

Blaine didn't mention this when I talked with him this morning. Evidently, he'd not read the paper and, since the storm, he'd had no visitors. Or maybe he had read it and that was the reason he was afraid of Jimmie marrying him. The guy who'd run out on her came home a hero. Now the big question—would she forgive him?

I read the article again and had just finished when the front door opened and closed. "Jimmie, you made it in."

"Finally. It took me awhile. I wouldn't have made it if not for the snowplow. How is everything here?"

"We got by, thanks to Benny and Bronc who worked every day. They said the new truck made the difference. How did you and Luke make out at the ranch?" Should I tell her about the article?

"It's a long story. Let's go eat in town, and I'll give you all the details. I'm starved for something good. We ate sandwiches the last four days." She turned to leave.

"Just a minute, Jimmie. I have something you need to see." I went to the lounge and brought the paper back, spreading it open and showing her the second page. She snatched it and sat down in the nearest chair. She must've read it twice with the amount of time she took.

She folded the paper up. "Let's go." She didn't comment about the article on the drive to the restaurant.

We spotted a secluded vacant booth. I had to hustle to keep up with her long strides as we zeroed in on our target.

She glanced at me. "I must look terrible and probably smell worse after all this time without a bath. I'm so hungry, I don't care. At least we're partly hidden."

We ordered, and she told me what happened at the ranch, emphasizing the trek to the house from the stalled Cherokee. She went into detail—too much so. By the time she finished, I was trembling. "Doesn't it frighten you to think what could've happened?"

She nodded. "I've thought of that many times. It didn't seem to bother Luke. That was the second time he saved my life. Plus—he was mad at me. I'd told him Drake was back." She smiled. "It's a wonder he didn't leave me out there."

Our meal was delivered, and after we finished eating, she leaned back and said, "That was good. You must be wondering what I think about the newspaper article. I was surprised, mostly because he's considered a hero. That's a long stretch for me."

I was going to take a chance; hopefully, she wouldn't take it the wrong way. I told her about Angie coming to stay with us after Evert left. I pointed out that she was about the same age as Jimmie, that Angie had made a mistake in marrying him, and now she was paying the price, looking at being a single mom.

Obviously, she understood what I was saying. "I know, Grace. Everything and everyone tells me I'd be making a mistake to allow Drake back into my life. He came along when I'd just about given up on finding someone. I thought he was so perfect, and it's hard to admit I was wrong. I'm going to be honest with you. I'd like to think there was a possibility of a future with Luke. He finally—and I do mean finally—provided a small amount of hope for that to happen during the time we spent at the ranch this week. It's a long shot, however, and I'm probably a fool for thinking it."

"I know Luke better than anyone, Jimmie. He's honest to the point of—I don't know a word to describe it. Maybe unreal would fit. When he tells you something, it's what he'll do. He's improving, thanks to you. He's still not the way he was before Vietnam, but he's much closer."

She didn't comment, but I hoped I gave her something to think about. She took me back to the Auction and said as soon as the roads were clear she was going after her dad.

Her parting words gave me reason for encouragement. "Thank you, Grace. I appreciate all you've done for Dad. Thank you, too, for giving me some insights into Luke."

When she drove off, I prayed that she wouldn't make the same mistake my Angie did.

# 46

# MORE THAN A HAIRCUT

 LUKE

It was the Saturday after the storm. Jimmie became angry when I referred to her as a girl, which wasn't an insult. In fact, I'd begun to think of her as my girl. Now, I understood that wasn't what she wanted. What she had in mind was becoming someone's wife, and at almost twenty-four she was on the verge of desperation. I'd never thought about her as anything but a girl—not ever referring to her as a woman, even in my thoughts.

Here I was sitting on my rear, when I had another load of hay to put out. "Let's go, Bull. We've got more work to do. It was amazing what a difference two days made. The snow was melting at an unbelievable rate. Maybe it was the work, it didn't matter—I continued to improve. I still would have sudden visions of the incidents that happened in Vietnam and would dream at least one night a week, but I recovered more quickly from the after-effects.

After delivering the second load of hay, I drove by the wheat field. I needed to get the calves back into the field, but it would take horses and someone helping me. They'd stayed together, but I found six dead after the storm ended.

It was Saturday and my work was finished. Didn't people who worked all week go to town on Saturday? I guess it was time for me to get my hair cut, in order to resemble an ex-Marine more than a hippie demonstrating on the campus of a California university.

Back at the house I bathed, shaved, and put on a clean shirt and pants. I started out the door, but Bull didn't move from his place in front of the stove. "What're you doing in front of a cold stove? It's springtime in the Arctic Circle." I'd heard several truck drivers bringing cattle to the Auction from South Texas refer to Dalhart by this title. "Well, are you going with me, or not?"

He got up slowly, stretched, and followed me out the door, less than enthusiastic. I decided Clayton rather than Dalhart would be my destination and forty minutes later walked into the Martinez Barber Shop and climbed into a chair.

"Been awhile since you've seen clippers or scissors," the barber said. "How do you want it cut?"

"A little above my collar and same above my ears. Block it in the back." I was hoping that would end the conversation.

"When'd you get your last haircut? You know some people sell their hair. You might've considered that."

"My last haircut was free—courtesy of Uncle Sam and the United States Marines."

He stopped the clippers. I looked in the mirror and saw the expression on his brown, friendly face change. "I'm sorry, soldier, for being so nosey. A barber has a boring job and making small talk helps a little."

He must've taken close to an hour to cut my hair without saying another word, and when he finished it looked like a large hairy animal had died and deteriorated on his floor. He swung the chair around so I could see the results in the mirror. I was impressed, realizing it'd taken so long to allow him to make it look this good. I'd never had a better haircut. "It looks great."

"I'm glad you like it."

I reached for my billfold, still admiring the image in the mirror. "How much do I owe you?"

"Were you in Vietnam?" he asked, quietly.

"Yeah. Got home in late August." I looked back at him and saw tears.

"No charge, son. My boy was killed three months ago over there. My wife and I are having a hard time."

"I'm sorry. I was fortunate to get home without an injury."

He grabbed a towel and wiped his face. "Would you consider having supper with me and my wife? It would mean a lot to her. It's already four o'clock and we usually eat around six. I would be very grateful."

The last thing I wanted was to join a grieving family to talk about the war, but I had no choice. "Yes, I'll be glad to do that." That wasn't the truth, but it was the right thing to say.

He smiled and wiped at his face again. "Thank you. I close at five, and if you'll meet me back here you can follow me home."

I left the barber shop, depressed and dreading the evening. How do I get myself in these situations? The poor man and his wife had lost their son—why should I not try to bring them some happiness? I'd been surprised at how minority soldiers were overrepresented compared to white soldiers in Vietnam. Half the men in my platoon were minorities. I promised myself to do the best I could to relieve their grief for one evening.

❋❋❋

I was waiting in my pickup, actually it was Granddad's, when the barber put a closed sign on his shop window. He'd never introduced himself, so I didn't know his name. He waved at me and got in his car, backing out and heading south on Main Street. I guess every town had a Main Street. I followed him through a red light and two stop signs before turning right down one of the few streets in town which had trees. He pulled into the driveway of an older wooden house that needed painting.

I met him as he got out of his car. "My name's Luke." I offered my hand, which he accepted.

"Juan," he replied. "I called my wife, and she's expecting us. I see you have your dog with you. Bring him in, and he can meet the family."

Bull and I followed him into the house, and I was surprised when the person who greeted us was far too young to be his wife. "Hi. I'm Ana. Welcome to our home. Miguel was my little brother." She turned to an older woman. "This is my mother, Maria."

She came to me, tears streaming. I accepted and returned the hug. She stepped back, wiping away the tears with the back of her hand. "I'm sorry, please forgive me. Thank you for blessing us with your presence this evening."

Juan, Maria, and I spent the next hour sitting in the living room talking while Ana stayed in the kitchen. They explained that Ana was a married daughter who lived in Clayton. Her mother had asked her to come over and cook supper since they had a special guest. Of course, Bull remained in the kitchen where there was food. I listened as they talked of Miguel from his childhood through high school, showing me pictures of him in his football uniform and proudly displaying the one taken in his suit his senior year.

He was a handsome boy, larger than his dad, with a wide smile, and I couldn't help but think—what a terrible tragedy for this young man with his whole life ahead of him to lose it in that horrible war. Several times his mother tried to bring up the war, but each time Juan changed the subject, finally telling her that I wouldn't want to talk about it.

The hour went by quickly with Maria carrying the brunt of the conversation, always about Miguel. My heart went out to them as I kept imagining my mom, dad, and granddad having to deal with my death if I'd been killed over there while Dad was alive, even worse if it had been after his death.

The daughter interrupted us to say that supper was on the table. She was an attractive lady with short black hair and a smile that brought some light into this dismal atmosphere.

Miguel said the blessing, and we started in on a delicious meal, which had been in short supply at the ranch. The main course was a Mexican casserole, salad, and guacamole with the best tortillas I'd ever eaten. Dessert was some kind of chocolate pudding. Bull sat next to Ana and received small pieces of food. I was hoping that he'd hold the gas until we were home or at least in the pickup.

There were few interruptions during the meal. I imagine they saw how I devoured the food and hated to disturb me. After we finished, it was back to the living room with Ana joining us and Bull clinging to her like stink on a skunk. She was his devoted friend for life.

The discussion continued, but thanks to Ana more in my direction. I covered everything beginning with my youth up until the time I was drafted. I skipped that and went to my current job at the Auction and finally to the ranch. They were interested in my mother's and Blaine's racehorse, asking several questions about Lady.

They finally gave me an opportunity to ask some questions, which I directed at Ana. She was a nurse at the clinic here in Clayton and had one boy who was three. "I left him home with his dad. If I'd brought him, we wouldn't have been able to have enough peace and quiet to visit. He's a holy terror and spoiled rotten, thanks to these two." She smiled and nodded to her parents.

Watching her, I thought how important she was to her parents at this time and how thoughtful it was for her to come over here to cook supper. I guessed her to be about the age of Jimmie. She was confident and articulate, never at a loss for words, even the right words.

I was surprised to see that it was already ten and told them it was time for me to get back to the ranch. They expressed their appreciation for me coming and Ana and Bull accompanied me to my pickup.

"You'll never know how much it meant to my mom and dad to have you come to our house tonight. They have grieved unbelievably since receiving word of Miguel. Tonight was the first time I'd seen them anywhere close to normal. Please come back to visit again."

"I don't come to Clayton very often."

"Will you please come back again?" she repeated.

"Definitely." I smiled. "I'll need to get another hair cut."

"Thank you again." She moved forward and hugged me.

I opened the pickup door. "Load, Bull." He just stood and looked at me like he was hard of hearing. I said, "Load, Bull!" He looked up at Ana, as if saying, "I'm staying with her."

She reached down and rubbed his head. "Load, Bull. I'll see you again." She turned and left, with his eyes following her.

"You'd better load, buddy, or I may feed you to the coyotes. Now, load!"

On the drive to the ranch, I had to roll the window all the way down. I seriously considered putting him in the back of the pickup. "She wouldn't think you were so cute if she was with us now." He responded by reaching over and giving me a wet kiss covering the entire side of my face.

# 47

# INDECISION

JIMMIE LYN

After taking Grace to the Auction, I started back to my apartment, thinking about what she'd said. The only person that would be happy with me marrying Drake was my mother, not because of my happiness, but because she'd look better to her friends. I admit that Grace's opinion had more credibility than my mother's did by a wide margin. I just felt like no one understood my position.

Drake's car was at my apartment and, when I pulled into my parking space, he opened my door before I could turn off the ignition.

"Good morning. I've been waiting for you a couple of hours." He reached for my arm to help me out of the car, but I pulled it away.

"I've had a busy morning," I said. "I thought the road was closed to Amarillo."

"Snowplows were out early. I was anxious to see you. Could we talk again? I'll leave the minute you say to."

"It'll need to be short. I have a busy afternoon." That wasn't the truth, but I didn't want him to think my time wasn't valuable.

"No problem. I need to get something out of my car."

I went on into my apartment, wondering if I was doing the right thing. It was difficult to imagine what else he could say that hadn't already been said.

He returned holding an Amarillo paper that was folded. He handed me the paper before he sat down. "I'd like you to read page two."

I opened it but didn't tell him it was old news to me. I stared at it several minutes pretending to read, but the phone interrupted me. I answered it in the kitchen.

Dad issued no greeting, going right to the point. "Have you seen the Amarillo Globe?"

"Yes. Drake's here now."

"Honey, please be careful. I don't trust him. Call me when he leaves. I'm ready to get out of this hospital."

I hung up, surprised that he was so calm. I returned to the living area and gave the paper back to Drake. "That's impressive. How did they find out?"

"After my law firm in Amarillo heard my story they gave it to the paper, thinking it would be good publicity. I haven't told them I'm leaving, waiting until you accepted my marriage proposal. Have you thought about it?"

"Yes, but I haven't made a decision. I need more time. This came about so suddenly." Why couldn't I just refuse the offer and tell him to go away?

"That's fine. Since I made the dangerous drive from Amarillo, will you have lunch with me? I'll leave after that."

Before I could answer, the phone began ringing again. I returned to the kitchen.

"Jimmie Lyn, have you seen the paper? I can't believe it! He's back! Have you seen him?"

"Yes, and yes, Mother. We are about to go eat lunch." I had a pretty good idea of what was coming next.

"Oh, Jimmie Lyn. This solves everything!" And she went on and on about how everyone would know he didn't leave on his own, and she wouldn't be embarrassed to see people in town. When she started in on the wedding, I ended the call.

We went to the Ranch House Café for lunch, and it seemed that everyone in town had decided to eat there today to celebrate the end of the storm and the sun coming out. We had to wait for a table, and I felt the stares of the people—some familiar, others not. When we were seated and looking at menus, people I knew started coming up to the table introducing themselves to Drake. This continued throughout the meal with several congratulating me on our upcoming marriage. I didn't taste a bit of my food and thought we'd never get out of here.

On the contrary, Drake was in no hurry to finish his meal, ordering a dessert and taking his time. I realized it was a mistake to accept the lunch invitation. I should've known that so many people in town read the Amarillo paper.

We finally left the restaurant, and went back to my apartment, and he followed me into the house. I sat down in a chair, not wanting to take the chance that the couch would be an invitation for him.

"How long are you going to keep me waiting?" he asked.

I looked him directly in the eye, hoping to appear defiant. "I don't know, Drake. You've kept me waiting for months. I'll let you know when I've made a decision. It may be next week or it could be next month."

"I'm ready to marry you, Jimmie. I'm surprised that after finding out the reason for my absence you're having a difficult time making a decision. Is there someone else?" The smile had disappeared.

I didn't know how to answer the question. "No, I don't think so—not at the moment. There could be—later."

"That's not an answer. Either there is someone or there isn't."

"He's not what's keeping me from saying yes. You hurt me so much, Drake. I can't forget that even with you back. Maybe in time, but not now. I need to think about it and try to come up with an answer. I told you to give me some time. Now you need to leave. Thank you for the lunch, even though it was awkward."

"Can I call you tomorrow?" The smile returned.

"I guess so, but don't expect anything."

I stood, thinking he would start to the door. Instead, he walked over to me, and I made a terrible judgment call. Looking up at him, I let him kiss me. He turned and left, with me standing there feeling like the fool I was.

**✳✳✳**

I spent a sleepless night, tossing and turning, alternating between indecision and anger. I got up at five, drank coffee until six, and called Benny, who I knew would be up. He answered on the first ring.

"Benny, can you meet me at the Auction?"

"Sure. You gonna bring some of those donuts I like?"

Even with all my stress, I smiled. "Yeah. See you in half an hour."

I dressed and went out just as the sun was coming up. It was cold but was supposed to be above freezing by noon. There was a lot of snow but by mid-afternoon, with the temperature in the 40s some of it would be melted. Mother Nature was about to reinstate spring.

Benny was waiting on me, and we spent an hour discussing the days I'd missed. We still had an unusually large number of cattle on the grounds due to several truckloads that had arrived for this week's sale which, of course, was cancelled.

He took out a cigarette and tapped it on the table where we were sitting. "Having Dewayne start cattle was the right move. Auctioneering and starting cattle is a little much, Missy. Dewayne won't complain because he knows you're in a bind. I've found my place in the pens. That's where I'd like to stay. However, I could start cattle until Blaine returns and Bronc could oversee the pens. It's just a suggestion but something to think about. You might want to ask your dad what he thinks."

I knew what my dad would say. You're the boss, Jimmie Lyn. "I don't need to think about it, Benny, or consult my dad. That's what we'll do starting next week. I appreciate you doing this."

He lit his cigarette and inhaled. "Changing the subject, Missy—do you ever wonder why we live in this God-forsaken country? Deep freeze one day and spring the next."

"It's the people, Benny. The friendly, good-hearted, honest people who have inhabited this country." I didn't say this because it sounded good. I really believed it.

"I've worked here many years, Missy. I guess you could call me a company man. I love the High Plains Cattle Auction and hope that one day, when Blaine retires, you're my permanent boss."

With all the emotion and stress of the last few days, I almost cried. "Thank you, Benny. I needed to hear that more than you'll ever know."

The meeting ended, and I went to my apartment and called Dad. He was watching a basketball game on television. I told him about talking to Benny and what we'd decided.

"You did the right thing, Honey. It's exactly what I would've done. See, I told you that you could run this Auction. I'm proud of you. What's funny is that I've tried to get Benny to start cattle for years, and he refused. Now, with you running the business, he volunteers. That should hurt my feelings, but actually it pleases me.

"What did Luke think about Drake coming back?"

"He was angry." I'd hoped we would avoid the subject of Drake. I should've known it wouldn't happen.

"What did you expect him to do? He killed two men protecting you, and Drake was the reason."

"I don't want to talk about it, Dad. I'm sorry. The roads should be clear by ten in the morning. I'll be there to get you by noon if you're ready to come home." I was joking. I knew the answer to that.

"Can't you get here sooner? I watched the weather, and it's going to warm up to 50 degrees tomorrow. I'm about to go crazy in here. I don't even like basketball, and here I am watching it."

I told him not to look for me before eleven. I could just imagine the expression on his face. I'd put a cup in the car tomorrow, so he could have his dip on the drive home.

I hung up and that seemed to be the cue for the doorbell. Surely, Drake wouldn't have come back. I opened the door and Sterling was standing there looking like a lost puppy. "Come in, Sterling."

"Could I talk to you?"

"Certainly. Take off your coat and sit down." He removed his long coat revealing a suit and tie.

I'd never seen anyone so uncomfortable, sitting in a soft chair. He shifted around in the chair like the seat was too hot. "I'm at my wit's end. I don't know what to do about your mother. I do love her, but she treats me terrible, like she despises me. I expect her to ask for a divorce any time. I'm sorry for bothering you with my problems. I have no one else to talk with."

This poor man suffered because of my mother. She had no shame, thinking only of herself. He was a good man who loved her and here he was begging for help. Suddenly, out of the blue, came an idea. "Sterling, would it offend you if I made some suggestions? They are quite personal, but it might help."

"I'll do anything if it will help. Please tell me what I can do." He was sitting on the edge of the chair.

"Do you have any jeans? What about a flannel shirt?" At this point I think he had been humiliated by Mother to the point that nothing would bother him.

"No. Would that help? I could buy some jeans and a shirt." I was afraid he was going to fall off the edge of his chair he became so excited.

"That's not all. Exchange your silk pajamas for flannel ones. They're warmer, anyway. Exchange your Old Spice for English Leather after shave."

"I'll do it! I'll try anything."

I included further instructions, and he agreed to follow all of them on the time-line suggested. He left the house a different man—filled with hope.

# 48

# NURSE

⚜ GRACE ⚜

The weather warmed quickly after the storm, and I rode Lady most days after work and on weekends. The wind was relentless every day, and it helped to have the indoor arena that Blaine had secured.

Jimmie had brought Blaine home, and he did fine until his second chemo treatment when he became deathly sick. It was the second week in March, and the number of cattle being brought in to sell had doubled. She asked me to look after her dad on Tuesday, Wednesday, and Thursday of that week.

When I arrived Tuesday morning, he didn't answer the doorbell. The door wasn't locked, so I went in and called his name. Receiving no answer, I started down the hallway to his bedroom, but I heard gagging sounds coming from the bathroom. "Blaine, are you all right?"

"Just sick." More gagging. "Be out shortly."

I went to the kitchen and put the coffee on. I was familiar with the set up since Jimmie had shown me where everything was earlier. There were dirty dishes in the sink, and I'd just finished washing them when Blaine came in.

"You didn't hire on as a housekeeper, Grace."

"It was no problem. Would you like some coffee while I cook breakfast?" I was shocked at how he looked, not having seen him in a week. He was in his housecoat, but I could tell he'd lost weight.

"No. I can't keep anything down. Not even water. I'm going back to bed. You go ahead and make yourself breakfast." He turned and went back toward his bedroom.

I had a recipe for chicken noodle soup that worked for my dad when he was sick, so I went to the grocery store to buy the ingredients. Of all people, I ran into Blaine's ex who was shopping. I was going to ignore her, but that didn't work. She had the aisle blocked. "Are you still playing nursemaid to Blaine?"

"Jimmie asked me to stay with him on days she's busier than usual, especially on sale day." I attempted to move on, but she was still blocking the aisle.

"Are you staying with him today?" she asked.

"Yes. He's not feeling well after his chemo treatment yesterday." I was losing patience with this lady.

"Pretty convenient for you, isn't it? You get to stay in the same house with him."

"I don't like what you're insinuating. I miss my late husband and am not interested in another relationship. You need to take your rudeness and anger somewhere else." I turned my buggy around and left, not giving her a chance to say anything else. Thankfully, I was able to avoid her while finishing my shopping.

Blaine was up when I returned, sitting at the kitchen table with a glass of water. "I'm going to try to keep some water down. This treatment is turning out to be something else. I've never been this sick. Last week's treatment wasn't bad—now this."

I set about making the soup. After getting it started, I sat down at the table and moved the topic to something more positive. "Jimmie seems to be handling your job well."

He broke into a smile. "Isn't she something? I'm so proud of her."

Talking about his daughter and the High Plains Auction seemed to help. An hour later, when the soup was done, he was able to eat a small bowl and keep it down.

By Thursday, Blaine was able to stay by himself, and I went back to work in the office. I could tell that something was bothering Madge. When it was time for our break, we were alone in the lounge. "How're you doing, Madge?"

"It's obvious, isn't it? I have a problem, Grace. Maybe you can help me." She took a sip of her Diet Coke. "I've been seeing Bronc for some time. I like Bronc and enjoy his company." She hesitated.

"And?"

"There's someone else. This boy I dated in high school. I was crazy about him, and then he went off to college. I thought that was it. My heart was broken, and it took me a long time to get over him. He's back in town and wants to get together."

"And?"

"I thought I was over him but. . .

"You're not."

"No. I was thrilled when he called me. When I saw him, it was just like a dream come true. But what about Bronc?"

"Is this guy here to stay?" I asked.

"Definitely. His dad owns a ranch between here and Amarillo. His dad's in poor health, and he's taking over the ranch."

"Looks like you have a decision to make that would thrill a lot of young ladies your age. Two men, and you have to make a choice." I didn't feel as sorry for her as I did Bronc. There was no doubt as to what decision she was going to make. Her true love had returned.

"Aren't you going to give me some advice?" she asked.

"Nope. You don't need advice. You've already made a decision. You just want me to agree that it was the right one."

My answer was short and probably hurt her feelings, but Bronc was Luke's friend and a good man. I hated to see him hurt, and that was going to happen. We went back to work—me disappointed and Madge frustrated.

✳✳✳

Angie coming to live with us had worked out better than I expected. She was a big help to me with the cooking and housekeeping. My dad moved back into his trailer, and no amount of talking could dissuade him. She was showing more each day, and I was anticipating the day I would be a grandmother.

Angie was a pretty girl, inheriting the dark complexion that ran in the family. She had many of the same features as Luke with a narrow face, thin lips and a wide mouth. She was small, being only a little over five feet and weighting a few pounds over a 100 before her pregnancy. It was hard to believe that a sweet, attractive girl like her could end up with someone like Evert.

We had changed her doctor to one in Dalhart. I couldn't imagine having to drive ninety minutes when she went into labor.

She and Luke had always been close, and he was pleased that Evert had left and she'd come to live with us. Luke had come in several times to visit, and it pleased me to see the close relationship renewed.

After Madge told me about her problem, she stayed away from me, but the change in Bronc was obvious. He seldom came into the office and, when he did, stayed only long enough to complete his business. My heart went out to him, and I suspected Madge was making a poor choice. However, it was none of my business.

# 49

# MOVING CATTLE

LUKE

The days after the storm were busy. One of the priorities was to repair the pipes that had frozen and busted on the windmills. I'd never considered myself a plumber, and this chore reinforced that opinion. I had to make several trips into town to get materials. After that I had to drag the dead calves into a pile to burn. If I didn't their carcasses would have every coyote in the country on this ranch, and with calving season about to start that could be a disaster.

The calves that we'd turned out due to the storm, for the most part, had stayed together. I was going to need horses and some help to drive them back into the wheat field.

Jimmie visited occasionally, but since she'd taken over the Auction and runs had increased, she couldn't be away very long.

It was Friday, March fourteenth, and I'd made arrangements to eat supper with my mom, sister, and granddad. I'd been in several times since Angie had come to live with us, which pleased me, and I hoped we'd seen the last of Evert.

I was there before dark, and Mom insisted that we go see Lady. She looked better each time I saw her, and everything looked positive for a return to the track. "Are you still planning on going to Ruidoso in May?"

"Yes. Of course, it depends on when the baby comes. I haven't said anything to Angie or your granddad about my plans. I'd like for Angie and the baby to go with me to Ruidoso. It would be better for everyone. I'd be there for her, and it would relieve your granddad of an additional responsibility. And selfishly, I'd have my grandbaby with me."

"Do you think she'll go? That trailer's not very big for the three of you."

I smiled and shook my head. "Blaine's bought a small house right across the highway from the track. He said it was for himself when he came to watch his horses run. I doubt if he's telling the truth about that.

"We'd better get to the house. Angie's cooking tonight and it should be ready."

I looked forward to these meals since it was a treat not to eat what I prepared. I left Bull at home since he'd beg, and they'd feed him from the table, and we'd suffer the consequences.

Angie was putting it on the table when we entered. I was amazed that she was not larger than she was, being seven months along.

She looked up when we came in. "Hungry?"

"I'm starved. I had a bologna sandwich for lunch. It smells good." I was almost drooling over the fried pork chops and gravy.

"You didn't bring Bull? I was looking forward to seeing him. He's so sweet."

"No, Angie. Bull is at home where he needs to be. I fed him an extra helping of dry dog food before I left."

Granddad came in from his trailer and hugged me. "It's always good to see you, Luke." He glanced at the table. "Fried pork chops and gravy. When I dream about food—that's it."

When we were seated, Mom asked Granddad to say the blessing. "I'm going to pass it to Luke tonight."

He knew I wouldn't turn him down, so I delivered the blessing. The food was great, and I complimented Angie. I asked her to come out Sunday and stay a couple of days. Two men were coming out to help me drive the calves back into the wheat field. I also wanted to pen at least two dozen cows which were not going to calve. They were older and needed to be sold and replaced with younger cows.

"I'd be glad to do that. I'd like to do more to pull my weight around here. I'll come out Sunday night and bring enough groceries for Monday and Tuesday. Will I need to do breakfast or just lunch?" she asked.

"Let's provide breakfast also. We're going to start early, and it's not going to be easy. The least we can do is feed them good. It's going to be a job for the three of us." That was an understatement.

I was pleased that she'd been willing to help. It'd also give us a chance to have some time together which had been in short supply since I returned from Vietnam. It was still a mystery how she could choose such a mate as Evert, but on the other hand there was Jimmie who was considering the same or worse.

I didn't stay long after supper since I was going by to visit with Blaine and give him a report on the ranch. This would be the first time since he came home we'd had a chance to talk.

I went by Jimmie's apartment before going to Blaine's, and Drake's car was there. I suspected it since she hadn't planned on coming out to the ranch tonight. We didn't talk about him, so I had no idea what she was going to do.

Blaine answered the door quickly. "Luke. Come in. I've been wanting to talk with you."

He looked much worse than the last time I'd seen him but was in good spirits, offering me a drink which I refused. After the pork chops there was no room for anything.

We talked for over an hour, mostly about the ranch. I told him about the plans next week. He seemed pleased, saying, "Good for you. We need to replace the older cows. Are you okay with staying at the ranch? I understand that the boss didn't give you much choice."

"It's no problem. In fact, I'm enjoying it and have done better. Your advice about hard work was right on. There's always work to be done at the ranch and little time to sit around and think of the past."

"I'm glad to hear that. I love the ranch and one day I hope to live there. After this illness, I'm more determined than ever."

We finished with a handshake and Blaine telling me how much he appreciated my mother and me.

I left the house the next morning to look for the calves we'd turned out in the wheat pasture. If I could locate them, it'd make it easier for us Monday to get them back where they belonged. Bull came to attention in the front seat and started barking. He'd spotted a jack rabbit sitting out to the right of us. "Okay, I'm going to let you out so you get him." I reached across and opened his door and the chase was on. The rabbit didn't move until he saw him coming and then took off. Bull had about as much chance catching him as I would've. Bull's heart was in it, but he was no greyhound and, after seeing it was hopeless, he returned with his tongue hanging out, defeated but happy.

We located most of the calves grazing at the far west end of the ranch. There was a windmill not turning in that vicinity, and I spent several hours getting it to pump.

✳✳✳

It was noon, and we'd just gotten back to the house for lunch when I saw a car coming. I waited by my pickup until it arrived and was startled by the man who got out. Only one man could be that tall—Drake Davis.

He walked up, saying, "Luke?"

"Yeah, that's me." I was eye level with his neck.

He looked down at me. "I'm Drake Davis. I'd like to visit with you a few minutes. You've probably already guessed what it's about or, better yet, who it concerns."

I was surprised that he'd be so bold as to come out here. Bull was usually friendly with visitors but not this one. The growl was so deep and low Drake probably didn't hear it. "Sure. It's a nice day, we can sit out here."

I motioned toward the two metal chairs on the front porch.

Bull lay down beside my chair, and I reached down and rubbed his head, hoping that would improve his attitude.

Drake moved one of the chairs so he'd be facing me and didn't waste any time getting right to the point. Sitting down, he was so tall his knees were high, so in order to appear threatening he had to part his legs to lean forward, like he was going to pounce. "I'm here about Jimmie Lyn. I plan on marrying her but she's putting me off. I believe you're the reason. You need to say that you're not interested in her and suggest she get on with her life."

This guy was something else. "Does she know you're out here?"

"No, and I don't expect her to find out. This is between you and me. Do you understand what I'm saying, or do I need to spell it out for you?"

I tried to choose my words carefully. "What gives you the idea that I'm not interested in her?"

He leaned even further. "I was afraid you wouldn't understand. I was being polite and asking you to cooperate. I'm telling you to leave her alone—stop seeing her. I'm going to marry her, and not you or anyone else is going to get in my way. Now, is that plain enough even for a country boy that only graduated from high school?" He wasn't finished. "I just returned from a dangerous assignment. I put some criminals in prison. I kept Jimmie Lyn out of it to prevent her from being in danger."

Bull sensed the hostility in his voice, and his growl became louder. I reached down to scratch his head and noticed the hair rising on his neck.

"What's the matter with that mutt? Does he have a bone in his throat?" he asked with a sarcastic smile.

"He doesn't like you. You better leave before I turn him loose on you. The way you're sitting in that chair he's looking right at his target. You know when a Pit Bull locks on to something he doesn't turn loose."

He quickly put his legs together. He shook his finger at me but left one hand in his lap. "I'm warning you. I'd hate to see you get hurt, but it could happen and quickly if you don't do what I say."

Bull stood, took a step forward, and his growl became even louder. It didn't take Drake long to get to his car, glancing over his shoulder a couple of times.

Bull moved over to Drake's chair and lifted his right leg—his favorite for accuracy.

✳✳✳

Angie came out late Sunday afternoon with my car loaded with groceries. She started cooking right away and created a casserole that was delicious. I convinced her not to give Bull any samples.

We talked for two hours about the past and the memories. We had shared so much the first part of our lives with Mom and Dad being gone much of the time when we were in high school. She brought up things I'd forgotten, most of which caused me to smile.

She took the one bedroom, and I slept on the couch. Bull joined her since the bed was more comfortable.

I was sleeping better and didn't wake up until my alarm went off at five the next morning. I made the coffee and Angie came in at five-thirty and started breakfast. My two guys were supposed to be here at six.

By the time she had the bacon fried and the biscuits out of the oven, I heard them drive up. I went out and helped unload and tie the three horses to the trailer. "Y'all ready for coffee?"

"I'm not used to getting up this early. I need something to get me going," Bronc said. "Spoon says he gets up at five every morning. Of course, he's not married and has to cook his own breakfast. He hasn't found anyone he loves as much as that old car."

Spoon was the older man who came with him. He'd been at the Auction for years and was a trusted employee.

They followed me in, and I introduced them to Angie. She was making the gravy to go with the scrambled eggs, biscuits and bacon. When she had everything on the table we sat down, and I said the blessing. Angie didn't eat with us, keeping the coffee cups filled, acting as waitress.

"Angie, that was the best meal I've had in a long time," Bronc said. "Your husband is a fortunate man. I've eaten with Luke before, and believe me it doesn't run in the family."

"I taught her everything she knows," I said, laughing. We all thanked Angie and left. They'd brought me a horse, also, and the sun was just coming up when we rode off toward the day's work.

We found the calves where I had expected, but it took us several hours to bunch them together and head them toward the wheat field. We arrived with thirty-two, which wasn't bad for a morning's work.

On the ride back to the house, I told Bronc that Angie was separated from her husband and was expecting a baby in May.

"That guy must be crazy," was his only comment.

***

We spent the remainder of the day getting the other twelve head into the wheat pasture, and the next day we were able to pen the older cows that were going to the sale. All in all, it was a productive two days. Angie fed us well, and the two men probably would've volunteered to come back anytime if she was cooking.

After they left, late Tuesday afternoon, I told Angie how much I appreciated her helping out.

"I enjoyed it, Luke. Those men were so nice. Is everyone at the Auction that way?"

"No. Afraid not. These guys are two of the best. Bronc has been a good friend from the beginning of my stay and Spoon is always willing to help out.

"I'd forgotten that men could be so polite and gracious. The last two days were my best in a long time, Luke.

"Now tell me about Jimmie. Do you love her? Remember, I'm your big sister, and I know you better than anyone. Don't try to lie to me."

"Probably. I'm just now getting my life back together. She's two years older than me and is desperate to get married. I'm not capable at the moment of making that kind of decision. If she'd give me a little time, maybe it would happen."

"Have you told her that?" she asked.

"Yeah. In a roundabout way."

"What's that mean? I don't understand."

"I didn't make any promises. I just told her I needed more time."

"Who's this other guy? Is he as bad as Mom says?"

"Worse. But he wants to marry her immediately." Enough of the questions. I changed the subject. "What about Evert? What're you going to do?"

Her expression changed drastically. "I'm going to file for divorce. He deserted me. I'm through with him. I should've done it a long time ago."

"Good for you. That's what I wanted to hear."

"You changed the subject. We were talking about Jimmie. Now, are you going to tell her you love her or let her marry this despicable person?"

"I just don't know. Maybe she'll see through him, and I won't have to do that."

Angie left late that evening, and I went to bed early, expecting to sleep well. Instead, I spent one of the worst nights since coming home. Dreams of the war would wake me, and after going back to sleep they would come again. Each of the episodes where my five men were killed replayed throughout the night, but the worst was Louis, who I had allowed to take the point. I woke up, thinking how horrific it must've been for his parents, not even being able to view the body of their son. And it was my fault.

# 50

# THE SET UP

JIMMIE LYN

My mother called me Wednesday morning at work during one of the busiest times of the day—thirty minutes before the beginning of the sale. She asked about Dad, then described her encounter with Grace at the grocery store yesterday. She was pleased with herself for, as she put it, telling her off. Rather than get mad, I asked her to have lunch with me Saturday, at the Ranch House at noon. I think she was surprised that I didn't scold her for treating Grace the way she did.

Things had gone well the last several weeks, with the exception of Madge and the bookkeeping. I couldn't spare Grace to help her, and she fell behind. I would stay and work each day in an effort to catch her up.

I'd been out to the ranch a couple of times, but it was hard to get away. Dad's treatment each week would make him ill. When he was feeling better, it was time for another one. He still had at least three more treatments remaining.

Drake had only been over twice in the last two weeks, mainly because I was too busy during the day and tired at night. I'd been so occupied with the Auction that there was little time for anything else. It didn't seem to bother Luke, but Drake was a different matter. He didn't try to hide his frustration.

Today we had over 1,500 head to sell, which was a good run for us. I always tried to take time before the sale to see as many buyers as I could.

I'd just ask them how they were doing, give them an update on Dad, and tell them I appreciated their presence. A half dozen buyers would buy a majority of the cattle, with area farmers and ranchers taking the rest.

Dewayne was setting up and testing his mic when I entered the area behind the ring. "Jimmie Lyn, we have a good run today."

"Yes. I hope everything goes well. I still get nervous on sale day."

He laughed, shaking his head. "Benny's doing a good job. It's amazing what the person starting cattle can do. Of course, everybody knows and trusts him, and when he puts a price on a cow, they start bidding. It's unreal, but last week he didn't catch but half a dozen or so. That's better than your dad does most of the time."

I turned as Benny came up behind me. "We were just talking about you, Benny. Dewayne was bragging on you."

"Don't get used to me sitting up here in this chair. When Blaine returns, it's back to the pens for me. That's where I belong—with the dust and manure."

I patted him on the shoulder. "Just the same, we appreciate you."

✳✳✳

Saturday came quickly, and I arrived ten minutes early at the restaurant, where I was to meet my mother. I picked out a table toward the back and waited on her. She was there shortly, dressed like she was going to a social event. I led the way to the table, making sure she sat where there was a view of the front booths and tables.

She immediately started in on Sterling. "I'm going to leave Sterling. I've made up my mind. I don't enjoy his company in the least. I've thought of a word that describes him—stuffy. He's no fun and so predictable it's unbelievable. I can tell you what he's doing just about every minute of the day. Right now, he's probably eating a ham and cheese sandwich that he takes for lunch every day. For dessert he'll have a banana. I don't know why . . ." She stopped, staring at the front.

Sterling had come in and was going toward a booth. He had on jeans and a flannel shirt with a High Plains Auction cap. "What's he doing here, dressed like that? He doesn't even own that kind of clothes. He doesn't ever eat here at lunch."

I thought of my last visit to the dentist—to keep from smiling. "I guess he felt like eating out today. He looks nice in those clothes. He's even got a cap from the Auction."

The waitress was standing there waiting for us to order, but my mother didn't pay any attention to her. "He wasn't wearing those clothes when he left for work this morning. Something's not right."

While my mother focused on the booth where Sterling was sitting, I ordered for us. "I'm going over there, Jimmie Lyn, to see what's going on. He may have lost his mind."

I took her arm. "Leave him alone. You wanted him to do something different. Maybe he's just trying to please you." Keeping a straight face was a challenge.

"Who's that at his booth? Can you see who that is?" she started to get up again, but I put my hand on her arm.

"I believe that's Piper. Yes, I'm sure. No one else dresses like that. I guess she came for lunch. She's probably just saying hello to Sterling." I turned my head so Mother wouldn't see my face.

In full view of my mother and a good many citizens, Piper reached and took Sterling's hat, placing it on her head and sat down opposite him.

"Well! Well! I-I never! Why would she act like that with him? She's married!" She tried to rise again, but I grabbed her arm.

"Our food's here. Let's eat and you can ask Sterling about it when he gets home tonight. Don't pay any attention to Piper. She's always been a flirt. She has a preference for older men. After all, her husband is twelve years older than she is."

I ate all of my lunch, but my mother barely touched hers. I stalled as long as I could, hoping Sterling would leave before us. It worked out even better than expected. They left together with Piper still wearing the High Plains Cattle Auction cap.

When I stopped by Piper's house on the way to my apartment, she came to the door laughing. "That was so much fun, Jimmie Lyn. My One Act Play experience proved beneficial. Sterling's such a sweet man. He blushed every time I said something. Did we fool your mother?"

"You were perfect. She left like she was going to a fire, headed toward Sterling's office. I told him to be cool and act innocent when she started with the questions. When we were planning it, I told him not to apologize. Did you tell Daniel about the plan?"

"Yes. He thought it was hilarious. He's known your mother for years and has always felt sorry for Sterling. I hope this helps her realize what she has and appreciates it."

I thanked her for the performance and left. When I drove up to my apartment, Drake's car was there. I wasn't in the mood to see him and had planned on going to the ranch, anxious to tell Luke about the trick on my mother.

He approached me saying, "I should've called before coming, but I knew you were busy. I need to talk with you." He was different today, and the smile was absent.

He followed me into the house and sat down without an invitation. I could tell this was going to be a serious discussion. "I need for you to make a decision. I've been patient, but it's time for me to get on with my life. We can be married immediately or have a church wedding in the near future. It makes no difference to me, but I want an answer today."

This was unexpected. He was not the same person, and it frightened me. "Why the hurry? I thought you were going to give me some time."

"I've given you time. Something has been holding you up, and I know what it is—rather who it is. It's humiliating for you to be withholding your decision because of this boy. You're several years older than he is and besides that—taller. I'm not going to continue to compete with this kid."

I stared at him, seeing a totally different Drake. The longer I went without responding the more irritated he looked.

He continued. "I went to see him today. That guy threatened to put his dog on me. He was scared, and he should've been. I doubt if he has anything to do with you after my visit. I told him to stop seeing you."

If he only knew this so-called kid who he thought was afraid of him. "You've had your say. You can leave now. I'm not going to marry you."

I'd never seen such hate as he rose. "No woman has ever turned me down! You and that—that boy will be sorry. I promise you that!" He left, slamming the door.

I tried to stand but my legs were shaking, and I had to sit back down. My heart was racing, and I felt like my skin was crawling. I didn't know what to do. "Calm down," I said aloud. "It's over, and you'll never see him again." But didn't I hear him threaten me and Luke?

After getting myself together, I left for the ranch, wondering what Luke would think of Drake's visit. When I drove up, Bull came to meet me, anxious for my attention. I was glad to catch them at the house, since Luke usually went back to work right after lunch.

Luke came around the house and I smiled, thinking, *so this is the kid who's shorter than me, who is the reason I'm not marrying Drake Davis.* He had on jeans that were dirty but fit well, since he gained weight, and an old black hat that needed throwing away, and there was only one description that fit him—heavenly.

# 51
# THE TEST

"Do you think she's ready, Daughter?" He had his window rolled down, to allow the smoke to escape, even though this morning it was still chilly.

I stared straight ahead, being extra careful, since I was carrying valuable cargo. "If she's not, she never will be. She's sound as she ever was. I just don't know how she'll run. After all, it's been eight months since the injury, and we've done everything the vet asked of us."

It was the third of May, and we were on the way to a place where we could give Lady an out before taking her to Ruidoso. It was a long trip to Central Texas from Dalhart, but it would be worth it to find out if she was going to come back after the layoff. To be exact, it was 328 miles to Trent, a small town west of Abilene. Luke had described the little country racetrack, and after calling the owner of the track earlier in the week, he'd discovered that they were racing today. My dad and I were on the way and should be there by eleven this morning, which would give Lady several hours to rest. It wasn't an ideal situation since the drive was long, but Lady was a good hauler and should be fine.

I'd been riding her every day that the weather allowed and galloping her every other day. Blaine had cleared a half mile route west of the Auction, and I used that area to gallop her. I'd even started riding her with my exercise saddle and had no problems. I'd breezed her 200 yards a number of times, and she'd felt awesome.

I tried not to become too excited, but I was losing the battle. Blaine didn't help me either, constantly predicting she was going to come back even better. I continued to be amazed that I now owned half of this beautiful animal.

We stopped at a roadside park on the south side of Plainview, unloaded Lady and walked her around for fifteen minutes. A bathroom stop wasn't necessary for Dad and me since we took turns using the trailer. I smiled, thinking of what Blaine's ex would think about me being so crude.

We didn't stop again until Post, where we filled up with gas. Luke had written down directions for us, and two hours later we found the racetrack without any problems. We arrived a little after twelve, going past a three-horse starting gate, and had our choice of parking among the scattered mesquite trees since the place was vacant.

After we unloaded Lady next to a shady area, I walked her up and down the quarter-mile track, which was about thirty feet wide, with a cable on each side. The ground was excellent—sandy, yet firm enough to get a good hold. As I was going back to the pickup, a man drove up on a Farmall tractor. He stopped a good way from me, turned it off and walked over to me.

"I was afraid your horse would spook at my tractor."

"You must be, Mack," I said extending my hand.

"That's right."

My dad had come over. "This is my dad, William. Most call him Willie."

A handshake later my dad said, "Getting ready to plant cotton?"

"In the next couple of weeks. We need a rain, but that's not unusual for this country. Y'all had a long drive. You must've got away early. Have you had lunch? You're welcome to join us."

"Thank you, but we brought sandwiches. What time does the crowd usually arrive?" I was hoping we'd have several hours for Lady to recover from the long ride.

"Around two. It usually takes another couple of hours before we have any races." He walked around Lady. "That's a nice filly. I assume she's the one that had the fracture. Luke spent the afternoon with us in October, on his way back home with her. He's a nice young man."

"Yes. She fractured her leg at the track the first of September. We just need to see how she comes back before taking her to Ruidoso."

He looked at her again and smiled. "I'm guessing she can run a little."

Dad couldn't resist telling him. "She ran second in the New Mexico Futurity last year. That's when she was injured."

Another smile. "I thought so. I kinda put two and two together. She looks like a scorpion. We'll keep it to ourselves, and it shouldn't be hard to match her. How much money do you want to put up?"

"We don't have much. I guess we could come up with $100. We're more interested in seeing how she does after the long layoff."

"I know just the people that have a horse that would give her a good test. They've come down from Big Spring the last couple of times and matched horses they outran easily. I need to get to the house. Wanda will have dinner ready."

I was afraid our expectations were too high and we were going to be disappointed.

✳✳✳

By three o'clock there were at least twenty-five pickups with trailers, some carrying two horses. We were standing by our rig when I heard someone call my name. I looked up in surprise and saw, of all people, Kenneth, our regular jockey. I'd forgotten that he was from Abilene.

"Grace, what're you doing here?" he asked, hugging me. "Is that . . . Is that her? She looks awesome."

"We brought her for a work after surgery and the layoff. I'm glad to see you. Could you help us get a race? We're new at this." What a stroke of good fortune to find Kenneth here.

"Sure. I know just the horse and the horse's rear. Just stay here and wait. He'll be around soon, harassing you. I have a race coming up. Just be patient, and we'll get you fixed up."

"Can you believe it, Grace? Kenneth being here is bound to be a good sign."

"I know, Dad. I'd forgotten that he's from Abilene, and since Ruidoso hasn't opened yet, he's riding at this country track."

We watched the first race, and it was close, but the horse Kenneth was riding won. We returned to our pickup and found a tall thin man wearing a big black hat surrounded by silver conchos at the crown—his jeans stuffed into his knee-high boots, examining Lady.

He offered no introduction or greeting. "What'cha got here? Looks like she's taking a nap. Is she a kid pony? Looks too calm to be a racehorse. I bet she couldn't outrun a fat man. She's what I'd expect around this rat-hole place. I come down here and nobody wants no part of old Dust Devil. I don't guess you'd be interested in losing some money today, would you?"

Before I could find words to answer this rude man, Kenneth walked up. "You look'n to make some easy money, Brinson?"

"Probably not. Everybody's afraid of old Dust Devil. I don't know why I bother coming to this place. There're no good horses and no money either." He pointed to Lady. "Do you know anything about this kid pony?"

"A little. She's a nice three-year-old filly that's recovering from a fracture. They just want to see how she comes back. She might be willing to work against your horse. Of course, it would only be a work, and she wouldn't put up any money."

"You gotta be stupid! I don't run Dust Devil for less than $200. She shouldn't bring a cripple out here." He turned and started to walk off.

"Wait a minute!" Brinson turned around. "I hate to see you come all this way without matching Dust Devil. What about giving the crippled filly daylight and going 300 yards? I've got $100 to put up if you'll give me 2-1 odds, and you might find some other suckers."

Brinson licked his lips and smiled. "That might work. Give me half-an-hour to see if I can get some more money put up. I'll give 2-1 odds to anyone—for any amount."

He left and Kenneth said, "He gives this sport a bad name. See what I mean by horse's butt. I have a feeling he's going to get a lot more takers than he planned on."

I brushed Lady, including her mane and tail before cleaning out her feet. That guy was something else. I didn't know anyone could be that rude. Thank goodness for Kenneth. After I finished grooming Lady, I walked over to where Brinson had drawn a crowd, talking loud enough to be heard in another county.

"What I want to know—where's the money? I'm giving this lady's horse daylight and 2-1 odds to you would-be gamblers. What's the matter with you people? What else can I do to get you to turn loose of your money?"

Mack then stepped forward with a handful of bills. "I'll take some of those 2-1 odds."

After that, several other men came forward with money. A man next to Brinson was writing down the bets and holding the money in a small box. Brinson was not yelling anymore.

Kenneth was at the trailer when we returned. "If you want me to, I'll go bet your money for you. Getting 2-1 odds against this filly shouldn't even be called gambling but a great investment."

I gave him my $100, and he left. I got a cloth out of the pickup seat, wet it with our drinking water, and cleaned Lady's nose and face. "Pretty girl. Let's show this bully what you can do."

Kenneth returned with his saddle. "Your $100 wiped him out, Grace. He got his wish. I imagine there's at least $2000 bet." He put a blanket and then the saddle on Lady. "Has she been gated since she was injured?"

"No. She's always been calm. It's been so long though, today may be different." He finished saddling—I gave him a leg up, and he rode off toward the track, leaving me with my heart in my throat. Could she really come back?

I didn't go to the finish line. I could see the race better standing back fifty yards or so about midway between the start and end of the race. Dad had gone to the finish line. I'd never been this nervous before a race—even the Futurity last year.

They were loading in the gates, and I was taking deep breaths trying to relax. They were in the gates! Why was it taking so long? The gates opened with a clang and both broke good. They were running side-by-side at first, and Lady hit another gear, pulling away, and by the time they passed me, the halfway mark, she was already ahead by two lengths. I didn't go to the finish line but went back to the pickup.

Kenneth came up several minutes later, slid off and turned to me. "Grace, she's even better than last year. I clicked once and she jerked his head off. She's an amazing filly."

I tried to find words to thank Kenneth but nothing seemed enough, so I hugged him with tears flowing. He seemed to understand.

He took his saddle off and said he was going to get our money.

Dad came back shaking his head. "Can you believe it, Daughter? She's awesome. I can't wait for you to call Blaine."

Kenneth returned with our money but wouldn't take anything for his jockey fee, saying he'd won $200. I assured him that we would be in Ruidoso for the Derby, and he would be up on Lady.

Mack and his wife, Wanda, offered to let us stay the night with them. I took them up on Lady, but said we already had reservations at the

Merkel Motel. It was five o'clock when all this was happening. Wanda rode to their house with us, and we stalled Lady and put out feed for her.

After taking care of Lady, we went into Merkel, checked into the motel, and I called Blaine. I tried to sound normal, but it was no use. He quickly picked up on my excitement as I described the race against a solid AAA horse. I had trouble ending the call because he kept talking about taking her to Ruidoso. I finally told him we needed to go eat and hung up.

We went across the motel driveway to a restaurant. We each ordered chicken fried steak, which was very good. We finished and were about to leave when a man came up to our table, introducing himself as Dean Smith. He reached and picked up our ticket. "I was out at the racetrack today. I bet on your filly, and I'm going to buy your supper. Brinson has been coming out and bullying everyone. He got what he deserved today."

✳︎ ✳︎ ✳︎

Lying in bed that night, I thought of the wonderful, kind people who'd made our trip successful. I went to sleep knowing Lady was in good hands with Mack and Wanda and thinking of how Henry would've enjoyed today.

# 52

# UNCLE LUKE

It was Saturday, the third of May, and a great time to be at the ranch. Calves were being born every day, and the grass was beginning to turn green, eliminating the need to put out hay. I still caked them every third day, but that was easy. I spent my days repairing fence and the wooden pens that were located on three parts of the ranch. It was no problem staying busy with miles of fence and the pens which had been neglected. Mom and Granddad had taken Lady to the little racetrack in Trent. I was tempted to go but knew I needed to stay close.

Jimmie came out late in the afternoon, bringing our supper. Today, it was fried chicken and biscuits she'd bought at the grocery store deli. Nothing smells as good as fried chicken, and I was hungry. I'd gained at least ten pounds the last month and was wearing some of the older jeans that had been too large earlier.

We'd developed this ritual of hugging as our greeting and today was no exception, with her holding the sack of chicken. "Are you glad to see me, or are you just lusting after the fried chicken?"

"Is it okay to say both? Would that get me in trouble?"

She held on to me a little longer than usual. "I'll accept that."

It was still early, but I couldn't wait to get at the chicken, so we went ahead and ate. Bull had developed this gift of looking so pitiful, even managing some moisture in his eyes, that Jimmie gave him a chicken leg, which he promptly carried off out of our sight.

"Would you like to go for a ride and look at the new babies? We're getting a new batch every day."

"I'd love to do that," she said.

We left the house with Bull riding in the back of the pickup. I think he understood but thought the chicken leg was worth the sacrifice. For the next hour we saw newborn calves from the age of three weeks to a day.

"They're beautiful, Luke. It gives you an appreciation of life and the mysteries of birth. How could anyone witness this and not know there is a God? Thank you for sharing this with me."

I turned off the ignition on my pickup, which was facing west. A few clouds brought out the contrasts of purples and pinks to the oranges and reds as the sun sank lower. I turned toward her. "What made you change your mind about Drake."

"Oh, Luke why do you have to ruin a perfect evening by bringing him up? I just decided he wasn't the person I thought he was."

I had to ask. "Was Blaine the only reason that's made the decision difficult? I mean, if your dad had given you the go-ahead, would it have been easy for you?"

She turned her head away from me, gazing out the window. "Why do you have to ask all these difficult questions about the past? The answer to both questions is no." She sniffed and paused. "There's someone else I care about. But he's been very careful not to give me any hope that we might have a future together. In fact, we had this discussion months earlier and agreed it wasn't serious for him. Maybe, more like a high school romance." More sniffs.

I slid across the seat, put my arm behind her back and pulled her to me.

✳✳✳

We had our coffee outside the next morning, watching the sun come up. Afterwards, she cooked pancakes, which turned out perfect. I already thought domestic life looks good.

We'd talked until well into the night about plans for the future. The only time she mentioned Drake was to say he'd threatened us, and she feared he might do something terrible. I felt good about being at the point where I could finally make a life altering decision. I thought, *it's not any too soon, Luke Ranker.*

After breakfast, we were standing by her car as she was getting ready to leave. We saw a pickup coming, kicking up dust it was going so fast. When it came closer, I could make out who it was. "That's your dad, and he's in a hurry."

He came to a sliding stop, getting out. "Luke, it's your sister! She's gone into labor and is at the hospital. You better get to town, quick."

"Get in, Luke! You can ride with me." She was turning her car around, and we drove past her dad before he was back into his pickup.

"Mom and Granddad are out of town. Of all times for her to go into labor. She's not due for another two weeks. I should've stayed with her."

"I'm sure she'll be fine, Luke."

It was the quickest trip to town I'd ever made. We were at the hospital in fifteen minutes. We were directed to the emergency room where we found her on a bed enclosed with curtains. Bronc was standing by the bed, holding her hand.

He looked up as we entered. "She called me, Luke. She found my number in the phone book. She was frightened, but we made it to the hospital in plenty of time."

"I didn't know what to do. My water broke, and I was afraid to drive." She still held on to Bronc's hand. "He was at the house five minutes after I called him. The doctor said it could still be a while."

I thought, *what a picture. My married sister whose husband deserted her, in labor, with a single cowboy holding her hand and comforting her. It could only happen in fairy tales.* "It looks like to me that y'all have everything under control."

I took Jimmie's arm. "We'll be in the waiting room if you need us."

Blaine came in a few minutes later and sat down beside us. We were the only people in the room. "I couldn't begin to catch up with you. How's she doing?"

Jimmie laughed. "Dad, I'd say she was in good hands. It's still going to be some time before they take her to delivery."

Blaine told us about talking with Mom and gave us the details of Lady's performance. "She has no idea she's about to become a grandmother. They're on the way home and won't be here for several more hours." He looked at his watch. "It's a little after eight. They won't be here until noon at least. Have y'all had breakfast?"

"Yeah. We'd just finished, and Jimmie was about to leave when you drove up," I said.

"Well, I haven't. I'm going to find me something to eat. It makes me nervous hanging around where babies are being born."

After he left, Jimmie took hold of my arm. "Oh, Luke, wasn't that sweet of Bronc?"

✳✳✳

Bronc waited with us after they came for Angie. The baby arrived at 10:09 and was a six pound three-ounce boy. We went in to see Angie an hour later. She was doing fine and managed a smile. While we were there they brought the baby in and gave him to Angie. "Isn't he beautiful?" she asked.

"He's gorgeous," Jimmie replied.

I couldn't see anything resembling beautiful, so I kept quiet.

"Have you thought of a name?" Jimmie asked.

"His first name is going to be Henry, after my dad. I don't know about a middle name."

I asked Jimmie to stay and told her I was going to the house and wait on Mom and Granddad. They should be home within the next hour or two.

It was such a nice day I sat outside and didn't have long to wait. Mom drove up and was out quickly, probably anxious to tell me about Lady's race. She greeted and hugged me before beginning. "I wouldn't have believed it if I hadn't seen it. She was awesome, Luke. Kenneth was there and he rode her, saying she was even better than before the injury."

I held up my hand to stop her. "I thought you might like to go see little Henry. He was born this morning and weighted six pounds three ounces."

She squealed and put her hand to her mouth. At first, she couldn't talk but that didn't last long. The questions poured from her like water out of a faucet. "Is Angie all right? Is the baby healthy?" The questions continued, but she didn't give me time to answer. Granddad had not said anything and just stood back smiling.

"Wouldn't you like to see him?" I asked. "I'll put Lady up while you and Granddad go to the hospital." They left immediately.

I drove the pickup and trailer over to Lady's stall and put her in the pen while I loaded up her hay rack. When she was taking a huge bite out of the hay, I rubbed her on the neck. "You're not as important as you were a few minutes ago."

✳✳✳

Angie stayed in the hospital a week due to the fact the baby came early. She decided on Luke for a middle name which pleased me. Henry Luke Ranker had a nice, solid sound to it. He was going to be called Hank, and for the week, at least, my mom's world changed. I'd come in from the ranch each afternoon to see about Angie, and my mother was always at the hospital, most times holding Hank. Granddad said she hadn't seen Lady since Hank was born, and he'd been doing all the feeding.

Blaine was back working full-time which freed Jimmie to spend more time at the ranch. Benny had gone back to the pens, and High Plains Cattle Auction had returned to normal.

My work at the ranch reached peak demand beginning the middle of

May with the haying season. Our hay barn was almost empty, and we had a hundred acres of wheat which hadn't been grazed to bale. Beginning the second week in May, it was cut and raked into windrows. Three days later the baling started, and Blaine sent a flat bed truck out with a driver and three hands to begin loading. It was important to get it out of the field as quickly as possible in case it rained.

With two loading and two stacking we put 500 bales on and took it to the Auction. We were able to unload and stack it in their barn, return to the ranch and load another 500 bales before quitting for the day. With rain in the forecast, Blaine hired another truck and hands to help us. With the additional truck, we were able to put 2,500 bales at the Auction and the same number in the ranch barn in five days. Mother Nature smiled on us, and the rain held off until we had the field cleared.

I'd never been so tired in my life when we finished on Friday, May twenty-third. Jimmie came out that evening and informed me she was taking me out to eat. I would've preferred to take a bath and sit down in front of the radio to listen to country music, but she was insistent.

"You need a reward for working so hard. There's this new Mexican food place in town that we need to try out. I'll have you home by ten, and you'll have the weekend to rest."

I was too tired to argue. The bath and clean clothes revived me somewhat and it turned out to be a nice evening. Just knowing that the hay hauling was over was a reason to feel better. When we left the restaurant going back to the ranch it was already dark and, with Jimmie driving, I leaned my head back and was almost asleep.

"What's he doing?" she screamed. "Move over!"

I bolted up to see a truck moving over into us, and the last thing I remembered was Jimmie's scream as we went off into the ditch.

# 53

# CLOSE CALL

☙ JIMMIE LYN ❧

She stood in a corner at the junior high dance, watching the other girls bunched up and giggling, waiting for a boy to ask them to dance. No one would ask her because she was a head taller than everyone. Her best friend, Piper, had talked her into coming, and Piper was on the dance floor every time the DJ put on a new song. Why did she give in and come in the first place, knowing what would happen? Besides hearing the whispers of giraffe, she had just gotten braces last week, and her mouth was full of wire. She kept wishing it would be over, and she could go home.

The music ended and Piper came over with a boy following her. "Jimmie Lyn, Delbert wants the next dance." She turned to him. "Delbert."

"Would you like to dance, Jimmie Lyn?" he held out his hand.

She took his hand and the music began. It was a slow dance—two-step. It was awkward, but they made it through a country song by Hank Williams.

After the song finished, she started back to her corner but was intercepted by another boy. This next dance was more to her liking. The song was "Great Balls of Fire" with Jerry Lee Lewis and the dance was the swing. She was not that close to her partner, so her height wasn't that obvious. She was having fun!

For the next three songs, different boys came and asked her to dance. She couldn't believe this was happening! The third song ended, and her partner left the floor in a hurry headed toward the door. She saw Piper waiting for *him, and they left, going outside.*

*She saw Delbert standing off to one side. Going over to him she asked what was going on.* "When one of us dances with you, she takes them outside and kisses them. She's awesome. Could I have the next dance?"

✱✱✱

I came to, not knowing where I was. It was dark and something wasn't right. I heard strange noises—someone talking and a grinding sound. A light shined in, and all I saw was the floor of a car. Then I remembered a truck ramming the car, and flying off into the ditch. I was trapped inside and my head hurt. I felt something warm and sticky on my face. Blood!

I heard someone else move and moan next to me. Luke was with me! Now I was fully awake and realized someone was trying to free us. The car was upside down, and we couldn't get out. I smelled gasoline. "Help us, please! Help!"

The light shined inside again. "Stay calm. We'll have you out in a minute." It came from a voice outside.

The car door was jerked off and hands reached inside, took hold of me and pulled. I felt the rush of night air and saw lights flashing all around. The next thing I remembered was being inside a car with a siren blaring. After that, everything was foggy, and it seemed like I was dreaming again.

✱✱✱

I woke up smelling alcohol and couldn't remember where I was. A woman was rubbing my face with a cloth. She had on a white dress, and I realized she was a nurse, and I was in the hospital. Someone had a cuff on my arm that was becoming tighter. A doctor was taking my blood pressure.

"You're going to be fine. We need to take some stiches and make some x-rays. Are you hurting anywhere?"

"My head." Everything was becoming clearer. The wreck, flashing lights, and the ride. Where was Luke? Was he here? Was he hurt?

"Luke. Where's Luke?" I asked, looking at the doctor.

"He's receiving treatment. Don't worry, we're taking care of him."

What did that mean? He was hurt too. How bad? The doctor was gone before I could ask him any more questions. The nurse was still in the room. "How bad is Luke hurt?"

"You heard the doctor. He's being taken care of. That's all I know." She left, evidently not wanting any more questions.

I tried to get up, but the doctor came back in. "What're you doing? You're not in any shape to go anywhere." He turned my head to examine the cut.

"I want to know about Luke. Where is he?"

He stopped his examination and stepped back. "Amarillo. We couldn't treat him here. Now, I need to stich up that cut."

He stepped forward with a needle and I jerked away. "You're not doing nothing to me until I know about Luke. How bad was he hurt?"

"Worse than you. He had injuries that needed more than we had to offer here. I don't know the extent of them. All I can say is they were serious and life threatening."

I stiffened with fear. Luke was going to die. He might already be dead and they're lying to me. Tears burned when they entered the cut on my face. After all we'd been through and now this. I heard loud talking outside the room.

The door opened, and my dad came in followed by the nurse. "How're you, Honey?"

"Blaine, she's going to be fine. Just some cuts and bruises. Probably a slight concussion. We're going to take some x-rays just as a precautionary measure. She's going to be sore for some time." The doctor turned back to me. "Now, are you going to let me stitch you up?"

"Dad, they won't give me information about Luke."

He moved to the bed and took my hand. "He's hurt bad, Honey. Grace has gone to Amarillo. She promised to call when she found out something. Do you remember what happened?"

"Not much. We were on the way to the ranch. A big truck run into us, and the last thing I remember is going off into the ditch. It happened so fast. I think Luke was asleep." Then I remembered more. "The truck did it on purpose. I remember screaming for him to stop and trying to move over away from him."

Dad continued to hold my hand. "Lie still and let the doctor do his job. We'll hear from Grace shortly."

After the doctor finished, they took me to a room and gave me something that knocked me out. The last thing I remembered was asking Dad if there was a telephone in the room.

I must've slept for hours because when I woke up, the sun was shining through the window. I moved and it hurt. I moved again and it hurt more. I was sore from head to toe and as long as I was still it was okay. I tried to sit up but fell back moaning in pain.

"What is it, Honey?" Dad was evidently in the chair, and I hadn't seen him.

"Just hurts all over when I move. Have you heard from Grace?"

"Not yet. She knows to call the hospital though."

There was a knock and Benny stuck his head in the door. "Missy, I had to come see about you."

"I'm sore and that's about all. I'll be fine. It's Luke I'm worried about."

"What happened, Missy?" Benny asked.

I told him everything I remembered. Then he asked me who would've done such a thing on purpose. I didn't know whether to tell him or not. I'd already thought about it, and Drake's threat kept coming to mind. He was the only person who would want to hurt me and Luke.

"I can't say for sure, Benny. I believe it was probably Drake." Of course, it was Drake, I thought. Who else would do such a thing?

"Do you remember what kind of truck it was?" Benny asked.

"It was dark and all I could see was a form of a truck. I knew it was a truck because it was much taller than my car. I may remember more later." It seemed my mind was becoming clearer all the time.

Benny left, telling Dad to get in touch if we needed anything. The doctor came in and told me that it was time for x-rays. I'd never felt such pain as when they helped me out of bed into a wheelchair. The x-rays were even worse. Having to get up on the table and change positions brought excruciating pain. They finally finished and wheeled me back to the room.

Dad was on the phone and hung up just as I entered. "That was Grace. Luke still hasn't regained consciousness. They know he has a broken collarbone and wrist but are puzzled why he hasn't come to. She promised to keep us informed."

I wondered if Grace had told them about his previous concussion. I asked my dad to call her back and remind her. One thing for sure—if my x-rays showed no fractures, I was getting out of here and going to Amarillo. I was the reason this had happened, and Luke was suffering and might die.

My next visitor, my mother, flew into the room surrounded by drama. My dad left immediately. She carried on over me like a mother is supposed to do except she kept inserting herself into the sympathy. She and Sterling were supposed to leave on a two-week cruise Sunday, but it would be postponed until I was well, even though the cost of the trip was not refundable at this late date.

"Mother, I'm fine. Don't cancel your trip because of me."

"Well, Sterling would be disappointed since it was his idea we take this vacation. He's been working so hard and needs some time off."

Ever since the episode at the restaurant she had nothing bad to say about Sterling. Evidently, he'd handled her questions about Piper well. She left after I assured her it would be fine for her to go ahead with the cruise.

The doctor returned an hour later with the results of the x-rays. "You're fortunate. There are no broken bones but only severe bruising. You do have a slight concussion. We'll keep you a couple of days just to be on the safe side."

"No. I'm leaving today. If you'll write me a prescription for a pain killer, I'd appreciate it. I'm going to Amarillo to be with Luke."

✲✲✲

We stayed in the intensive care waiting room until Grace came out. We hugged, and she said that Luke was conscious. I breathed a sigh of relief as she continued to explain. "The doctor said he had a severe concussion and, coupled with the one back last fall, was the reason he was out for so long. His injuries included a broken collarbone, wrist and ankle. His memory right now is fuzzy, but he did know me. When you see him don't be shocked. His face is cut in several places, evidently glass from the windshield did that.

"Thank the Lord you're all right, Jimmie. Luke is already asking about you. I told him you were fine, just bunged up a little. They're going to keep him in intensive care for another couple of hours before they move him into a room."

"Grace, why don't you and I go get something to drink in the cafeteria while Jimmie Lyn stays with Luke?" asked my dad.

"That sounds good," Grace said. "Visitors are only allowed for fifteen minutes, but maybe they'll stretch it a little."

Luke had his eyes closed when I went into the room. I studied him, lying there in critical condition with wide cuts on his forehead, below his right eye, and on his left cheek, all because of me. The wounds had been sewn up, and it had taken at least thirty stitches. I moved to him, leaned over, and kissed him lightly on the lips. He didn't wake up, so I kissed him again with a little more pressure.

He opened his eyes, looking confused, and then smiled. "Hello."

"I'm so sorry, Luke." I took hold of his hand.

"What happened? I just remember you screaming and then going into the ditch."

I told him everything I knew including my opinion that it was Drake or someone he'd hired. I continued to remember a little more each time I went over it. The truck was solid, much shorter than an eighteen-wheeler. It was more the size of a bread truck as I remembered the outline in the darkness.

"Are you sure it was Drake?" he asked.

"Who else would it be? It could be that he hired someone. I have no doubt he was behind it, one way or the other."

A nurse came in, and said it was time for me to leave. I was tempted to argue, but then I thought she might not let me back in again. I squeezed his hand, bent down, and whispered, "I love you, Sergeant Ranker."

# 54

# RUIDOSO

GRACE

It was June eighteenth, and we were packing for the move to Ruidoso. I don't know who was more excited—me or Angie. Hank was six weeks old, and we thought he was old enough to make the change. My dad wasn't going. He was happy here and enjoyed working at the Auction. The first thing on the agenda when we arrived in Ruidoso would be to locate a doctor for the baby. I'd been concerned about leaving Luke, but it had been three and a half weeks since the wreck, and he was under Jimmie's care. She had insisted—no, demanded—that he stay with her since our little house would've been crowded. Luke protested, but it was feeble, and he was recovering nicely. With the broken ankle, collarbone, and wrist he was pretty much helpless. Angie had been taking Hank and staying with Luke during the day while Jimmie was at work. The main problem we encountered with the set-up was Bull, who went on a hunger strike and wouldn't eat. We finally took him to Jimmie's to be with Luke, and he was satisfied.

Jimmie insisted that the wreck was no accident and Drake Davis was responsible. Blaine had done some checking and found that Drake was still in Amarillo but had no way to prove he was involved. I'd thought that when Luke returned from Vietnam he'd be out of harm's way, but it'd been just the opposite. He wasn't happy being confined to a recliner but was accepting it better than I would've thought.

Blaine had done well after the treatments ended, and the number of cattle being brought to the Auction increased weekly with the runs now consisting of around 2,000 a week. He'd returned for his three-week check-up the first of June and received a positive report.

I'd anticipated being a grandmother would be rewarding, but it turned out to be beyond description, and holding Hank, looking into those big blue eyes, filled my heart. We've had our share of heartache the past several months, however, as my dad had reminded me many times, there is a silver lining in every cloud. Hank was a good baby, sleeping most of the night and seldom crying.

Bronc had been coming around often, with the pretense of seeing the baby but spent most of his time talking to Angie. When I said something to the effect that it looked as if she had an admirer, she denied it. "Mother, he wouldn't be interested in me. He's only being nice. I'm a single mother—why would he even consider me?"

"Well, let's see if I can think of a reason. You're a beautiful young lady who is intelligent, sweet, and would make someone a wonderful mate. I believe that Bronc is smart enough to see these characteristics. Just think what you like, and we'll see who's right."

We had everything loaded in my pickup and ready to go by late that afternoon, with plans to leave early the next morning. I was taking my trailer and hauling Lady. Blaine would hire someone to bring the other three horses within the next few days. I didn't trust anyone with Lady. Besides, it would be good to have my two-horse trailer available.

Jimmie and Luke came out that night to say goodbye. It was Luke's left wrist and collarbone that were broken and his right ankle. He could hobble with a crutch at a snail's pace and was able to get into the house with Jimmie's help. His face had healed from cuts but did leave scars that would be permanent. However, with his dark complexion they didn't take away from his looks. Jimmie's scar was visible, also, but it was above her right eye and was barely noticeable. It seemed that every time I saw her, the more beautiful she became. When she was with Luke, she reminded me of a rose in full bloom.

Hank was passed around throughout the evening, giving everyone an opportunity to hold him. Even Luke had his turn, cradling him in his good arm. After hugs and well wishes they said goodbye at nine. I noticed that Angie had a long face. "Bronc didn't come to tell you and Hank 'bye, did he?"

She looked up surprised but recovered quickly. "Oh, Mother, I didn't expect him to come. He has better things to do than waste his time with me."

I moved over and hugged her. "You're too transparent and honest to fib, Angie, especially to your mother."

She left quickly saying she needed to check on Hank, whom she'd put to bed an hour earlier.

***

I was up by five the next morning. I made the coffee and finished loading the last- minute items in the pickup. We'd hooked the trailer on last night and put in bedding to give Lady a comfortable ride. I included my exercise saddle, chaps, and helmet in the tack compartment when no one was around. I was going to continue to ride Lady for at least a month.

With Lady loaded, I drove back to the house to pick up Angie and the baby. She walked out of the house, carrying a bag, followed by Bronc with Hank. I smiled—he'd shown up this morning to have a little private time. Angie got in and he handed the baby to her, saying, "I'll see you soon."

Pulling away, I glanced at Angie, who was smiling. "He wants to come see me in Ruidoso. I couldn't very well say no, could I, Mother?"

I laughed. "No, Angie, you did the only thing you could."

Our route took us to Tucumcari, New Mexico, through Melrose and on to Roswell. From there it was only about seventy miles to Ruidoso. We stopped several times but were at the track by one in the afternoon. We'd kept the same stalls for years in Barn C. I'd called in May before the meet opened and reserved them for this year. When we arrived at Barn C, the stalls were full on both sides. There was only one thing to do. I drove to the office and spoke to a man behind the counter. "I had the stalls on one side of Barn C reserved for the season. Both sides are in use."

He asked for my name and went over to a filing cabinet, thumbing through it until he came out with a folder. Opening it, he frowned. "You didn't show up at the beginning of the meet."

"No. I made it clear when I called in May I was going to be late arriving."

"There is no record of that request. I'm sorry but there's nothing I can do. We don't have any stalls available on the grounds."

I didn't expect it to start this quickly. "My husband and I have had Barn C for years. I have a filly in the New Mexico Derby. You're going to find me stalls for my horses!"

A man who must've heard me came out of a back office. "Is there a problem?"

"She says she reserved Barn C in May, but she didn't show up and we gave it to someone else."

"I did reserve the barn and told them I'd be late getting here," I repeated.

"What's your name?" asked the new arrival to the debate.

"Grace Ranker."

He looked surprised. "Henry's wife? I should've remembered you. I'm so sorry for your loss." He turned to the other man. "Find this lady some stalls."

It took someone who remembered Henry to get something done. "Thank you."

The stalls I received were about as far away from the track as possible.

I could see why they were vacant since there were knee-high weeds covering the area. I checked the stalls and then unloaded Lady, putting out some hay and water for her. I would find someone to mow the weeds.

After unhooking my trailer, we left to find our residence. Blaine had given me directions and the address. We found the road which twisted among random pines toward the little cream-colored frame house snuggled beneath the mountain overlooking the racetrack several miles below us. We stopped in front and admired it. The large picture windows held long flower boxes containing what looked like multicolored zinnias. A stone wall pushed forward concealing some kind of roofless deck. In front of the deck Shasta daisies bowed and swayed in crowded masses. I felt like a little girl looking under the Christmas tree seeing her perfect doll house, except this was reality.

"Mother, it's beautiful. He must've hired someone to landscape. Let's go inside."

Clutching the key in my hand, I couldn't wait to see behind the sky-blue door. Stepping back in time, an oak grandfather clock looked down on me. To the right a round oak claw-footed table and chairs sat flanked with a matching mirrored china hutch. Victorian furniture surrounded the den walls. A white fireplace captured the attention of the north wall. Floor to ceiling white book shelves stood on each side of it. The small kitchen, bath, and two bedrooms in the antique style completed our residence for the summer. The back door revealed a rose garden. Honeysuckle covered the feet of beautiful shrubs and trees I couldn't name. A path led around a bend to the mountain trail behind the tiny secret garden. It was me—a perfect fresh start.

"I didn't expect anything like this. It's wonderful," Angie said.

"It's hard to believe we're going to live in something like this after spending so many years at the track in a travel trailer." I was at a loss for words.

✳✳✳

The next several days were busy, cleaning up the stall area, buying feed and getting our other three horses settled in after they arrived. I'd rise early, go to the track, and feed Lady. Every other day I exercised her. Usually by eight o'clock I'd go back to have breakfast with Angie and Hank. They would return with me to the track, weather permitting. Angie had grown up around horses and was a big help. She was a willing worker, cleaning stalls and doing other jobs that came up while I took care of Hank. Late in the afternoon we would sit on the deck and enjoy the gorgeous view of the mountains to the south and west. I began to feel guilty for being so happy and thinking less often of the past as I held my sweet grandson.

The little house had a telephone, and we talked with my dad or Luke every few days. The second week Bronc called, and I took Hank out on the deck to allow them privacy. Blaine had called several times inquiring about Lady and asking if we needed anything. He hadn't even seen the house, which he bought through a realtor. I described it to him, trying to help him visualize its simplicity and charm.

I hadn't planned on entering Lady until the Derby but, looking at the race schedule, saw there was an allowance race the Fourth of July for three-year-old non-winners of a race this year. The purse was $5,000 which was too tempting to pass up, and I decided to enter her. I'd saved some money, but it would run out soon, and the purse would be a welcome addition to my bank account if she could win. Another factor in my decision was that Angie had decided she wanted to start divorce proceedings when we had the money. I was making an effort to justify entering her but the real reason was that I was anxious to see how she would run.

# 55

# DETECTIVE

 LUKE

I'd been waiting to be dismissed for two hours and was getting impatient. I needed to get out of here into some fresh air. It was Wednesday, May twenty-eighth, and I'd been here for five days. I'd gone through almost two years in a war zone and returned without a scratch, and now I had a cast on my wrist and ankle with my arm in a sling, nursing a broken collarbone. I could play the role of Frankenstein with my face sewn together. One man was responsible, and I was helpless. How long would I be in this shape? What if he wasn't satisfied with what he'd done to us?

"What are you thinking about?" Jimmie asked. She was waiting with me and was my ride back to Dalhart.

"What I must look like. The guy in the mirror this morning scared me. You sure you want to be seen with me?"

"You look good to me, Luke Ranker. You'll be as good as new in no time."

A nurse came in with papers for me to sign, followed by a guy pushing a wheelchair. I put my name on the dotted lines, managed to get in the wheelchair, and was on my way to freedom.

\*\*\*

For the next month, I stayed with Jimmie. She fed me, washed my clothes, helped me get dressed and undressed and cared for me like we were married. She would go to work each day but make sure I was comfortable in front of the TV and would come home and prepare lunch for me. From time to time Angie would stay with me during the day. I came to depend on Jimmie more than anyone else in my lifetime.

My mother left for Ruidoso on June nineteenth with Angie and Hank. Hank was only six weeks old but both were confident he'd be fine. I'd become a devoted and loving uncle to this little boy. I hated to see them leave, but Mom was excited, and I promised to come see them as soon as I was able. Angie was as happy as I'd ever seen her. She planned to file for divorce and, of course, Bronc had been coming around often, even though he'd taken my place at the ranch.

Finally, on June twenty-fifth, the doctor removed the cast on my ankle and the one on my wrist, but I continued to wear the sling since the collarbone was the most serious of my injuries. I moved back in with my granddad despite the protest of Jimmie and was determined to do something useful rather than sit around all day. I'd questioned Jimmie often about the accident and had some idea of what kind of vehicle rammed us into the ditch. She kept insisting it was a short truck with solid sides which were tall, and I came to the conclusion that it fit the description of a U-Haul truck. It would've been a perfect vehicle to use for such a crime since it was from a rental agency and would be hard to trace.

On Monday, June thirtieth, I left for Amarillo to do some investigating. It would give me something to do until I could go back to work; however, there was slim chance of discovering anything useful. I looked up the address of the U-Haul place and found there were two. The first was on the north side of town, which was easy to locate.

A woman was sitting behind a desk when I entered. "Can I help you?"

"Yes ma'am, I hope so. Would it be possible to see who had trucks rented on the twenty-third of May? All I need to know about is the large trucks."

She frowned. "That's not public information. Why would you want to know?"

I told her what had happened and my suspicion that it could've been a U-Haul truck. "Both me and my friend were injured."

"So, you're doing a little detective work. I'm sorry I can't help you."

Her determined look revealed that it was useless to argue further, and I left, going to the other location which was across town. I met with similar results from a woman who could've been a sister to the first. When I told her about the attempt on our lives, she indicated some interest.

"Do you really believe they were trying to kill you, and it wasn't an accident?"

"Yes ma'am, I have no doubt. They rammed into the side of our car and drove us off the road into the ditch."

"I'd like to help, but there's a chance of losing my job if I let you look at our books. I do have a suggestion. You say he rammed your car, so there was probably damage to his vehicle. You might check with the body repair shops in town and see who had brought in damaged vehicles. That's the best I can do."

I thanked her and left, wondering how many body shops were in Amarillo. It took me some time, but I found a phone booth that still had a phone book attached to a chain. I looked in the Yellow Pages and found a dozen body shops listed, and there was no telling how many were unlisted. I wrote down the addresses and left, not being optimistic about my chances.

I spoke with the owners of the shops, not receiving any more cooperation than from U-Haul. I found several trucks but none fit Jimmie's description. I'd visited ten locations, and it was five in the afternoon when I gave up and started back home. I'd not been successful, but I was doing something instead of sitting in a recliner watching television.

I'd promised Jimmie to be at her apartment this evening at seven to eat supper with her and was on time. When she came to the door she had on shorts and half a white t-shirt. "I've been on my three-mile run and haven't had time to change. What're you staring at?"

"You're not dressed to go out in public. You could've caused a wreck."

"Oh, Luke, I had warmups on over this. I just wanted to see your reaction.

"Come on in, and I'll fix you a drink while I shower and change. It won't take me long, and then we're going out to eat. I always feel good after my run."

I avoided the recliner since most of my last month had been spent in it. She said it wouldn't take long, but an hour later she came out and announced she was ready. On the drive to the restaurant, she asked me about my day, and I told her of the trip to Amarillo searching for the truck that hit us. "It's kinda like looking for a needle in a haystack."

"Luke, the chances of us proving it was Drake are slim. I have no doubt he was responsible, and he meant to kill us. If it wasn't him, it was someone he hired. In a way, it might be better if we never found out. I'm afraid of what you might do."

"What if he's not satisfied? He may try again and be successful this time," I said. When we arrived at out eating place, she hadn't answered my question.

✳✳✳

I went back to Amarillo the next day and this time took Bull. I'd left him home yesterday, but he looked so pitiful I let him go with me. I had two more body shops to visit and after that, no plans. Number eleven was about three miles out on the highway to Canyon. When I reached the

Southside Body Shop I let Bull out, thinking he probably needed a break. He followed me to the office where I met a man coming out.

"Hey, that's a Pit Bull. I love those dogs. They have a bad reputation, but they are the sweetest dogs." He reached down and rubbed Bull on the head. "How you doin' boy?"

"Are you the owner of this shop?" I asked.

He was still rubbing on Bull but looked up. "Yeah, that's me. What can I do for you?"

"Could I have a few minutes of your time? I need to ask you some questions. I'll explain the purpose of my visit."

"Are you selling something?" he asked.

"No. It's personal and won't take long."

"Come in and bring your dog. I have some coffee on."

We sat down with Bull close enough to him to get his ears scratched and head rubbed. I told him about the incident, and the reason for checking out body shops.

"I haven't had any in that would fit that description. My brother-in-law runs a body shop on the east side of town and he sorta specializes in large vehicles. If you'd like to check there, I'll call him."

"I'd appreciate that. I haven't had much success talking with shop owners."

I listened as he called his brother-in-law telling him to expect me to come by with some questions. I thanked him and left, glad that Bull had been along.

I found the shop which had all kinds of vans and trucks parked around it. Several people were inside the office, and I had to wait my turn to talk with the owner. I explained that his brother-in-law had sent me, and he motioned for me to follow him to a back room, which I assumed served as his office. I told him the reason for my visit and waited—hopeful.

He leaned back in his chair rubbing his two-day stubble as if in deep thought. "There was a man who came in a couple of weeks ago, maybe longer, who asked for an estimate to repair a dented fender. He didn't like my offer and left. I've heard some things about the guy, mostly bad. He supposedly is an electrician but is rumored to deal in drugs and other shady activities. He has a truck that would fit your description." He sat up in his chair. "I can give you his name but that's about all. The truck has the picture of a lightning bolt on its side. His name is Biggert. I don't know his first name." He reached for a phone book on a shelf behind him, thumbing through it. "He's not listed. Not in the Yellow Pages either."

"I appreciate your help. Do you have any idea where I might find additional information?"

"I'd start at the police station. From what I've heard they probably know him well."

I thanked him again and left, feeling like I was making some progress. I followed his suggestion and went to the police station, going in the entrance where I was taken after my accident in January. I had another stroke of good fortune, finding the man behind the counter was the one who called Jimmie to come after me. I introduced myself, reminding him we'd met before.

It took him a minute but he recognized me. "I remember you. The pretty girl came to pick you up after you tail-ended that car."

I described the reason for coming in and asked him about Biggert.

"Did you file a complaint?" he asked.

"No. I didn't have any idea who did it. I'm just trying to locate the truck that hit us."

"Biggert's bad news. We know he's involved in all kinds of illegal schemes. We just haven't been able to gather enough evidence to arrest him. I'll tell you this—the guy's capable of anything."

"Do you know where I could find him? At least look at his truck. Maybe I could file a complaint then."

"A bunch of his kind hang out at a bar just off Amarillo Boulevard.

It's called the Swinging Sister, but I'd be careful going in there. It's a close-knit group who aren't friendly to strangers. From the looks of you, the last thing you need is more trouble."

I thanked him and left. It didn't take long to find the Swinging Sister. It didn't look like a place you'd want to take a date. It had no windows and a solid door, looking like one of those places during the prohibition era that you saw in the movies. Several cars were parked out front and I noticed an alley leading around to the back. I took that route. Only one vehicle was parked behind the bar—a truck with a lightning bolt on the side. I parked and got out, followed by Bull who'd been whining for some time needing a potty break. I walked around to the other side of the truck and inspected the damaged fender. There was blue paint on the white fender—the color of Jimmie's car.

A voice startled me. "What're you looking for?" He was short, overweight, and had a full beard.

"Just admiring your truck. Looks like you had a little fender bender."

He took a step closer. "What's it to you?"

"Would you be interested in selling it?" I felt Bull's presence by my leg.

"No. People can get hurt snooping around here. You're lying. You're not interested in buying my truck."

His threatening tone did it. Bull began that low deep rumble that was his warning. I reached down and scratched his head. "We're leaving now since you're not interested in selling your truck."

When I turned, I heard the truck door open, and he came out with a tire tool moving toward me. "I'll teach you to come snooping around here."

Bull met him before he was close enough to use the tire tool, grabbing him above his left knee. He was on the ground in a second screaming, "Get him off me! He's tearing my leg off!"

I reached and picked up the tire tool he'd dropped and grabbed Bull by the neck. "No! Bull. That's enough." I pulled back on Bull, and he released his grip on the leg.

The man stayed on the ground groaning in pain. "Get him away from me. He was gonna kill me."

"I don't know, fellow. When he gets a taste of blood it's hard to control him. I need to ask you a few questions and maybe Bull will get in a better mood.

"How'd you get the bent fender?"

"None of your damn business." He was holding his leg which was bleeding."

I pointed to him. "Get him, Bull."

Bull grabbed the man's arm that was holding his leg, igniting the screams again. "Get him off! Please, get him off!"

I reached and grabbed Bull pulling him back. "Now you want to tell me how you got the bent fender."

He was willing to talk with Bull standing over him, blood dripping from his mouth. A man had paid him $2000 to run a car off the road. He didn't know who the car belonged to, only her address, and the make, model, and license plate of the car. Davis was the name of the man who paid him.

I left him lying on the ground, needing medical attention. I was sure he could get back inside for help. On the drive home, I looked down at Bull who was asleep with his head in my lap. "You're going to get a can of Spam tonight—maybe two."

# 56
# THE VISIT

JIMMIE LYN

Luke came by Tuesday evening and told me about discovering Drake was responsible for running us off the road. He wouldn't provide details, only telling me the name of the man Drake hired to do it. I couldn't imagine the guy telling him voluntarily, so violence must've been involved. Since Luke's arm was still in a sling, I didn't see how he could've been very persuasive.

When I asked him what he planned to do, his response was, "Nothing for the time being. I'm limited until I'm able to use my arm, and then I'll go see him." I knew what that meant, and it frightened me. When I tried to reason with him those gentle brown eyes turned black, and I knew it was useless.

There was only one thing for me to do—go talk with Drake. I'd wait until Thursday, since tomorrow was sale day and we already had a big run of cattle with more coming in.

The next morning, I went to work early and caught my dad before he got busy. I told him about Luke finding out that what we suspected was true and Luke's plans to go see Drake when his arm healed.

"We can go to the law with this, Jimmie Lyn. Send him to jail before Luke does something that will destroy his life." He rubbed the back of his neck like he always did when stressed.

"I suggested that, but Luke said the man who did it would never confess. Which made me wonder why he told Luke everything. Luke scares me when he becomes angry. It's not outward, in fact he remains calm, but something within him is terrifying. Do you have any suggestions, besides going to the law?"

"Let me think about it. I'm afraid Drake will try to hurt you again if we don't do something. But that something is not Luke killing him. What makes it worse—this guy's a hero. After thinking about it, Luke's probably right. We couldn't get anything done through the law."

"I'm so sorry for getting Luke involved in this. You warned me, but I didn't listen. Now we're all paying the price."

"I'm not sorry, Honey, as long as it all works out. It's brought you and Luke together. The future looks promising for y'all and that pleases me."

"Dad, I believe the trip to Louisiana will be good for Luke. I wish we could go immediately, but he keeps putting it off until his injuries heal. He still has this fear that the parents will blame him for their son's death."

I changed the subject, sorry to have laid this problem on my dad with a busy day ahead. "I understand Lady is in Thursday."

That immediately brought a smile. "Yes, I'm leaving tomorrow at noon. I'm excited and know that Grace is too."

"Enjoy yourself. We'll make out, without you for a few days." I left him in a better mood after bringing up Lady.

❋❋❋

I reached Amarillo in time for lunch. No way was I going to his apartment. I planned to see him in his office surrounded by other people, and leave afterwards. I rehearsed my speech, trying to assure myself that it might do some good.

I became more nervous the closer it came to a face-to-face meeting. After all, he wanted us hurt, and it would have pleased him even more if we'd been killed. I had to be strong, not just for myself but for Luke as well. I kept asking myself, how could I be so wrong about someone? My face was damp, which meant my makeup was going to be ruined. It was hot and my air conditioner was on, but nerves were wrecking havoc on my body. I kept telling myself aloud, "I can do this."

I arrived at the building which housed the Becket and Becket Law Firm. I sat in the car a few minutes, gathered my thoughts, and tried to boost my courage. "It's now or never," I mumbled, getting out and heading toward the glass-door entrance.

The building was cool and after taking the elevator to the second floor, I entered office 2 B. A secretary greeted me. "Can I help you?"

I took a deep breath. "I'd like to see Drake Davis."

"Do you have an appointment?" she asked.

"No, just tell him that Jimmie Lyn Waddell would like to see him."

She rose and left, coming back in a few minutes. "You'll have to wait. He has someone in his office."

Of course, he'd make me wait, knowing I'd be nervous. I sat down and thumbed through a magazine taken from a nearby rack. I didn't see anything, even the pictures. I looked at the clock on the wall—10:23. At 11:04 the secretary told me that I could go in.

Drake was standing behind his desk. "Well, this is a surprise. What brings you to see an old flame? Change your mind?"

*I hated him* and that thought somehow calmed me. "No, I haven't changed my mind, Drake. This is not a social visit. You threatened me the last time I saw you. Remember that?"

"Aw, I was just upset. I didn't mean it." He leaned back in his chair and smiled.

"No. You meant it. In fact, you carried out your threat on May twenty-third. I was taking Luke home, and a truck ran us off the road, injuring both of us—Luke worse than me."

Then he laughed. Not just a chuckle, a roaring laugh. "You're imagining things. I remember being at a friend's house that evening."

I looked him directly in the eyes. "You paid a man named Biggert $2,000 to do your dirty deed."

He looked away not meeting my glare. Suddenly, he was serious, the laughter turned to hate. "You can't prove anything. I don't even know a man named Biggert."

"You're a liar, but you're right—we can't prove it. The purpose of my visit is to warn you. Go away, for your own good."

Again, the smile. "You threatening me?"

"No. I'm trying to save your life and keep Luke from killing you and going to prison."

"You talking about that kid you've been shacking up with at the ranch? You must be joking trying to scare me with that threat." He stood up. "You can leave now. And don't be surprised if you and that kid have another accident."

I staggered out of the room and down the elevator before my legs gave out, and I collapsed on a bench in the lobby. I was shaking and trying not to cry, hoping to make it to the car.

A woman came over to me. "Are you all right?"

"Yes. I just need a minute." Thank goodness she left, and I sat there for several more minutes before going to my car. I didn't trust myself to drive, so I sat and considered what'd happened. Why didn't I describe Luke to him and tell him about the Russians who came for me? Simple answer—he wouldn't have believed me. Also, it would give Luke the advantage because Drake was grossly underestimating him. I didn't accomplish anything today, or did I? He was at least made aware that we knew it was him. No doubt, Biggert wouldn't have told him what happened with Luke. Whether I did any good or not—I had to try.

✳✳✳

Luke came by my apartment Thursday evening on his way to the ranch and asked me if I wanted to go. I accepted the invitation and on the way asked him about his arm.

"I'm getting rid of this sling. I'm not doing any good sitting around. My arm is going to be weak since I haven't been using it. I need to go back to work. Most of all I'm bored."

That meant I didn't have long to do something that would keep him from going after Drake. He was driving with his right arm since his left was in a sling. I moved over closer to him. "We haven't done any courting lately. I'm beginning to wonder if you find me attractive. I wore that skimpy outfit the other day, and all you said was I shouldn't wear it in public. It kind of disappointed me."

"No, that's not all I said. I said you could cause a wreck wearing it in public. If I saw you jogging down the street in that getup, I'd be distracted. I'm pretty stove up to do any heavy courting."

I touched his arm. "I'd be gentle with you. By the way, since you're about to get rid of the sling, what about going to Louisiana? It'd be kind of a celebration of you getting back to normal."

He took so long to answer I thought he was going to avoid the issue. "I have something to do before the trip to Louisiana. We can't just do nothing and wait around until he tries to kill us again. And he will try again."

"Luke, he wouldn't even know where we were if we went to Louisiana. It would also give you another couple of days to heal. Please, let's go next week. Today's Thursday, let's leave Monday." Maybe pleading with him would help.

"I'll think about it."

Bronc was at the house when we arrived. It was late afternoon and with the sun going down it had cooled off. We sat outside, and they talked about the ranch and Bronc's rodeo schedule with the subject coming back to Luke's mother and Angie often. It was only a little over a month until the XIT Rodeo, which Bronc always entered. The rodeo had put Dalhart on the map, and the attendance usually was three times the size of the town.

Bronc went into the house and came back carrying a letter. "I received this from my brother before he returned from Vietnam. I want to read part of the last page.

*You have mentioned a friend of yours whose name is Luke Ranker. I ran into a couple of men who served in his platoon. The way they described him you would think he was superhuman or something. They swore he saved their lives more than once, and they sent a letter requesting he receive a medal. Please tell Luke these things—I know it will make him feel better about his service in this terrible war.*

"See, Luke. You need to accept the medal. Your men knew you deserved it," I said.

Luke looked off into the distance. "When the subject of the war comes up, all I can think about is those five men in my platoon who were sent home in body bags. They were the heroes and deserved a medal, not the ones who came home to their families. Maybe one of these days, when enough time has passed, it'll be different."

We left shortly after that and on the drive back to town, Luke was silent. When we drove up to my apartment, I expected him to let me out and leave. Instead, he turned to me with that mischievous smile. "Let's go inside and catch up. Remember you have to be gentle."

# 57

# STANDING UP

It was Thursday morning, the Fourth of July, and I was enjoying my coffee while sitting on the deck. I'd already been to the barn and fed the horses and was waiting for Angie and Hank to get up so we could have breakfast. The flowers were beautiful, and the cool breeze from the southwest was carrying the sweet aroma of the honeysuckle. It was going to be an exciting day with Lady entered in the fourth race on a twelve-race card. She'd been training well and was ready to show us what she could do on a fast track, which wasn't unusual for July since in southeastern New Mexico this was the dry season.

Blaine had called yesterday at noon and said he couldn't come to Ruidoso for the race. His daughter, who lived in California, had gone into labor and he was leaving immediately. His flight from Amarillo was scheduled to leave at three in the afternoon. I could tell he was excited about his new grandchild even though he was going to miss the race. He gave me a phone number, and I promised to call him after the race.

I'd forgotten how much I missed the racetrack and this lifestyle. The smell of the stable area resurfaced memories of Henry and our life together, scraping to get by yet happy. I'd admitted to myself that Henry would remain in my thoughts for the rest of my life. Angie had asked me about Blaine, saying it was obvious that he was enthralled with me and was there any chance of us having a future. I wasn't as sure of myself as previously, when Luke had asked the same question.

I'd been exercising Lady for over three months, and Kenneth had given her a work, out of the gates last week going 220 yards. She had a bullet time, out of thirty other horses, and Kenneth was pleased with her performance. I'd picked up a program yesterday, and her opening odds were 2-1 based on last year's race record and her workout. I couldn't help but wonder if I was doing the right thing entering her before the Derby Trials, which were only six weeks from now.

I kept thinking my good fortune couldn't hold out after all the problems last year. Angie and Hank's presence and this wonderful little house were almost too good to be true. Now, if only Lady could stay sound and win the money back that Blaine had put into her. Not everything had gone well, as we drew the 2 gate for today's race. It was disappointing that the powers that be hadn't improved the track to the point where it was fair to all the horses. The constant pounding of the inside by the thoroughbreds caused the first four lanes to be much slower than the outside.

My dad was doing well, feeling useful again and working fulltime. Blaine had kept him busy on the off-sale days, driving the feed truck, hauling cattle to and from the ranch, and other odd jobs. He was happier than he'd been since Mom passed, which was another reason to be thankful to Blaine.

Then there was Luke, who had finally confessed to me that he planned to marry Jimmie, but he hadn't told her yet, needing a little more time. I was worried about Luke and Jimmie being in danger from Drake, who must be an evil person. Luke hadn't told me the details, but Blaine told me everything.

✻ ✻ ✻

We were at the barn by nine o'clock, sitting in our outside chairs, watching Big Boy and Candy Man trudging along on the walker. It was a beautiful day and appeared to be perfect for the afternoon races.

Our perfect morning was interrupted when a pickup drove up and Oliver Knox exited. He sauntered over to where we were sitting. "Good morning, how's everybody today?"

I remained seated. "We're good, just sitting out here and enjoying this beautiful day."

"That is a sweet baby. I guess you're the proud grandmother?"

"Yes. He's been a blessing. I only wish that Henry was here to enjoy him." I wished he'd just say what he wanted and leave. He must have something on his mind in order to come down here. My feelings about him hadn't improved.

"Grace, I need to explain my actions last year before the Futurity. I was under a lot of pressure. My decision to give Miss Jet a substance to enhance her performance was a reflection of that pressure. Under ordinary circumstances, I wouldn't have done it."

I stood up, hopefully to appear more confident. "I want you to understand my feelings toward you, Oliver. You were a friend before Henry died. After that you took advantage of a grieving widow. You would've never, and I mean never, done anything like you did if Henry had been alive. You came close to killing a beautiful animal and broke the law doing that. There was no justification for your actions.

"If you want to apologize, I will accept it and maybe we can at least be civil to one another again. If you are determined to continue making excuses for your behavior, you can leave. Now, I've had my say, you need to make a decision."

"I thought you would understand. Evidently, I was wrong." He left without further comment.

"You were wonderful, Mom. That'll give him something to think about," said Angie.

I didn't expect Oliver to come around but was glad he did. I needed him to understand how strongly I felt. In a sense I was relieved to have it over and hoped that was the end of it. "Thank you, Angie. I believe your dad would've been proud of me."

I had one other mission before the race and left Angie and Hank, going to the racing office where the stewards met each race day. It was ten o'clock and there were only two present, each with a racing form.

"Excuse me," I said.

They both lowered their forms. "Can we help you?" one of the men asked.

I introduced myself as a trainer and went right into the reason for my visit. "I know a woman trainer is an oddity, but I have just as much of a right to train as the men." I then went into my experience at the Albuquerque Meet which ended with Big Time Boy being taken down. I encouraged them to look at the video and determine if I was correct in that there was no foul. I finished by saying I understood they were not the stewards at Albuquerque, but I wanted to make my position known. "All I want is to be treated like the male trainers. I will not be cheated again without a fight."

The two men looked at one another. "We always try to be fair," the older one said. "It sounds like you're threatening us. We could turn you in to the Racing Commission, and you could lose your license."

"Go ahead if you believe that's the appropriate move. Review the race at Albuquerque first to determine if I'm justified. I assure you if I go before the Racing Commission, they'll see the replay and that is going to be an embarrassment to all racing stewards."

"We'll pull up that replay and go from there," said the younger man.

I left, satisfied with my message, which I believed was necessary even though it could mean a reprimand or worse from the Racing Commission. I was already stressed after my lecture to Oliver and, now after this encounter, was more so and the race was coming up. I wasn't accustomed to being this aggressive; it definitely was out of character for me.

✷✷✷

We were so far from the track that it was difficult to hear the announcer, but we were able to hear the first call. Fifteen minutes later Lady waited in the saddling paddock before Kenneth arrived carrying his saddle. "Grace, it's a big day for you and Lady. If it's agreeable with you, I'll move her over to better ground. I looked at the racing form and the 3 and 4 horses are not much. I should be ahead of them enough the first fifty yards to move to the middle of the track."

"Sounds good. I'm a nervous wreck, Kenneth. Your judgment is better than mine." I had two things going for me—a great rider and a fast horse.

After we finished saddling and the announcement, "Riders up" was made, I went to my pony horse and waited for Kenneth on the track. As we passed the tote board, I noticed the odds had moved up to 4-1. Someone was betting a lot of money on another horse to move the odds that much.

My stomach was turning flips as Lady was loaded. Behind the gates, I had to rely on the call of the race since nothing could be revealed watching through all that metal.

**"They're all in line. A good break for all and it's Miss Jet on the inside going to the front and My Azure on the outside, and Rocket Man moving up. It's now Miss Jet pulling away and winning easily, with Rocket Man to place and Miss Wrangler to show."**

My heart was pounding as I made my way to the finish line. Kenneth rode up, all smiles. "She's awesome, Grace."

Immediately the announcement; **"Ladies and Gentleman the inquiry sign is up. Please hold all your tickets."**

The jockey on the second-place horse, Rocket Man, had not dismounted but was walking his horse in a circle. Evidently, he was the one claiming a foul against Kenneth who exclaimed, "We didn't touch anybody!"

Sure enough, the trainer of the second-place horse, Rocket Man, was the same one who had lodged a complaint at Albuquerque when Big Time

Boy was taken down. Within a minute the announcement; **"Ladies and Gentlemen the Fourth Race is now official."**

Looking at the tote board the Number 2 horse was in first place. I breathed a sigh of relief. The jockey on Rocket Man slid off and walked by us and Kenneth didn't miss the opportunity. "Hey, Felix. You lodge another foul toward me that is totally unjustified, and I'm going to whip you like a stepchild." Kenneth looked at me and grinned. "I'll do it too, Grace."

As always, the win picture was full of people, some whom I hadn't ever seen before. I could care less since my daughter was beside me, and I was holding my grandson who was posing for his first win picture. After the picture, I did a quick calculation coming up with our share being $3,000 minus $300 for Kenneth, which left us $2,700 with my half being $1,350. That would get me through the rest of the meet.

I gave Hank back to Angie and started to the test barn with Lady. On the way, I was intercepted by Lynda, Oliver's wife. She started right in without a greeting. "I guess you think you're smart today. Oliver told me you chewed him out. You should be ashamed of yourself for talking to him that way. If it hadn't been for him, you wouldn't even have this horse." She continued to talk, but I just kept walking until she gave up, shouting a number of curse words at me from a distance.

I had a pleasant surprise at the test barn when the vet greeted me. "Grace, congratulations. Every once in a while, something happens to restore my faith in this profession that wears me out sometimes. Today was that something."

"Thank you. You certainly deserved a bunch of the credit," I said.

"I'll accept that compliment with a smile. Now, let's see if we can get this pretty girl to pee."

# 58

# THIBODAUX, LOUISIANA

✎§ JIMMIE LYN ﻉ✎

It was the morning of July fourteenth, and Luke had finally consented to make the trip to Louisiana. He'd gotten his sling off and pronounced himself as fit as ever. Packed and ready to go, I waited. I'd insisted that we take my car since it was newer and would be more dependable on the long Louisiana trip. I tried not to think about Drake and the threat he posed and was thankful we would be out of the area for at least a few days.

Luke was stubborn, and we still argued a good part of the time we spent together. Usually the opposing views didn't last long before one of us gave in, with the outcome about an even split. We'd been through so much together that we'd developed a mutual respect.

Dad had been all for the trip and told me not to be in any hurry to get back. Of course, he was ecstatic about being a granddad and confessed that the little girl was beautiful. He hadn't stayed but a couple of days since my mother was also there. That event, coupled with Lady's win on the Fourth, had put him somewhere in the clouds. He talked with Grace every day. She must've been tired of going over the race that many times, but not on comparing what it was like to be a grandparent. He'd continued to improve, and his checkups showed no signs of cancer.

My mother was a different person after the incident she witnessed at the restaurant between Piper and Sterling. I thought it might help but had no idea it would create a complete transformation. She hadn't spoken a negative word about Sterling since that day.

The honking of the car announced Luke's arrival. I grabbed my suitcase and was out the door with the horn still blaring. "I'm coming!" I stopped short of the car. "I told you, Luke, we're taking my car. Load your stuff, and leave your car right where it is."

For once, he followed my orders without arguing. In the car, he turned to me. "You gonna drive the whole way?"

"No, of course not. We'll take turns. I looked at a map, and we'll drive to Tyler today. Dallas is about halfway, but we can go farther. It's nine and we should be in Tyler by seven this evening. If we get a good start, we could be in Thibodaux, Louisiana, by early afternoon. You're quiet this morning. You sick or something?"

"I knew it'd be this way if we took your car."

"I'll let you decide where we eat. Will that help?"

"Wake me up when it's my time to drive." He leaned his head back against the seat.

Driving gives you time to think, and I did a lot of it the next hour. Every time the thought of Drake and the way he'd treated me came into my thoughts, I immediately dismissed it and moved to something else. That was my way of dealing with it—or not dealing with it.

Something caused me to turn toward Luke who appeared to be asleep. He didn't bring Bull—a surprise. I didn't think he'd be away from his dog that long. The haircut made him look younger, more like a teenager.

A few minutes later, I looked in my mirror and saw flashing lights. It was the Highway Patrol. Why were they stopping me? I pulled off to the side of the road. He walked up and immediately asked me for my license. My hand shook as I searched for it in my purse. "I know it's here. Just give me a second." I couldn't believe this.

"What'd you do wrong?" Luke asked. "Here, give it to me."

I passed my purse to him. It only took him a few seconds to bring out the folder that contained my license, which I gave to the officer. "Sorry it took so long."

He took down the information on my license and handed it back to me. "Have you been drinking or taking medication?"

"No, of course not."

"I was following, and it appeared you were under the influence of drugs. Were you getting sleepy?"

"Maybe, a little." This was better than anything else that came to mind. I sure didn't want to tell him I'd been studying my passenger.

"I'm just going to give you a warning ticket. It might be a good idea to let the guy drive. Is he your little brother?" I signed the ticket he presented to me.

"No. He's my friend." Why couldn't he just say brother and leave off the *little*. It was humiliating that he must think I was the *big* sister.

"Be careful and drive safely." He walked back toward his patrol car.

Luke and I changed places, and he was smiling as he slid in behind the wheel.

We were in Tyler before dark and stopped at a Holiday Inn to see about a room before finding a place to eat. Luke went in and was gone longer than I expected. He returned and presented me with a key. "The rooms are expensive, but I got one anyway."

After eating at a Pizza Hut, we returned to the motel room, which included a bed, chair, and couch. I turned on the television but left the sound down. I thought it would be a good time to talk about his visit with Louis's parents. "I understand why you need to make this trip. How do you plan to go about telling the parents that you were the blame for his death? I mean, are you just going to come right out and tell them?"

He sat down, placing his arm on the back of the couch, looking at the silent screen. "I've gone over it a thousand times and still haven't decided the best way to do it. I've tried to imagine how they'll react, being face-to-face with the person responsible for their son's death. In a way it's selfish of me to tell them, hoping it will make me feel better. I can't see it giving them any satisfaction. Maybe it'll harm them. I keep telling myself it might help them to express their anger and hurt. I don't know."

"Won't it be hard to see the grief that you're blaming yourself for?" I asked.

He continued to stare at the television. "Yeah. But I don't know what else to do. I thought about seeing a counselor, but they'd only try to convince me not to blame myself." He rose abruptly. "I'm going for a walk."

When I went to bed Luke wasn't back. He must've gone for a long walk.

***

We drove into Thibodaux a little after four in the afternoon. We stopped at a locally-owned motel and reserved a room, which was cheaper than the Holiday Inn. Luke said the name of the family we were seeking was LeBlanc. He did have an address, but we had no idea where to start. A sign when we entered town, announced the population at 15,241, much bigger than he'd anticipated.

The address was 4605 Lafourche Drive. I stopped and filled my car up with gas, giving Luke the opportunity to ask directions. I could hear only part of the conversation.

With Luke guiding, we soon found the place. The white house was perched on top of huge poles several feet above ground level. Six floor to ceiling windows flanked by forest green wooden shutters—real ones, not fake—faced the front. A sunflower yellow door smiled behind a screen. One car sat in the driveway. I suggested Luke go to the door by himself, while I stayed in the car.

"No. I want you with me. His dad's name is Jules and his mother's is

Lucille. Now, come with me."

I followed him up the stairs to the house, where he knocked. The door opened, but the screen remained closed. "Yes. What do you need?"

"Ma'am, I'm Luke Ranker and this is my friend, Jimmie Waddell. I was in the service with your son."

"Sergeant Ranker?"

"Yes ma'am."

She flung the screen door open and cried, "Cher." She hugged him, crying at the same time. Next, I received a somewhat lesser hug.

She was about five feet tall and heavy with short hair, which made her round face even more so. "Come see, please. Welcome to my home."

We followed her into a kind of living room with padded chairs and a couch. She explained that Jules was working and wouldn't be home for another two hours. We both declined her offer of something to drink.

Her excitement showed as she fanned her pink face with a newspaper that was on the couch. "Sergeant Ranker, you came to see us. It makes me so happy." Then she burst into tears again.

We carried on a broken conversation for fifteen minutes, intermittent with crying episodes. Each time I thought she was over the shock of seeing Luke, she would break down again.

"Mrs. LeBlanc, we need to go back to our motel and rest awhile. We'll return in a couple of hours when Jules is home," Luke said.

"Yes. Jules will be home and you can eat dinner with us." She came over and hugged both of us when we stood.

In the car I asked Luke if Louis talked the way his mother did. "It's hard for me to follow her. I have to concentrate on every word, and sometimes I still don't know what she said."

"Louis's accent was worse than his mother's. We had to tell him to slow down and repeat what he said. It got better with time. They also have different ways of saying things. You noticed that she said, 'come see' instead of 'come in' when inviting us into the house."

I drove and couldn't see Luke's expression when I asked him if the reception was what he expected. "Not at all. I thought they'd be angry with me. It may be different with his dad. They're good people, which I expected." He reached over and squeezed me on the arm. "Thank you for coming with me. I was afraid of what would happen when I told them who I was."

Luke afraid? He'd killed two men, showing anything but fear. He cracked the bully in the Pizza Hut over the head without even flinching. How strange. "You've got it through your head that they'll blame you for his death because you blame yourself. I'd suggest, Luke, that you don't apologize until they have a chance to show you how they feel."

The motel room was nice and the first thing we did was turn on the air conditioner. It was warm and humid, totally different from the climate we'd left yesterday.

"How long are we going to stay?" I'd planned on being back for the sale. That was going to be difficult and near impossible since today was Monday.

"Just tonight. I know you need to be back by Wednesday. We'll probably leave early enough in the morning to make it a one-day trip. We wouldn't get home until late tomorrow night, but you'd be there for the sale."

I breathed a sigh of relief. He was doing that for me since it wasn't necessary for him to return. We had about an hour before going back to the Le Blancs. "I'm going to shower and change clothes. These I have on are clinging to me. I can't believe it's so hot and humid."

"It's a different world down here. Weather, traditions, language, and food are not the same as where we came from." He left, saying he was going for a walk.

I took my shower, dressed, put on makeup, and sat down to do my nails. Here I was, 900 miles from home, having dinner with strangers.

# 59

# CONFESSING

Nervous on the way to the LeBlancs, I kept rehearsing what I was going to say. After all these months, I continued to feel unsure and thought the trip may have been a mistake. Jimmie drove and I looked over at her, finding it hard to believe that I'd taken so long to see that she was beautiful.

"You're staring at me again. Is something wrong? Is my makeup showing?"

"Nothing wrong. Just admiring you." I turned toward my window, embarrassed she'd caught me.

"Thank you—I guess. For someone who's stingy with compliments you can drop some bombs."

We arrived, and Mrs. LeBlanc opened the door before we knocked, giving us a welcome similar to the first one. She said that her husband wasn't home yet, but we could wait for him in the backyard. We followed her outside and down a walkway to a boat ramp on the river. She motioned for us to sit down in some outdoor chairs. "Jules comes home in his boat. He's a fishing guide. The bayou runs into some good fishing areas. He should be home anytime."

While we waited, several boats passed us, slowing down when they approached the dock. I expected any one of them to pull into the boat slip built into the dock. I could tell Mrs. LeBlanc was becoming anxious.

After fifteen minutes she rose and pointed. "Here he comes."

A boat turned toward the dock, slowed, and coasted into the boat slip. Jules was short and stocky with several days of peppered whiskers. He was shirtless and the hair on his chest matched that on his face. He pitched a rope to Mrs. LeBlanc who held the boat steady while he climbed out.

As he looked at us a wide grin stretched his tan face. "Nous avons des visiteurs, Lucille." (We have visitors, Lucille.)

She took him by the arm. "Ce sergent de rang. Il est venu nous rendre visite." (This is Sergeant Ranker. He's come to visit us.)

He blinked several times and made an inhuman sound, lunging forward and grabbing me. At first, I thought it was anger, and then realized it was raw emotion which resulted in a hug that squeezed the breath out of me. He let go and stepped back. "My Loo-ee loved you, Sergeant Ranker. He talks about you in every letter he wrote." He wiped at his eyes. "You came to visit us. Thank you so much."

We went back up the ramp to the house with Jules hanging on to my arm. Inside we sat down at the kitchen table with a Bud Light magically appearing before us. In the time spent in South Louisiana I'd discovered that was the drink of choice. Jules told us of his guiding business and went on to say that Louis had planned on joining him after he got out of the service.

Suddenly he perked up. "We're going fishing tomorrow. Loo-ee told me he was taking you after y'all got out. I'm going to cancel my schedule and keep his promise to you. That would please Loo-ee."

I started to object, and Jimmie kicked me under the table, mouthing, "Yes."

"Won't your clients be mad that you canceled their fishing trip?"

"Doesn't matter. I'll tell them I have a special guest. They'll be okay. Everyone wants to fish with Jules. You and Miss Jimmie need to be here at six in the morning. Lucille will have coffee and breakfast for you."

We sat at the table and talked while Mrs. LeBlanc finished cooking supper. Unlike the Martinez family I visited in Clayton, Jules wanted to know everything about me. He would occasionally ask Jimmie a question to be polite but most of the focus was on me. I kept trying to think of a way to confess my responsibility in Louis's death but finally gave up, thinking maybe Jimmie was right, and I should wait.

He told me about his family, which was large with many living in the area. Louis had two older brothers, both of whom worked offshore on drilling rigs. The longer he talked the better I could understand him, remembering how long it took us to understand Louis.

Supper waited on a beautiful table cloth covered with every type of china imaginable. Tall crystal glasses held drinks . . . not like the jelly jars I had at the ranch. Jules asked us to join hands and said the blessing. The meal was delicious, consisting of a fresh salad and some kind of rice-shrimp dish with lots of seasoning and crusty garlic bread. Dessert was the best pecan pie I'd ever eaten, topped with whipped cream.

After the meal, we went to the sitting room and Mrs. LeBlanc had her opportunity to tell us about Louis growing up. She proudly showed us pictures of him in elementary, junior high, and high school. One of his pictures, when he was about ten, showed a cast on his arm. I asked her what had happened.

"Loo-ee was a sweet boy but stubborn." She threw up her hands to emphasize her point. "I mean stubborn. He wanted a motor scooter. We told him it was too dangerous, but he wouldn't leave us alone. Night and day he begged, pleaded, and made us feel guilty for not giving in. Finally, we gave up just to shut him up. The third day he had the scooter, he wrecked it and broke his arm. We were thankful it was only his arm. That didn't slow him down. He rode that scooter to school until we bought him a car his senior year."

Jules picked up where his wife left off, describing how they begged him not to join the Marines, but he did anyway. "He'd wanted to be a Marine since he was a small boy, and the dream never left him. Me and Lucille have talked often of how we regretted not trying harder to convince him to do anything but go into the service. Maybe we gave up too quickly." He gazed off in another direction as if remembering.

We stayed until nine, thanked them for the amazing supper, and promised we would be here by six in the morning.

On the way back to our motel, Jimmie had me drive, saying, "Two beers and all that food has done me in. Aren't they wonderful people?"

"Yeah. But I still didn't tell them I was the blame for Louis's death. That's what I came to do." I pulled into the parking lot of the motel and stopped. "I'm telling them tomorrow."

"Are you deaf? Didn't you hear what they said about Louis? He begged them just like he begged you, and they gave in. Why should you not do the same?"

"Mine was life and death. That's the difference."

"You're not listening, Luke. They begged him not to join the Marines. He did anyway. If he'd listened, he wouldn't have even been in Vietnam."

"Doesn't matter. I shouldn't have let him take the point. I knew it was a mistake even before he was killed."

"I don't want to argue with you. I'm still miserable from all that food. Could we go for a short walk?"

"Sure." We made three trips around the motel. It was dark, and after the first one, she slipped her hand into mine.

The phone woke me up the next morning. We'd asked the motel to give us a wake-up call at five-fifteen which would give us time to get ready for our fishing trip.

I'd slept on the couch and saw that Jimmie hadn't moved. Standing by the bed I gently shook her arm. She didn't move. I shook her again, harder.

She moaned. "Leave me alone."

She'd turned over, away from me. On an impulse, I bent down, put my mouth on her neck and blew as hard as I could, creating a loud noise.

She bolted up in bed. "What're you doing?"

"You've got a gorgeous neck. I couldn't resist. Time to get up. We're going fishing today. You're the one who told me what to do. I was going to refuse and get you back for the sale. Remember?"

"Ohhhh. It's too early, Luke. Couldn't you go without me?"

"Nope. Get up! You want me to blow on your neck again?"

"She smiled, "I've been woken up in worse ways."

### ✲✲✲

Jules and Lucille were waiting on us when we arrived. They served coffee and donuts without holes. They called them beignets—unbelievably delicious. We visited over our breakfast, and half an hour later were seated in Jules's boat headed west, I think. We seemed to be going fast and with spray showering us occasionally, it was a little scary. The sun was just coming up when we slowed and finally stopped. Jules dropped an anchor over the edge. "Now, we fish."

He rigged up a rod and reel for me, putting a small crab on the hook. "We're going for redfish today. This is one of my favorite places. Now the tide is moving out. Just cast your line out a short way, and let the tide carry it out further. He then prepared a rod and reel for Jimmie, casting it a short distance, before handing it over to her.

We watched the beautiful morning with the sunlight dancing over the water. Seagulls were swooping down all around us, hoping for a handout, Jules explained. Suddenly, Jimmie screamed, the rod jerked out of her hand. Jules caught it before it went over the side. He handed it back to her.

She tried to reel, but the drag wasn't set tight enough, and the line continued to stream outward. Jules reached over and adjusted the drag, and she was able to stop the line from peeling out. For the next twenty minutes she struggled to get the fish to the boat. She'd get it right up to Jules, who was holding a net, and it would be gone again. Finally, Jules netted the fish and brought it into the boat. It was huge.

She exclaimed, "I should've brought my camera!"

"Bull Red." Jules handed the fish to Jimmie and pulled a disposable camera out of a tackle box snapping several photos. Then he reached over, took the hook out of its mouth, and threw it overboard. "Too big. Not good to eat. Probably has worms."

"He was so big. I've never caught a fish like that!"

"No worry. Plenty more. We need smaller for good eat'n."

My rod jerked, but I caught it and the fight was on. It didn't take me as long, but my fish wasn't as large. Jules netted it and tossed it into the huge ice chest.

It was no wonder that everyone wanted to go fishing with Jules. We caught fish all morning until we stopped to eat the sandwiches Mrs. LeBlanc had sent. I'd always heard that after you fish on the coast it'd ruin you from fishing in fresh water. I believed that now.

"I'm exhausted," Jimmie said, taking a bite of her sandwich. "I've never had this much fun."

Jules laughed. "Can you believe I get to do this for a living? It's a good life living on the bayou. The tide is changing. We'll go for a boat ride, and you can relax. I have some things to show you."

He drew in the anchor and we were off, going into a larger body of water. He slowed down and pointed. "Look, it's dolphins, three of them swimming together. Suddenly, one of them leaped out of the water, his whole body becoming visible. Jimmie, lowered her voice. "They're beautiful."

We continued into different canals and larger bodies of water. He slowed the boat again. "Over there, at the edge of the water—alligator."

"Louis told us about wrestling alligators. Did he really do that?" I asked.

Jules roared with laughter. "That boy could tell some tall ones. He did wrestle alligators." Then he spread his arms apart about two feet as he continued to laugh. "He just didn't tell you how big they were."

By mid-afternoon we were back at the dock. Jules told Jimmie to go on up to the house that we had to clean fish. It took both of us to lift the cooler out of the boat. A small sink and table occupied a corner of the dock. He opened a drawer on the table and took out a long thin bladed knife. He then took a fish out of the cooler and placed it on the table. A few seconds and four cuts later, two large fillets appeared on the cutting board and the remains were pushed into the water. I would've just got in the way trying to help.

In fifteen minutes, thirty fillets were returned to the ice chest. "That's a lot of fish," I commented.

"That's some mighty good eat'n. I'm going to freeze these. When you start back, we'll pack them in dry ice. They'll make the trip home with you in good shape."

After a Bud Light on the patio we left, promising to be back at 6:00 for supper. I drove and Jimmie actually went to sleep on the short drive to the motel. When we pulled into the parking lot, I reached over and poked her in the ribs.

"I've never been this tired, Luke. It was so much fun. I had no idea fishing could be like that. Could we come back again, sometime?"

"It depends."

"On what?" she asked.

"If we can come in my car."

# 60

# CRAWFISH

 JIMMIE LYN

*I could live down here,* I thought as I applied fresh makeup, getting ready for dinner at the LeBlancs. These people had fun, and they made me feel good about myself without really understanding why. They were honest, unpretentious, and not shy about showing affection. I had a feeling they'd let you know too, if they disapproved.

The last twenty-four hours, I'd stopped thinking about Drake. Maybe he'd be gone when we returned. Luke had been sweet the entire trip and didn't seem like the same person. The LeBlancs kept referring to me as his missus, which pleased me. Luke seemed also to accept the term.

Looking in the mirror, I was satisfied with what I saw. My face was a little pink due to the fishing trip but overall—not bad. I pulled my naturally curly shoulder length hair back with a little leather headband instead of fighting it. I'd packed a hip-hugger denim mini-skirt with a red-bandana paisley halter top which tied behind my neck and in the back. It accented my Texas tan. Luke had been ready ever since I started my preparation. He had on new jeans and a white long-sleeved shirt. I guess he didn't have any with short sleeves, like my dad. The white brought out his dark skin. He was handsome, and Piper's description fit him perfectly.

He told me again I looked nice as we prepared to leave. I returned the praise, thinking he might've blushed but his dark face hid it. "You've complimented my looks twice recently. What's the deal? We've spent all this time together, Luke. Why now?"

"I don't know. I just see you differently than I used to. You grew on me, I guess," he grinned. "We better be going, or we'll be late."

He said on the way to the car he'd drive and then, of all things, he opened my door for me. What was going on? Was this a date? Well, I could play this game. When he was under the wheel, I moved over next to him.

When we turned on to the lane where the LeBlancs lived, cars were lined up for two blocks on both sides of the street. "Looks like someone's having a party," he said. "There's no place to park." He drove on to the house finding a parking space in their driveway. "Wow! What about that? We must be living right."

Jules must've been watching for us because he opened the door as we were going up the steps. He met us with his arms wide open. "Laissez les bons temps rouler! (Let the good times roll) This is a Cajun Party in your honor, Sergeant Ranker!" He ushered us through the house and into the backyard. There must've been at least a hundred people flowing from the long screened-in back porch onto the cemented patio and sprinkled under enormous trees draped with southern moss. The crowd stopped whatever they were doing and looked at us, applauding.

Lucille came forward, grasping both my hands. "We're doing a Crawfish boil for our new friends from Texas." She pulled me forward and started to introduce me to the women. I didn't feel under or over dressed as the women's apparel varied from shorts to jeans to flowery dresses. Everyone had a smile and a warm greeting. At least half the guests were introduced as kin. Across the yard, Luke was going through the same ritual with Jules guiding him.

After the endless introductions, I settled on two ladies about my age to visit with. We traded information about ourselves, with them asking questions about Texas and where I lived. One was married, the other single. They were talkative, which made it easy for me since there were no awkward silences.

The one who wasn't married startled me with a sudden observation. "Your Boo, mon loup, is fine. You need to stay close to him with all these Cajun women."

I must've looked confused. The married one translated. "Your man reminds my friend of a wolf. Don't be offended; that is a compliment in French culture."

I didn't try to explain that we weren't married. Jules and Lucille had never accepted it and neither would these women. My eyes found Luke in the crowd and maybe he did resemble a wolf.

As shadows overtook the area, lights appeared like beacons from the back porch and dock. The arms of the oaks held strings of light bulbs illuminating a festive atmosphere with clusters of friends gathered at their feet. Men began setting up tables in the yard and spreading newspapers on them. After the tables were set up, two men came through the gate in the backyard carrying a burlap sack in each hand. Several others came to assist, pouring out crawfish on the tables until they were covered. Mixed in were corn on the cob and potatoes.

Jules was trying to get everyone's attention. "Listen everybody! Listen! I need to say something!" Quiet finally settled in. "We are about to suck the heads and pinch the tails of these delicious crawfish. First, we must offer our thanks to our Lord. I'm going to ask my friend, Marseilles, to do the honor."

With all heads bowed, Marseilles began.

**Bless us O Lord, and these crawfish**
**that we are about to enjoy.**
**bless those who caught them,**
**and those who prepared them,**
**and give crawfish to those**
**who have none.**

**We thank you, O God for this**
**wonderful world, and for all that you have put on it**
**and we give you special thanks, O God**
**for having put the Cajuns and the crawfish**
**down in the same place.**

**Amen**

My stomach was turning over as I looked at what lay on the table. Suck the heads—I don't think so. Like every other time I was in trouble, I went searching for my protector. I found him, taking his arm and pulling him aside, whispering, "I can't eat those things."

For one of the very few times since I'd known him, he laughed, whispering back, "We've got to. This is what they do for friends who visit, Jimmie. I'll help you. Come on." He led me over to a table.

I swear, one of them moved. "They're not all dead!" I said, choking back a scream.

"Yes, they're very dead and cooked," he whispered, picking up one and pinching the tail off. He dipped it in a small bowl of sauce. "Open up." He stuck it in my mouth and, holding back a gag, I started chewing.

All I could taste was *hot*. I finally got it down. "I need a beer, quick!" I tried to whisper, but it came out louder than expected, and the group around me burst into laughter. A kind man nearby handed me a Bud Light and I downed half of it, putting out the fire. For what seemed like hours and several beers, I ate crawfish tails, but unlike the men and women around me, I didn't suck the heads. I also ate corn and potatoes which meant less tails, but they also were seasoned with fire. I looked around and the tables were piled high with crawfish remains.

Luke did much better than me, eating his share of the tails but passing on the heads. The meal ended, and I was tipsy. I supported myself by leaning against Luke who seemed to understand. The tables were moved, the patio was cleared and three men appeared—one with an accordion, another with a fiddle, and a third with a guitar.

Jules called for quiet again. "Now we gonna move to a Fais-do-do (Cajun dance party). Our dance floor is not big enough for everybody. After one dance move off the floor and give someone else a chance."

Before the band even started playing, the unmarried woman I was visiting with earlier, grabbed my support and pulled him onto the patio, causing me almost to fall. She wrapped her spidery arms around Luke and began bobbing around the floor dragging Luke along. I tried to understand the steps connected to the peppy music, but the best I could make of it was a Texas two-step with fancy steps in between. Luke seemed to be catching on fast—too fast.

The music ended and Luke came back over to me. "What'd you think? Ready to give it a try?"

I spotted another woman moving toward us. I didn't have much time to decide. I slipped out of my sandals. "I'll try, but you may have to hold me up." The next song was slower and required less movement, thank goodness. We stayed with the traditional two-step, and it was fun. The longer we danced the closer he held me, and I was sorry when it ended. We moved off the floor to make room for someone else.

He held onto my arm even after leaving the patio. "Would you like another beer?"

"No. Definitely not. A Coke would be great, though." He started off in the direction of the refreshments and was intercepted by another woman. I saw him shake his head and continue on. He needed a cattle prod to keep them off.

He returned with my Coke. "Here you are. I put a little bourbon in it to give it a kick. Have you noticed some of the young men staring at you—the way I do?"

"The last thing I need is a little more kick. No, I haven't noticed anyone staring at me. I have noticed the ladies stalking you like a cat on a mouse."

He smiled and pulled me to him. "It's that backless top. I knew it was going to happen. Let's just find a couple of chairs and watch for awhile."

The party lasted until around midnight, but we only danced a few times content with just sitting and enjoying the music.

Jules tried to get everyone's attention again, but it was futile. The noise was loud and people were having too much fun. He finally stood up on one of the tables that'd been moved off the patio and hollered, "Listen up friends! Quiet! I need to speak!" Slowly the noise ceased. He held up a paper. "This is our last letter from Loo-ee. I have asked Marseilles to read it for you."

Marseilles came forward and climbed on the table, which was no easy task, since he probably weighed at least 300 pounds. There was complete silence when he cleared his throat and began reading.

**Dear Momma and Daddy,**

I am doing good. I hope you are doing good also. I miss the Boudin and crawfish. The food here is terrible. The weather is worse than the food since it rains all the time and my clothes never are dry. The first thing I'm going to do when I get home is go fishing. I promised my Sergeant to take him fishing, too.

Everyone in my platoon has signed a letter requesting that Sergeant Ranker receive a medal for what he recently did. We were on patrol when we were ambushed by Gooks. There had to be several hundred. That's the only way we ever found them is when they ambushed us. We only had twenty-two men in our platoon. They had us surrounded on three sides. We were in some dense brush. Sergeant Ranker called us together and ordered us to retreat. We had one M60 machine gun in our patrol and the Sarge ordered it left behind with him. When the Gooks saw us retreating they became careless, coming out in the open to pursue us. We stopped and watched what happened from a quarter of a mile away. The Sarge let them get within about a hundred yards before he opened up with the M60. Sitting on the revolving tripod, the gun was deadly and the Gooks immediately took cover leaving a number of their comrades lying in the open field. Sergeant Ranker joined us later and we escaped to safety. Had we stayed, all of us would have been killed. I am fortunate to serve under such a leader as the Sarge. I keep pestering him to let me take the point but he refuses. I will not give up until he allows me to be treated like the other men.

I miss you and love you. Please give my love to my brothers. I will see you in three months.

Your son,
Louis

The quiet was eerie as Jules got back on the table and took the letter from Marseilles. He wiped at his eyes and spoke loudly. "Sergeant Ranker and his missus came to see us. My Lucille and me see the guilt in his eyes. I am guessing that he finally gave in and let my Loo-ee take the point and he was killed. We do not blame this brave man for our son's death even though I imagine he does. Please understand, Sergeant Ranker, Loo-ee loved you and we do also. Thank you for coming to visit us."

The second he stopped, the applause began with whistling and cheering. I thought it would never stop. When it did, a long line formed with each man and woman coming by to speak to us. Most of the men shook hands and thanked Luke, but of course, most of the women hugged him. I received my share of handshakes and hugs, also.

It was one o'clock before we said goodnight to the LeBlancs and went to our car. Luke opened the door for me again. I responded by moving over as close to him as I could, putting my head on his shoulder. People observing us would've thought we were high school sweethearts going steady. I smiled—that was fine with me.

# 61
# REDEMPTION

I left Thibodaux early Wednesday morning, feeling like a heavy burden had been lifted. We'd promised to come back once a year to go fishing and stay at least a week, which wasn't going to be difficult for either of us. After the late night and liquor, Jimmie was asleep, with her head in my lap. I brushed the hair from her face, gently, to keep from disturbing her. For the past eight months, I'd seen all her moods—anger, happiness, disappointment, hurt, and excitement. I knew now that I wanted to spend the rest of my life with her. My doubts had been removed. Maybe because, finally, I was at peace with myself.

The first thing I needed to do was address the problem of Drake, who I knew would continue to be a threat, to her especially. I needed some kind of plan to stop him, and the answer was not the law. He was too smart for that, and it would only delay what would have to be done eventually. It was not unlike war—you had to destroy the enemy.

She stirred and moaned, opening her eyes. "Where're we?"

"Lafayette. You hungry?" We'd left early and hadn't eaten.

"No. My stomach's still burning. I'd like a Coke—a king size."

I stopped at a store, filled up with gas and brought her a Coke. From there we only stopped for bathroom breaks, gas, and snacks and were in Dallas by four in the afternoon. I went through Dallas instead of turning north toward Wichita Falls.

"You missed the turn-off," she said.

"Nope. We're going to make a detour. How's your stomach?"

"Much better. Where're we going? I thought we were going to drive all the way home today."

"Are you in a hurry to get back? I know you think they can't do without you at the Auction."

She moved over next to me, putting her hand on my leg. "I'm yours, Luke, to do whatever you feel like doing. The High Plains Cattle Auction can do without me. Now, what do you have in mind?"

"Ruidoso. We've been in the heat, and I'd like to visit the mountains. Is that okay?"

"That's better than okay. It's fantastic. Are we going to stop or drive straight through?"

"Let's drive as long as we can. If need be, we can stop somewhere and spend the night. If not, we can eat breakfast with Mom, Angie, and Hank. It's hard to explain. Maybe I feel so good about the trip to Louisiana that I'm putting off going back to Dalhart and facing my big problem."

"You're talking about Drake. Just leave him alone, Luke. Maybe he'll go away and forget about us."

"You don't believe that. He's planning at this minute to hurt you one way or another. I won't let that happen."

✷✷✷

We were in Post by ten that evening, and she wanted to call her dad and tell him our plans. We found a phone booth, and she returned a few minutes later saying her dad was fine with the delay of our return, encouraging her to be gone as long as she wanted. We ate supper at the Dairy Queen and at 10:45 were climbing the hill, putting us on the Caprock or Escarpment on the plains.

"Roll your window down," I said.

She did as I asked. "It's cool. Oh, it feels so good. So different from a few miles back."

In New Mexico, we stopped in Tatum for a restroom break, gas, and coffee. We sat in the car, drinking our coffee. "What do you think, Jimmie Lyn Waddell?"

"What a wonderful surprise! I'm excited. I never dreamed we'd go by Ruidoso."

We left Tatum and were in Ruidoso three hours later. I knew we couldn't find the house in the dark, so we stopped in a restaurant parking lot and slept in the car until the sun was up. We didn't have any problem finding the house, and as we drove up, we spotted Mom on the patio. She met us before we reached the house, hugging us. "Luke, Jimmie what a nice surprise! Where did you come from? I thought you were in Louisiana."

"We were twenty-four hours ago," I replied. "We decided to make a slight detour and come see you."

We joined her on the patio, and she got us coffee. "I can't wait to show you the house when Angie and Hank are awake. Your dad did really good, Jimmie."

We told her about our visit to Louisiana. Jimmie did most of the talking which was fine with me, spending more time on the fishing trip and party than anything else. "We ate crawfish, Grace. Can you believe that? We only ate the tails but they, ugh, sucked the heads."

"Are they anything like the crawdads that we have in our tanks that we use for fish bait?" Mom asked.

Jimmie looked at me to provide the answer. "Mom, they're exactly the same critter. Jimmie had to drink a lot of beer to get them down. Actually, they were pretty good. A little spicy but good."

"It sounds as if it was an exciting and successful trip," Mom said.

"Absolutely. I should've gone earlier. My fear was not justified. By the time we left, they made us feel like we were a part of the family. I wish you could've met them. They're the nicest people that I've ever been around.

Everybody we came into contact with were nice and treated us like royalty."

Jimmie nodded at Luke. "Yes, especially the younger women who were a little bit too nice to Luke," and she added defensively, "I didn't drink that much beer either."

We heard Hank crying, and Mom was up and gone in a second. I asked Jimmie if she was tired. "Not really. It'll probably hit me later, but right now, I feel good. Maybe it's this mountain air."

Mom returned carrying Hank, who was latched on to a bottle. "He wakes up hungry. Hasn't he grown, just in the last couple of weeks?"

"He's beautiful. I think he looks like his Uncle Luke. Could I hold him?" Jimmie took him without Hank losing his grip on the nipple.

Angie joined us and, as we visited, Hank was passed around so everyone had a chance to hold him, even me.

When Mom left for the track, Jimmie and Angie went with her, taking the baby, of course. I begged off saying I had some shopping to do in town. I dodged questions saying it wouldn't take long, and I'd be out to the track shortly. I found the store in town I was looking for and entered with a total of $86 in my pocket.

✱✱✱

That afternoon, instead of going back to the track, Jimmie and I stayed at the house with the intent on catching up from the all-nighter. She was on the couch, and I was in a soft chair with my feet propped up on a hassock when the phone rang. I was closer and answered.

"Luke, Blaine here. Y'all make it okay?"

"We got here early this morning. Long trip but worth it. How's everything at the Auction?"

There was a pause, and I was about to repeat, thinking he didn't hear me. "Fine. Is Jimmie close by?"

She was awake and listening. "Yeah. You want to talk to her?"

"Sure. Put her on," he said.

They talked long enough for her to tell him about our trip to Louisiana and the house he'd bought. Before hanging up, he asked to speak with me again. Jimmie gave me the phone and left, going outside.

"Is Jimmie still in the room?" Blaine asked.

"No. She went outside."

"Luke, somebody vandalized her apartment last night. They made a mess and it'll take several days to get it back together. I have Benny and Bronc over there cleaning it up. Try to keep her out there at least three more days. More if possible. I don't want her to see the apartment as it is."

I stiffened. "Drake was responsible." I had no doubt.

"Probably. I've reported it to the law, but there's little chance of proving it was him. In fact, he probably hired someone to do it."

"I'll make sure we don't return for at least three days. Do you think Drake knows where we are?"

"I don't see how, Luke. I didn't even know until late last night. I was expecting you home today."

We ended the call, and I joined her on the patio and, of course, Jimmie asked about what her dad wanted. I expected the question and was ready. "Business mostly and he inquired about Lady and how she was doing."

She wasn't convinced. "It took a long time for him to ask you about that."

"You're nosey. It's not necessary for you to know everything Blaine and I talk about."

She came over and sat down in my lap, putting her arms around my neck, changing the topic. "I appreciate you coming by Ruidoso. I'm enjoying it so much. Could we stay a few more days?"

Sometimes, things just work out.

✳✳✳

I called Blaine back later when Jimmie went to town with Angie and Mom and asked for more details about the apartment. It was even worse than I'd thought. They'd taken red paint and written obscenities all over the walls and threats like you're going to die and so is he. They'd taken a knife and cut up the living room furniture, doing as much damage as possible.

The fear and desperation in his voice was evident. "I don't know what to do, Luke. The authorities said they'd look into it. That gives me zero confidence. I definitely don't want Jimmie Lyn to see what they did. This guy must be crazy or full of hate or both to do such a thing."

"Don't worry. We're safe out here. I don't plan on us coming back for a week."

"Be careful, Luke. I wouldn't put anything past this guy. Call me every other day or so and let me know y'all are okay."

After the call ended, I went to the car and opened a small metal box containing the pistol I'd taken from the Russians. I checked the clip, which held eight shells. That would have to do. No way could I find ammunition here that would work. When we returned home, I'd have my 12 gauge, still at the ranch.

My mind went quickly to other thoughts—much more positive thoughts. I had to decide how to approach this event. I'd volunteered to cook hamburgers tonight on the outside grill. It was still only five o'clock, and I had plenty of time, so I returned to the patio. They were racing today and, looking across the highway, I saw horses warming up for a race. The distance was too far to make out anything other than tiny figures moving up and down the track.

Blaine had made a good purchase with this house. It was a nice location, with a great view, and the landscaping was beautiful. I realized how much more content I was after visiting the LeBlancs. I never dreamed of the type of response I received. And then, like a black cloud, the thought of Drake Davis blanked out everything positive in my life.

# 62

# BAD NEWS AND
# GOOD NEWS

 GRACE

I seldom went downtown, but having Angie and Jimmie with me shopping was fun. We made most of the stores on one side of the street and then moved to the other side. It wasn't crowded since the races weren't over. I only bought a few knickknacks for the baby, but Jimmie's and Angie's arms were loaded.

"Grace, I want to get something special for Luke. Do you have a suggestion? I'd rather it not be clothes but something he wouldn't buy for himself."

"He likes to fish. Of course, you know that. He didn't bring his fishing tackle to Dalhart and has said a number of times he regretted it."

"We'll pass a sporting goods store on the way back. I can buy something for him there," said Jimmie.

Luke had the outside grill going when we returned and came over to the car to help us carry in our bags. "Looks like y'all did some shopping."

Something was going on with Luke. He had that look I hadn't seen in years—excitement combined with mischievousness. After we were inside and Luke had returned to his grilling, I told Jimmie and Angie. "I don't know what it is, but something's going on."

The phone started ringing and stopped me from going further into Luke's mood. It was my dad and the concern in his voice frightened me, thinking it must be bad news. "We've got a problem, Daughter. I don't know what to do. Bull has stopped eating and I mean anything. We've got to do something, or he's going to starve."

I breathed a sigh of relief, thinking it could've been a lot worse. "Just a minute, Dad, and I'll get Luke."

I listened in on the conversation and from what I could tell, Luke was going to meet my dad in Melrose and pick up Bull. That dog was something else. I guess he was worth it considered how much he'd helped Luke when he returned from Vietnam. They helped to heal one another and that bond was incredibly strong.

Luke confirmed what I'd heard. He'd meet his granddad at eleven tomorrow morning in Melrose to pick up his dog. That meant he'd need to leave early since it would only be ten New Mexico time.

Luke had said that supper would be ready at six, which was early for us to eat. I didn't remind him since he was cooking tonight. At precisely six he came in and told us to sit down at the table. He was cooking and serving tonight. I rounded up Jimmie and Angie, and we all had a seat at the table when Luke came in carrying our plates with the burgers.

"Nobody eats until I bless the food," he said. He began as if in a hurry. **"We give thanks for all our blessings, especially family. We are thankful that given time, everything usually works out for the best. We ask that we continue to relish life and be joyful in what it brings. Bless this food to the nourishment of our bodies and us to thy service. Amen.**

We all had burgers and chips on our plates, but they were covered with a napkin, which was confusing since flies were not a problem. We removed our napkins.

"What's this little box on my plate?" Jimmie asked. She picked it up and removed the lid. She went silent as we watched. "Oh, oh, my. I-It's a r-ring." Then she started crying but managed to say, "It's b-beautiful!"

We all got up and gathered around her to get a better look. It had the smallest stone in it, I'd ever seen. It could've come out of a Cracker Jack's box. Now, it was clear what Luke's mood was all about.

"Oh, Luke. It's beautiful," she repeated, slipping it on her finger. "It just fits."

Hank started crying from the other room, like he wanted in on the excitement. Angie went in to see about him and Jimmie left, going outside, followed by Luke. I wiped away a tear and smiled, thankful for the future that awaited our family and anxious to give the news to my dad and Blaine.

***

Luke was up early the next morning, and I joined him on the patio for our coffee. "What time did y'all go to bed last night?"

"Around three this morning. We stayed up talking and making plans. She insisted that she's in no hurry to get married, but I don't want to wait. I asked her about having a small ceremony here at the little Presbyterian Church in town as soon as possible. She agreed, so it's settled. She's going to call her dad today."

"I'm happy for you, Luke. She's a wonderful girl." I'd be delighted to have her for a daughter-in-law.

"I'm going to leave her here while I go pick up Bull. She can sleep late and go to the track with you. In fact, while I'm gone all of you need to stay together." He went on to explain the phone call from Blaine and the damage to Jimmie's apartment, emphasizing again the need for none of us to be left alone while he was away. "Blaine doesn't want her to know, and I agree."

This wonderful moment suddenly turned dark. How could any man be this evil and yet portrayed as a hero? "Are you afraid he'll show up here?"

"Probably not, but there's no use taking any chances. I should be back by two this afternoon."

After this news, the mood changed and little was said before Luke left. I had to stay upbeat around Angie and Jimmie so as not to give any indication of a problem. The celebratory mood needed to continue and not be erased by this potential threat.

The horses were usually fed by now, but they'd just have to wait. It was race day anyway, and the only exercise for them would be on the walker. After breakfast, we'd all go to the barn together.

Jimmie joined me later on the patio, fully dressed and still excited. "I hardly slept any. I was surprised. No, I was shocked! You said something was going on with Luke. How did you know?"

"I'd seen it many times when he attended high school. I had no idea what his intentions were. I was as surprised as you. What're your plans?" Luke had told me, but I knew she wanted to share them with me.

"A small wedding, here in Ruidoso—soon. Grace, I'm thrilled and couldn't be happier. I'm going to the church today and talk with the pastor. We'll have to work around his schedule. What time did Luke leave?"

"He's been gone about an hour. He said to expect him back around two this afternoon. Maybe you can wait and let him go with you to see the pastor." I held my breath, hoping she'd agree.

"Oh, I don't know. I may just go ahead without him. We agreed on everything, so he doesn't need to go with me. I can have all the information when he returns." She held up her hand, studying the ring. "Isn't it beautiful?"

All I could think of was, *beauty is in the eyes of the beholder.* "Yes, it is." Now, I had a problem. How was I going to get her to go with us to the track?

I went for more coffee and Angie was in the kitchen. I looked, to make sure Jimmie hadn't followed. "Angie, I need your help. I don't have time to explain. When we get ready to leave this morning, ask Jimmie if she'll watch Hank for you at the barn while you clean stalls. Add anything to make this more convincing. Don't ask me why. Just do it."

She looked confused, started to reply, and I put my hand to my lips as Jimmie came in. "I'm not hungry this morning. Luke and I had a midnight snack. I'll be glad to cook breakfast for y'all."

"Tell you what. Let's just stop and get some pastry for breakfast." Maybe Angie would take the cue.

"Sounds good to me," Angie said. "Jimmie, do you mind watching Hank for me this morning at the barn. I need to clean stalls and Mom has some errands. I've neglected doing my part lately. I'm afraid she's going to start charging me rent."

The disappointment showed. "Sure. I was going to see the pastor but that can wait."

✳✳✳

Luke was at the barn a little after two, with Bull clinging to him every step. Jimmie met him with a hug. "We made it. I had to stop and get Bull a couple of cans of Spam, so you know what that means."

Bull had this wide grin like he understood what'd been said. He rubbed up against Jimmie's leg, turning his rear to her—an invitation for a little scratching.

"I missed you, too, Bull." She bent down and vigorously rubbed him.

"How was your granddad?" I asked.

"As happy as I've ever remembered him. Excited about my marriage to Jimmie. Of course, he quoted Scripture; Proverbs 31." Luke pulled out a scrap of paper from his jean pocket. "He wrote it down for me. Verses 10-12. 'Who can find a virtuous woman? For her price is far above rubies. The heart of her husband doth safely trust in her, so that he shall have no need of spoil. She will do him good and not evil all the days of her life.'" He tucked it back into his jeans. Luke continued. "With his job, Granddad feels useful. I hope at seventy-six I'm in the same shape. Blaine's done a lot for all of us, including Granddad."

Jimmie asked him about going to visit with the pastor and he agreed. They left, with Luke assuring us they wouldn't be gone long. No way was

Bull going to be left and, as they drove off, I wondered if he was going to be in the wedding.

I told Angie she'd done well getting Jimmie to come with us to the barn. I continued and told her the reason it was important, including the threat Drake posed.

"Is he really that dangerous?"

"Evidently. I hope that the law catches up with him," I said.

"This is unreal. It sounds like something out of a movie. Does this mean that we're all in danger?"

"I don't know, Angie. Luke said we weren't taking any chances. I worry about what Luke might do. He's had so much violence in his life the last several years. I'm glad they're getting married here and not in Dalhart."

"Speaking of their marriage, I would've been glad to give Luke my wedding ring to give her. It would've been much better than what he gave her," Angie said.

I laughed. "Nothing would be more beautiful than what he gave her, Angie. It's not the size of the diamond. It's how she views what he selected. She wouldn't trade that ring for one that cost thousands."

✳✳✳

That afternoon, sitting on the patio with a breathtaking view of Sierra Blanca, Jimmie gave us the particulars of the wedding. It would be Saturday, July twenty-fifth, at six in the evening at the First Presbyterian Church here in Ruidoso. Bronc would be Luke's best man and Piper would be maid of honor. The honeymoon would follow at the Waddell Ranch in Dallam County with Bull in attendance.

# 63

## A WEDDING AND A PROMISE

~❦ JIMMIE LYN ❦~

It was Saturday, July twenty-fifth, at 5:05 p.m. and I was dressing for our ceremony but not wearing the gown that Mrs. Proctor created for me. I selected something much simpler. At a small dress shop in town, The Treasure Chest, I found a jewel. A simple lavender linen dress caught my eye. I held my breath, hoping it would fit. Perfect! Satisfied with how I looked, I knew Luke would also enjoy the backless view. Piper had come in yesterday, and we'd stayed up most of the night at her motel talking about the past, present, and future. She was delighted that Luke was the groom and continually referred to him as heavenly. If she was delighted, my dad was ecstatic, repeating over and over how pleased he was. My mother, of course, was disappointed that we weren't having a big wedding but eventually accepted my decision and was here with Sterling.

We'd heard nothing from Drake, but I knew that Luke would find him immediately after the week-long honeymoon at the ranch. I'd do everything possible to dissuade him, but it would be futile. I'd finally been told of the destruction to my apartment before going back for clothes. There was no way to repair the damage in that short amount of time. The walls had been repainted, but some of the writing bled through, and I shivered each time I thought of it.

I still couldn't make up my mind about whether or not to wear heels.

Luke had never once referred to my height. I'd be taller than he was if I wore the heels, but they were more appropriate for a wedding. I sat down on the side of the bed and made a decision. I would wear heels and stand straight. We were going to spend a lifetime together, and he'd made the decision to take me as I was—all six feet of me.

The ceremony we'd chosen was simple and short, yet perfect for us. I was nervous until Dad and I started down the aisle and saw Luke staring at me. I knew what that look meant—he was thinking about how good I looked. I straightened up and smiled back at him.

Most dads are sad about giving their daughters away. When the pastor asked the question, "Who gives this woman?" My dad's answer shocked everyone. "Her dad is happy to do so." Laughter followed.

Standing side by side we exchanged vows and finally the words, "I now pronounce you man and wife." I looked at Luke. "You may kiss the bride."

It was a perfect kiss—not too long or too short. The pastor addressed the audience. "I now give you Mr. and Mrs. Luke Ranker." We turned and, to applause, started up the aisle toward our future.

✵✵✵

*Meanwhile, three hundred and eight miles southeast of Ruidoso.*

*It was eight o'clock, and the wedding was over. He would've liked to have gone, but he had more important things to do. It was time to get ready and, with a timeline to follow, he went to the top drawer in his bedroom chest and took out the Colt .45 that his granddad had left him. Picking it up, he was always surprised at how heavy it was. He checked, and it was loaded with five shells, but the hammer sat on an empty chamber, like his granddad had taught him.*

*He went to his phone and called the Old Man who was going to help him. "Are you ready to go?"*

"As ready as I'll ever be. Are you sure about doing this?"

"Yeah. I don't have any doubt. I'll be there in a few minutes."

He'd made up his mind when he saw her apartment, which had made him so angry he became sick, going outside and throwing up. She'd been raised around the Auction and was like family to him, and he loved her like a granddaughter. His wife had passed over twenty-years ago, and the Auction and Missy helped him get through the devastating loss. It was time to give back to these people who'd given him so much.

*** 

He drove up to the Old Man's house and parked. They were taking his car, a 1958 Cadillac Deville. He called him the Old Man, but actually they were close to the same age—mid-sixties. They'd worked at the Auction a combined sixty-five years and had been friends the entire time.

He met me at the door. The Old Man asked if he wanted a drink. He declined saying that would come later after this was over. The car parked in his garage was seldom driven. It was special and a prized possession of the Old Man who'd never been married. He'd actually measured the car, and it was over twenty-one feet long. The back seat was larger than some bedrooms he'd been in.

On the drive to Amarillo, he went over everything again. He'd been planning this for some time and had been to Amarillo every day studying his subject's schedule and habits. He pretty well knew what time the man came and went. They were in Amarillo at 10:20 and fifteen minutes later we were at his apartment. They drove by and his car wasn't there, just as he'd planned. They stopped two blocks away, and he got out, telling his friend to be back at eleven-thirty to pick him up in front of the apartment.

He made his way to the apartment, going around to the back. The front door had a dead bolt, but the back entrance had a sliding glass door. He took the gun and using the butt broke the glass, enough to reach through and *unlock the door. He was inside, what appeared to be the kitchen. He had a small flashlight but didn't turn it on until he was out of the kitchen. He made his way to the front, turned off the flashlight, and waited by the front door. He looked at his watch—10:50. He still had forty minutes or so to wait.*

*He sat down on the carpet, took a paper sack out of his back pocket and placed the gun inside. If the plan worked, Missy and her new husband would never have to worry about this evil man again. She would take her daddy's place in a few years when he retired, and the Auction would continue to flourish.*

*He waited patiently until lights came through the window, indicating that the man was home. He held his flashlight on top of his watch and saw it was 11:23—perfect. He stood, so he would be behind the door when it opened. He heard the click as the door unlocked, before removing the gun from the sack. The door opened, followed by the sound of the light switch. The door closed and he stepped out, confronting Evil.*

*He pushed the gun into his ribs—hard. "Move and you're a dead man."*

*"What? Who?"*

*He pushed the .45 harder. "Just do exactly as I say. You need to understand. There's a good chance you will die tonight. Move slowly and turn off the light."*

*The light went off. So far so good. "Now we're going to walk to the car parked out front." He continued to have the gun in his side as they slowly walked to the Cadillac. "Open the door and get in, slowly."*

*Evil, found his voice. "Where're you taking me? Who are you? You can't get away with this?"*

*He slid in beside Evil and in the same motion swung the two-and-a half pound Colt and caught him across the face, causing blood to gush from his nose. "Shut up! I'll do the talking from now on."*

*Evil slumped over in the seat with his hand covering his face. He wasn't out, just addled a little. Now he had Evil's attention. "Sit up."*

*Evil straightened up but still had his hands over his face with blood* streaming. He produced a towel from the floor board and gave it to Evil. He placed the .45 on the side of his neck below his jaw. "If you move suddenly, this will just about take your head off. Hopefully the driver won't hit any bumps in the road, or it might go off accidentally. He pushed harder burying the barrel in his neck and cocked the hammer.

"We're going for a ride. Relax and pray it's a smooth ride."

Everything was going good until they slowed and turned into a lane which had a speed bump. The Cadillac jolted and the hammer fell with a loud click. "Damn, you're a fortunate man today. The chamber was empty. The next five chambers have live ammunition. Watch those speed bumps, driver!"

The question came from the driver. "What's that smell?"

"We had an accident back here. Just keep your eyes on the road." The lane led up to a parking lot which had few cars but was well lit. They came to a stop, and it was time for the final stage of the plan—the tricky part.

Evil's nose had stopped bleeding, but he was whimpering like a child. The gun was still pressed against his neck, and it was time for the final instructions.

"You've threatened and injured people that are dear to me. You're going away and never set foot in this area again. If you do, I promise, you will be killed on sight. We are at the airport, and in my pocket is a one-way ticket to London with a stop-over in New York. We're going to get out and walk to Gate 4 where you will board. I imagine you'll think about running—if you do I'll shoot and kill you. I'm an old man and what happens to me doesn't matter in the least. I probably should just go ahead and kill you right now, but you're going to get a chance to live. Do you understand?"

Still whimpering, he nodded his head.

From then, everything went as planned. They walked to Gate 4 with the gun in a paper sack, waited a few minutes until the call for boarding, and Evil left, walking through the entrance. He waited until the plane taxied down the runway and lifted off before leaving. He returned to the Cadillac *sat down in the front seat, and lit a cigarette. Benny took a deep drag and, letting it out slowly, relaxed—the plan completed. "It's time for that drink now."*

✳✳✳

The Waddell Ranch 12:32 A.M.

They didn't stay long after the wedding, anxious to start the honeymoon. It was a beautiful night in the Texas Panhandle, and when they walked up to the back door of the little ranch house, with Bull close behind, he reached and picked her up—she squealed and grabbed him around the neck as he carried her inside.

Maybe it was an accident or fate but at that very moment, a light in the sky revealed a plane on the way to New York.

# Epilogue

## AUGUST 31, 1969
## RUIDOSO, NEW MEXICO

I sat on the patio drinking my morning coffee thinking of the past and the upcoming day. Henry had been gone for a year and three days. What a year it had been—filled with sorrow, uncertainty, fear, excitement, and finally joy. I shivered, not knowing if it was the early fall mountain air or the emotions of the memories.

Luke and Jimmie were happily married and living at the ranch with him looking after the cattle and her driving back and forth to work each day. Luke had agreed to accept his medal in a ceremony, September twenty-seventh. Luke sought out Drake but he'd disappeared, and the law firm told him that Drake hadn't shown up for work on Monday, July twenty-eighth, and they'd assumed he'd gone back to some kind of undercover work for the law.

Jimmie had changed the most since the marriage. With an unfolding of confidence came the beauty which she had denied.

Luke now had the look I remembered so well, which he carried in high school—the wide smile and mischievous brown eyes.

My dad continued to do well and was pleased with himself for cutting down to a pack a day of Camels. He still read the Bible daily and was always ready with a scripture for any occasion.

Angie was waiting on her divorce to become final. She and Bronc reminded me of two junior high kids, swooning over each other, waiting around for the other to make some kind of romantic move. And, of course, there was Hank, who was now four months old and able to roll over. He filled my heart to overflowing, and I had to discipline myself not to hold him all the time and look into those beautiful, inquisitive blue eyes.

Blaine was doing well, having another positive checkup before coming to Ruidoso for the weekend. He continued to treat me like someone special, but I wasn't ready for a relationship. However, I'd quit thinking that it would never happen. He'd announced that he was going to retire within the next three years, and Jimmie would take over the Auction.

Bull was still Bull. Too much table food and watch out. Jimmie had been taking him with her on sale day. The first time she turned him loose, and he was given leftover hamburgers and chips all day. He was sick that evening as were Luke and Jimmie. The next sale day she put a sign on his neck—don't feed the dog.

Lady, the reason I was sitting out here on the patio this beautiful morning, had qualified nine days ago for the Derby which had a purse of $90,000 this year. She barely made it, holding on to the eight spot out of ten. She had the 1 Gate which Kenneth attributed to her not doing better. Today she'd drawn the ten spot which thrilled us all. The family was all here for the big race. Blaine had gotten rooms at a nice motel for everyone except me, Angie, and the baby. I objected, telling him he should be able to stay in his own house, but to no avail.

Everyone was meeting for breakfast at a local restaurant except me. I was going to the track to feed and stay with Lady. I picked up the program on the table beside me and looked at the 11th race. My eyes moved to the 10 horse—Miss Jet, owned by Grace Ranker and Blaine Waddell, and trained by Grace and Henry Ranker. Blaine had insisted, to my joy, that Henry be included as the trainer. The opening odds were

10-1 which were accurate according to her performance in the trials.

*** 

The afternoon was excruciatingly long. Finally, at 4:45, the first call was made for the 11th Race. Luke stayed with me and had the pony horse saddled and ready to go. I waited for the second call and Luke handed me Lady—my hand was shaking as I accepted the lead rope, which was attached to the only calm thing in the family. Lady was acting like it was just another day. "Pretty girl. If you only knew how important this race was to us."

We reached the saddling paddock and Kenneth was already waiting. "She looks good, Grace. You need to relax and enjoy this day. I'm going to tell you something—if she breaks clean, nothing—and I mean nothing—in this field can touch her."

"I can't help it, Kenneth. I know we should be happy just to be here, but this means so much to me. The fact that Henry's name is on the program makes it even more important. It's a dream that we shared, and I know he's watching. I know it's strange, but I feel his presence and have all day."

"I'll say it again, Grace. If we break good, you can go ahead and start for the Win Circle."

Luke helped us saddle and I went to my pony horse. The announcement was made—**"Riders up"**— and Luke took Kenneth's foot and lifted him into the saddle. I met them on the track, taking the lead rope for the post parade. As we passed the tote board the odds had dropped to 5-1. Someone had made a huge bet, most likely Blaine. We were conservative in the warm-up, and when we reached the gates Lady had only broken a light sweat. I handed her over to the gate person and rode back a good distance.

The voice came over the speaker. **"Ladies and Gentlemen, the** horses are loading for the running of the New Mexico Derby. They're having trouble with Jack of Diamonds, the number 5 horse. Numbers 8, 9, and 10 are in. They're all in line. The flag is up!" A loud bang as the gates opened— "It's a good break for all except number 5 who stumbled, and Miss Jet on the outside is going to the front . . ."